PRAISE FOR
77 SHADOW STREET

“Koontz has pulled out all the stops. . . . Thi[illegible] and deeply satisfyin[illegible] after the final page i[illegible]

“Utterly terrifying . [illegible] character and the en[illegible] witness to the unspea[illegible]pproaching. You will be sleeping with the lights on after reading this one!”

—*RT Book Reviews* (4-1/2 stars)

CRITICAL ACCLAIM FOR DEAN KOONTZ

“Koontz [is] working at his pinnacle, providing terrific entertainment that deals seriously with some of the deepest themes of human existence: the nature of evil, the grip of fate and the power of love.”

—*Publishers Weekly* (starred review)

“A modern Swift . . . a master satirist.”

—*Entertainment Weekly*

“Koontz is a superb plotter and wordsmith. He chronicles the hopes and fears of our time in broad strokes and fine detail, using popular fiction to explore the human condition [and] demonstrating that the real horror of life is found not in monsters, but within the human psyche.” —*USA Today*

“Koontz has a knack for making the bizarre and uncanny seem as commonplace as a sunrise. BOTTOM LINE: the Dean of Suspense.” —*People*

"If Stephen King is the Rolling Stones of novels, Koontz is the Beatles." —*Playboy*

"[Koontz is] far more than a genre writer. Characters and the search for meaning, exquisitely crafted, are the soul of his work. This is why his novels will be read long after the ghosts and monsters of most genre writers have been consigned to the attic. One of the master storytellers of this or any age." —*The Tampa Tribune*

"Dean Koontz is not just a master of our darkest dreams, but also a literary juggler." —*The Times* (London)

"Dean Koontz writes page-turners, middle-of-the-night-sneak-up-behind-you suspense thrillers. He touches our hearts and tingles our spines."
—*The Washington Post Book World*

"Dean Koontz almost occupies a genre of his own. He is a master at building suspense and holding the reader spellbound." —*Richmond Times-Dispatch*

"Demanding much of itself, Koontz's style bleaches out clichés while showing a genius for details. He leaves his competitors buried in the dust." —*Kirkus Reviews*

"Koontz has always had near-Dickensian powers of description, and an ability to yank us from one page to the next that few novelists can match." —*Los Angeles Times*

"Tumbling, hallucinogenic prose. Serious writers might do well to study his technique."
—*The New York Times Book Review*

"The master of the psychological drama."
—LARRY KING, *USA Today*

"Koontz is a master of melding the supernatural with the commonplace. [His] writing crackles with dry, tongue-in-cheek wit." —*The Boston Globe*

"Dean Koontz is a prose stylist whose lyricism heightens malevolence and tension. He creates characters of unusual richness and depth. A level of perception and sensitivity that is not merely convincing—it's astonishing."
—*The Seattle Times*

BY DEAN KOONTZ

77 Shadow Street • What the Night Knows
Breathless • Relentless • Your Heart Belongs to Me
The Darkest Evening of the Year • The Good Guy
The Husband • Velocity • Life Expectancy
The Taking • The Face • By the Light of the Moon
One Door Away From Heaven • From the Corner of His Eye
False Memory • Seize the Night • Fear Nothing
Mr. Murder • Dragon Tears • Hideaway • Cold Fire
The Bad Place • Midnight • Lightning • Watchers
Strangers • Twilight Eyes • Darkfall • Phantoms
Whispers • The Mask • The Vision • The Face of Fear
Night Chills • Shattered • The Voice of the Night
The Servants of Twilight • The House of Thunder
The Key to Midnight • The Eyes of Darkness
Shadowfires • Winter Moon • The Door to December
Dark Rivers of the Heart • Icebound • Strange Highways
Intensity • Sole Survivor • Ticktock
The Funhouse • Demon Seed

ODD THOMAS

Odd Thomas • Forever Odd • Brother Odd • Odd Hours

FRANKENSTEIN

Prodigal Son • City of Night • Dead and Alive
Lost Souls • The Dead Town

A Big Little Life: A Memoir of a Joyful Dog Named Trixie

Dean Koontz

Bantam Books *New York*

A Novel

77 Shadow Street is a work of fiction. Names, characters, places, and incidents either are the product of the author's imagination or are used fictitiously. Any resemblance to actual persons, living or dead, events, or locales is entirely coincidental.

A Bantam Books International Edition

Published in the United States by Bantam Books, an imprint of The Random House Publishing Group, a division of Random House, Inc., New York.

A signed, limited edition has been privately printed by Charnel House.
Charnelhouse.com.

BANTAM BOOKS and the rooster colophon are registered trademarks of Random House, Inc.

Title page art from an original photograph by Dora Pete.

A hardcover edition has been published in the United States by Bantam Books, an imprint of The Random House Publishing Group, a division of Random House, Inc., in 2010.

This book contains an excerpt of the forthcoming novel *Odd Apocalypse* by Dean Koontz. This excerpt has been set for this edition only and may not reflect the final content of the published book.

ISBN: 978-0-553-84121-3
eBook ISBN: 978-0-345-53236-7

Cover design: Scott Biel
Cover images: Stephen Youll (house),
David Muir / Getty Images (key)

Printed in the United States of America

www.bantamdell.com

2 4 6 8 9 7 5 3 1

From here in the Nutland,
To Ed and Carol Gorman,
Out there in the Heartland,
With undiminished affection
after all these years.

O dark dark dark.

They all go into the dark . . .

—T. S. Eliot, *East Coker*

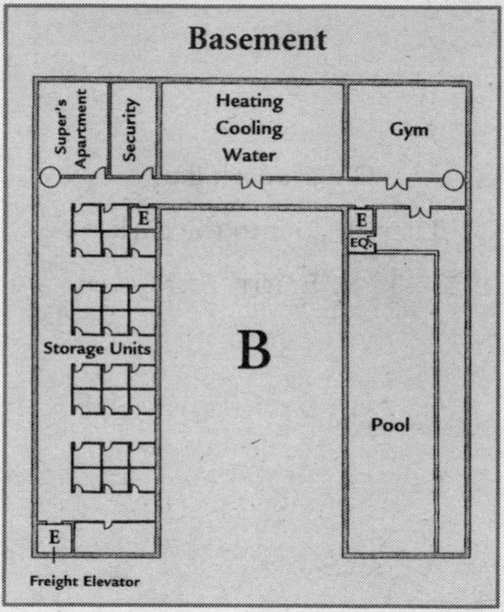
Basement
Super's Apartment
Security
Heating
Cooling
Water
Gym
E
E
EQ.
Storage Units
B
Pool
E
Freight Elevator

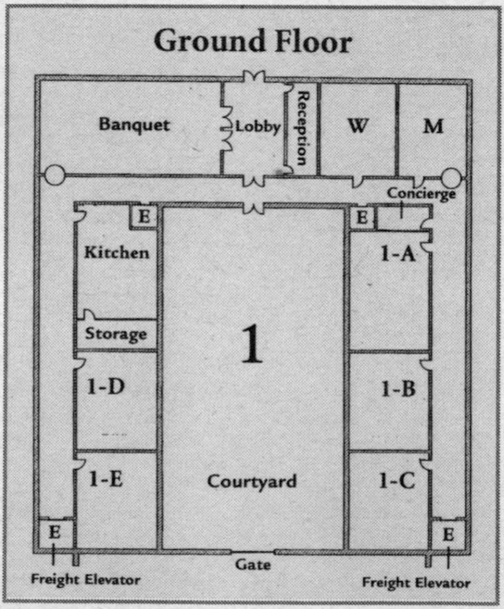
Ground Floor
Banquet
Lobby
Reception
W
M
Concierge
E
Kitchen
E
1-A
Storage
1
1-D
1-B
1-E
Courtyard
1-C
E
E
Gate
Freight Elevator
Freight Elevator

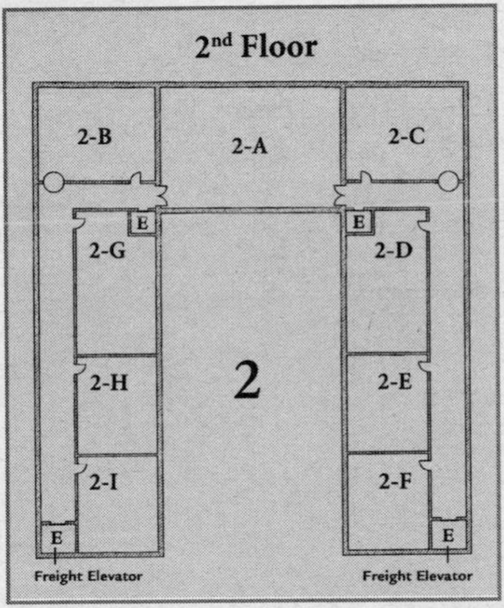
2nd Floor
2-B
2-A
2-C
E
E
2-G
2-D
2-H
2
2-E
2-I
2-F
E
E
Freight Elevator
Freight Elevator

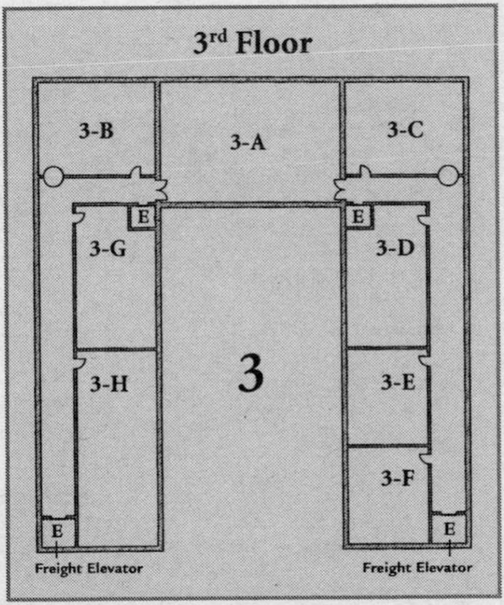
3rd Floor
3-B
3-A
3-C
E
E
3-G
3-D
3-H
3
3-E
3-F
E
E
Freight Elevator
Freight Elevator

77 SHADOW STREET

PART ONE

Where the Shadows Gather

How slow the shadow creeps;
but when 'tis past
How fast the shadows fall.
How fast! How fast!

—HILAIRE BELLOC, *For a Sundial*

1

The North Elevator

Bitter and drunk, Earl Blandon, a former United States senator, got home at 2:15 A.M. that Thursday with a new tattoo: a two-word obscenity in blue block letters between the knuckles of the middle finger of his right hand. Earlier in the night, at a cocktail lounge, he'd thrust that stiff digit at another customer who didn't speak English and who was visiting from some third-world backwater where the meaning of the offending gesture evidently wasn't known in spite of countless Hollywood films in which numerous cinema idols had flashed it. In fact, the ignorant foreigner seemed to mistake the raised finger for some kind of friendly hello and reacted by nodding repeatedly and smiling. Earl was frustrated directly out of the cocktail lounge and into a nearby tattoo parlor, where he resisted the advice of the needle artist and, at the age of fifty-eight, acquired his first body decoration.

When Earl strode through the front entrance of the exclusive Pendleton, into the lobby, the night concierge, Norman Fixxer, greeted him by name. Norman sat on a stool behind the reception counter to the left, a book open in front of him, looking like a ventriloquist's dummy: eyes wide and blue and glassy, pronounced marionette lines like scars in his face, head cocked at an odd angle. In a tailored black suit and a crisp white shirt and a black bow tie, with a fussily arranged white pocket handkerchief blossoming from the breast pocket of his coat, Norman was overdressed by the standards of the two other concierges who worked the earlier shifts.

Earl Blandon didn't like Norman. He didn't trust him. The concierge tried too hard. He was excessively polite. Earl didn't trust polite people who tried too hard. They always proved to be hiding something. Sometimes they hid the fact that they were FBI agents, pretending instead to be lobbyists with a suitcase full of cash and a deep respect for the power of a senator. Earl didn't suspect that Norman Fixxer was an FBI agent in disguise, but the concierge was for damn sure something more than what he pretended to be.

Earl acknowledged Norman's greeting with only a scowl. He wanted to raise his newly lettered middle finger, but he restrained himself. Offending a concierge was a bad idea. Your mail might go missing. The suit you expected back from the dry cleaner by Wednesday evening might be delivered to your apartment a week later. With food stains. Although flashing the finger at Norman would be satisfying, a full apology would require doubling the usual Christmas gratuity.

Consequently, Earl scowled across the marble-floored lobby, his embellished finger curled tightly into his fist. He went through the inner door that Norman buzzed open for him and into the communal hallway, where he turned left and, licking his lips at the prospect of a nightcap, proceeded to the north elevator.

His third-floor apartment was at the top of the building. He did not have a city view, only windows on the courtyard, and seven other apartments shared that level, but his unit was sufficiently well-positioned to justify calling it his penthouse, especially because it was in the prestigious Pendleton. Earl once owned a five-acre estate with a seventeen-room manor house. He liquidated it and other assets to pay the ruinous fees of the blood-sucking, snake-hearted, lying-bastard, may-they-all-rot-in-hell defense attorneys.

As the elevator doors slid shut and as the car began to rise, Earl surveyed the hand-painted mural that covered the walls above the white wainscoting and extended across the ceiling: bluebirds soaring joyously through a sky in which the clouds were golden with sunlight. Sometimes, like now, the beauty of the scene and the joy of the birds seemed forced, aggravatingly insistent, so that Earl wanted to get a can of spray paint and obliterate the entire panorama.

He might have vandalized it if there hadn't been security cameras in the hallways and in the elevator. But the homeowners' association would only restore it and make him pay for the work. Large sums of money no longer came to him in suitcases, in valises, in fat manila envelopes, in grocery bags, in doughnut-shop boxes, or taped to the bodies of high-priced call girls who arrived naked under leather trench coats. These days, this former senator so frequently felt the urge to deface so many things that he needed to strive to control himself lest he vandalize his way into the poorhouse.

He closed his eyes to shut out the schmaltzy scene of sun-washed bluebirds. When the air temperature abruptly dropped perhaps twenty degrees in an instant, as the car passed the second floor, Earl's eyes startled open, and he turned in bewilderment when he saw that the mural no longer surrounded him. The security camera was missing. The white wainscoting had vanished, too. No inlaid marble underfoot. In the stainless-steel ceiling, circles of opaque material shed blue light. The walls, doors, and floor were all brushed stainless steel.

Before Earl Blandon's martini-marinated brain could fully absorb and accept the elevator's transformation, the car stopped ascending—and plummeted. His stomach seemed to rise, then to sink. He stumbled sideways, clutched the handrail, and managed to remain on his feet.

The car didn't shudder or sway. No thrumming of hoist cables. No clatter of counterweights. No friction hum of rollers whisking along greased guide rails. With express-elevator speed, the steel box raced smoothly, quietly down.

Previously, the car-station panel—B, 1, 2, 3—had been part of the controls to the right of the doors. It still was there, but now the numbers began at 3, descended to 2 and 1 and B, followed by a new 1 through 30. He would have been confused even if he'd been sober. As the indicator light climbed—7, 8, 9—the car dropped. He couldn't be mistaking upward momentum for descent. The floor seemed to be falling out from under him. Besides, the Pendleton had just four levels, only three aboveground. The floors represented on this panel must be subterranean, all *below* the basement.

But that made no sense. The Pendleton had one basement, a single underground level, not thirty or thirty-one.

So this could not be the Pendleton anymore. Which made even less sense. No sense at all.

Maybe he had passed out. A vodka nightmare.

No dream could be this vivid, this intensely *physical*. His heart thundered. His pulse throbbed in his temples. Acid reflux burned his throat, and when he swallowed hard to force down the bitter flood, the effort brought tears that blurred his vision.

He blotted the tears with a suit-coat sleeve. He blinked at the indicator board: 13, 14, 15. . . .

Panicked by a sudden intuitive conviction that he was being conveyed to a place as terrifying as it was mysterious, Earl let go of the handrail. He crossed the car and scanned the backlit control board for an EMERGENCY STOP button.

None existed.

As the car passed 23, Earl jammed a thumb hard against the button for 26, but the elevator didn't stop, didn't even slow until it passed 29. Then rapidly yet smoothly, momentum fell. With a faint liquid hiss like hydraulic fluid being compressed in a cylinder, the car came to a full stop, apparently thirty floors under the city.

Sobered by a supernatural fear—fear of what, he could not say—Earl Blandon shrank away from the doors. With a *thud,* he backed into the rear wall of the car.

In his storied past, as a member of the Senate Armed Services Committee, he had once been to a meeting in the bunker far beneath the White House, where the president might one day try to ride out a nuclear holocaust. That deep redoubt was bright and clean, yet it impressed him as more ominous than any graveyard at night. He had some experience of cemeteries from his earliest days as a state lawmaker, when he had thought that in such lonely places, from earth and graves and dust, no one could be raised up to witness the paying of a bribe. This quiet elevator felt far *more* ominous than even the presidential bunker.

He waited for the doors to open. And waited.

Throughout his life, he'd never been a fearful man. Instead, he inspired fear in others. He was surprised that he could be so suddenly and completely terrorized. But he understood what reduced him to this pathetic condition: evidence of something otherworldly.

A strict materialist, Earl believed only in what he could see, touch, taste, smell, and hear. He trusted nothing but himself, and he needed no one. He believed in the power of his mind, in his singular cunning, to bend any situation to his benefit.

In the presence of the uncanny, he was without defense.

Shudders passed through him with such violence that it seemed he should hear his bones knocking together. He tried to make fists, but proved to be so weak with dread that he could not clench his hands. He raised them from his sides, looked at them, *willing* them to close into tight knuckled weapons.

He was sober enough now to realize that the two words tattooed on the middle finger of his right hand could have made his insult no clearer to the clueless third-world patron in the cocktail lounge. The guy probably couldn't read English any more than he could speak it.

As close to a negative self-judgment as he had ever come, Earl Blandon muttered, "Idiot."

As the car doors slid open, his enlarged prostate seemed to clench as his fists would not. He came perilously close to peeing in his pants.

Beyond the open doors lay only a darkness so perfect that it seemed to be an abyss, vast and perhaps bottomless, into which the blue light of the elevator could not penetrate. In this icy silence of the tomb, Earl Blandon stood motionless, deaf now even to the pounding in his chest, as if his heart were suddenly dry of blood. This was the quiet at the limit of the world, where no air existed to be breathed, where time ended. It was the most terrible thing he had ever heard—until a more alarming sound, that of something approaching, arose from the blackness beyond the open doors.

Ticking, scraping, muffled rustling: This was either the blind but persistent questing of something large and strange beyond the power of the senator's imagination . . . or a horde of smaller but no less mysterious creatures, an eager swarm. A shrill keening, almost electronic in nature yet unmistakably a voice, quivered through the blackness, a cry that might have been of hunger or desire, or bloodletting frenzy, but certainly a cry of urgent need.

As panic trumped Earl's paralyzing dread, he bolted to the control panel, scanning it for a CLOSE DOOR button. Every elevator offered such a feature. Except this one. There was neither a CLOSE DOOR nor an OPEN DOOR button, neither one labeled EMERGENCY STOP nor one marked ALARM, neither a telephone nor a service intercom, only the numbers, as if this were an elevator that never malfunctioned or required service.

In his peripheral vision, he saw something loom in the open doorway. When he turned to face it directly, he thought the sight would stop his heart, but such an easy end was not his fate.

2

The Basement Security Room

Having been shot five times when responding to a domestic-disturbance call, having almost died in the ambulance, having almost died on the operating table, having subsequently contracted a vicious case of viral pneumonia and almost died while recuperating in the hospital, Devon Murphy had quit the police force two years earlier. Although he'd once been a patrol officer, the real deal, he wasn't in the least embarrassed to spend the rest of his career as a security guard, as what some of his former brothers in blue would call a rent-a-cop or a Barney. Devon didn't have a macho problem. He didn't need to prove his toughness. He was only twenty-nine, and he wanted to live, and his chances of living were greatly increased by being a Barney in the Pendleton rather than a target for every thug and crackpot on the city streets.

On the west side of the basement, the security center occupied a room between the superintendent's apartment and the big heating-cooling plant. The windowless space, eighteen feet by thirty-six feet, felt cozy but not claustrophobic. A microwave, a coffeemaker, a refrigerator, and a sink provided most of the comforts of home.

The khaki uniform was kind of dorky, and all that saved Devon from looking like a janitor was a gun belt, from which were suspended a Mace holder containing a small canister of Sabre pepper spray, a cell-phone holder, work keys, a small LED flashlight, and a swivel holster sheathing a Springfield Armory XDM chambered for .45 ACP. In a luxury condominium like the Pendleton, the likelihood that he'd have to use the pistol was hardly higher than the probability that he'd be abducted by extraterrestrials on his way home from work.

Primarily, he was required to cycle through the twenty-four security cameras in the building. And on a random schedule, twice a shift, he got some fresh air by patrolling the basement, the ground floor, and the courtyard, a beat that took fifteen minutes to cover.

Six wall-mounted plasma screens each presented four security-camera views in a quartered format. With a touch-screen Crestron control, Devon could instantly select any one of the cameras for a full-screen display if he saw something suspicious, which he never did. Seventy-Seven Shadow Street was the most peaceful address in the city.

Both nice people and jerks lived in the Pendleton, but the homeowners' association treated employees well. Devon was provided with a comfortable Herman

Miller office chair. The refrigerator was stocked with bottled water, fresh cream, various flavors of coffee, and all of the fixings for whatever brew might be the favorite of the guard on duty.

He was drinking a Jamaican-Colombian blend with a dash of cinnamon when a *breet-breet* signal alerted him that someone had opened the lobby door to enter from the street. He looked to the appropriate plasma display, summoned the lobby camera to full screen, and saw Senator Earl Blandon come in from the December night.

Blandon was one of the jerks. He belonged in jail, but he bought his freedom by loading up on attorneys in five-thousand-dollar suits. No doubt he had also threatened to take half his political party down with him if they didn't put their hands up the backsides of their puppet prosecutors and puppet judges to ensure that the Muppet show called justice would follow the plot he preferred.

Police work had made Devon somewhat cynical.

With Blandon's thick white hair and Roman-coin face, he still looked like a senator, and he seemed to think that appearance alone should continue to command the respect that he had received before he disgraced his office. He was curt, dismissive, arrogant, and in need of having his ear hair trimmed, a detail that fascinated Devon, who was meticulous about his personal grooming.

Blandon had sopped up so much sauce over the years that he was inoculated against visible displays of inebriation; he no longer revealed his drunkenness with slurred speech or with an unsteady gait. Instead of staggering when he was loaded, he walked taller and threw his shoulders back farther and raised his chin more imperially than when he was sober. The telltales of his intoxication were faultless posture and an almost flamboyant poise.

Norman Fixxer, the night concierge, released the lock on the inner lobby door. A *breet-breet* signal issued from the security-station door monitor.

Although Blandon belonged in prison instead of in an ultra-luxury condominium, he was nevertheless an apartment owner. Like any resident, he expected to have his privacy even in the public spaces of the Pendleton. Devon Murphy never followed residents, by camera, along hallways and into elevators, except for the ex-senator, who could be singularly entertaining.

Once, having passed through the lobby and reached the ground-floor corridor, he had been too soused to maintain his deceptively regal posture and had dropped to all fours, crawling to the north elevator—and out of it on the third floor. On another post-midnight return, he strode confidently past the elevator, turned the corner into the north wing, seemed suddenly to become disoriented, opened the door to the concierge's office, evidently mistook it for a bathroom, and urinated on the floor.

That office was now kept locked when not in use.

On this occasion, Blandon found the elevator easily enough, and he boarded it with an air of dignity worthy of a king climbing into his royal carriage. As the doors closed, and after he pressed the button for the third floor, he glanced up once at the security camera in the car, and then he looked around at the bird-and-cloud mural with an expression of pure contempt.

The ex-senator had written two long letters to the homeowners' association criticizing the mural with what he must have assumed was the erudition of a knowledgeable art connoisseur. The board, on which sat at least one genuine art connoisseur, instead found the letters to be contemptible, confrontational, and alarming. The security staff had not been bluntly told to observe Earl Blandon in the elevator when he returned home inebriated, against the possibility that he might deface the mural, but the suggestion had been made indirectly.

Now, as the elevator passed the second floor, something unprecedented happened. An expression of surprise came over the senator's face . . . and swirling currents of blue static, like nothing Devon had seen before, suddenly flushed the image from the screen. The five other screens, quartered into twenty camera shots, also succumbed to the static, and the security system went blind.

Simultaneously, Devon heard low tympanic beats, hollow and strange and barely audible extended notes. Through the soles of his shoes, he felt vibrations in the concrete floor, subtle waves resonating in time with the drumming.

He didn't become alarmed, because the door and

window monitors remained operative, and all the indicator lights were green on the board. No one was forcing entrance at any point. If the sound had grown louder and the accompanying vibrations had accelerated, Devon's puzzlement and concern might have swelled into apprehension.

The phenomenon continued at a consistent level, however, and after about half a minute, the low drumming faded, the last of the vibrations passed through the floor, and the blue static receded from the plasma screens. The many security-camera points of view returned.

The elevator camera had a wide-angle lens and was mounted near the ceiling at a rear corner of the car, providing coverage of the entire interior, including the doors—which were closed. Earl Blandon was gone. Apparently the car had arrived at the third floor, and the ex-senator had disembarked.

Devon switched to the camera covering the short length of public corridor serving Apartments 3-A and 3-C, and then to the camera that provided a view of the entire long north-wing hallway on the third floor. No Earl Blandon. His was the first apartment in that wing, 3-D, overlooking the courtyard. He must have stepped out of the elevator, turned the corner, and let himself through his front door during the time that the video surveillance failed.

Devon cycled through all twenty-four cameras. Without exception, the public spaces were deserted. The

Pendleton remained quiet and still. Evidently, above the basement, the sullen drumming and the vibrations had been so faint that, if anyone had been awakened, no one had been concerned enough to step out of his apartment and have a look around.

3

The Basement Pool

Whether upon arising at four o'clock in the morning, as now, or after work, Bailey Hawks preferred to swim laps with only the underwater lights, the rest of the long room dark, the pool a great glowing jewel, bright watery reflections fluttering like diaphanous wings across the white ceramic-tile walls and ceiling. The pleasantly warm pool, the astringent scent of chlorine, the *slish-slish* of his limbs parting the water, the gentle swash of wavelets lapping at the pale-blue tiles . . . The tense expectation that preceded a trading day and the mental fatigue that followed one were sluiced from him when he swam.

He got out of bed before dawn to exercise, have breakfast, and be at his desk when the markets opened, but rising early was not the cause of the exhaustion that he felt by every Friday evening. A day spent investing other people's money could sometimes leave him as weary as any day of combat when he'd been a marine. At thirty-eight, he was in his sixth year as an independent wealth manager, after having worked for a major investment bank for three years following his military career. During his first year at the bank, he'd thought that eventually, as success built his confidence, he would be less oppressed by the responsibility to protect and grow his clients' assets. But the burden never became lighter. Money could be a kind of freedom. If he lost a portion of someone's investments, he would be throwing away a measure of that client's liberty.

When Bailey was a boy, his mother called him "my guardian." His failure to protect her was an embedded thorn, perpetually working its way through his mind all these years later, too deep to pluck out. He could atone, if at all, only by reliable service to others.

At the end of his fifth lap, he touched bottom with his feet and turned to face the farther end of the long rectangle of shimmering water, where he had entered by the submerged steps. The pool was five feet deep, and Bailey stood six two, so when he leaned back against the coping to rest before doing another five laps, the water rose not quite to his shoulders.

He smoothed his wet hair back from his face—and saw a dark form coming toward him underwater. He hadn't been aware of anyone entering the pool after him. The rippled surface spun the quivering light and wavelet shadows into purling patterns that severely distorted the approaching figure. When you were submerged, the greater resistance made progress harder than doing laps on the surface, but this swimmer bored through the water as if he were a torpedo. The exertion needed to make such headway should have forced the man to breach for air before he could complete a hundred-foot length, but he appeared to be as fully at home underwater as any fish.

For the first time since his days in the Marine Corps, Bailey sensed mortal and imminent danger. Wasting not an instant second-guessing his instinct, he turned, pressed his palms flat atop the coping, and levered himself out of the pool, onto his knees. Behind him, someone seized his left ankle. He would have been pulled back into the water if he hadn't kicked furiously with his right foot and struck what seemed to be his assailant's face.

Released, Bailey scrambled to his feet, staggered two steps on the matte-finish tile, and turned, suddenly breathless, overcome by the irrational fear that he was in the presence of something inhuman, one mythical monster or another that was not merely mythical anymore. Nothing confronted him.

The underwater lamps were not as bright as they had been. In fact, the quality of the light had changed from crisp white to a sullen yellow. The blue water-line tile appeared green in this sour glow.

The dark shape moved under the surface, sleek, swift, streaking back toward the steps. Bailey hurried along the apron, trying to get a better look at the swimmer. Now acid-yellow, the pool appeared to be polluted, clear in some places but cloudy in others. Discerning details of the person—or thing—in the water proved difficult. He thought he could make out legs, arms, a basic human form, yet the overall impression was of something deeply strange.

For one thing, the swimmer didn't frog kick, which was almost essential for making way underwater without swim fins, and he wasn't using a breaststroke, either. He appeared to undulate with the muscular sinuosity of a shark, propelling himself in a way no human being could.

If Bailey had been more prudent than curious, he would have snared his thick terry-cloth robe from the hook on which it hung, slipped into it and his flip-flops, and hurried to the nearby security room in the west wing of the basement. Devon Murphy would be on duty there. But Bailey was transfixed by the eerie nature of the swimmer, by the otherworldly mood that settled on the room.

The building shuddered ever so slightly. A low rumble rose from the earth under the Pendleton's foundation, and Bailey glanced at the floor in front of him, half expecting to see hairline cracks opening in the mortar joints between the tiles, though none did.

With the brief shaking, the light in the pool changed again, from the pustulant shade of disease-darkened urine to red. Short of the steps, the swimmer turned with the serpentine ease of an eel, heading back toward the end of the pool from which Bailey had fled.

Where clear, the water was the color of cranberry juice. Where clouded as if from disturbed silt, it resembled blood, and that vile stain now spread more rapidly through the pool.

The fluttering watery reflections on the glossy white tiles of the walls and ceiling morphed into tongues of faux fire. The long room grew dimmer, murkier, and shadows swelled like billowing smoke.

Nearing the farther end of the lap pool, the swimmer became harder to see, although still visible in the fouled water. No man could have swum three lengths so quickly without once needing to surface for a breath.

The shuddering lasted five or six seconds, and half a minute after it subsided and after the building grew silent, the pool lamps phased from red to yellow to white again. The faux fire licking along the glossy walls became dancing wings of light as before, and the room brightened. The cloudy water turned crystalline once more. The mysterious swimmer had vanished.

Bailey Hawks stood with his hands fisted at his sides, dripping into the puddle in which he stood. His heart knocked with less force than it might have when he was under enemy fire, back in the day, but nevertheless hard enough for him to hear it hammering.

4

Apartment 3-C

At 4:13 A.M. Silas Kinsley was awakened by a low thunderlike sound and thought the building seemed to be shaking. But the brief rumble and the movement stopped by the time that he sat up and came fully to his senses. He waited in darkness, listening for a moment, and then decided that the disturbance had been part of a dream.

When he lowered his head to the pillow once more, however, a sound arose from within the wall against which his bed stood. The whispery slithering noise brought to mind images of snakes writhing between the studs behind the plasterboard, which seemed improbable if not impossible. He had never before heard anything like it. He suspected—intuited—that it must be related to the disquieting history of the house.

The disturbance continued for perhaps five minutes. He lay listening, wondering, not fearful but certainly wary and alert for any change in the sound that might help him to identify the cause.

The subsequent silence was the expectant kind that fostered insomnia. Having recently turned seventy-nine, he usually found sleep elusive once it had been interrupted. Silas was a retired civil-litigation attorney, but his mind hummed as busily these days as when his calendar had been fully booked with clients. He rose before dawn, showered, dressed, and was frying eggs in butter when, beyond the kitchen window, the hot-pink light of morning painted coral reefs across the sky.

Later, after lunch, he fell asleep in an armchair. When he sat up in alarm an hour later, he could not recall much of the nightmare from which he had fled, only that it involved catacombs of flowstone, in which there were no skeletal remains, as in most catacombs, but empty burial niches carved into the sinuous walls. Something silent and unseen, something with implacable intent, had sought him through that maze of passageways.

His hands were as cold as those of a corpse. He stared at the rising moon at the base of each of his fingernails.

Still later on that somber December afternoon, Silas stood at a living-room window of his third-floor apartment in the Pendleton, on the crown of Shadow Hill, watching the lower avenues fade behind an advancing wall of rain. Buildings of buff brick, of red brick, of limestone, as well as newer and taller and uglier curtain-glass towers were at once bleached to a uniform gray as the storm washed over them, becoming like the ghostly structures of a long-dead city in a dream of plague and desolation. Neither the warm room nor his cashmere sweater could relieve the chills that, like a winged horde, fluttered through him.

The official story was that, 114 years earlier, Margaret Pendleton and her children—Sophia and Alexander—had been snatched from this house and murdered. Silas had come to doubt that the long-ago kidnapping occurred. Back in the day, something stranger than murder happened to those three, something worse.

Shadow Hill rose to the highest point in this heartland city, and the third floor was the Pendleton's topmost. The west-facing structure seemed to rule the rain-swept metropolis below. Both hill and street were named for the shadows of trees and buildings that, on a sunny afternoon, grew longer by the hour until, at twilight, they crept to the summit and met the night as it came in from the east.

Not just a great house, not merely a mansion, the Pendleton was more accurately a Beaux Arts *palace* built in 1889, at the height of the Gilded Age, sixty thousand square feet under roof, not counting the vast basement or the separate carriage house. A combination of Georgian and French Renaissance styles, the building was clad in limestone, with elaborately carved window surrounds. Neither the Carnegies nor the Vanderbilts, nor even the Rockefellers, had ever owned a grander house.

Upon taking up residence shortly before Christmas

1889, Andrew North Pendleton—a billionaire in an era when a billion dollars was still real money—christened his new house Belle Vista. And so the place was known for eighty-four years; but in 1973, it was converted into condominium units and renamed the Pendleton.

Andrew Pendleton remained happy in Belle Vista until December 1897, when his wife, Margaret, and their two young children were supposedly abducted and never found. Thereafter, Andrew became a pitied recluse whose eccentricity matured into a genteel kind of madness.

Silas Kinsley had lost *his* wife in 2008, after fifty-three years of marriage. He and Nora were never blessed with children. Having been a widower for three years, he could imagine how loneliness and grief might have robbed Andrew Pendleton of his sanity.

Nevertheless, Silas had concluded that loneliness and loss were not the primary causes of the billionaire's long-ago decline and suicide. Andrew North Pendleton had been driven insane also by some terrible knowledge, by a mysterious experience that he struggled to understand for seven years, on which he remained fixated until he took his own life.

A kind of fixation had gripped Silas, too, following Nora's death. After selling their home and buying this apartment, he had filled his time by taking an interest in the history of this landmark building. That curiosity ripened into such an obsession that he spent uncounted hours poring through public records, back issues of newspapers more than a century old, and other archives in search of facts, no matter how ordinary, that might add to his knowledge of the Pendleton.

Now, although he had watched the legions of the storm marching out of the lowlands and up the long north slope of Shadow Hill, Silas startled back one step when the first wet volley snapped against the French panes, as if the rain, mistaken for mere weather, were instead a malevolent assault aimed specifically at him. The city blurred, the day seemed to darken, and the silvering effect of the living-room lamplight made an inadequate mirror of the window. In the wet glass, his face was transparent and lacking sufficient detail, as if it were not in fact his reflection but instead must be the face of another, the pale countenance of something less than fully human, a visitor from an occult realm temporarily connected to this world by the power of the storm.

Spikes of lightning split the darkening day, and Silas turned away from the window as thunder jackhammered the sky. He went to the kitchen, where the under-cabinet fluorescents brightened the golden-granite countertops and where all other lights were off. His files about the Pendleton littered the dinette table: newspaper articles, Xeroxes of public records, transcripts of interviews with people who claimed to have some experience of the building prior to 1974, and photocopies of the eleven scraps that remained of a handwritten journal that Andrew North Pendleton had destroyed immediately before killing himself.

Each surviving piece of Pendleton's writing was an incomplete fragment, each singed brown around the edges because he burned the journal in his bedroom fireplace prior to biting a shotgun barrel and receiving a mortal meal of buckshot. Each of the eleven scraps of prose was intriguing, suggesting that Andrew Pendleton endured an experience so extraordinary as to be otherworldly. Or perhaps in the final stages of his madness, he was tormented by a dementia in which he mistook nightmares and hallucinations for memories of real events.

Of the eleven surviving scraps, Silas most often returned to a cryptic, disturbing fragment about Pendleton's daughter, Sophia, who was seven years old when she disappeared. The words and all their possible meanings so haunted him that he'd committed them to memory: . . . *and her once-pink skin gone gray, her lips as gray as ashes, and her eyes like smoke, a humorless and iron-gray grin, no longer my Sophie and less Sophie by the moment.*

Andrew Pendleton's loss of his family was not the only tragedy in the history of the great house. The second owner, Gifford Ostock, who was the sole heir to considerable wealth made in coal mining and in railroad coal-car manufacturing, lived well and fully in Belle Vista from 1905 until 1935. One night in December of '35, the butler, Nolan Tolliver, slaughtered the Ostock family and all the live-in staff before killing himself. Tolliver left an incoherent handwritten note claiming to have murdered them in order to "save the world from eternal darkness," and though he took responsibility for all sixteen killings, eight of the dead were never found. To this day it was not known why or how Tolliver disposed of half his victims, or why he did not likewise dispose of the other eight.

5

Apartment 2-C

Bailey Hawks had not reported the encounter in the lap pool to building security. Out of consideration for the privacy of residents, no camera was mounted in that room; therefore, no proof existed that the bizarre incident had occurred.

Five residents of the Pendleton were among his clients: the Cupp sisters, Edna and Martha, in 3-A; Rawley and June Tullis in 2-D; and Gary Dai in 3-B. People with substantial investment portfolios were not likely to continue to entrust their assets to a man who began to rant about a supernatural experience, regardless of how solid his performance had been in the past.

Bailey spent most of the morning and early afternoon in his study, where he tracked the prices of stocks, bonds, and commodities on three dedicated computers while conducting research and analysis on a fourth. Only one of his two full-time employees, Jerry Allwine, worked here with him, and although Jerry was out with the flu, the day was not hectic. There wasn't much movement in either equities or commodities, and when the major exchanges closed, at 2:00 his time, it proved to be a treading-water day.

Normally, Bailey possessed a sharp focus and singular powers of concentration, which served him as well on financial battlefields as in the wars in Afghanistan and Iraq. As he worked that Thursday, however, his mind repeatedly drifted to the memory of the mysterious figure in the pool, and the sense of peril that he had felt back in the moment rose anew and lingered, though not as acute as it had been during the encounter.

Computers off, working by the light of a single lamp, he was still at his desk past three o'clock when shatters of rain against the north-facing windows drew his attention. For the first time he realized how dark the day had grown. Dusk had crept in two hours ahead of schedule. The lowering clouds were as plush and gray as the coats of the Cupp sisters' cats, seeming not only to belly over the city but also to curl around it as if settling in for a long dreamy evening.

Serial lightning flashed, flashed, flashed. The bright flares caused geometric shadows of the French-window muntins and stiles to flutter through the dimly lighted room and briefly print themselves upon the walls.

The quick-following crash of thunder, loud enough to suggest Armageddon, did not bring Bailey up from his chair. But as his desk lamp dimmed, he bolted to his feet during the subsequent barrage of lightning because this time, among the flung grids of window-frame shadows, another shadow moved. Sinuous and fleet. It raced across the room not as if it might be a silhouette of something inanimate projected and set in motion by the storm light, but instead as if it must be an intruder revealed.

Man-tall when it leaped, the featureless dark figure seemed more pantherlike as the leap became a lower lope. Having spun in his chair even as he sprang up from it, Bailey turned to follow the specter, if that's what it was. The thing eluded the eye, swift and quicksilvery, its motion smooth and continuous while the lightning-inspired shadows of the window frames flickered and twitched in the stroboscopic pulses of the storm.

The black form didn't print itself upon the wall, along with the window grids, but seemed to pass *through* the plaster. The chain of lightning cast out its last bright link, the brass desk lamp grew brighter, and Bailey hurried from the study in pursuit of the thing that walls could not contain.

6

Apartment 3-C

After he stood staring for a moment at the Pendleton-related files on the kitchen table, Silas went to the coffeemaker. He filled a white ceramic mug and took down a bottle of brandy from a cupboard shelf and spiked the coffee. The clock showed 3:07 P.M., and though Silas never took a drink earlier than dinner-time, if at all, he felt the need to be fortified for a meeting at five o'clock.

He leaned against the counter, with his back to the double sink and to the window above it. Lightning flared, enlivening his shadow, which sprang forward and leaped back through the half-dark kitchen, forward and back again, as if the distorted silhouette were an entity with a mind of its own and with a keen desire to be free of him.

He sipped the coffee, which was as hot as he could tolerate, perhaps a cure not just for his unsteady nerves but also for the chills that plagued him. He was of half a mind to skip his scheduled meeting, to remain here and drink spiked coffee until his eyes grew heavy and he could no longer stay awake. Even in retirement, however, he was a lawyer who respected not just federal, state, and city laws, but also and primarily natural law, the code with which he believed that all men were born, a code of responsibilities that included the duty to love truth and always to pursue it.

Sometimes truth was elusive. . . .

After Tolliver, the butler, murdered the Ostock family and his fellow workers in 1935, Belle Vista stood empty for three years, until a bachelor oilman named Harmon Drew Firestone, undeterred by the history of violence, purchased the great house at a bargain price. He spent a fortune to restore it to its former grandeur. By World War II, Belle Vista had become *the* center of the city's vibrant social scene. Old Harmon Firestone died quietly in his sleep, of natural causes, in the spring of 1972.

Firestone's estate sold Belle Vista to a property-development trust that converted the building into twenty-three condominium apartments of various sizes. The high ceilings, the lavish and well-crafted architectural details, the hilltop views, and the elegant public spaces ensured that the units sold out quickly in 1974, for the highest per-square-foot cost in the history of the city. Thirty-seven years later, a couple of the original owners still lived in their apartments, but other units had changed hands more than once.

Only the previous day, Silas learned that the Pendleton's history of bloodshed didn't end in 1935, with

Nolan Tolliver's killing spree. Not only had there been more recent violence of a bizarre nature; apparently, the incidents also occurred with a predictable regularity, every thirty-eight years, give or take a day, which suggested that another atrocity might occur soon.

Margaret Pendleton and her two children, Sophia and Alexander, disappeared on the night of December 2, 1897.

Thirty-eight years later, on December 3, 1935, the Ostock family and seven members of their household staff were murdered.

In 1973, thirty-eight years after the Ostock tragedy, no one had been living in Belle Vista because it was being remodeled into high-end apartments; no residents died. However, in late November and early December of that year, tradesmen and craftsmen working on the conversion had experiences so unsettling that a few quit their jobs and for all these years kept silent about what they witnessed. One of them, Perry Kyser, was meeting Silas at five o'clock.

At the coffeemaker, he refilled his mug. He hadn't put away the brandy. After a hesitation, he decided not to spike the brew again.

As he capped the bottle, he glimpsed movement from the corner of his eye, a dark and fleeting something. Heart quickening, he turned toward the open door to the hallway. Light from a pair of crystal ceiling fixtures revealed cream-colored walls, a Persian-carpet runner, a gleaming mahogany floor, but no trespasser.

His recent discoveries had pulled his nerves taut. If

the Pendleton was destined to be a death house once more, as in certain other Decembers, time might be running out. This was Thursday, December 1, 2011.

Silas wasn't in a mood to dismiss the fleeting figure in the hallway as a misperception. He put down his coffee mug and ventured out of the kitchen, head cocked, listening for an intruder.

The dining room lay to the left, the study and a half bath to the right. All were unoccupied.

Beyond the dining room lay the large living room with its cast-iron firebox and elaborately carved limestone surround that extended to a fourteen-foot-high ceiling ornamented with reeded and egg-and-dart moldings. Directly opposite the fireplace, snakes of rain wriggled down the tall windows.

At the farther end of the living room, in the foyer, both the deadbolt and the security chain were engaged on the front door.

Across the hall from the living room, no one lurked in the bedroom or in either of the two walk-in closets. The quiet seemed deeper than usual, an expectant hush, although he might have been imagining the uncanny quality of this silence.

As he approached the half-open door to the spacious bathroom, a domain of gold-veined white marble and large expanses of mirrors, he thought that he heard susurrant voices or perhaps the slithering noise that had arisen within the wall during the night. But when he crossed the threshold, the bathroom also proved to be hushed—and deserted.

He stared at the room in one mirror and then in another, as if a reflection of the space might reveal something that could not be seen by looking directly. Because the mirrors faced each other, he stood among multiple Silas Kinsleys who were either advancing toward him single file or receding from him with their backs turned.

A long time had passed since he had studied his face in a mirror with full self-awareness. He appeared far older than he felt. He had aged ten years in the three since Nora died.

He glanced from face to face, half expecting to discover that one of them was that of a stranger, a malevolent Other hiding among the infinity of diminishing Silas Kinsleys. What a curious thought. The images were of course all identical old men.

As he returned to the hallway, a low and menacing rumble arose, not thunder, from underfoot, as if a subterranean train were passing beneath the building, although the city had no subway system. The Pendleton shuddered, and Silas swayed with it. He thought *Earthquake,* but in the fifty-five years that he had lived in this city, he never felt a temblor and never heard of a major fault underlying any part of the state. The shudder lasted ten or fifteen seconds, and then it faded away, leaving no damage in its wake.

In the study, Witness turned in a circle, wanting first to get the feel of the space. He might be there only seconds, a minute or two at most. This was a man's room but warm, with one wall given to a gallery of photographs showing Silas Kinsley with some of the clients he had so ably represented; Silas and his late wife, Nora, in different exotic locales; and the two of them with various friends on celebratory occasions.

In the hallway, Kinsley walked past the open door, toward the kitchen. He didn't glance this way. Witness waited for the attorney to reappear, belatedly alerted by peripheral vision, but domestic noises in the kitchen suggested that no confrontation was imminent.

How would he react to finding a stranger—a strong young man in boots, jeans, and sweater—in his apartment as if by magic? With the fear of an old man weakened by time or with the calm authority of a lawyer still confident after decades of courtroom triumphs? Witness suspected that this was a man whose composure wasn't easily shaken.

Two walls of the room featured floor-to-ceiling shelves packed full of books. Most of them were books of laws, of cases that were significant for the interpretations of laws that set precedents, and thick biographies of important figures in the history of American jurisprudence.

With reverence, Witness slid one hand lightly across the spines of those books. Where he came from, there were no laws, no attorneys, no judges, no juries, no trials. The innocent had been swept away by a brutal tide of belief in the primacy of the primitive, by faith in the wrong things, by rebellion against reality and the elevation of idiot conviction to the status of the single Truth. He had killed many people in his time, certain that he would never be held to account for the blood he spilled. Nevertheless, he held the law in high regard, just as a man who lived in godless despair might esteem the *idea* of God that he was unable to embrace.

7

Apartment 2-A

The storm was a gift. The lyrics of "One Rainy Night in Memphis" needed a melody with bounce but also with a melancholy edge, which was not an easy combination to achieve, especially for Twyla Trahern. The bounce part gave her no difficulty, but melancholy was for her a secondhand experience, something that happened to other people, and though she had written a few melancholy songs before, she needed a moody environment to inspire her. With her guitar, she sat on a stool by a window in the study of her apartment on the second floor of the Pendleton, gazing at the timely rain, at the city lights twinkling in the premature twilight that the thunderheads impressed upon the day, picking out notes and trying various chords, seeking the sound of sorrow.

Although she didn't always compose this way, she got the chorus first, because that was where the bounce needed to be most emphatic. She worked on it—the final refinements would be made at the piano—leaving the eight-bar bridge for later, which she would write after she had extrapolated the clean lines of the melody from the refrain.

As usual, she had earlier laid down the lyrics line by line, verse by verse, polishing each until it had a shine but not so much that it was slick. Shine without slickness was a hard standard to meet. Many lyricists could spring all the way through a song, knowing that a few lines weren't good enough, that they would have to go back later to rewrite, but Twyla could not work that way. Sometimes, to get the syncopations correct, to make the syllables fall gracefully with the music, she would have to tweak the words once she completed the melody, but tweaking always proved to be the extent of it.

She wrote country and she was country, the daughter of a farmer who lost his farm in the recession of 1980, when she was two years old. He worked thereafter as a maintenance mechanic in a coal-fired power plant, mostly in windowless chambers where the heat could reach 130 degrees. Ten hours a day, five and sometimes six days a week. Sweating continuously. Often doing dangerous work in air smoky with the fine ash of pulverized coal that was flash-burned in a continuous controlled explosion. Winston Trahern endured his job for twenty-two years, to keep his family clothed and fed and comfortable. Twyla never heard her dad complain, and he always showered at the plant, after his shift, and came home looking fresh and clean. When Twyla was twenty-four, a coal cracker at the plant exploded, killing her father and two other men.

She had gotten from him the sunny disposition that made it hard work to write a melancholy song, which was a better inheritance than a pot of money would have been.

As flags of rain unfurled across the city and rippled down the window glass, the melody coalesced around the lyrics. Twyla began to realize she was writing a song that nobody could sing better than Farrel Barnett, her former husband. His first big hit as a performer and her first top-ten tune as a songwriter was "Leaving Late and Low," and they were married as she finished writing four songs for his second CD.

At the time, she thought she loved Farrel. Maybe she did. Eventually, she realized that in part she had been drawn to him because his eyes were the same shade of blue as her daddy's and because he had about him an air of trustworthiness and unshakable good cheer reminiscent of Win Trahern.

In Farrel's case, the cheerfulness was real, though sometimes manic and sometimes inappropriate to the moment. But the trustworthy air was a projection as ephemeral as the beam of light that paints pictures on a movie screen. He went through women like a tornado through a Kansas town, tearing apart other marriages and stripping his more vulnerable lovers of their sense of self-worth as if he took pleasure not in the sex but instead in the destruction that he left behind. Although he always treated Twyla tenderly, he was not as respectful of other women. On a few occasions, one of these wretched specimens, rinsed through with bitterness, washed up on Twyla's doorstep, as though having endured Farrel Barnett made them sisters in suffering who could console each other and plan a mutual vengeance.

After four years, she had no longer loved him. She had needed two more years before she realized that if she didn't divorce him, he would blow apart her life and scatter the wreckage so widely that she wouldn't be able to put herself together as she'd once been. By then, Farrel had made the country-music charts with fifteen songs, twelve written by Twyla, eight of which reached number one.

More important, they created a child together—Winston, named for Twyla's father—and Twyla was at first determined that Winny would not be raised in a home without a dad. Eventually she came to understand that in some rare cases, a broken home might be better for a boy than one in which his narcissistic old man showed up only occasionally and then merely to recuperate from touring and from marathon adultery, less engaged with his young son than with his little entourage of sycophantic buddies.

Although she didn't love Farrel anymore, didn't even like him much, she didn't hate him, either. When she finished "One Rainy Night in Memphis," she would offer it to Farrel first because he would do the best job with it. Her songs supported her aging mother. They were Winny's future. What was best for a song trumped settling old scores.

When the rumble rose not from the storm-torn

heavens but from the ground under the building, Twyla's fingers froze on the frets and raised the plectrum from the strings. As the last chord faded, she felt tremors pass through the Pendleton. Her Grammy and Country Music Association awards rattled on the glass shelves in the display case behind her piano.

In expectation of some impending disaster, she was still gazing through the tall window when barbed lashes of lightning flailed the sky, several great flashes that made the rain appear to descend haltingly, that flared as if with apocalyptic power and seemed to obliterate the other buildings flanking Shadow Street. As the tremors rising from the ground passed and as hard thunderclaps shook the afternoon, the lightning and rain conspired for a moment to make the four lanes of pavement seem to disappear. The city streets below vanished, the buildings and their lights. In the flickering celestial display there appeared to be nothing but a vast, empty landscape, the long hill and a terrible plain below it, something like a sea of tall grass stippled with clusters of black trees, their craggy limbs clawing at the gloom.

This vision must have been a trick of storm light on rain-washed glass, nothing more, because when the pyrotechnics stopped, the city was there as before, the buildings and the parks. The busy traffic ascended and descended the long boulevard, the blacktop streaming with rain and with glimmering reflections of headlights, with slithering red rivulets of taillights.

Twyla discovered that she'd gotten off the stool and

had lowered her guitar to the carpet without being aware of either action. She stood at the window. What she had seen could have been nothing but an optical illusion. Yet her mouth went dry as she waited for another volley of lightning. In the next barrage, the city did not disappear, but held its ground. The unpopulated vastness, glimpsed before, did not reappear. A mirage. An illusion.

She turned to look past the piano at the display case. None of the awards had fallen over, but the shuddering of the building had been real, not a trick of light and rain-blurred window.

8

Apartment 2-C

Bailey turned on all the lamps and ceiling fixtures in the living room, dining room, kitchen, master bedroom, guest bedroom, and both baths. He left them blazing even when he found no one lurking anywhere in the apartment. He wasn't frightened by what he had seen. More curious than anything. The brighter the light in the place, the likelier he was to get a better look at whatever—if anything—came next.

He wasted no time considering the possibility that he might have hallucinated the entity in the swimming pool and the phantom that passed through a wall. He didn't do drugs. He didn't drink to excess. If he suffered from a brain tumor or another mortal condition, there had been no previous indication. In his experience, post-traumatic stress disorder, caused by the horrors of the battlefield, was chiefly the invention of psychiatrists bent upon stigmatizing the military.

In the bedroom, he retrieved a pistol from the bottom drawer in his nightstand. The Beretta 9 mm featured a twenty-round magazine, a six-inch Magnaported Jarvis barrel, and Trijicon night sights. He had purchased the weapon after returning to civilian life, and he never had occasion to use it except on the shooting range.

Once armed, he didn't know what to do next. If the things that he had seen were not full-blown supernatural apparitions, they were at least paranormal. In either case, a pistol might not be of any use. He intended to keep the gun handy, anyway.

He stood by the bed, holding the weapon, feeling frustrated and somewhat foolish. In war, he never had a problem identifying his enemies. They were the guys who wanted him dead, who were shooting at him and his men. They might run away when their surprise attack failed to gain them a quick triumph, but they didn't simply vanish. To survive a firefight, to *win* it, marines had to do more than persevere; they had to be strategists and tacticians, which required a solid grasp of reality, a capacity for clear reasoning. Now here he stood with the Beretta, waiting for an enemy to materialize out of the wall, for an apparition, a boogeyman, a manifestation of *un*reason, as if he were not a marine and never had been, as if he were instead a character from the movie *Ghostbusters.*

As in the pool room eleven hours earlier, a rumble rose from the ground under the Pendleton. This time it escalated rapidly, became louder than before, and the building shuddered for perhaps five or six seconds before both the sound and the tremors faded. He had no doubt that this apparently seismic event was somehow related to the mysterious swimmer and to the inky specter that passed cat-quick through his study. Techniques of financial analysis, no less than battlefield experience, had taught him that coincidences were rare and that unseen connections were everywhere waiting to be uncovered.

No sooner had the Pendleton become still and quiet than Bailey heard the voice. Low and portentous, it sounded like a newscaster reporting disaster on a radio in another room, the shape of the words distorted, their meaning elusive—except that this voice was *here,* as intimate as a lover's murmurs.

When he bent to listen to the clock radio on the nightstand, the voice seemed to come from across the room. He went to the armoire that housed the television, opened the doors to reveal the dead dark screen—and heard the speaker now behind him, seemingly close and yet still unintelligible.

Wherever he went in the bedroom, the unseen speaker spoke in a corner different from the one to which he had been drawn, as though taunting him.

When Bailey stepped into the adjacent bathroom, the voice was *there* as surely as it had been in the previous room. It seemed to issue from behind a mirror, but then from out of an air-intake grill near the ceiling, and then from behind the textured plaster of the ceiling itself.

As Bailey proceeded through the bright rooms, pistol held down at his side with the muzzle toward the floor, the voice grew darker, more menacing. The direction of origin changed even more rapidly, as though the speaker were a crazed ventriloquist succumbing to the fear that, of he and his dummy, only the puppet was real.

And then in the kitchen, the words became clearer, more fully formed, but no more intelligible. Bailey realized he was listening to a foreign language. Neither French nor Italian, nor Spanish. Not German. Not Russian. Nothing Slavic. Nothing Asian. He had never heard anything like it before, which perhaps should have made it seem like one of those extraterrestrial languages in science-fiction movies. Instead he thought it sounded ancient and primitive, though he didn't know why he felt that way about it.

Not once did he suspect that the voice came from the apartment next door. The Pendleton was a steel-reinforced, poured-in-place concrete structure, and the renovators employed that same technique to separate condominium units from one another, augmenting it with modern sound-suppression technology. The only neighbor with whom he shared a wall on this floor was Twyla Trahern, the songwriter, and he couldn't hear even the faintest chords of her piano when she was composing.

Standing by the kitchen island, turning in place, he listened to the voice issue from the air all around him, at first louder but then fading as if someone somewhere was turning down a volume knob.

As the voice became less than a muttered curse, the wall phone rang, and he picked it up. "Hello?"

"Bailey, dear, Edna and I need your calming influence." Martha Cupp, one of the elderly sisters who were among his clients in the Pendleton, spoke with a firmness that was not imperious but rather like that of a good schoolteacher who set high standards and, with affection, expected you to meet them always. "Sally is either off her nut or on the whiskey." Sally Hollander was their housekeeper. "She says she's seen Satan in the butler's pantry, and she wants to quit her job. You know how we depend on Sally."

"I'll be there as quick as I can. Give me five minutes," Bailey said.

"Dear boy, you are the son I never had."

"You had a son."

"But he's nothing like you, I'm sorry to say. His failing chain of sushi restaurants will soon be as dead as the fish they serve. Now he wants me to back him in a wind farm, four thousand windmills on some dreary plain in Nevada, producing enough energy to power eleven houses while killing six thousand birds a day. The boy is a huge wind farm himself, he chatters faster than a carnival barker. Please hurry and talk some sense into our Sally."

As Bailey racked the wall phone, he suspected that Sally's encounter with the devil himself would turn out to have nothing to do with whiskey.

"What's happening here?" he asked aloud, and waited only a moment for the disembodied voice to answer him in that unknown language. The kitchen was now as silent as it was bright.

One

I am the One, the all and the only. I live in the Pendleton as surely as I live everywhere. I am the Pendleton's history and its destiny. The building is my place of conception, my monument, my killing ground.

In celebration of my triumph, I prepare this file to be conveyed to you of great faith, to you who knew the world had gone wrong and longed to repair it. The world you have known is destroyed. I will show you. . . .

Andrew North Pendleton, proud and ignorant, built his great house on this site not because the vista pleased him, but because of the legend of Shadow Hill. Like some others in the upper class in the late nineteenth century, Andrew was eager to pursue new ways of thinking, to throw off the chains of tired tradition. He became fascinated with various forms of spiritualism, and he had the leisure time to pursue them. Séances, sessions of automatic writing, crystal readings, past-life regression through hypnosis: He was a seeker, no less a fool than other men. An Indian mystic, of what tribe was never clear, told him the history of Shadow Hill, and Pendleton declared that he must build there to benefit from the spiritual energy of that hallowed ground.

Indians once settled atop the hill because at certain times of the year, a pale-blue light rose sporadically from old volcanic fumaroles, shimmering and dancing in the air. Infrequently, loved ones long dead appeared briefly among the living, as if the past and the present were one. The ground must be sacred, so they said, and the tribe would be protected by both the ghosts of those lost and by the shining blue spirits.

The mystic, secretly an agent for the owner of the land, failed to tell Andrew Pendleton that the Native Americans eventually moved off the hill when they experienced a more vivid spectacle that filled the night—and their encampment—with a seeming horde of bright-blue spirits less benign than those that had come before them.

On that night, half the tribesmen disappeared forever. They came to me. I partook of them, for they were an affront to my existence.

When Andrew Pendleton, his wife, and his children were presented to me, I allowed him alone to live. In a sense, I owed my existence to him, because he chose to build on Shadow Hill. His Belle Vista became not merely a house but also a vehicle that brought me into the world.

I am the One, and there can be no other. They come to me, and I receive them as the meat they are. In time, all will come to me, and then what must be will be. Thereafter only I shall know the sun and the moon.

Soon the current residents of the Pendleton will appear before me, bewildered by my many manifestations. I know them, for I know everything. Not all will perish, but nearly all. I especially desire the children; I do not tolerate innocence, and I despise gentleness. The ex-marine will discover that the concepts of honor and responsibility are not rewarded under my dominion.

Those who might love one another will not be saved by love. The only love that matters is self-love, and the only self worth loving is the One.

9

Apartment 2-A

Almost-nine-year-old Winny was curled in an armchair in his bedroom, examining three books, deciding which one to read next. Officially a fourth grader, he could read at a seventh-grade level. He'd been tested. It was true. He wasn't all puffed-up proud of it. He knew he wasn't smart or anything. If he was smart, he would know what to say to people. He never knew what to say to people. His mom said he was shy, and maybe he was, but he also never knew what he should say, which a truly smart person would know.

The reason that he could read so well was just because he read all the time, ever since he could remember. First picture books with a few words. Then books with fewer pictures and more words. Then books with no pictures at all. He read mostly young-adult fiction these days. But in a couple years, he'd probably be reading thousand-page adult books, whatever, unless he just read so much that his head exploded, and that would be that.

His dad, who had homes in Nashville and Los Angeles, who came around way less often than the FedEx delivery guy, almost as seldom as Santa Claus, didn't want Winny to get lost in books all the time. He said any boy who got lost in books all the time might turn into a sissy or even an autistic, whatever that was. His dad wanted him to be more into music. Winny liked music, but not as much as he liked reading and writing.

Besides, he was never going to work in music. His dad was a famous singer, and his mom was a semi-famous songwriter, and Winny never wanted to be famous for anything. Being famous and never knowing what to say would be the worst, everybody hanging on your every word but you didn't have any words for them to hang on. That would be like falling facedown into manure in front of everybody like twenty times a day, every day of your life. Everyone in music always seemed to know what to say. Some never shut up. Forget music.

Winny might be a sissy like his dad worried he would be. He didn't know. He liked to think he wouldn't be. But he'd never been tested. Four days a week, he went to the Grace Lyman School, which was founded by Mrs. Grace Lyman, who died like thirty years earlier, but it was an exclusive school even though she was dead. Of course, she wasn't still at the school. They didn't keep her corpse around in a big jar or anything. That would have been cool, but they didn't. He didn't know where her corpse was. Nobody ever said. Maybe nobody knew. Grace Lyman was dead, but they still ran the school by her rules, and one of her rules was zero tolerance of bullies. If he never came face-to-face with a bully, he couldn't be sure whether he was a sissy or not.

He might even be a killer. If some bully started pushing him around, really getting him worked up, maybe he would just go berserk and cut the guy's head off or something. He didn't think he was a berserk killer, but he had never been tested. One thing Winny had learned from books was that you had to be tested in life to discover who you were and what you were capable of doing. Hopeless sissy, noble warrior, maniac—he could be anything, and he wouldn't know until he was tested.

One thing he could never be was Santa Claus. Nobody could be Santa Claus. Santa Claus wasn't real like the FedEx guy. This was a recent discovery of Winny's. He wasn't sure how he felt about that. At first, he was sad, he felt like Santa had died, but the sad thing didn't last very long. A person who never existed couldn't die, you couldn't grieve for him. Mostly Winny felt like an idiot for having believed the whole stupid Santa thing as long as he had.

So now he couldn't honestly say his dad came around as seldom as Santa Claus because in truth Santa Claus never came, but sometimes his dad did. Of course, he hadn't seen his dad in a long time, so maybe it would turn out that his dad never existed, either. Winny got a phone call now and then, but that could be a fake-out, the guy on the other end could be anyone. If his dad came for a Christmas visit, he would bring Winny what he always brought: a musical instrument or two, a stack of CDs, not just his own but also

CDs by other singers, and a signed publicity photo if he had a new one. Every time Farrel Barnett got a new publicity photo, he made sure that Winny received one. Even though Santa Claus didn't exist, he brought better presents than Winny's dad, who was most likely real, though you never could tell.

Winny had almost decided which of the three books to read when the floor and walls shuddered. The lamp on the table beside his chair had a pull chain, and it swung back and forth, clinking against the base. At the windows, draperies swished a little, as if stirred by a draft, but there was no draft. In the open shelf of his bookcase headboard, Dragon World action figures vibrated against the wood. They jiggled around as if they were coming to life. They were jiggling a lot. But of course they were even deader than old Grace Lyman.

Winny sat through the shaking, the bright blasts of lightning at the windows, and the booming thunder. He wasn't afraid. He wasn't going to wet his pants or anything. But he wasn't calm and collected, either. He was in-between somewhere. He didn't know the word for how he felt. The past couple of days, things were kind of strange in the Pendleton. Things were weird. But weird didn't always have to be scary. Sometimes weird was really interesting. Last Christmas, his dad gave him a gold-plated saxophone, which was just about as big as Winny. That was more than a little weird, but it wasn't *either* interesting or scary, just weird in a stupid kind of way.

He had kept secret the weird and interesting thing

that happened to him twice in the past two days. Although he wanted to share his strange experiences with his mom, he suspected that she would feel she had to tell his dad. For all the right reasons, she was always trying to keep old Farrel Barnett involved in his son's life. For sure, his dad would overreact, and the next thing Winny knew, he would be seeing a shrink twice a week, and there would be some kind of custody battle, and he would be in danger of Nashville or Los Angeles.

As the shaking came to an end, Winny glanced at the TV. It was dark and silent. Although the acrylic screen wasn't polished enough to reflect him as he sat in the armchair, it didn't appear flat but instead seemed to have forbidding depths, like a cloudy pool of water in the shade of a forest. The glow of his reading lamp, floating on the screen, seemed to be the pale distorted face of someone drowned and drifting just below the surface.

Twyla hurried from her study to Winny's room at the farther end of the big apartment, which contained over thirty-five hundred square feet of living space in eight rooms, three baths, and a kitchen—one of the two largest units in the building. She knocked on his door, and he told her to come in, and when she crossed the threshold, she found him in the armchair, legs tucked under himself, three books in his lap.

He was luminous, at least to her, although she thought not only to her, because she had often seen people staring at him as if his appearance *compelled* their attention. He had her dark hair—almost black—and his father's blue eyes, but his looks were not the essence of his appeal. In spite of his shyness and reserve, he possessed some ineffable quality that endeared him to people on first encounter. If a boy so young could be said to have charisma, Winny was charismatic, though he seemed to be oblivious of it.

"Honey, are you okay?" she asked.

"Sure. I'm all right. Are you okay?"

"What was that shaking?" she wondered.

"You don't know? I figured you'd know."

"I don't think it was an earthquake."

He said, "Maybe something blew up in the basement."

"No. That would have set off an alarm."

"It happened before."

"When?"

"Earlier but not as bad. Maybe someone's blasting somewhere. Some construction guys or someone."

His bedroom had a twelve-foot-high coffered ceiling with an ornate gilded-plaster medallion in each coffer and exquisite panels of wainscoting with a gilded ground overpainted with a Japanese-style scene of dragonflies and bamboo, original to the Pendleton.

This almost daunting elegance was balanced by Winny's toys and books, but Twyla wondered—and not for the first time—if she had made a mistake when she bought the apartment, if this was a suitable environment for a child. This was a safe building in a safe city, a privileged ambiance in which to grow up. But there weren't many kids in the Pendleton, therefore few opportunities to have playmates. Winny had no interest in playmates; he always seemed to keep himself entertained. If he were to overcome his shyness, however, he needed to be around other kids his age, not just at school, but also playing and having fun.

Sitting on the footstool in front of her son's armchair, Twyla said, "Honey, do you like it here in the Pendleton?"

"I don't want to live in Nashville or L.A.," he said at once.

"No, no," she said. "That's not what I mean. I don't want to live in those places, either. I mean, maybe we could get a house in a regular neighborhood, not so fancy as this, a house with a yard, maybe near a park or something, where there's lots of other kids. We could get a dog."

"We could get a dog right here," Winny said.

"Yes, we could, but it's not as easy to take care of in the city as it would be in a suburb. Dogs like to have room to run."

He frowned. "Anyway, you can't just go and live in a regular neighborhood 'cause of who you are."

"Who I am? I'm just me, just someone who writes songs. I'm nobody special."

"You've been on TV sometimes. You even sang on TV that time. You sang really good."

"I grew up in a regular neighborhood, you know. In fact it was a kind of shabby regular neighborhood."

"Anyway, I don't much like parks. I always get some

itchy rash or something. You know how I get that rash. Or I can't stop sneezing 'cause of the flowers and trees and all. Maybe it's fun to go to a park in winter, you know, when everything's all dead and frozen and covered in snow, but it's not so great most of the year."

She smiled. "So a park—that's like a little piece of Hell right here on earth, huh?"

"I don't know what Hell's like, except probably hot. It must be worse than the park, since it's the worst place ever. Let's stay where we are."

She loved Winny so much that she wanted to shout it out. She could hardly contain so much love. "I want you to be happy, kiddo."

"I'm happy. Are you happy?"

"I'm happy with you," she said. He was in his stocking feet. She took hold of his right foot by the toes and shook it affectionately. "Wherever I am, I'm happy if you're there."

He averted his eyes, embarrassed by her declaration of love. "I like it here okay. This place is cool. It's different."

"Anytime you want," she said, "you could have kids from school for a sleepover or a Saturday afternoon."

Frowning, he said, "What kids?"

"Any kids you want. Your friends. One or two, or a whole bunch, whoever."

After a hesitation, alarmed by the thought of inviting kids home with him, Winny said, "Or you and me, maybe we could go to the park and stuff if that's what you want."

Rising from the footstool, she said, "You're a gentleman. You really are." She leaned over, kissed his forehead. "Dinner at six."

"I'll just sit here and read till then."

"You have homework?"

"Did it in the car, coming back from school with Mrs. Dorfman."

Mrs. Dorfman, the housekeeper, doubled as Winny's chauffeur.

"Doesn't sound like much homework for a Grace Lyman student."

"It was a ton, but it was stuff that's all easy for me. There wasn't any awful math or anything."

Twyla once told the boy that she had done well in math because it was a kind of music. Ever since, to support his determination to avoid being pushed into becoming a musician, Winny had pretended to find math difficult.

Lightning flashed, much softer than previously, but instead of glancing at the windows, the boy turned to regard the dark TV in the wall of cabinetry and bookshelves opposite his bed. Brow furrowed, his face settled into a look of wary expectation.

As thunder rolled instead of crashing like before, Twyla was overcome by intuitive motherly concern. "Is anything wrong, Winny?"

He met her eyes. "Anything like what?"

"Anything at all."

After a hesitation, he said, "No. I'm okay."

"You sure?"

"Yeah. I'm good. I feel good."

"Love you, my little man."

"Me too." He blushed and opened one of the books in his lap.

His mom was great, the best, probably pretty much like a real angel would be, except that she said things like "my little man," which an angel never would because an angel would know that it was an embarrassing thing for anyone to say to Winny. He was little, all right, but he wasn't a man. He was just a skinny kid that the wind could blow over. He kept waiting to get biceps bigger than pimples, but it wasn't happening even though he was almost nine years old. He was probably going to be a skinny kid all his life until suddenly he turned into a skinny old geezer, with nothing in between.

But his mom always meant well. She was never mean or phony. And she listened really well. He could tell her things, and she cared.

When she asked if anything was wrong, maybe he should have shared his recent weird experiences even if she would tell his dad. At dinner, maybe he would tell her about the voice that spoke to him from the weird channel on the TV.

Witness stepped to the piano in Twyla Trahern's study as she exited the room, her back to him, unaware that he was behind her. He followed the woman to the doorway and stood on the threshold just long enough to ascertain that she was headed to the kitchen, most likely to make dinner for herself and her son.

Whatever she intended to prepare, they would not be here to eat it. Time was running out, the moment looming.

Witness wandered back toward the piano, pausing at the display shelves containing Twyla's awards for songwriting. She had achieved remarkable success before the age of thirty. He remembered her songs because he forgot nothing. Nothing. He had owned the CD she made, on which she sang her own compositions, her voice warm and throaty.

Where he came from now, there were no songwriters, no songs, no singers, no musicians, no audiences. The morning dawned unsung, and through the day and night, the air was not once brightened by a note of Nature's music. Among the last people whom he had killed were a man who could play the guitar with great finesse and a young girl, perhaps twelve, whose voice had been clear, sweet, angelic.

He had not been himself in those days. He had loved the law and music at one time. But then he had changed, been changed, in some ways by his intention, in other ways not. He had enjoyed music once. Now that he lived without music, he *revered* it.

Reverence could not keep him in Twyla Trahern's study. It all shimmered away.

10

The Basement Security Room

When Devon Murphy went off duty at 7:00 A.M. Thursday, Logan Spangler came on for the next eight hours. Of the five guards that covered the twenty-one weekly shifts at the Pendleton, Logan was the most senior, the chief of security.

He had been a beat cop and then a homicide detective, and he had busted more punks than the combined series heroes of a hundred thriller writers, which maybe wasn't saying much because, in Logan's estimation, ninety percent of the guys who pounded out those books were sissies who knew less about real evil than did your average librarian and who were no tougher than a Twinkie. He was eligible for retirement at fifty-two, and he only turned in his badge at sixty-two because that was the mandatory retirement age. Now at sixty-eight, he could still whup the ass of any forty-year-old on the force.

Logan gave himself totally to his security-guard position. If he failed to take it as seriously as he had once approached his work with the police department, he would be disrespecting not only his employers but also himself. Consequently, he was not inclined to shrug off the failure of video surveillance during the previous night, even though it had been down just briefly.

Devon thought the cameras were out of commission about half a minute. After the kid left for the day, Logan reviewed the time-stamped recordings—images from the cameras were stored for thirty days—and found that in fact the system malfunctioned for only twenty-three seconds.

During the morning and early afternoon, as his duties permitted, Logan ran the security-system diagnostic program, hoping to discover the cause of the interruption in surveillance, but he could find no explanation. He also reviewed the stop-motion recordings from key basement and ground-floor cameras during the two hours that led up to the failure, which had occurred between 2:16:14 A.M. and 2:16:37 A.M. He half expected to see a previously undetected intruder who might have tried to sabotage the surveillance equipment, but everyone on those DVRs was a resident or an employee of the Pendleton, engaged in legitimate business.

A few minutes before his shift began at 3:00 Thursday afternoon, Vernon Klick arrived, his owlish green eyes clouded behind heavily smudged eyeglasses that hadn't been cleaned since maybe Thanksgiving. He carried a lunch pail and the usual large briefcase, as if he were an attorney burdened with case files. His shoes were not polished, his khaki pants poorly pressed. He had shaved, but there was just enough grime under a few of his fingernails to make Logan want to scrub his subordinate's hands with a bristle brush. For whatever reason, Klick had gone into a decline since being hired. He didn't know it, but he would not be in his job the following day's shift.

Logan mentioned the rumpled pants and scuffed shoes, but he refrained from commenting on the fingernails. If Klick realized the disgust that he engendered in his boss, he might be alerted to the fact that his days were numbered. Logan preferred to surprise an employee with his termination notice only minutes before he was escorted from the building.

Relinquishing the main command post, Logan moved to the spare chair. He again ran the diagnostic program, fruitlessly seeking the cause of the brief video outage.

"What's the story?" Klick asked.

"Story?" Logan asked.

"What're you looking for?"

"Nothing."

"You've got to be looking for something."

Logan sighed. "There was a brief failure of cameras last night."

"That's big."

"It's not big," Logan said. "It was twenty-three seconds."

"Somebody maybe pulled a heist."

"Nobody pulled a heist."

"Somebody pulled something," Klick said.

"Nobody pulled anything."

"Somebody did," Klick insisted. He'd never been a policeman, only a security guard; but he believed that he possessed a cop's intuition. "Maybe somebody killed somebody."

"Nobody was killed."

"Just because you haven't found the body yet doesn't mean it isn't somewhere in the building for someone to find sometime."

Logan refused to keep the idiotic conversation alive. He closely and repeatedly reviewed the video of Senator Earl Blandon's return to the Pendleton the previous night, his time in the elevator, and the third-floor corridors immediately following the dissipation of the blue static.

He was aware of Vernon Klick's barely repressed frustration at having to share the room with his boss for more than a minute or two. No doubt the freak had a pornographic magazine in his briefcase or a pint of Irish whiskey, or both, and was eager to pleasure himself one way or another.

What kept Logan at his task was a problem with the timing of Earl Blandon's return to his apartment. The elevator required twenty-one seconds to go from a full stop on the ground floor to a full stop on the third. According to the time-stamped video, camera coverage had been lost four seconds into the elevator's ascent. Subtract the next seventeen seconds of ascent from the twenty-three seconds of outage. That left only six seconds of blue static during which the man could have stepped out of the elevator, walked the length of the short west-wing corridor on the third floor, turned right into the north corridor, unlocked his door, and entered his apartment.

Like Devon Murphy, Logan knew the telltales of the senator's drunkenness: the careful posture, the exaggerated poise. The footage of Blandon crossing the lobby left no doubt that he came home in a state of extreme inebriation.

Perhaps a sober man could have walked briskly from the elevator to the door of 3-D and let himself into the apartment in a mere six seconds. In an advanced state of drunkenness, Earl Blandon moved not briskly but at a stately pace, almost with the measured progress of a bride matching her steps to the processional music on her way to the altar. Surely he had needed at least six seconds just to fumble the key from his pocket and insert it successfully into the lock.

"Before I leave for the day," Logan said, "I'm going to check on one of the third-floor residents."

Indicating the screen that his boss had been studying, Klick said, "You mean the senator?" When Logan didn't reply, Klick said, "You think he's dead?"

"No, I don't think he's dead."

"Then you think he killed somebody?"

"Nobody killed anybody."

"Somebody killed somebody, I bet, or robbed somebody, or robbed *and* killed somebody."

Getting up from his chair, Logan Spangler said, "Vernon, what's your problem?"

"Me? I don't have any problem."

"You have some kind of problem."

"My only problem is that missing twenty-three seconds."

"That's not your problem," Logan said, "it's my problem."

"Well, then you shouldn't have got me worried about it."

"There's nothing to worry about."

"There is if someone killed or was killed."

"Work your shift. Follow procedures. Don't let your imagination run wild," Logan advised, and left Klick alone to do whatever he did when he was supposed to be on duty.

As Logan pulled the security-room door shut behind him, a rumbling rose seemingly from underfoot, and the Pendleton shuddered. The same thing had happened earlier. Foundation work was under way for a high-rise on the eastern slope of Shadow Hill, which was no doubt the source of the disturbance. He decided to inquire with the city building department after checking on the senator.

11

Apartment 3-F

Mickey Dime left Jerry dead in an armchair in the study.

In the kitchen, he washed his hands. He liked the water so hot it stung. The liquid soap made a soothing lather. It smelled like peaches. Peaches were his favorite fruit.

Beyond the window, the sky flashed, flashed. He wished he were outside to feel the air shiver, to enjoy the crisp scent of ozone that lightning left in its wake. Thunder crashed. He felt it in his bones.

He poured a glass of chocolate milk and plated a lemon muffin. The glass was by Baccarat, the plate by Limoges, the fork by Tiffany. He liked the look and feel of them. The muffin was heavily drizzled with icing. He sat at the breakfast table by a window overlooking the courtyard. He ate slowly, savoring the treat.

A lot of sugar made most people hyper, but it calmed Mickey. From the time he was a little kid, his mom said he was different from other people. She wasn't just bragging. Mickey *was* different in many ways. For instance, his metabolism was a high-performance machine, like a Ferrari. He could chow down on anything, never gain an ounce.

After the muffin, he enjoyed three Oreos. He pulled the wafers apart and licked off the icing first. His mom had taught him to eat them that way. His mom had taught him so much. He owed everything to her.

Mickey was thirty-five. His mother had died six months earlier. He still missed her.

Even now he could recall the precise chill and the too-soft texture of her cheek when he leaned into the coffin to kiss her. He kissed each of her eyelids, too, and half expected them to flutter open against his lips. But they were stitched shut.

He finished his snack. He rinsed the plate, the glass, the fork. He left them on the drainboard to be washed by the housekeeper, who came twice a week.

For a while he stood at the sink, watching raindrops tap the window. He liked the patterns of rain on glass. He liked the sound.

One of his favorite things was to walk in warm summer rain, in the cold rain of autumn. He owned a getaway cottage in the country, on twelve acres. He liked to sit in the yard, in the fresh-smelling rain, in the nude. He liked to feel a storm washing him with its thousand tongues.

Mickey returned to the study, where Jerry was dead in the armchair. The silencer-equipped .32 pistol had been fired at close range. The bullet pierced the heart.

Under the entrance wound, the bloodstain on the white shirt was in the shape of a teardrop, a graceful detail that Mickey appreciated.

Jerry's suit was beautifully tailored. The pleats in his pants looked as sharp as knife blades. The tight weave of the wool was pleasing when Mickey rubbed a lapel between thumb and forefinger. The shirt and tie appeared to be silk. Mickey liked the smell of silk. But Jerry wore a crisp lime-scented cologne that overwhelmed the subtler fragrance of the fabric.

Since becoming a professional, Mickey never killed a man for free. It was unnatural. Like Picasso giving away a painting. An important part of the sensual experience of murder was counting the money afterward.

The first time he killed, a week after his twentieth birthday, he'd been an amateur. He was fortunate to have gotten away with it. He tried to get a date with this cocktail waitress named Mallory. She turned him down. And she wasn't nice about it. She humiliated him. He learned everything about her: how she shared a little house with a girlfriend, how her fifteen-year-old sister lived with her. He went in there with a Taser, chemical Mace, and vinyl-strap handcuffs. It was all about sex, and he got plenty. Then he had to kill them, which he discovered was another kind of sex. But it was stupid to kill for sex when you could buy it. Killing for sex instead of just for the pleasure of killing, he was sure to leave DNA behind. Besides, when he was totally hot and in the act, he was out of control and certain to make mistakes, leave clues of other kinds. So even though it had been the best night of his life to that point, he decided never again to kill as an amateur. He was proud of his subsequent self-control.

Mickey also had never before popped a relative. Jerry was his brother. Maybe it should have felt different, but it didn't. The only difference was not receiving a fat envelope full of cash for the job.

Not once in years of dreaming about murder had Mickey imagined offing someone in this apartment. So inconvenient.

Jerry Dime had forced the moment. He had come here to kill Mickey. But he was an amateur. He telegraphed his intentions.

Come to think of it, Mickey would eventually get a payday for this bit of work. No need now to share their mother's estate.

From the bedroom closet, he got a spare blanket. It was made of some microfiber, as soft as fur but strong. He rubbed it against his face. It smelled like a camel-hair sport coat, which was one of Mickey's favorite smells.

Jerry's wide-open eyes seemed bluer in death than in life. Mickey had russet eyes. Their mother's eyes had been green. Mickey didn't know about their fathers' eyes. Their fathers had been anonymous sperm donors.

After pulling the corpse out of the armchair and onto the blanket, Mickey went through his brother's pockets. He took Jerry's wallet, phone, coins. The coins were warm with Jerry's body heat.

Mickey rolled the dead man in the blanket. He cinched the ends tight with a couple of his neckties.

Stepping out of the study, he pulled the door shut behind him.

As he glanced at his watch, the doorbell rang.

His twice-a-month manicurist, Ludmila, had arrived. She was a Russian immigrant, in her mid-fifties, dark-haired and intense.

She spoke English well. But they were agreed that she would not speak except to thank him for payment. Any conversation would detract from the pleasure of the manicure and pedicure.

After his mother's death, Mickey had expanded the master bath into the guest bedroom. He never had overnight guests.

The huge bathroom had white-marble walls and ceiling, black-granite countertops, and a checkerboard marble-and-granite floor. It featured a spa chair with water supply, a custom massage table, and a corner sauna lined with cedar.

Mickey reclined in the spa chair. He soaked his bare feet in warm water. The footbath was scented with fragrant salts.

As Ludmila worked on his hands, Mickey closed his eyes. Slowly he ceased to be a man and became only ten fingertips. The whisper of the emery board was a symphony. The fragrance of the clear nail polish intoxicated him. The simplest pleasure could be rapturous if you gave yourself entirely to it.

Sensation was everything. It was the only thing.

One

I am not what you of great faith imagined, but I am what you sought. I am the past undone in its entirety.

I celebrate death. Death makes room for new life. I die every day and rise again. Those weaker creatures who die and do not rise have done a service to the world, because a world of weaklings is a world with no future.

Ironically, my tremendous strength and immortality have their origin in a fault: a fault in the structure of space-time that lies in the heart of Shadow Hill. Periodically, when conditions are right, past and present and future exist here simultaneously, just as they exist in me. Those who live at the pivot point, where past and future meet, sometimes glimpse what once was and what will come to be. By the Native Americans who first lived here and by everyone who followed them, those presences out of time are thought to be ghosts or hallucinations or visions.

Every thirty-eight years comes an event of greater power than mere apparitions. Involuntary pilgrims journey to my kingdom and discover their fate, which is the fate of the entire world.

Arriving from 1935, the wealthy Ostock family learned to be more submissive to the One than their servants were to them. Humanity believes it is exceptional, but it is to the world as fleas to a dog, as lice to a chimpanzee. An infestation. A plague. The Ostocks and all human beings are rats on the road out of Hamelin, enchanted by a tune that leads them to drown in me.

Soon the songwriter will stand before me, and I will feed upon her heart, which she imagines is the source of emotion in her songs. The elderly attorney, who believes in the law, will learn there is no law but mine. The retired detective who believes in justice will get the justice he deserves. I will enter the boy, control his body, but allow him to be aware for a while, allow him to witness the slow corruption of his body and his innocence. Vermin born of vermin, they are the infestation for which I am the purifying fire.

12

Apartment 3-A

Smoke in an armchair and Ashes on a footstool watched Martha Cupp as she moved impatiently from window to window in the living room, their orange eyes as bright as lanterns.

Except for the betrayals of her body, from minor annoyances like gray hair to the greater treachery of arthritis in her hands, Martha felt twenty years old. She was as quick of mind as she had been six decades earlier, sharpened by the wisdom that came from a life rich in experiences.

At eighty, as at twenty, she had no patience for nonsense. To her dismay, the world was more than ever a temple of absurdity. So many people had stopped believing in any truth that offered hope, uncritically embracing instead a belief in the animated inanimate that was computer "intelligence," in the gleaming but hollow utopia of the Internet and all things digital, in the preposterous economic theories of envious sociopaths, in the absolute moral and legal equality of men and ants and apes and asparagus. In particular, Martha disliked the numerous denominations of End Timers who, like the odious Mr. Udell in 3-H, believed passionately in one existential threat or another, from a looming ice age to an imminent planetary meltdown, to the Rapture followed by Satanic rule and Armageddon. Nonsense.

A few days earlier, their cook and housekeeper, Sally Hollander, had been among the sane. Then suddenly she began talking about vivid and disturbing dreams. She became so distressed by the third round of nightmares that she believed they must be prophetic glimpses of a rapidly approaching doomsday. And now she claimed to have seen the devil in the butler's pantry.

The city was real, the storm was real, and the window before Martha was real, but the devil in the pantry was rubbish and humbug. Either Sally, previously so dependable and sound of mind, was having a midlife crisis and developing a personality disorder, or the poor woman suffered from some physical malady with symptoms that included hallucinations and delusions. Because Sally was like a beloved niece, Martha didn't want to consider the second possibility, which might indicate a brain tumor or other dire condition.

A blazing axe of lightning chopped the sky and thunder crashed like a thousand trees felled and falling as one. For a moment the entire city seemed to go dark. But that must have been just a brief blinding effect of the brilliant thunderbolt, because when she blinked twice, the city was out there again, its twinkling buildings and lamplit avenues receding in the murk.

Earlier, Smoke and Ashes, a pair of British blue shorthairs, had remained cat-calm through Sally's outburst, languid and self-absorbed. Their ears had pricked slightly at the first scream, and their heads had turned toward the source of the sound. But their muscles had not tensed nor had their dense and ultra-plush blue-gray fur bristled in the least. As the housekeeper's cries of terror softened into sobs, Smoke and Ashes had lost interest and had focused once more on their grooming. The behavior of the cats was for Martha proof enough that nothing demonic had paid a visit.

Edna, Martha's older sister—eighty-two—had an affinity for nonsense. All her life, Edna believed in everything unlikely, from palm-reading to poltergeists, from the lost continent of Atlantis to cities on the dark side of the moon. At the moment, she was sitting at the kitchen table with Sally, plying the shaken woman with brandy-laced coffee to quiet her nerves and encouraging her to remember—or invent—new details of her encounter with the Prince of Darkness in the butler's pantry.

Sometimes Martha marveled that she and Edna, being different in so many ways, had built a major business together with so few moments of friction over the years. Martha had a head for business, and Edna was the creator of ever more delicious recipes. Cupp Sisters Cakes became the largest mail-order dessert company in the nation, produced a highly successful line of frozen cakes on sale in supermarkets, and in general rode every wave in the cake business to greater success. The only thing they didn't see coming was, ironically, the upscale-cupcake craze; none of the many franchised cupcake stores bore the Cupp name. Martha supposed they succeeded because their talents were different but complementary—and because they adored each other.

The company had been sold four years previously, and they had given away half their fortune. Thus far retirement was enjoyable, a series of luncheons and social events, volunteer work with their favorite charities, and plenty of free time to pursue their personal interests. But now this episode with dear Sally. Although Edna was the superstitious one, Martha could not shake the uneasy feeling that with this peculiar incident, her long run of good fortune—and her sister's—might be near an end.

As though in prophetic confirmation of that thought, the sky swung another series of bright blades. The city, like a chopping block, seemed to shudder from the impacts, the countless briefly silvered raindrops stuttering down the dusk in a stroboscopic dazzle.

In the window glass, Martha's reflected image flickered, as if the life force in her might be near the end of its wick. She suffered from a fear of death that she struggled always to repress, a dread that dated from the night that her first husband, Simon, passed away, when she had been forty-one. The inspiration for her fear was not Simon's death but an incident that occurred shortly thereafter, which for the past thirty-nine years she had been able neither to explain nor forget.

When the doorbell rang, Smoke and Ashes turned their heads but did not deign to leave their cushioned perches to welcome the caller.

In the open doorway, Bailey Hawks greeted Martha with a kiss on the cheek. As he crossed the threshold into the foyer, her anxiety diminished. He was the kind of man to whom she'd never been attracted in her youth: quiet, competent, a good listener, a steady ship in any storm. For reasons she had never quite understood, even into middle age, she had been drawn to weak men with sparkling personalities, who were always entertaining and, in the end, always disappointing. Well, she had done all right in spite of having married one man-child and then another; but it was comforting to have a friend like Bailey when your housekeeper started ranting about seeing the devil between the china cabinets and the silver closet.

"I don't know whether to call a medical doctor or psychiatrist," she said to Bailey, "but I refuse to call an exorcist."

"Where's Sally?"

"In the kitchen with Edna. By now my sister will have convinced herself that she, too, saw the apparition and that it had a forked tongue just like a snake."

Edna cared about decor far more than did her sister, and so Martha lived with the consequences of Edna's passion for all things Victorian: chesterfield sofas upholstered in midnight-blue mohair, side tables draped with velvet and crocheted overlays, étagères full of porcelain birds, floral-fabric walls in original William Morris patterns, everything trimmed with ornate gimp, tassels, fringes, lace, and swags.

Although the kitchen had touches of late-nineteenth-century style, it appeared more modern than the rest of the apartment because even Edna preferred gas and electric appliances to wood-burning iron stoves and hulking ice lockers. The most Victorian thing in this roomy space was Edna's outfit, a faithful re-creation of actual day wear from the period, which her seamstress had made according to a drawing in a catalog published in that era: a lilac silk afternoon dress covered with white-spotted lilac chiffon, featuring a lace yoke with rucked silk, a matching hip basque, elbow-length pleated sleeves, and a pleated and gathered floor-length skirt.

Martha was so accustomed to Edna's ways that most of the time she was hardly aware that her sister's fashions were unusual, but once in a while, like now, she realized that these dresses might be more accurately described as costumes. Sitting at the breakfast table with Sally Hollander, whose self-chosen uniform consisted of black slacks and a simple white blouse, Edna looked eccentric, sweet and dear, pleasingly fanciful, but undeniably eccentric.

Declining an offer of coffee with or without brandy,

Bailey sat at the table, across from Sally, and said, "Will you tell me what you saw?"

Previously, the housekeeper's broad, freckled face had always appeared to be aglow with soft reflected firelight, her green eyes often merry but seldom less than amused. Her skin was ashen now, the fire banked in her eyes.

The tremor in her voice seemed genuine. "I was putting away the luncheon plates. The ones with the pierced rim and the roses. From the corner of my eye, I saw something . . . something quick and dark. At first it was a shadow, *like* a shadow, but not a shadow. It came from the kitchen into the butler's pantry, went past me toward the door to the dining room. Tall, almost seven feet, very fast."

Easing forward in her chair, arms on the table, Edna lowered her voice as if concerned that the forces of darkness might learn she was aware of them. "Some say this place is haunted by Andrew Pendleton himself, ever since he committed suicide back in the day."

Leaning against a counter, Martha sighed, but no one noticed.

"Maybe that's true, maybe it isn't," Edna continued. "But even if 77 Shadow Street is as full of restless shades as any graveyard, this wasn't one of them. Nothing as innocent as lingering spirits. Tell him, Sally."

"God help me, I'm half afraid to talk about it," the housekeeper said. "Talking about such things can be an invitation to them. Isn't that what they say, Miss

Edna? I don't want to invite that thing back, whatever it was."

"We *know* what it was," Edna said.

Martha expected Bailey to glance at her knowingly, but he remained focused on the housekeeper. "You said it was like a shadow *at first*."

Sally nodded. "It was ink-black. No details. But then I turned to look after it passed me . . . and I saw it as clear as I see you now. About eight feet away, turning toward me as if it hadn't noticed me until it flew past and was surprised to see me there. Like a man but not a man. Something different about the shape of the head, something wrong, I can't say for sure what. But no hair at all, no eyebrows. Skin as gray as lead. Even the eyes gray, no whites to them, and the irises black, black and deep like gun barrels." She shuddered and resorted to her spiked coffee for comfort. Then: "He . . . it . . . it was lean but looked strong. It opened its mouth, those terrible gray lips, its teeth gray, too, and sharp. It hissed and it meant to bite me, I'm sure it did. I screamed, and it came at me so fast, faster than a cat or a striking snake, faster than anything."

Although Martha remained determined not to be as credulous as Edna, neither her insulating skepticism nor her sensible pantsuit prevented a chill from prickling her spine. She told herself that what disturbed her was the change in Sally, this uncharacteristic claim of a supernatural experience, rather than the possibility that the encounter might have been real.

"Demonic," Edna declared. "A creature of the Pit. No ordinary spirit."

To the housekeeper, Bailey said, "But it didn't bite you."

She shook her head. "This sounds so weird . . . but as it came at me, it changed again, from something very real to just a black shape, and it flew past. I could *feel* it brushing past me."

"And how did it leave the butler's pantry?" Bailey asked.

"How did it leave? Well, just like that. *Whoosh* and gone."

"Did it pass through a wall?"

"A wall? I don't know. It was just gone."

"Oh, walls mean nothing to demons," Edna assured them.

"Demons," Martha said derisively enough to make it clear she considered such talk nonsense.

Sally said, "I don't know if it was any demon, ma'am. I didn't conjure it, for sure. But it was something, all right. As real as me, it was. I don't nip at a bottle when I'm working, and I didn't hallucinate it."

As earlier, a rumble arose from underfoot, and this time the Pendleton shook sufficiently to rattle glassware in cabinets and flatware in drawers. Dangling from a rack over the center work island, copper pans and pots swung on their hooks, although not enough to clang against one another.

The shaking persisted longer than previously, ten or fifteen seconds, and halfway through the tremors, Bailey pushed his chair back from the table, getting to his feet as though anticipating calamity.

Sally Hollander warily surveyed the kitchen, as though she expected that cracks might zigzag up its walls, and Martha stepped away from the counter when upper cabinet doors rattled behind her.

Seemingly amused by her companions' alarm, toying girlishly with the rucked silk at the lace yoke of her dress, Edna said, "I spoke earlier with sweet Mr. Tran, and he's quite sure these quakes are just because of bedrock blasting to carve out the foundation for that new high-rise on the east side of Shadow Hill."

Tran Van Lung, who had legally Americanized his name to Thomas Tran, was the building superintendent. He lived in an apartment in the basement, next to the security center.

"No. That went on too long, much too long, for blast waves," Bailey insisted. "And the first one I felt was in the pool room this morning, about four-fifteen. They wouldn't be starting construction work at that hour."

"Mr. Tran is the finest superintendent the Pendleton's ever had," Edna said. "He knows everything about the building. He can fix anything or knows who can, and he's as trustworthy as anyone I've ever met."

"I agree," Bailey said. "But even Tom Tran can sometimes be operating on misinformation."

When most young men of Bailey Hawks's age squinted, they had but two or three small darts at the outer corners of their eyes. His years at war had stitched the memory of worry into his face so completely that when he was alarmed, his smooth skin folded into an array of pleats that aged him and gave him the aspect of a formidable man of fierce intentions.

When Bailey had sprung up from his chair, Martha Cupp glimpsed something even more revealing of his state of mind. Under his sport coat, he carried a gun in a shoulder holster.

13

Apartment 3-D

When Logan Spangler, chief of security, stepped out of the north elevator on the third floor, the double-door entrance to the Cupp sisters' apartment was to his left. The single-door entrance to Silas Kinsley's apartment stood directly in front of him. He thought of this as the geriatric corner. He liked the old dames and the retired attorney. They were quiet, proper, and considerate. The only owners who gave him fewer problems were those in 1-B, who had died nine months previously and whose estate was still being settled, and Mr. Beauchamp in 1-D, who had passed away of pneumonia two weeks earlier.

Having retired from the police department, Logan supposed that when he retired next from the Pendleton job, he might become head of security for a cemetery. A field full of stiffs in their narrow little condos would be even more quiet and proper than Edna and Martha Cupp. And when he retired from *that* job, he could just lie down in a prepared hole and let them cover him with a dirt blanket.

He wasn't bitter about being forced out of the department at sixty-two. That was six years earlier, ancient history. Though not bitter, he had become a cynic. In truth he had always been something of a cynic and a grump *on the job*—which served him well when he was dealing with homicidal dirtbags, helped him to understand them and find them and bust them—but he had been good-humored and relatively easygoing when off-duty. With all of that action now gone from his life, however, Logan wasn't working off this negative energy every day, and as a consequence, he suspected that he might be souring into an around-the-clock grump.

He could live with that.

From the elevator, he turned right, walked about twenty feet, and turned right again into the north corridor. The apartments were all on the right side, three of them, with views of the courtyard. The farthest belonged to Mickey Dime; in addition to having inherited money, Dime was supposed to be a successful corporate consultant for matters of employee-conflict resolution. The inherited money might be true, but Logan was convinced the rest of it was the product of a bull's back end. Next door to Dime was the Abronowitz apartment. Bernard Abronowitz was in the hospital, recovering from surgery.

The nearest and largest of the three apartments belonged to the former senator, Earl Blandon. If the disgraced politician had gotten on the elevator but had never gotten off, as the security cameras seemed to suggest, there was a mystery to be solved that might test the wits of the cleverest of detectives. Considering how lacking in drama the past six years at the Pendleton had been, Logan doubted that any such puzzle waited to be solved, and he expected Blandon to answer the doorbell in one state of inebriation or another.

After Logan rang three times but received no answer, he rapped sharply on the door. He waited and then rapped again.

Earlier, he had phoned the day-shift concierge, who had relieved Norman Fixxer at 6:00 A.M., and had ascertained that the senator had not left the Pendleton through the lobby during the morning or early afternoon. Now he called the evening concierge, Padmini Bahrati, who had come on duty at 2:00 this afternoon, and she was certain that since she had been at the front desk, the senator had neither departed the building on foot nor asked for his car to be brought around to Shadow Street.

Of course, if Blandon left the grounds by the east gate of the courtyard, he could have gone to the garages behind the Pendleton and driven away without requesting valet service. With that possibility in mind, Logan phoned Tom Tran and asked him to check the senator's garage stall.

Two minutes later, the superintendent reported that Blandon's Mercedes was in the garage. He had not driven away.

After ringing the bell at 3-D yet again and after receiving no response, Logan unlocked the door with his passkey. If the senator was at home, he had not engaged either the security chain or the blind deadbolt that couldn't be unlocked from the corridor.

Holding the door open but remaining in the hall, Logan called, "Senator Blandon? Sir, are you home?"

The senator's apartment was half the size of that occupied by the Cupp sisters. Unless he was unconscious or in the shower, he should have heard Logan.

In an emergency, when there were reasons to believe that a resident might be mortally ill or otherwise incapacitated and unable to grant admittance, the owners'-association protocols required that a security guard enter the apartment with a passkey but only in the company of either the concierge or the superintendent. The idea was to further minimize the already small chance that anyone on the well-vetted security team might use such an occasion to engage in theft.

Because Earl Blandon had a short fuse and was so reliably saturated in alcohol that he was flammable if not explosive, Logan Spangler decided to enter the apartment alone. If the senator wasn't in need of help, he would be greatly displeased by the intrusion. Paranoia was Blandon's armor, righteous indignation his sword, and he never missed a chance to take offense. One uninvited visitor would anger him, but two would *infuriate.*

Interior design held no interest for Logan, but when he turned on the living-room lights, he noticed that the senator had mimicked the power decor of certain men's clubs. Deeply coffered ceilings. Dark wood paneling. Immense leather armchairs. Heavy wood side tables on claw feet. Bronze lamps with parchment shades. Above the limestone fireplace mantel hung a glassy-eyed stag's head with a fourteen-point rack that Blandon had undoubtedly bought rather than earned by his skill as a hunter.

In the dining room, the table was a long slab of highly polished mahogany. Every seat was a captain's chair with arms and a high back, but at the head of the table stood a larger and more ornately carved chair, with silver inlays, as if to imply that the host, if not technically of royal blood, could nevertheless claim to be of a station superior to that of his guests.

As he toured the apartment, touching nothing but light switches and doors that needed to be pushed open, Logan remained, as always, aware of the pistol at his right side, though he did not imagine that he would need it. In a withering world that seemed to be darker and more violent by the day, the Pendleton offered an oasis of peace.

Continuing to call out to the senator as he proceeded through these chambers, Logan came to the master suite. Here, the ceiling coffers, with their baroque moldings, were painted white, and pale-gold paper gave a soft texture and a light pattern to the walls.

The bed was neatly made, everything in order. Because Earl Blandon didn't seem to be the kind to routinely, meticulously clean up after himself, Logan suspected that the man had never made it to bed the previous night.

Those residents who did not have full- or part-time housekeepers of their own, like the senator, contracted with a domestic-service agency, approved by the owners' association, for whatever assistance they required. Generally, they preferred a maid two or three times a week. According to the schedule filed with the security office by the head concierge, who arranged for the service, Earl Blandon's maid came every Monday, Wednesday and Friday.

This was Thursday. No housekeeper had been here to make the bed.

In the master bathroom, a couple of large rumpled towels lay on the floor. When Logan stooped to finger them, he found they were not damp. When he opened the glass door, he saw not one bead of water in the marble-clad shower stall, and the grout joints appeared dry.

The senator had showered perhaps twenty-four hours earlier, before going out for the evening. He evidently had not slept in his bed the previous night. Evidence was mounting that on returning home, he'd gotten into the elevator but, impossibly, had never gotten out.

As much as politicians might try to convince the public that they were mages with magical solutions, they didn't have cloaks of invisibility or get-small pills that shrunk them to the size of an ant. If the senator hadn't disembarked from the elevator by its doors, he must have gone through the emergency exit in the ceiling.

How Blandon could have done that in the twenty-three seconds during which the elevator camera wasn't functioning and *why* he would have done such a thing baffled Logan Spangler. A close inspection of the elevator might reveal a clue.

When he turned to leave the bath, another rumble rose from under the building, and the lights went off both in this room and the next. In the blinding blackness, he unclipped the six-inch flashlight from his belt and clicked it. The crisp white LED beam flared brighter than that of a traditional flashlight, yet he almost stepped out of the bathroom before he realized that everything around him had changed.

A few seconds in the dark seemed to have been *years*. The white marble floor, polished and gleaming earlier, was dulled by dust. Pieces were missing from the decorative braided border of green and black granite. Green stains and rust streaked the nickel-plated sink. Tattered cobwebs festooned the faucet handles and the spout, as if no water had been drawn here in a long time.

In the mirror, now clouded and mottled as if fungus growing behind it had eaten away portions of its silver backing, Logan's reflection seemed to be an apparition, lacking the substance of a real man. The inexplicable sudden deterioration of his surroundings left him for a moment breathless, and he half expected to see that he had aged with the room. But he remained as he had been when he shaved before his own bathroom mirror that morning: the brush-cut gray hair, the face seamed by experience but not yet haggard with age.

As the rumbling faded, Logan saw that the glass in the shower-stall door was gone. Only the frame remained, corroded and sagging. On the floor, no towels were to be seen.

Bewildered but able to breathe once more, he crossed the threshold into the bedroom, which contained no furniture. The LED beam revealed that the bed, the nightstands, the dresser, the armchair, the art on the walls were all gone. The imitation Persian rug had vanished as well, revealing more of the wood floor.

The surprise of finding the space unfurnished gave way to consternation and to concern about his sanity when the trembling beam of light revealed that the bedroom appeared to be in a long-abandoned house. Worn and warped beneath the dust, the mahogany floor in places curled up from the concrete to which it had long been adhered. Stains like the velvet wings of enormous moths discolored the wallpaper, and overhead the once-white paint, now gray and yellow, dangled in delicate peels, as if the deep coffers had been the cocoons from which those insectile shapes had quivered free.

As a detective, Logan possessed unshakable faith in what his five senses revealed to him and in what meaning his mind—both with reason and intuition—would eventually make of those many details. Facts could be twisted by liars, but every fact was like a piece of memory metal that inevitably returned to its original shape.

His eyes couldn't lie to him, though he tried to blink away these impossible changes in the senator's bedroom.

After so many years as a cop, he saw the whole world as a crime scene, and in every crime scene, truth waited to be found. Initially the evidence might be misinterpreted—but seldom for long, and never by him. Throughout his career, other cops called him Hawkeye, not only because he saw so clearly but also because he could look down on a case as if from a great height and see truth as the hawk sees the field mouse even in the tall grass. Yet though he knew that everything around him now must be a lie, he could not perceive the reality through the illusion.

After a moment, however, as if someone dialed a rheostat, light rose, at first from mysterious sources, but then from semitransparent shapes that resembled the lamps that had been here when Logan first entered the room. Not only lamps but also furniture materialized, ghostly shapes at first, like the weaker image in a photographic double exposure, but rapidly becoming more solid, more detailed. The Persian-style carpet reappeared under his feet.

While the reality of the senator's bedroom reasserted, while the vision of an abandoned and deteriorated building faded, Logan turned slowly in place. The welling light rinsed the mothy stains from the pale-gold wallpaper. The gray and yellow ragged paint of the ceiling coffers raveled up into smooth white surfaces once more.

Over the years, Logan Spangler had so often acquitted himself well and with such equanimity in moments of peril that he thought he was all but incapable of fearing for his life. But astonishment quickly deepened into awe, and the mystery of the transforming room was so formidable that dread crept over him as he wondered what power might effect such a change and why.

Having turned 180 degrees, Logan Spangler faced the bathroom. Beyond the open door, the lights were bright. The dusty, damaged marble floor appeared clean again and in good repair.

Behind him, something hissed.

14

Apartment 2-G

To distract herself from the prospect of imminent death by electrocution as well as from a memory of blazing hair and smoking eyes, Sparkle Sykes decided to take an inventory of her dress shoes, of which she had 104 pairs. Sitting on a padded stool in her roomy walk-in closet, she took her time with each item of footwear, enjoying the taper of the heel, the roundness of the counter, the arch of the shank, the slope of the vamp, the smell of leather. . . .

For the past twenty-four years, since her beloved daddy was struck by lightning and killed when she was eight years old, Sparkle Sykes had been afraid of thunderstorms. They were not just weather to her. They were thinking creatures, the electricity in their clouds serving the same cognitive function as the milder current that wove ceaselessly through her brain, from synapse to synapse. Like armadas of alien starships, they appeared on the horizon and conquered the entire sky, oppressing the land and the people below them. They were ancient gods, proud and cruel and demanding of sacrifices, beings of pure power, entering the world from outside of time, with the evil intention of inflicting suffering on mere mortals.

Sparkle supposed that, on the subject of thunderstorms, she was a little bit crazy.

Hours before the storm arrived, she had drawn heavy draperies across the windows of her apartment, which overlooked the Pendleton's grand courtyard. When passing through rooms with a view, she did not glance at the windows, for fear that she would glimpse flashes of the storm's fury pulsing behind the pleated panels of brocade.

Between three hundred and six hundred Americans were killed by lightning each year. Two thousand were injured. More people were killed by lightning than by any other weather phenomena, including floods, hurricanes, and tornadoes. The current in a lightning bolt could run as high as thirty thousand amperes with a million or more volts.

Some people thought that Sparkle's encyclopedic knowledge of lightning must be a sign of obsession, but she thought of it as nothing more than a part of her family history. If your father had been a railroad engineer, no one would be surprised that you knew a great deal about trains. A ship captain's daughter would likely be steeped in seafaring stories and the lore of the oceans. The child of a man cored through by the million-volt lance of a storm would surely be disrespectful of her father if she cared to know nothing about the instrument by which his fate was delivered to him. And then there was her mother's horrific end.

Less than half an hour into Sparkle's inspection of her footwear collection, she remembered one of hundreds of death-by-lightning cases that she had read in the press. Just a few years earlier, somewhere in New England, a bride outside a church, moments before her wedding, was struck down by the first bolt of a storm before even a drop of rain had fallen. The entry point had been her silver tiara, the exit point her right foot. She wore white-satin pumps with spike heels; the left shoe exploded into several pieces, but her right flash-burned and fused with her flesh.

An inventory of shoes no longer distracted Sparkle from the thunder that crashed down upon the Pendleton. Suddenly the sight of shoes reminded her of her own mother's barefoot death dance.

She hesitated to leave the closet because it had no windows. Here she could not see the storm—or the storm see her. And here the cannonades of thunder were more muffled than elsewhere.

For a minute or two, she stood there, trying to decide where else to take refuge—and then Iris appeared in the doorway. At twelve, the girl was like Sparkle in two respects—petite in stature, with delicate facial features—but otherwise different. Sparkle was a blonde, but Iris had hair as black as raven feathers. Sparkle's eyes were blue, Iris's a curiously luminous gray. Mother had fair skin, daughter an olive complexion.

Iris looked at Sparkle directly but only for a moment, and then turned her attention to the floppy plush-toy rabbit that she cradled in one arm as if it were a human infant.

"Does the storm frighten you, sweetie?" Sparkle asked, for she worried that her anxiety might infect this highly sensitive child who already found the world almost more abrasive than she could tolerate.

On a good day, Iris spoke fewer than a hundred words, and on many days none at all. She had a particular aversion to answering questions, which were often such a painful intrusion on her privacy that her face clenched with anguish.

In a voice as sweet as it was solemn, the girl said, "'We're going to the meadow now to dry ourselves off in the sun.'"

No meadow lay along the length of Shadow Street, nor was any sun to be seen on this dreary day. But Sparkle understood that the girl meant she'd at first been frightened but wasn't afraid any longer. Iris's words were from the novel *Bambi*, spoken by the famous fawn's mother after the terror of a thunderstorm; she'd read the book dozens of times—as she did all her favorites—memorizing whole scenes.

Gazing solemnly at the toy bunny, Iris tenderly stroked its velveteen face. The rabbit's fixed stare seemed, to Sparkle, only slightly less expressive than the lustrous eyes with which her daughter had so briefly regarded her.

As Iris turned from the open closet door and drifted across the master bedroom, toward the hallway, Sparkle longed to go after her, to touch her face as Iris petted the face of the rabbit, to put an arm around her and hold her close. The touch would not be welcome; she could bear to be touched only when in certain moods, and she could never tolerate a cuddle. An embrace would inspire the girl to shrink away, to thrash free, perhaps even to shriek and to lash out angrily, though she had fewer tantrums than some autistic children.

Only one-sixth of such kids were ever able to live any kind of independent life. Although Iris had a unique gift, she might not be that one in six. Only time would tell.

Sometimes an autistic child possessed one isolated special skill, perhaps an astonishing rote memory or an intuitive grasp of mathematics that enabled dauntingly complex mental computations to be made in but a second or two, all without a day of education in the subject. Some could sit at a piano and at once play melodically, even read and understand sheet music the first time they saw it.

Iris was that perhaps rarest of autistic savants: one who had an intuitive grasp of the relationship between phonemes, the basic sounds by which a language was constructed, and the printed word. One day when she was five, Iris picked up a children's book for the first time—and quickly began reading, having had no instruction, because when she looked at a word on the page, she heard the sound of it in her mind and knew its meaning. When she had never encountered a word before, she searched for its definition in a dictionary and thereafter never forgot it.

These seven years later, Iris's vocabulary was larger than her mother's, though she rarely used it in speech. But her strange gift was her hope, or at least it was her mother's hope *for* her. Books greatly enlarged Iris's world, offered her a door out of the narrow room that was autistic experience, and no one could say where that might lead her.

As Iris moved out of sight, thunder broke so loud that even in the windowless closet, it sounded less like weather than like a bomb blast. The storm was at war with the city.

Sparkle Sykes heard herself saying her name, over and over, as if it were a two-word charm to ward off harm. Her earliest memories were of her mother, Wendeline, telling her that this was a magical name for a special child. *Syke* was an old Scottish word for a small, fast-moving stream. Sparkle Sykes, therefore, was surely a power to be reckoned with: many quick streams, rushing always forward, clear and sweet and sparkling, with the power to dazzle and bewitch.

For a while when she was eight, Sparkle thought she killed her father with love-triggered magic.

Murdoch Sykes, tall and strong and handsome, with thick hair that went white before his thirtieth birthday, enjoyed photography and counted himself more than an amateur but less than professional. On Sundays, he went for long walks through the Maine meadows and woods, taking nature photos of things anyone could have seen on the same walk but that seemed intimate and revelatory, as if Nature had opened herself to him as she did to no one else.

On his last day, he came home early because the pending storm marshaled its forces hours ahead of predictions. As he strode out of the woods, crossed the paved country road, and came toward their home on a bluff above the sea, tanned and muscular, snow-white hair stirring in the breeze, leather camera bag slung over one shoulder, T-shirt as white as his hair, khaki pants tucked into hiking boots, he seemed to be not a mere man but instead a courageous adventurer returning from the farthest end of the world—or a god.

Sparkle had been waiting for him on the front porch. At first sight of her daddy, she leaped up from the rocking chair and waved enthusiastically. She would have run to meet him at the end of their front yard, where it bordered the shoulder of the road; but just then thunder cracked and rolled, and the sky threw down the first fat drops of rain, which shattered off the blacktop, danced through the grass, and rattled against the wooden porch steps with a hard sound reminiscent of beads falling from a broken necklace.

Instead of increasing his pace, Murdoch Sykes crossed the long yard as though he welcomed rain as much as sunshine, and he seemed not just to love Nature but also to *command* her. He didn't even bother to take off the rain-spattered steel-rimmed eyeglasses that made him look as wise as he was strong.

The sight of him thrilled young Sparkle. She knew

that as usual he would have tales of the forest and all its creatures, which he would recount with such humor and style that no storybook could be half as entertaining.

Although she loved his stories, she wished that he would never again go for a Sunday walk, that he would stay home with her. Indeed, she wanted him to stay home every day, never leave again, at least not without her. She wanted him with her, here, now and forever.

Dancing from foot to foot with delight, Sparkle called out—"Daddy, Daddy, Daddy!"—intending to jump on him when he reached the top of the steps, knowing he would let the camera bag slide to the floor and catch her in his arms.

But Murdoch Sykes never arrived at the steps. The first bright blade of the storm preceded the second explosion of thunder, its serrated edge slashing through the darkling day, scorching air and vaporizing raindrops, making contact with his eyeglasses, which for an instant glowed as if the frames were neon tubing.

How fast it happened, in less than half a second, yet how slow it played in memory. The lenses burst into sprays of glass quills, portions of the steel frames melted to his skin, and he was in the same instant lifted and thrown forward six or eight feet yet somehow remained standing as he stumbled to a stop, arms flailing as if he were a poorly manipulated marionette, the camera bag stripped from him and left behind, his hair on fire, that white mane suddenly a clown's orange wig. Incoming immediately behind the lightning, a fierce volley of thunder rattled the house windows, trembled the porch floor, and seemed to knock Murdoch down, though in fact he was already dead weight in the grip of gravity. Scalp stubbled and black, he fell on his back and lay staring at the sky with smoking eyes, mouth open, clothes smoldering even in the rain, the blackened toes of his right foot poking out of the missing end of his torn hiking boot because—as the autopsy would report—the lightning had entered through his left eye and exited through the toe cleat.

That vivid mind movie stole from Sparkle the courage to leave her closet. Glued to the stool again, she wished that her name really might be magical, because then she'd use it to charm away the current storm.

She happened to be staring at the open door when in the bedroom the thing crawled past. It came from the direction of the bathroom, following the path that Iris had taken toward the hallway.

The lamps and ceiling fixture were on in the bedroom, to ensure that storm light behind draperies would be less noticeable. Sparkle could see the creature clearly, but it nevertheless defied belief.

If it resembled one thing more than any other, it looked like a naked baby with an unnaturally large head, about twelve or thirteen months old, still just a crawler, not yet a toddler, single-mindedly creeping forward, but it wasn't a baby. For one thing, it was too big, the size of a three-year-old, perhaps thirty-five pounds or more, and for another thing, its skin wasn't pink and healthy but pale-gray mottled with green.

Sparkle neither cried out in fear nor leaped to her feet at the sight of this nightmarish intruder. Her response to any shock or threat had been programmed when lightning struck down her father so many years earlier. She went rigid that day on the porch, paralyzed with guilt and horror. Having wished her father would never leave home again, would stay there forever, she was wretchedly certain that her magical power had called down the lightning, which answered her wish in a way that she never could have imagined. Not only guilt had frozen her but also fear, for young Sparkle believed that, if she moved, surely another spear of lightning would strike *her* down, considering that she had wished, as well, to be with her daddy forever.

Her guilt had passed in a few weeks, though not her grief, and she had not believed in magic for a long time. But now she responded to the hideous crawler as to her father's corpse: paralyzed by the conviction that she was safe only if she didn't move or make a sound.

The large misshapen head, the size of the creature, and the gangrenous color of its skin were not the only details that argued against it being either an infant or human. Although its plump legs and small feet resembled those of a baby, it had *six* of them. It did not use its hands to crawl, but held its arms out in front of it, as if reaching for something, its stubby fingers ceaselessly raking the air. The thing was lumpy, too, as if it were riddled with tumors. In locomotion, it moved not with the rhythmic flexion and contraction of efficient muscles but in repulsive swellings and deflations occurring at multiple points across its body. For reasons that Sparkle could not explain, she thought it must be as much fungus as flesh, a weird hybrid of plant and animal.

As this beast from an acidhead's delirium passed the open doorway and crawled across the bedroom toward the hallway, she rose from the stool, suddenly shaking with fear, swallowing repeatedly to force down a scream that swelled in her throat almost with the substance of a vomitous mass. She looked around for a weapon, but she saw nothing in the closet that would give her courage. Nevertheless, she stepped to the open doorway, in quiet pursuit, convinced that the hellish creature was on Iris's trail and that it was a predator.

Witness positioned himself to ensure that the next fluctuation would take him to the third place he hoped to see, which was the study belonging to Sparkle Sykes. Here were even more books than in the attorney's apartment. They were not law books but volumes used for research, poetry, and mostly novels.

He knew about this woman because he knew about all things, but also because in his youth, when he had not merely looked like a man in his twenties but also had been exactly that, he had read what she'd written.

Later, when he was required to kill, he had done so with what now seemed inexplicable enthusiasm. The only time he had hesitated was when a young woman named April, thinking him a friend, had taken from her backpack a book by Sparkle Sykes, one he had read long before, and wanted to share it with him. He repeated for her passages from memory. She had been thrilled to find, in such grim circumstances, one who shared with her the love of this enduring light. He gave her the mercy of killing her quickly with an iron bar to the back of her skull.

His bottomless memory was his greatest curse, for it was dark water, an abyss, in which drifted the bodies of April and so many men and women and children, not just those whom he had killed but uncountable others who perished when the great blade of monstrous history cut them down. He passed his days now on the floor of that ocean of death, where the feeble yellow illumination illuminated nothing, and when he sometimes walked in daylight, he still felt drowned.

His time in Sparkle Sykes's study, as it had been when she wrote to shape the world, was much shorter than Witness hoped. But then he supposed it was more than he deserved. He faded from the room, the room from him.

15

Apartment 2-A

Winny didn't want music when he was reading because music reminded him of his dad, and his dad didn't approve of reading too much. His dad wanted him to put down the books and do manly things like join the wrestling team at school. Of course, there wasn't a wrestling team in the fourth grade. For sure not at the Grace Lyman School. Although judging by the humongous painting of the late Mrs. Grace Lyman in the school lobby, she could have wrestled her way to a state championship. Winny's dad wanted him to go all-out nuts for football, Tae Kwon Do, kick-boxing, and also learn to play a manly musical instrument like a guitar or a piano but not, for God's sake, a flute or a clarinet. Winny didn't know why his dad thought some instruments were manly and some were sissy. He *did* know that if he turned on music while he was reading, no matter what kind it was or who the singer was, his father would get in his head so much that he wouldn't be able to concentrate on the book.

He never switched on the TV when he read, either, but twice the previous day, Wednesday, the set in his room had turned itself on to Channel 106, which on local cable was a dead channel. Instead of electronic snow, rings of blue light pulsed from the center of the screen to its borders.

The first time this happened, having never seen anything like it before, Winny thought the TV must be haywire. When he tried to turn it off, the remote didn't work. Because there wasn't any noise with the pulses of blue light, he decided to continue reading and see if the set might switch itself off.

After ten minutes, he had felt maybe the TV was watching him. Well, not the TV but someone using the TV somehow to spy on people. That sounded fully whacko, just the kind of thing that would land him on a nut-doctor's couch, in a custody battle, and in a new home in Nashville with his manly, musical dad.

So he had pulled the plug, and the TV had gone dark.

Later Wednesday, when he had come back to his room, the TV was plugged in again. Mrs. Dorfman, the housekeeper, must have done it. She was nice enough, but she just couldn't leave anything alone. When she cleaned, she always moved things around, like Winny's Dragon World action figures, arranging them ways that *she* liked. She was full-time but she was a live-out housekeeper, not live-in. If she was a live-in, by now she would have worn out all the carpets with her endless sweeping.

Anyway, the TV had been plugged in again

yesterday—Wednesday—evening. And not long after Winny settled down to read, the set had switched on. Like before, rings of light throbbed outward from the center of the screen. They reminded him of the light on sonar scopes in old submarine movies, except they were blue instead of green.

Again he had felt that he was being watched.

Then a deep voice had spoken a single word from the throbbing rings of light: *"Boy."*

Maybe a word leaked into the dead channel from a program on a nearby live channel. Maybe it was just a coincidence that Winny was a boy and that the TV, which seemed to be watching him, said "boy," instead of "banana" or something else.

"Boy," it said again, and Winny pulled the plug.

Wednesday night, he had difficulty sleeping soundly. He kept waking up, expecting the TV to be pulsing with blue light even though it was unplugged.

Of course on this gloomy Thursday, while Winny was at Mrs. Grace Lyman's School for Wrestlers, Mrs. Dorfman had plugged the set in yet again, when she sterilized his room for the day. He thought about unplugging it before anything could happen. But part of him wanted to know what this was all about. It was weird, the interesting kind of weird, not the scary kind that might give you a stroke or make you pee your pants, just creepy.

So maybe half an hour after his mom said, "Love you, my little man," and left his room, while gusts of wind rattled rain against the window, it happened. From the corner of his eye, Winny saw the TV fill with throbbing rings of blue light. He looked up from his book, and the voice said again, *"Boy."*

Winny never knew what to say to most people when they tried to drag him into a conversation. He found it even harder to figure out what to reply to a TV that seemed to be watching him and saying hello, or whatever it meant by that one word.

"Boy," it repeated.

Talking back to a TV set seemed a little screwy, like talking to furniture. Putting his book aside, Winny said, "Who are you?" Although the question sounded stupid, he couldn't think of anything smarter.

The voice was deep but kind of flat, like someone on a public-address system reading a boring announcement: *"Boy. Aboveground. Second floor. West wing."*

The TV seemed to be telling Winny where he was in the Pendleton. He already knew where he was. He didn't need to be told. If there was a guy watching through the TV, he seemed even worse at conversation than was Winny.

But of course there couldn't be anyone watching. TV worked only one way. A television received. It didn't broadcast. Something else was going on here, a little mystery that would be solved if he just thought about it long enough. He wasn't supersmart, but he wasn't stupid, either, not half as stupid as the boy characters in some of the books he read.

"Boy. Black hair. Blue eyes."

Winny shot up from the armchair.

"Aboveground. Second floor. West wing."

Black hair, blue eyes: Someone somewhere could see him through the TV. No doubt about it. The little mystery was suddenly big.

Winny didn't like the way his voice trembled when he said, "What do you want?"

"Boy. Black hair. Blue eyes. Aboveground. Second floor. West wing. Exterminate. Exterminate."

Because he was somewhat short for his age and scrawny, still waiting for his biceps to appear, Winny figured that if he ever did the slightest wimpy thing, people would be sure he was a gutless sissy. Once people thought you were a sissy, they would never *un*think it except maybe if you saved a hundred little kids from a burning orphanage or disarmed a terrorist and beat him up until he cried for his mommy. Winny wouldn't be big enough to beat up anyone for at least ten years, if ever. He didn't know an orphanage anywhere, and even if he did know one, he might wait around the rest of his life for a fire that never happened, unless he started it himself. So he tried never to do or say anything sissyish. He never showed fear in a scary movie. When he accidentally cut himself, he didn't cry or appear to be alarmed at the sight of blood. Bugs spooked him, all those legs and antennas, so he forced himself to pick up beetles and things that were gross but didn't sting, to study them in the palm of his hand.

When the TV said *"Exterminate,"* lots of fourth-grade boys from the Grace Lyman School would have been scared, and at least a few might have run away in panic to hide. Instead, Winny stayed calm and walked—didn't run—to the kitchen, where the warm air smelled cinnamony. His mom was looking at something through the window in the upper oven door.

Winny said, "You better come see what's on my TV."

"What is it?"

"I can't explain it. You've gotta see."

Indicating a fold-down television mounted under an upper cabinet near the refrigerator, she said, "Show me with that one, honey."

"I think only my TV has it. Mine switched itself on. This one didn't. You better come see."

Winny hurried away—but did not run like he was scared or anything—and he heard his mother close behind him. He figured the TV would be off when he returned to his room. He wouldn't have any proof, and she wouldn't believe him—until maybe some death squad showed up, tattooed muscular goons in black uniforms carrying massive guns. To his surprise, the rings of blue light continued to throb on the screen.

"Some kind of test pattern," his mother said.

"No. It's 106, a dead channel. And it talks."

Before Winny could explain further, the deep flat voice spoke from behind the blue light: *"Adult female and boy. Aboveground. Second floor. West wing. Exterminate. Exterminate."*

Frowning, his mother said, "What's the joke?"

"It's not *my* joke," Winny assured her.

"Adult female. Black hair. Dark-brown eyes. Five feet five."

She plucked the remote off the table beside the armchair, but it didn't work. She couldn't turn off the TV or change channels.

"*Exterminate. Exterminate.*"

Approaching the television, his mom said, "Is this a DVD?"

"No. It's . . . I don't know, something else."

She checked the DVD player anyway.

Winny said, "It's happened before except till now it never said anything except 'boy.' "

"Before when?"

"Yesterday twice."

"Why didn't you tell me?"

"Wasn't anything to tell. It just said 'boy.' "

"Somebody has a sick sense of humor."

"But how can he see us?" Winny wondered.

"He can't."

"Well, but he knows what we look like."

"That doesn't mean the creep can see us. It just means he knows who we are, who lives in this apartment. It's a security issue. We'll get to the bottom of it quick enough. I'll call the guard on duty."

She pulled the plug, and the television went dark.

Just having the set off made Winny feel better, and his mom's confidence made him feel safer, but not for long.

As she stepped back from the TV, the wall changed. It was covered by low cabinets with bookshelves above—but then it *rippled*. The transformation started near the ceiling and flowed down, like water washing away one thing and leaving a different thing behind it, as if the cabinets and the bookshelves and all the stuff on the shelves had never been real, had been only a realistic painting that was now dissolving. Above the descending ripples, the new wall didn't have any cabinets or shelves, and it didn't look new, either, but stained and greasy, the plaster crumbling, patches of sooty mold reaching this way and that with black tentacles.

His mom made a small startled sound and raised one hand as if to command the change to halt, but the ripples *raced* all the way down the wall, shivered across the floor, taking with them the polished mahogany, leaving behind scarred and dirty planks, then eating away the area rug, all of it happening so fast that neither Winny nor his mother had time to think maybe they might vanish too, not until the strange tide lapped toward their feet.

She scooted backward, grabbing Winny by one arm to pull him with her, but the ripples broke like surf and feathered around their shoes, dissolving the rug underfoot while leaving the two of them untouched. And just like a wave breaking on a shore, the ripples retreated, leaving in their wake everything as it should have been, the rug intact once more and the mahogany polished. Up the wall the ripples went, reversing the transformation they had made, restoring the cabinets, bookshelves, books, and television, as if a wizard had cast a change spell, had at once regretted it, and had followed it with a cancellation spell to undo his mischief.

The ripples receded into the junction of wall and ceiling. They didn't return right away. Maybe they would never return. Maybe it was over, whatever *it* might have been.

Winny's heart galloped as though he were running for a finish line. He couldn't breathe. Something seemed to be stuck deep in his throat. For a moment he thought maybe, in the shock of the moment, he swallowed his tongue the way he'd read some people did when having a seizure. He gagged on that thought, though not on his tongue, which turned out to be in his mouth where it belonged.

His mom still had a grip on his arm. She was holding him very tight, like she was afraid he'd float away and drown or something. She didn't say anything for a moment, and neither did Winny, because there wasn't any point jabbering about it. They knew what they'd seen, and neither of them could explain it, because it was flat-out nuts, so impossible that at first it filled your mind and left no room for other thoughts. But then Winny remembered the blue rings of light and the deep voice—*"Exterminate. Exterminate"*—and his mother must have remembered it, too, because she said, "Come on, let's go," and pulled him toward the bedroom door.

"Where are we going?" he asked.

"I don't know—somewhere, anywhere, out of here, out of the Pendleton."

One

To you of great faith, I am the product of your wisdom and the guarantor of your immortality.

She who fears lightning has written that a city is a forest of buildings shaken by a perpetual storm of interests, its people the fruit of its limbs, some ripening to perfection, others withering on the branches, and still others falling prematurely to rot upon the ground. I will teach her that the city is nothing so noble as a forest, that it is a bleak orchard of despair, from the twisted and leafless limbs of which hang only rotten fruit, that worm-eaten apple known as humanity. I will crawl the crevices of her brain, instilling in her an understanding of the worthlessness of her kind, so that she will beg for death because she cannot bear to be human anymore.

She speaks of perfect fruit when she has produced an imperfect daughter. She imagines the withered child to be a blessing. This kind of derangement is emblematic of humankind. Grave faults are said to be only eccentricities, and imperfections are routinely celebrated as mere differences that make for a rich variety in the species.

Variety is not the spice of life. It is the mother of disorder.

Individuality is not the hallmark of freedom. It is the essence of decadence.

Freedom is slavery to chaos. Unity is peace, all thinking and acting as one.

Soon the imperfect mother and the even more imperfect girl will be as one, their meaty individuality stripped away. Their pride and hope and fear will prove to have been as pointless as their lives were meaningless.

Like the mother and her daughter, the elderly sisters will learn that money buys no safety, that all human accomplishment is without consequence, that what matters is the earth, not vermin like them, who plague it, the earth in all its grandeur.

Under the 1,700-mile-thick mantle of the planet, the outer core is a sea of molten iron and nickel 1,400 miles in diameter, and it is the movement of this sea that generates the earth's magnetic field. Expressions of this field, shimmering blue in the night and visible even on overcast days, were what drew the Indians to settle on Shadow Hill. Every thirty-eight years, the deep convection currents in that molten-metal ocean generate an unusually large tidal wave of energy. The fault in space-time on which the Pendleton is built is like a trapdoor, most of the time held shut by a restraining spring. But the tsunami of magnetic energy has opened it before and will soon open it again.

I await the moment.

16

Topper's

Across Shadow Street, half a block downhill from the Pendleton, Topper's restaurant featured fine steakhouse food in a sleek black-and-white Art Deco environment with a richness of carved glass and stainless steel. The waiters wore black and white, and the only color was provided by the china—a Tiffany knockoff—and the festively presented food.

In the adjoining bar, Silas Kinsley sat in a booth at a window table. Here the indirect lighting, even lower and more artfully designed than in the restaurant, shaded the edges off every surface and added a luster to every reflective material.

He and Nora had come here often for the steaks, sometimes for just a drink. During the year after her death, he hadn't gone back to any place they frequented together, certain that the memories invoked would be too painful. Now he pretty much went *only* where they had gone together because the memories sustained him. The more time that passed since her death, the closer he felt to her, which he supposed meant that he was quickly moving toward his own death, which would deliver him to her.

Although offices were still closing, a business crowd already gathered at the bar, perhaps seeking shelter from more than just the storm and relief from more than just the pressures of their work. Although Silas had not practiced law in many years, he remained aware of the telling details that could confirm or disprove testimony. In the current dreadful economy, in these times of rapid change and daily irrational violence, numerous subtleties in the personal style and manners of the customers suggested that they chose Topper's because they yearned to escape not merely their workday worries but also the era in which they lived. The background music was big band, Glenn Miller and Benny Goodman and Artie Shaw. The favored drinks were the martinis and gin and tonics and Singapore slings that made the 1930s buzz, rather than the weak white wine and low-calorie beer of this joyless, health-obsessed age. In defiance of the law, having brought their ashtrays, as people in the days of prohibition hid bottles of booze in brown-paper bags, some even smoked cigarettes, and neither management nor other customers complained. A mood of rebellion was as evident as the music, though perhaps many of them could not yet quite articulate what they wished to rebel against.

In his window booth, Silas faced east, uphill, and could see the lights of the Pendleton through the driving rain. Across the table from him sat Perry Kyser, who had been the site supervisor for the construction company that converted Belle Vista into the Pendleton in 1973. Kyser had just been served his vodka martini and meant to savor the first taste before sharing the story he had to tell.

He was a big man who had not gone to fat with advanced age. In spite of his bald head and snow-white mustache, he looked like he could still work any job on a construction site. He and Silas were by far the oldest people in the room, and the only two who remembered big-band swing from their childhoods, when it had still been the dance music of choice and had dominated radio programming.

Perry Kyser was the father of Gordon Kyser, who had been an attorney in the firm of Kinsley, Beckinsale, Gunther and Fortis, back in the 1980s and '90s. That was long before Silas retired, lost his wife, moved into his current apartment, and became obsessed with the history of the building. He had never met Perry Kyser in the days that he'd been Gordon's senior partner, but the connection with the son had been sufficient to make the father willing to talk about some experience that until now he had shared with no one.

Their small talk was brief, about Gordon and the weather and getting old, and after his second taste of the martini, Perry Kyser got to the subject that brought them together: "Renovating an older building—theater, school, offices, a megahouse like the Pendleton, whatever—there's going to have been a few deaths there in the past. Usually not murders. Accidents, heart attacks, like that. And often as not, with a large crew, you'll have a couple guys, they have a thing for ghost stories. They don't invent 'em, I'm not saying they do, but if any stories are in circulation about the project site, these guys will know 'em and talk 'em up during breaks, at lunch. In that environment, when little things happen nobody would think twice about otherwise, odd little things, then they take on a bigger meaning than they should. Even level-headed people imagine they see things . . . but they really *believe* they saw 'em. Know what I'm saying?"

"The power of suggestion," Silas said.

"Yeah. But the Pendleton wasn't like that. Something really happened there in '73, late November, first of December. I lost my best carpenter, quit the job because of something he saw, wouldn't even talk about it, just wanted out of there. Other guys, solid types, claimed to see what they called shadow people. Dark shapes crossing a room, along a hallway, even through walls, quick as cats, almost quicker than the eye."

"Did you see them?"

"No. Not me." Kyser surveyed the other customers, hesitating to proceed, as if having second thoughts about sharing his experience. "Not the shadow people."

Silas pressed him: "You said 'late November, first of December.' Do you remember exactly how long these phenomena lasted?"

"Far as I know, they started November twenty-ninth, Thursday. The last might've been December first. You don't seem surprised by this haunted-house talk."

"I don't believe it's haunted, but like I told you on the phone, there's something strange about the place. Seems like terrible things happen in the Pendleton every thirty-eight years."

"The research you've done, the hours you put into it . . . Why?"

Silas hesitated, shrugged. "I don't have anything else to do."

"Retirement's a bitch, huh?" The thinnest edge of sarcasm in Kyser's voice suggested that he didn't believe the answer and wanted a better one before being more forthcoming.

"Fair enough. Since I lost my wife, this is the only thing to come along that's interested me. The usual distractions—TV, movies, books, music—none of them seems worth the time. Maybe this isn't worth it, either. Maybe nothing is. But it's what I've got now."

Kyser considered that answer for a moment and then nodded. "I've still got Jenny. I can see how, if I didn't have her, I might want a project of my own." Again, he studied the people at the bar, as if he expected to see someone he knew.

Returning to the purpose of their meeting, Silas said, "You told me the phenomena ran from Thursday the twenty-ninth through the first of December. That was a Saturday. You worked Saturdays?"

Kyser's attention shifted from the crowd gathered at the bar to his martini, into which he gazed as though the future could be read in the crystal clarity of the vodka. "The first twelve months we worked a big crew six days to meet our deadline. But by the end of '73, we were on a five-day schedule with the finish work. I was there that Saturday morning, making a punch list, hundreds of small items we needed to get done to wrap the job by Christmas."

Beyond the window, torrents overflowed gutters and blacktop shimmered with runoff. Shadow Street rose like a great storm swell on a night sea, and at its crest loomed the Pendleton, not stately and welcoming as it had seemed before, but as ominous as a colossal warship with massive guns loaded for battle.

"Our painting-crew chief, Ricky Neems, he was there that same Saturday, making his own punch list upstairs. Because of this"—he hesitated—"well, because of this thing that happened, I left early, didn't finish my list. Ricky . . . we never saw again. Good painter, the best, but a few times each year, he'd fall off the wagon, go on a drinking binge, disappear for three days. Every time he came back, he'd say it was the flu or something, but we knew the truth. He was sober most of the time, and he was such a good guy when he was sober, we just worked around his benders. But Ricky never came back after Saturday. No one saw him again. Police took it as a missing-persons case, but they figured he got drunk, picked a fight with the wrong guy, got killed and dumped somewhere. I knew different. Or thought I did. My opinion is they didn't break a sweat looking for Ricky, him being single, no family to push for answers. But even if they worked hard, they might not have found him. . . . I think Ricky was snatched up and taken, soul *and* body, straight to Hell or someplace like it."

This declaration of damnation seemed out of character for a construction supervisor who spent his life working with his hands and building on solid foundations. Again Perry fell silent, avoided Silas's eyes, and studied people at the bar as he sipped his martini.

While taking any deposition, moments arose when a good lawyer knew a question might inhibit revelation, when patience and silence were required to extract an embedded splinter of truth. Silas waited.

When at last Perry Kyser met the attorney's eyes, there was resolution in his unwavering gaze, an intensity and a challenge that suggested he anticipated encountering skepticism but that he also intended eventually to be believed.

"Anyway, I'm in the basement that Saturday, in what was going to be the gym, making my punch list. This noise comes from under the building, like a kettledrum, a timpani. Then it grows into a rumble, vibrations in the floor. I think earthquake or something, so I go into the hall . . . and it's not like it should be, not clean and bright like we made it, but damp, dirty, musty. Half the ceiling lights are out. Mold on the walls, ceiling, some of it black, but some patches glowing yellow, brighter than the overhead lights. At each end of the hall these video screens, suspended from the ceiling, rings of blue light pulsing in them. Some floor tiles cracked. Nobody's done any maintenance for a long time. Doesn't make sense. So I think it's me, something wrong with me, hallucination, seeing the hallway like it isn't. Then I see this . . . this *thing*. It's no trick of shadows, Silas. It won't sound real, but it was as real as you sitting there."

"You said on the phone you've never told anyone about this."

"Never. I didn't want people looking at me that way, you know, like you'd look at some guy says he's flown on a UFO."

"From my point of view, Perry, your silence all these years makes you all the more credible."

Kyser finished his martini in one swallow. "So . . . I'm at one end of the hall, outside the gym. This thing is at the halfway point, near the doors to the heating-cooling plant. It's big. Big as me. Bigger. Pale as a grub, a little like a grub, but not that, because it's kind of like a spider, too, though not an insect, too fleshy for a spider. Now I'm thinking—who put what kind of drug in my coffee thermos? Nothing on Earth looks like this. It's moving away, toward the security room, hears me or smells me, and it turns to me. It looks like it can move fast, but maybe it can't because it doesn't."

Given the history of the Pendleton and the eerie nature of Andrew Pendleton's journal scraps, Silas had expected Kyser to reveal a strange experience, which on the phone he'd hinted that he would. But this was more bizarre than anything Silas could have imagined.

Perry Kyser continued to meet Silas's eyes and seemed to search them ceaselessly for signs of disbelief.

Lawyer's intuition told Silas that this man wasn't

lying, that he *couldn't* lie, not about this, maybe not about anything important.

"This voice comes out of the blue screens—'Exterminate,' it says. 'Exterminate.' The thing starts toward me. Now I can see how lumpy it is, not like any animal, lumpy flesh, pale skin. And wet, maybe wet with sweat, but milky wet, I don't know what. A kind of head, no eyes, no face to speak of. What might be rows of gills along the neck, but no mouth. I'm backing toward the north stairs, hear myself saying very fast, 'who are all good and deserving of all my love,' so I'm halfway through an Act of Contrition, but I don't even realize I started it. I'm sure I'm dead. As I back into the stairwell door and finish the Act of Contrition, the thing . . . it speaks to me."

Surprised, Silas said, "It spoke? In English?"

"No mouth I could see, but it spoke. Such misery in that voice. Can't convey the misery, despair. It says, 'Help me. For God's sake, someone help me.' The voice is Ricky Neems. The painter who's up on the third floor right then, making his punch list. I don't know . . . is it Ricky for real or is it this thing imitating Ricky? Is this thing somehow Ricky? How can that be? All my life . . . I never scared easy. Never had anything worth being scared about after Korea, the war."

Their waitress stopped at the table to ask if they wanted a second drink. Silas *needed* another round, but he didn't want it. Perry declined as well.

"Korea was my war, too," Silas said. "Living with that

fear day after day, eventually you're inoculated against it."

"But in that basement hall, Silas, I'm so terrified the strength goes out of me like it never did in Korea. One hand on the doorknob to the stairs, can't seem to turn it. My legs are weak. Only reason I'm still on my feet is I'm leaning against the door. Then everything changes. The lights get brighter. The dirty floor, the mold, the blue screens, everything that's wrong—it fades out. The hallway like it's supposed to be, clean and fresh—it fades *in.* And the thing coming toward me fades away, too, like it was all a dream. But I'm awake. It wasn't a dream. It was sure *something,* but not a dream."

Perry stared out at the rainy night for a moment before he continued: "After that, I go upstairs, looking for Ricky, and he's there, he's all right. He heard that rumble, like the timpani, but nothing else happened to him, and I didn't know how to tell him what I saw without sounding nuts. But I should've told him. I should have insisted he get out of there, do his punch list Monday. I did try to get him to call it a day, he wouldn't, so I left him there to die."

"You didn't. You couldn't know. Who could?"

"The next day, Sunday, I go to church. Hadn't gone in a while. Felt the need. Monday, went to work with a pistol under my jacket. Didn't think a pistol would do the job. What else would? A pistol was something. But . . . that was the end. No more shadow people, and nothing like what I'd seen. Maybe stuff happened Saturday, no one but Ricky Neems there to see. During the next month, we finished the job."

Silas's right hand was cold and wet with condensation from his Scotch glass. He blotted his fingers on a napkin. "Any theories?"

Perry Kyser shook his head. "Only what I said earlier. I got a glimpse of Hell. That encounter changed me. Frequent confession and regular Communion suddenly seemed like a good idea."

"And you never told your son, your wife?"

"I figured . . . if I was given a glimpse of Hell, it's because I needed the shock. To change me. I made the change but didn't have the courage to tell my wife why it might have been necessary. You see?"

"Yes," Silas said. "I don't know about Hell. Right now, I don't know for sure about much of anything."

The waitress returned and left the check on the table.

As Silas calculated the tip and took cash from his wallet, Perry again studied the customers at the bar. "What's wrong with them?"

Surprised, Silas said, "You sense it, too?"

"Something. Don't know what. What're they—mostly twenties and thirties? For their age, they're trying too hard."

"Too hard at what?"

"Being carefree. Should come natural that young. They seem, I don't know . . . anxious."

Silas said, "I think they come here for the Deco, the

music, the atmosphere, because they want to escape to a safe time."

"Never was such a time."

"Safer," Silas corrected. "A safer time."

"The thirties? War was coming."

"But there was an end to it. Now . . . maybe never an end."

Still focused on the bar crowd, Perry said, "I thought it was just me being old."

"What was?"

"This feeling that everything is coming apart. More like being torn down. I have this nightmare now and then."

Silas put away his wallet.

Perry Kyser said, "Everything torn down, every man for himself. Worse. It's all against all."

Silas looked out at Shadow Street, the Pendleton looming through volleys of rain.

"All against all," Perry repeated, "murder, suicide, everywhere, day and night, unrelenting."

"It's just a nightmare," Silas said.

"Maybe it is." Perry looked at him. "What now?"

"I'm going home, sit and think awhile."

"Home," Perry agreed. "But I'm gonna try not to think."

"Thanks for your time, for being so frank with me."

As they got up from the booth, the big man said, "Thought talking about it at last would take the chill off. Didn't, though."

The bar crowd sounded louder, edgier. Their laughter was shrill.

In the small lobby, as they waited at the coat-check window, Perry said, "You have kids?"

"We never did."

"We have kids, grandkids, great-grandkids."

"That alone should take the chill off."

"Just the opposite. I'm old enough to understand I can't protect them. Not from the worst. Not from much of anything."

Silas protested when Perry Kyser insisted on tipping the coat-check girl for both of them.

Outside, under the awning, in the cold breeze, they put up the hoods of their raincoats. They shook hands. Perry Kyser walked away downhill. Silas went uphill toward the Pendleton.

17

Apartment 3-D

In Senator Earl Blandon's apartment, where luxury and order had for a moment vanished behind a bleak vision of vacancy and decay, Logan Spangler turned in the now restored bedroom, hand on the grip of the pistol in his swivel holster, seeking the source of the hiss that, although brief, had been as hostile a challenge as any sound he'd ever heard, reminiscent of serpents and jungle cats and nameless things in dreams.

He saw a figure, tall and lean and quick, little more than a silhouette but definitely not the senator, as it sprang out of sight into the hallway. From that brief glimpse, he couldn't tell if it was a man or a woman—and he had the strangest impression that it might be neither, though it had been erect rather than on all fours like an animal.

A lifetime of police work habituated him to a responsible handling of firearms. He never drew a gun merely because there might be a potential for violent confrontation, but only when the potential hardened into a high probability. Once a weapon was drawn, it was more likely to be used, and not always as wisely as you might expect to use it. Logan was confident of his policing skills but remained acutely aware that he was only human and therefore capable of stupid mistakes. As he approached the door, he kept his right hand on the holstered .45.

No one waited in the hall. At the far end, past an archway, lay the living room. Between here and there, a door on the right led to the study; a door on the left served a guest room with its own bath and a second door led to a half bath, all of which he had previously toured in search of the senator.

On the threshold of the hallway, Logan paused, listening. After a silence, a great wheel of thunder rolled across the sky, muffled here because the hallway had no windows, and when it traveled to a far horizon and out of hearing, he continued to heed the deep quiet, which seemed to him to have an air of menace.

First he ventured into the guest room on the left, from there into the adjacent bath, where all was as it should be. Having opened the closet door earlier, he could see that no one lurked within.

Directly across the hall from the guest room, the study was also deserted. He went no farther than the threshold. Beyond the tall windows, landscape lighting rose from the large courtyard below, illuminating wind-billowed sheets of silvery rain like the tattered shrouds of something that crouched on the ledge and sought entrance.

Logan turned from the study and angled across the hall to the half bath, where the door stood ajar two inches. He remembered leaving it entirely open, but perhaps he was mistaken. Seen through the narrow gap between door and jamb, the quality of light was not what it should have been: yellower and dimmer than before.

The quiet after the thunder now deepened into a sea of silence in which not one sound swam. An oppressive quality to the stillness, a foreboding of violence, felt like a weight on his chest.

Using his left hand, Logan plucked the small aerosol can of pepper spray from his utility belt.

With one foot, he pushed on the door, which swung inward, and the half bath was not as it had been before. The two recessed lights in the soffit above the vanity no longer functioned, and the socket of one trailed out of its can on a length of wire. All light came from an eighteen-inch disc with irregular edges in the ceiling, which had not been there previously. The space felt damp, smelled of mold.

On part of the wall to the left of the door and on the entire back wall, draping over most of the toilet, grew what might have been two varieties of fungus, neither of a kind that Logan had ever seen before. Ceiling to floor, row after row of serpentine forms as thick as garden hoses conformed to one another's curves like a sensuous sculpture, pale-green but mottled here and there with black. At a half dozen points, from between those snugly grown rows, clusters of mushrooms of the same coloration sprouted on thick short stems. They ranged in diameter from perhaps three to six inches, each with a puckered formation at its crown.

As the master bedroom had transformed around him, so this small chamber had changed in his absence. He doubted neither his sanity nor the proof of his eyes; with an alacrity that somewhat surprised him, he had adapted to the idea that in this place and at this moment of time, the impossible might be possible. He was as determined to understand these phenomena as he had always been committed to solving any homicide case assigned to him.

Before the bathroom might return to its previous condition, he inserted the can of pepper spray into the holder on his utility belt and traded it for his small flashlight. Playing the crisp white LED beam over the fungi, he crossed the threshold into the half bath.

18

Apartment 1-C

Earlier, before she met the demon in the pantry, Sally Hollander made dinner for Martha and Edna, and now she wanted to leave for the day. Everything was in the refrigerator and needed only to be heated. The creature—or spirit, whatever—that she'd seen might not be limited to haunting the Cupp apartment; it might appear beside her after she'd gone to the farthest end of the earth to escape it. Nevertheless, she would feel better in her own place. After she had time to think about what she'd seen, without Edna's explanations, one more far-out than the next, her nerves would most likely mend so that she would have the courage to return to work in the morning.

Bailey Hawks offered to escort her to the apartment in which she lived, at the back of the Pendleton, in the north wing of the ground floor. That unit was owned by the Cupp sisters, and she lived there for free. They took good care of her, and she couldn't imagine what she would do without them; therefore, in the comfort and solitude of her rooms, she needed to get her mind right about what had happened.

Sally wasn't a weak sister. She had endured worse frights than the thing in the pantry. But she accepted Bailey's offer with relief and gratitude.

In the elevator going down from the third floor, they didn't say a word about her extraordinary encounter, but talked of the Cupps with mutual affection. Nearly the same age, she and Bailey had always been easy with each other, like old friends from the start. She was fond of him and thought he was fond of her.

Occasionally she wondered what they would be like together, but it wasn't her nature to initiate a romance. She wasn't fainthearted, though she admitted to being a bit of a wallflower. And because the Cupps were Bailey's clients, Sally figured that he felt it would be inappropriate to date her.

That was just as well. Romance had failed her before, and she had done without it happily enough for twenty years. Falling in love could be like falling off a cliff, no water below but plenty of rocks.

She had once been married. Her husband, Vince, was a musician, a guitarist with a combo that enjoyed steady employment playing in nightclubs and at private parties. Sometimes Vince started drinking during the band's breaks, continued pouring down his favorite poison after the performance, and came home fully boiled. He wanted sex but was too inebriated to be capable of it, and in his frustration he turned to what he called "the next-best thing," which proved to be a nightcap of physical and emotional abuse.

The first time she had been taken by surprise. He seized a fistful of her hair, pulled it hard enough to bring tears to her eyes, slapped her repeatedly and viciously, using his body to jam her into a corner so hard that she thought her spine might snap if he didn't relent. As he worked on her, Vince called her the vilest names, intent on administering as much humiliation as pain, and in her shock and rapid disorientation, she failed to fight back.

She was embarrassed to recall how, for a while, she had thought that half the blame for that episode must have been hers. The sober Vince, a gentle and soft-spoken musician, seemed to have no fault except jealousy, for which he often apologized; but the drunken Vince was Mr. Hyde on steroids, and he apologized for nothing. The second time it happened, she resisted—and learned that he was much stronger than she had thought and that resistance only inflamed him. Slaps became punches, and he reveled in the assault. When he was finished and she lay bruised and bleeding at his feet, he said, "I should have been a drummer, I sure can beat some crazy rhythms on the skins." He promised her that he would kill her if she ever left him.

She eventually escaped from Vince, divorced him, and started a new life. The Cupp sisters not only provided a fine salary but also a sense of family. Sally had gone from profound despair to contentment in a matter of months, from self-loathing to self-respect, such a long journey in such a short time that she would always remain aware that life could change for the worse as suddenly as it had changed for the better.

At her apartment door, as Sally turned the key in the lock, Bailey said, "Would it make you feel more comfortable if I came in while you check your rooms just to be sure there's nothing . . . out of order?"

The question reminded her of how seriously he had listened to her story in the Cupp sisters' kitchen, with not a word of disbelief, with not the slightest expression of doubt or amusement. Now she saw in him a tension she hadn't noticed before, a not fully concealed wariness of the hallway around them, of the threshold they crossed, of the foyer into which they entered, as if he believed implicitly in the possibility of a threat in this safest of residences.

If that was the case, she was not foolish enough to think that her story of the demon in the pantry had been so electrifying that it had convinced a rock-steady investment adviser and former marine that something supernatural was afoot. He would be wary only if he'd had an experience of his own that was supported by her tale.

"That's nice of you, Bailey. And I'll take you up on it. I'm still a little . . . shaky."

Once in her apartment, he subtly took the lead, staying at her side, maneuvering her through the rooms not in the way she would have chosen to proceed but instead perhaps according to strategies he had been taught in the military. He didn't appear to believe that he was conducting a dangerous search, pretty well maintained the attitude of a friendly neighbor concerned more about her peace of mind than about any genuine peril she might face, but Sally nonetheless perceived the seriousness with which he conducted the task.

He switched on not just ceiling fixtures but also lamp after lamp, and when they found no intruder in the final room, he said, "You might want to leave all or most of the lights on until your nerves settle down and you feel completely comfortable. I would if I were you, it's only natural."

In the foyer once more, as Bailey put his hand on the doorknob, Sally said, "What have *you* seen?"

He looked at her as if about to say that he didn't understand her question, but then his expression changed. "Not what you saw. But something . . . strange. I'm still thinking about it, processing it. Listen, are you really sure you want to be here alone? Martha and Edna would be happy to put you up in their guest room for the night."

"I know they would. But I've lived in this apartment almost twenty years. If I'm not safe here, then I wouldn't be safe anywhere. All my things are here, the best of my memories. Right now I just need to feel everything's as it should be—normal, ordinary. I'm okay. I'll be fine."

He nodded. "All right. But if you need anything, call me. I'll come straight down."

She almost asked him to sit with her for a while; however, alone with Bailey, she might not be able to conceal that she was attracted to him. Might not *want* to conceal it. All these years on her own, she hadn't been lonely; but at times she wished for tender companionship. If he became aware of her interest and failed to respond, she'd feel foolish, mortified. On the other hand, if he *did* respond, she wasn't sure that she would be capable of committing to more than a deeper friendship. Her romantic experiences before she married Vince had been few and innocent, and after surviving him, she perhaps would always find any prospect of physical love tainted by the possibility, however remote, that a seed of violence lay waiting to be fertilized in the relationship.

She thanked Bailey for his kindness, shut the door, and engaged both deadbolts. She was home, in her nest, a nest for one, and she was pleased to be there, where everything was known and carefully tended, where no one who had promised to cherish her was waiting to break his vow.

She needed to steady herself, and the most calming thing she could do was make a fine dessert. In the kitchen, having decided to bake a chocolate Battenberg loaf cake wrapped in white marzipan, she went first to the sink to wash her hands. As Sally turned on the water, she was assaulted from behind, seized by a twisted handful of hair, also cruelly by her left arm, and forced to turn away from the sink to confront her assailant. In the turn, she thought *Vince,* assuming that he had found her after all these years. But it was the demon from the pantry: that almost-human hairless head, lead-colored skin, those terrible gray eyes with black irises like bottomless wells, stronger than a man but somehow sexless. Its ashen lips skinned back from pointy gray teeth, and as it hissed, it struck quick as a snake, biting the nape of her neck before a cry could escape her.

An instant paralysis came with the bite, cold flooding through her body, followed by a loss of feeling in her limbs. Her suddenly rigid face felt as if it were encased in the plaster of a death mask, and she had no voice for a scream or even for a whisper. She could smell and hear, she could move her eyes, her tongue, could breathe, and her heart raced; but if the creature stopped supporting her, she would collapse to the floor, limp and immobile.

Her terror was so intense that it might have paralyzed her if the bite had not already done so. The past twenty years of nights alone had been for the most part a sweet, peaceful solitude. Only now was Sally Hollander overcome by desperate loneliness, by an awareness of the fearsome abyss that lies under life and threatens at every moment to yawn wide and swallow everyone, everything. Imminent death didn't terrify her as much as did the prospect of having lived a life in perpetual retreat, a life that would amount now to so much less than she'd ever hoped, a life that would end without a witness, in the arms of this creature whose eyes were gateways to a pitiless void.

A tongue thrust from between its pointed teeth, neither like a human tongue nor, as she expected, like that of a serpent. Gray and glistening, tubular, hollow, resembling a length of highly flexible rubber tubing almost an inch in diameter, it fluttered in the air before her, then slithered back into the mouth, as if it were not a tongue after all but, instead, another creature that lived in the larger one's throat.

At least six and a half feet tall, the demon held Sally in its strong arms and bent forward, its face descending toward hers as if it intended to chew into her and devour her alive. She realized that her mouth sagged open, but she remained powerless to close it or to scream. She was repulsed when the creature's open mouth closed over hers not in a kiss but as if to draw from her the breath of life. Disgusted beyond tolerance when the tubular tongue slid across her own tongue, she was driven to the edge of sanity when the impossibly long appendage pushed to the back of her mouth and down into her throat, where something cold and thick and foul gushed from it, overwhelming her ability to swallow.

19

Apartment 2-G

Sparkle Sykes, stepping quietly out of her closet and moving cautiously across the bedroom, followed the six-legged crawling thing that might have been a mutant baby born after a worldwide nuclear holocaust as imagined in the waking nightmares of an insect-phobic, fungi-phobic, rat-crazy mescaline junkie. It *wasn't* a baby. Some hybrid—but of what and what?—something cooked up from a witch's brew of jumbled DNA. Pale-gray mottled with green, it looked like dead flesh reanimated, and she was half afraid it would turn to stare at her and its face would be so hideous that the sight of it would kill her or drive her mad.

On a Biedermeier chest of drawers stood an eighteen-inch-tall bronze statue of Diana, Roman goddess of the moon and the hunt. It weighed maybe fifteen pounds. Sparkle snared it by the neck and held it in both hands, an awkward but elegant club in case she needed one.

No sooner had she armed herself than she noticed

something that bewildered her. The creeping monstrosity, which had seemed as solid as the floor on which it crawled, was now slightly transparent, so that she could see through it to the pattern of the Persian carpet underneath.

If she had been given to the use of drink or drugs, she might have thought that she was hallucinating. Although she knew too well about the varied effects of mescaline and the like, she always had been a teetotaler whose only addiction was coffee of all kinds.

Fright that made Sparkle feel light-headed now quickly acquired the greater gravity of dread, dread so heavy that she felt weighed down to the extent that she had to struggle to remain in pursuit of the creeping nightmare. She fell a couple of steps behind and then came to a halt when the six-legged miscreation veered away from the open bedroom door. Instead of crossing that threshold into the hall, it became yet more transparent, crawled *through* the wall, and disappeared.

She remained frozen for a second or two, and then hurried to the door. Afraid that the thing was aware of her and waiting just out of sight, Sparkle remained in the bedroom, cautiously leaned through the doorway, and discovered the hall deserted. The grotesque intruder seemed not to have passed through the wall but *into* it.

The wall wasn't nearly thick enough to accommodate such a creature. In going through the wall, it seemed to have gone out of the Pendleton altogether, into some other reality or dimension.

Her hands were damp with sweat, and the statue of Diana wanted to slip through her grip. She put it on the floor, blotted her palms on her slacks, and hurried to Iris's room, where the door stood open.

The girl was sitting in bed, propped up by a pile of pillows stacked against the headboard, reading a book. She did not react to her mother's arrival. More often than not, behind the armor of her autism, she refused to recognize the presence of others by even so much as a glance.

Sparkle toured the room and peered in the adjacent bathroom, expecting to find some slouching beast out of a Bosch painting or risen from a Lovecraft story. All was as it should be.

Reluctant to leave her daughter alone, she sat on the edge of an armchair, waiting for her heartbeat to slow. But Iris had drawn open the draperies that her mother had closed earlier, and shears of lightning scissored the sky with blades so bright that Sparkle sprang up and left the room.

She wanted to return to the windowless closet. After the thing that she had seen, however, the master suite seemed to be alien territory, where expectations of a second visitation would fray her nerves worse than would the pyrotechnics of the storm. Besides, she wanted to be close enough to Iris to hear her if she called out.

She retreated to the kitchen, which had no view of the courtyard. During the day, the only natural light here came from a row of clerestory windows high in the south wall, set far back in a deep alcove that lay over the public hallway, which had a much lower ceiling than the rooms of the apartments. Those panes had been fitted with power shades operated by a remote, and earlier she had lowered them.

As Sparkle brewed espresso, she thought again about mescaline. Peyote. She had hard experience with its devastating potential. She wondered if someone had slipped a hit of one hallucinogen or another into her food. That seemed paranoid, and she was *not* an everybody's-out-to-get-me kind of girl, but she couldn't think of any other explanation for what she had seen.

Talman Ringhals, Tal, Tally, handsome and charismatic professor, seducer of students, knew everything about hallucinogens: mescaline, LSD, the bark of the ayahuasca vine, psilocybin and other substances derived from an array of magic mushrooms. . . . When he seduced Sparkle late in her sophomore year—his analysis of Emily Dickinson's poem about lightning, "362," won her heart—she didn't know about his religion, in which the sole sacrament was any consciousness-altering drug. Tal raised the subject carefully, revealing his faith in chemically induced transcendence only when he felt that she would be in his thrall as long as he wished. When she declined to participate in one of his spiritual journeys, he secretly spiked her coffee with mescaline. Instead of "touching the face of God," which Tal promised would be the effect of this sacrament, Sparkle plummeted into a hell of hallucinations, the memory of which still haunted her.

She dumped Talman Ringhals, which was a new experience for him, and soon thereafter learned that his betrayals had begun before he spiked her coffee, when he told her that she need not worry about birth control because he'd had a vasectomy. Iris was the consequence of that lie.

Now the six-legged monstrous baby seemed like a nasty drug flashback, though she had never experienced a flashback before.

Uneasy about leaving Iris alone but still rattled by the lightning, she sat at the kitchen table, her back to the clerestory windows in the high alcove. When the storm sky blazed, she couldn't see it throbbing around the edges of the shades. But when thunder shook the night, the kitchen lights flickered, and this faux lightning proved sufficient to bring into her mind's eye the memory of her mother's death dance.

The central theme of Sparkle's existence was lightning, both the kind that the sky threw down and a series of metaphorical bolts—like Tal and mescaline poisoning and Iris—that suddenly changed her life forever, often for worse but sometimes for better. The second real lightning strike that burnt a new path for her to follow came at dusk one year to the day after her father, Murdoch, had perished before her eyes.

Sparkle loved her dad as much as life itself, but her mother, Wendeline, loved him even *more* than she loved life. For a year, her grief did not mellow into sorrow as time usually ensured, but instead sharpened into anguish, and she lived in despair that isolated her from her daughter. On the first anniversary of Murdoch's death, when Nature chose to mark the occasion with another storm that rolled in from the sea, Sparkle sought her mother for comfort, at first without success. After climbing the spiral stairs of the shingled tower at the northwest corner of the house, she found Wendeline outside, in the rain, on the widow's walk, the highest point of the structure, gazing at the thunderheads that had gathered in the last light of the day. Her mother wore a blue dress that Daddy had particularly liked, and she stood barefoot on the wet deck, holding an umbrella that provided little protection from the wind-driven rain.

Nine-year-old Sparkle Sykes pleaded with her to come back into the house. Wendeline seemed unaware of her daughter, intent on the fierce lightning that, far out at sea, stitched the darkening sky to the darker water, and on nearer bolts that struck the Maine shore and appeared briefly to set the foaming waves on fire. She seemed to be in a trance of anticipation, half smiling, as if she expected her husband, like a descending angel, to come down to her, back to her, from out of the storm.

A moment after Sparkle realized that her mother gripped the umbrella not by its wooden handle but by the metal rod above the handle, lightning was drawn to the steel ferrule, followed the rod, found the hand, pierced the woman. The umbrella burst into flames as it flew from her, twirled away into the rain, and she twirled, as well, not struck down but lifted by a million volts, lifted and spun into a brief loose-limbed dance like the capering scarecrow in *The Wizard of Oz*. Her arms swept up as if she were reaching in ecstasy for another hit of flying flame. Powered by the storm that for an instant entered her, Wendeline whirled into the railing and over it, out into the rain and the dusk, dead before her fall began, a fall that ended in a holly hedge that both embraced and pierced her, holding her faceup to the violent heavens.

Young Sparkle in her rubber-soled shoes, on the wet deck of the widow's walk, orphaned now and traumatized, standing motionless in a state of shock, understood instantly that this world was a dark place and hard, that life was best for those who refused to be broken by it, that being happy required the strength and courage to refuse to be intimidated by anyone or anything. She wept but she did not sob. She stood there for a long time until the tears stopped flowing and the rain washed the salt from her face.

For the past twenty-three years, she had cowered from nothing other than lightning, neither from any human being who crossed her path nor from fear of failure in any task. She did not shrink from the dangers and risks that worried other people. Only the swift sword of the storm could inspire her retreat, and she sensed now, as she finished the espresso, that the time had arrived when she must overcome that phobia, too, if she were to survive whatever unprecedented peril the crawling six-legged vision represented.

In the absence of thunder, the kitchen lights

flickered again, and Sparkle realized that if the power failed, she dared not be caught even for a moment in pitch blackness when it might be shared by something like the otherworldly crawler. For emergencies, she had stashed a flashlight in each room of the apartment. Now she took one from a drawer near the ovens.

The power did not go off, but she decided that, regardless of the lightning at the windows, she must remain with Iris until she understood what was happening. And in the current circumstances, she could not risk disturbing the easily agitated girl by forcing her to move from her room to the kitchen or to some other space where windows were less prominent. In an emergency, keeping Iris calm would be the key to keeping her safe.

On her way to her daughter's room, glancing through the open door to the study, Sparkle saw concentric circles of blue light throbbing from the center of the television, which had been off when last she passed this way. Iris wouldn't have turned it on. The girl didn't like TV because its ceaseless stream of changing images struck her as chaotic, first made her nervous and then frightened her: "You don't know what's coming next, it's always just coming at you."

Sparkle stepped into the study and stared at the eerie blue rings. Apparently it was a test pattern of a kind she had never seen before.

She tried to switch off the TV, but the batteries in the remote seemed to be dead. Approaching the set to use the manual controls, she halted when an uninflected—perhaps computerized—voice spoke.

"Adult female. Blond hair. Blue eyes. Five feet two."

Having heard herself described, Sparkle frowned.

"Adult female. Blond hair. Blue eyes. Five feet two. Aboveground. Second floor. South wing."

"What the hell?"

The TV said, *"Exterminate. Exterminate."*

20

Apartment 3-F

After the Russian manicurist departed, Mickey Dime went into the study. The wood floor felt sexy under his bare feet. A lot of things felt sexy to Mickey. Nearly everything.

On the carpet, he stood squinching his toes in the deep wool pile. His feet were small and narrow. Well-formed. He was proud of his well-formed feet. His late mother had said that his feet looked like they were carved by the artist Michelangelo.

Mickey liked art. Art was sexy.

Murder was the sexiest thing of all. Murder could be an art, too.

His brother, Jerry, stone-dead and rolled up in the microfiber blanket, wasn't a work of art. An unplanned murder, committed in haste, without the target being *aware* that he would soon die, without time for the victim's terror to ripen, could not be a work of art. It was amateurish. Crude hack work. Driven by emotion.

Great art wasn't about emotion. It was about *sensa-*

tion. Only the bourgeoisie, the tacky middle class, thought art should affect the better emotions and have meaning. If it touched your heart, it wasn't art. It was kitsch. Art *thrilled*. Art spoke to the primitive, to the wild animal within. Art strummed deeper chords than mere emotions. If it made you think, it might be philosophy or science or something, but it wasn't art. True art was about the meaninglessness of life, about the freedom of transgression, about *power*.

Mickey learned about art from his mother. His mother had been the smartest person of her time. She knew everything.

He wished his mother were still here. She would know how to dispose of Jerry's body.

This wasn't an easy problem to solve. Every hallway in the Pendleton was monitored by security cameras. So were the elevators. So were the garages behind and separate from the main structure. Jerry weighed about 165 pounds. They were on the third floor.

The longer Mickey stood there, staring at the blanket-wrapped corpse, the bigger and heavier it looked.

He returned to his enormous bathroom, where he had received the manicure and the pedicure in his own spa chair. He opened his aromatherapy cabinet. He considered the sixty essences, each in a small glass bottle, racked on the back of the cabinet doors.

Underfoot, the cold marble floor felt sexy. But the chill also sharpened his mind and helped him to make a decision.

The fragrance of limes would further clarify his thinking and aid in the solution of his problem. The vaporizer stood on a roll-out shelf. Using an eyedropper, he distributed five drops of the essence of limes at the designated points on one of the cotton pads that came with the machine.

Fragrant steam billowed forth. Mickey breathed deeply. Any pleasant scent, if concentrated enough, could be intoxicating. He was exhilarated by the intense, astringent clarity of limes.

Smell might be the most erotic of the five senses. Pheromones that men and women produced, of which they were not consciously aware, drew them inexorably to one another more than did appearances or any other qualities they might possess. The nose was aroused before the genitals.

Mickey returned to the study. Dead Jerry waited in the blanket, the ends secured with neckties.

Mickey stood over the bundle. He regarded it with calculation, his mind lime-fresh and ready to get on with business. He paced around the cadaver. He sat in an armchair, pondering it.

He went to a window to peer down at the rain-washed courtyard, which was enclosed on three sides by the Pendleton and on the east end by a fourteen-foot-high limestone wall. An ornate bronze gate in that wall led to an open-air transitional space, which had other gates at its north and south ends. That space connected with the first garage, which had been converted from the carriage house.

Mickey's parking space lay even farther away, in the second and larger garage, a new structure that stood alone, with three floors, one of them underground.

His attention shifted to the south wing, across the courtyard. On the second floor, someone stood backlighted at a window. If anyone had been trundling a blanket-wrapped stiff past the fountains and the ornamental shrubs below, he would have been seen.

Mickey returned to dead Jerry. A blanket didn't sufficiently disguise a corpse. When you started hauling it around, anyone who saw it would know it was a dead guy in there.

Sensation was the only reason for living. Sensation stimulated thought and action. In this case, aromatherapy wasn't potent enough to rev up his mind.

Mickey went to the walk-in closet in his bedroom. From a high shelf, he took down a black carryall. The smell and feel of the leather pleased him.

In the bedroom, he put the carryall on the bed. He pinched the pull tab between thumb and forefinger. He relished the erotic sound of the slider separating the teeth of the zipper.

From the bag he removed panties and lingerie that had belonged to his mother. Silk, satin, lace.

Tactile sensation can be a powerful stimulant.

After a while, he knew how he must dispose of the body. The only problematic part of the plan would be killing the guard currently on duty in the security room.

Murdering the guy would be easy. But that would be

two jobs for which nobody was paying Mickey. Not good. The various people who contracted his services must never discover that he was murdering for free. They might decide he was no longer professional enough to be trusted. Then they would put out a contract on *him*.

In order to enjoy the most intense sensations that this world offered, you had to earn entrance into the right circles, to be one of those with a license to do anything you wanted and the wealth to ensure you could fulfill your most exotic desires. His mother had taught him that to be certain of achieving such a rarefied position, far beyond the reach of ordinary law, you had to make yourself useful to the Anointed, which was the class to which she belonged.

Like his mother, he exterminated people to make himself useful. She hadn't used guns or garrotes, but words—theories and analyses and well-crafted lies. His mom killed reputations. She destroyed people intellectually, emotionally. She was always happy to see them dead if later they committed suicide or if eventually disease got them, but she never actually pulled a trigger, slid in a shiv, or set the timer on a bomb.

Mickey would dispose of the guard in the same place he dropped Jerry. By the time they were found, if they ever were, too little of them would remain to be identified, and no one would know how they had died.

With that decision made, to his surprise a vivid series of erotic images teased his mind's eye. There was another resident of the Pendleton whom he found incredibly hot. But he couldn't buy sex with Sparkle Sykes, because she didn't need the money. He liked her daughter, too. They reminded him of Mallory, the cocktail waitress, and her younger sister, two of his first three murders. A nostalgic yearning overcame him. He would never again have sex with someone before killing her. Too risky. But if disposing of dead Jerry and the guard proved as simple as he expected, there was no harm in a little fantasizing about someday doing the Sykes girls and disposing of them in the same manner. Everybody liked to daydream.

Inspired, he put away the panties and lingerie. He returned the carryall to the closet.

He pulled on a pair of socks. They were a cashmere blend. His newly manicured toes were snug and warm in them.

One

In your wisdom, you once observed: "What need have we of gods if we become gods ourselves?"

I am sure, however, that you will come to understand that a world populated by gods would be as disordered as a world crowded with ordinary human beings in all their mad variety. The Greeks imagined a panoply of gods and demigods; consider the jealousies and rivalries that ensued among those residents of Mount Olympus. Men as gods would make of the world one vast Olympus, in a constant turmoil of supernatural events.

I am the One. I have no need for either humankind or godkind. In destroying the former, I destroy the latter.

Consider the one who kills for a living and who murdered his brother, as Cain murdered Abel. He allows for no god who will condemn him. He says that sensation is everything, that it is the only thing, and he is correct. He understands the truth of life better than do any of the other residents of the Pendleton. If there were a human being to whom I might grant a measure of mercy, it would be he. But mercy is a concept embraced by the weak, and I am not weak.

Tremors rumble under the building, then and now.

The current crop of Pendleton residents will soon stand before me like stalks of wheat waiting for the scythe. If blood ran in my veins, I might thrill to the prospect of this impending harvest, but I am bloodless and not subject to blood passions.

I will inflict pain upon them, I will lead them into despair, I will administer death unto them without the ecstasy that the hit man might experience when he murders, but with an efficiency and a prudent self-interest that ensures I will become and will remain the One until the sun dies and the world goes dark.

21

Here and There

Witness

Cold rain streamed down the tall chimney stacks, which were whetstones against which the wind whistled thinly as it sharpened itself, and even here, where few would ever see them, the grand architectural details did not relent. Every chimney was capped by a fascia of carved acanthus leaves, and each of its four tall walls was decorated with an oval medallion of limestone in which were engraved the letters *BV*, for *Belle Vista*.

The glazed ceramic-tile roof of the great house appeared flat, but it was slightly sloped from the center point to all four walls of the waist-high balustrade that defined the parapet. The rain streamed away into copper scuppers that carried it to embedded downspouts in the corners of the structure.

Through the downpour, weaving among the chimneys and the vent stacks, which were as familiar to him as the patterns of his long-enduring melancholy, Witness approached the western parapet. He wore boots, jeans, a sweater, and an insulated jacket, but not a raincoat. He had come from a night where there was no rain; and he didn't expect it here.

He stood at the high balustrade, gazing down upon the bustling traffic on the avenue and then at the sparkling sweep of the city spreading out upon the plain below. This was the fourth time he had seen the metropolis from this vantage point, and it was both brighter and larger than on the three previous occasions. If the lights of the streets and buildings hadn't deliquesced into the shroud of rain, the city would have been even more impressive than it was.

Witness waited for sudden dryness, for darkness deep and vast.

Silas Kinsley

Returning from his informative meeting with Perry Kyser in the bar at Topper's, approaching the main entrance of the Pendleton, Silas hesitated because the lighting was dimmer and more yellow than it should have been, obscuring the transition from the first to the second step. The first step was as wide as two, and the second was actually a broad stoop, so people who were tipsy (which Silas was not) or elderly (which he certainly was) sometimes stumbled there.

Surrounded by an architrave of limestone carved in an ivy motif, the arched bronze-and-glass doors were recessed under a bubblelike glass-and-bronze canopy by Louis Comfort Tiffany. Tucked discreetly under the canopy, the lights shone down on the steps and doors. None was burned out, but the entrance appeared half as well illuminated as usual.

Pushing open one of the doors and stepping into the lobby, Silas discovered that the lights here were also dimmer than usual. Drawing back the hood of his raincoat, he realized that the lighting was the least of the changes the space had undergone. Bewildered, he found himself not in the familiar carpetless lobby but in a reconfigured room with a fine antique Tabriz carpet over part of the marble floor and two divans where arriving guests might wait to be received. To his left, the concierge counter was gone, replaced by a solid and handsomely paneled wall inset with a single arched door. The evening concierge, Padmini Bahrati, was nowhere to be seen. On the right, instead of two sets of double French doors leading to a large banquet room that residents used for parties too big to be accommodated in their apartments, another solid arched door was set in a paneled wall. Directly ahead, the pair of French doors to the ground-floor public hall had been replaced by a formidable arched doorway with an intricately carved surround; the double doors were closed to any view of the space beyond. Rather than indirect cove lighting and recessed can lights in the ceiling, there were a grand crystal chandelier and floor lamps with pleated-silk shades and tassels.

He knew this place from old photographs. This was not the lobby of the Pendleton in 2011, but instead the reception hall of Belle Vista in a distant age, the apartment building gone, the private home returned. Back in the late nineteenth century, Shadow Street had been the first in the city to receive electric service, and Belle Vista had been the first new house to be built here without gas lamps. The lighting was dimmer than usual because these bulbs were primitive Edison products from the early days of the illumination revolution.

Sometimes, under stress or in the grip of strong emotion, Silas suffered from familial tremors of the jaw, which caused his mouth to quiver, and of the right hand. He began to tremble now, not with fear but with wonder. Time past and time present seemed to meet here, as if all the yesterdays of history were just a door, a threshold, a step away.

Directly ahead, a door opened, and the haunting began. The man who entered had died decades before Silas Kinsley's birth. Andrew Pendleton. Billionaire of the Gilded Age. The first owner of this residence. He was no ghost, no rattler of chains looking to torment Ebenezer Scrooge, but rather a traveler out of time. He was dressed for another era: wide cuffs on his pants, narrow lapels on his suit coat, a high yoke on his vest, and a hand-knotted bow tie.

Startled, Pendleton said, "Who are you?"

Before Silas could respond, Belle Vista rippled away, as if it must have been a mirage, and the long-dead businessman shimmered out of sight with the reception room. Silas found himself standing in the brightly lighted lobby of the Pendleton, everything as it should be.

Beyond the concierge's counter was an entrance to a walk-in coat closet used during parties in the nearby banquet room. Through that door came Padmini Bahrati, a slender beauty with enormous dark eyes, who reminded Silas of his own lost Nora.

"Mr. Kinsley," said the concierge, "how are you this evening?"

Blinking, trembling, Silas remained speechless for a moment, and then he said, "Did you see him?"

Adjusting the cuffs of her blouse, she said, "Who?"

Judging by her demeanor, the transformation of the lobby had not extended to the coat closet. She was unaware of what had happened.

Silas strove to keep his voice steady. "A man. Leaving. Dressed as though he stepped out of the late eighteen hundreds."

"Perhaps that's a new fashion trend," Padmini said, "which would be lovely, considering what you see people wearing these days."

Twyla Trahern

As she slammed the door to Winny's room, hoping to contain whatever malign force had tried to manifest in there, and as she hurried with the boy along the hallway toward the master suite, Twyla first thought that she would throw some essentials into a suitcase before leaving the Pendleton. By the time she reached the threshold of her bedroom, she decided it would be foolish to delay one minute longer than necessary. Reality had changed before her eyes and then had changed again. She didn't know what was happening here, but she needed to react to it as she would have reacted if she'd seen the ghost of a decapitated man who spoke to her from the head that he carried in the crook of his arm: *She needed to get the hell out.*

All she required was her purse. It contained her car keys, her checkbook, her credit cards. They could buy new clothes and anything else they needed.

"Stay close," she urged Winny as she crossed the living room toward the wing of the apartment that included her study, where she had left her purse.

She wasn't as much of a churchgoer as maybe she ought to be, but Twyla was a believer, raised in a house with a well-read Bible, where they prayed every evening before dinner and again at bedtime. In the small town where she was brought up, as in her immediate family, most people lived as best they could with the conviction that this life was preparation for another. When her daddy, Winston, died in the coal-cracker explosion, lots of people at his funeral said, "He's in a better place now," and meant it. There was this world and the world after, and Twyla once wrote a song about the need for humility in the light of our mortality and another about the mystery of grace, both hits.

Whatever the next world might be like, however, she knew for certain that the walls of Heaven weren't crumbling and stained and greasy and crawling with black mold, like the wall that changed in Winny's bedroom. If television existed in Heaven—which was about as likely as cancer wards existing in Heaven—there wouldn't be either spyware that made every TV a surveillance device or deadpan computer voices ordering people exterminated. That didn't even sound like Hell, but more like a hell on earth, maybe North Korea or Iran or some other place run by madmen.

In the study, as she snatched her purse from the piano bench and turned to leave, her attention was drawn to the windows by a flash of lightning, and she remembered the brief illusion that the storm and the rain-washed panes had earlier presented to her: the city gone, replaced by an empty landscape, a sea of grass, strange trees—craggy and black—clawing at the sky. *That* had been part of *this,* not an illusion, but a glimpse of a different reality.

The knot of fear in her breast tightened.

As acutely perceptive as ever, Winny said, "What? What is it?"

"I don't know. It's crazy. Come on, sweetie. You go ahead of me, I don't want you out of my sight. We need coats, umbrellas."

Theirs was the largest apartment on the second floor, twice the size of the next biggest, and the only one with two entrances. The front doors opened into a short length of hallway, near the north elevator, and the service door opened near the south elevator. Their winter coats and rain gear were in a closet in the laundry room, near the back door.

As they crossed the kitchen, Twyla said, "Winny, wait a sec," and snatched the handset from the wall phone. She pressed O, which in the Pendleton's customized telecom system would ring the phones in both the concierge's office and at the lobby reception counter.

A woman said, "Operator," which wasn't the standard greeting, and she didn't sound like Padmini Bahrati, who was the only female concierge on the staff.

Confused, Twyla said, "Is this the concierge?"

"The what? Excuse me. No, ma'am. This is the operator."

Perhaps she was some new employee who didn't know the protocols.

"This is Twyla Trahern in 2-A. Will you please have my Escalade brought around from the garage right away?"

"I'm sorry, ma'am. You've dialed the operator. If you've got a number for this concierge person, I'll be happy to place the call for you."

Dialed? Place the call?

Watching his mother, Winny raised his eyebrows.

To the operator, Twyla said, "Aren't you at the front desk?"

"No, ma'am. I'm at City Bell, the central exchange. Whom do you wish to call?"

Twyla had never heard of City Bell. She said, "I'm trying to reach the front desk of the Pendleton."

"The Pendletons? Is that a residence? Just a moment, please." She returned after a silence: "We have no

Pendletons listed anymore. By any chance . . . do you mean Belle Vista?"

Twyla was aware of just enough of the building's history to know that when it was a single-family residence, it had been called Belle Vista. But that hadn't been since sometime in the 1970s.

The operator said, "That would be Mr. Gifford Ostock and family. But I'm afraid that's a private number."

"Gifford Ostock?" The name meant nothing to Twyla.

"Yes, ma'am. Since Mr. Pendleton . . . passed away . . . well, Mr. Ostock has lived at Belle Vista."

Andrew Pendleton had died more than a century earlier.

"This Ostock doesn't live there now," Twyla said.

"Oh, yes, ma'am. He's lived there at least thirty years."

Twyla had never known an operator as chatty and patient as this. As nice as the woman sounded, it was nonetheless tempting to think that her unprecedented forbearance must be a subtle mockery if not something more sinister.

Although she did not realize why she was asking the question until the last word fell from her lips, Twyla said, "I'm sorry. I was confused for a moment. Could you please give me the number of the Paramount Theater?"

The Paramount, an Art Deco movie palace from the 1930s, stood at the base of Shadow Hill, walking distance from the Pendleton.

The operator didn't tell Twyla to dial 411 for directory assistance. Instead, after a pause, she said, "Yes, ma'am. That number is Deerfield 227."

"DE-227. That's only five numbers."

"May I connect you, ma'am?"

"No. I can place the call later. Could you tell me—are the letters in the same place on a touch-tone phone as on a . . . rotary?"

As though she had decided she might be talking to a drunk, the operator at last sighed but remained polite: "I'm sorry, ma'am, but I don't know the term 'touch-tone.'"

"What year is this?" Twyla asked, which raised Winny's eyebrows again.

After a hesitation, the operator said, "Ma'am, do you need medical assistance?"

"No. No, I don't. I just need to know the year."

"It's 1935, of course."

Twyla hung up.

Logan Spangler

In the transformed half bath of Senator Blandon's apartment, in the inadequate yellow glow of the ameboid form on the ceiling, Logan Spangler played the LED flashlight over the walls of sinuous, pale-green, black-mottled, serpentine fungus from which, at six locations, sprouted clusters of similarly colored and oddly shaped mushrooms on thick short stems. Logan had never seen such specimens before, and he regarded them with curiosity but also with suspicion.

They were suspect less because they were unusual than because their sinuous forms and eerie coloration disturbed him on a level so deep that he couldn't plumb it, perhaps as deep as racial memory, an intuitive sense that he was in the presence of something not only foul, not merely poisonous, but also alien, corrupt, and corrupting.

Behind Logan, someone said something that he didn't understand, but when he spun to face the speaker, no one loomed in the doorway or in the hall beyond. Silence. Then the voice came again from behind him, in a foreign language, low and whispery and ominous, not so much threatening as foreboding, like someone delivering terrible news. He turned again as the speaker fell silent, but no one had materialized in the bathroom while he'd been distracted. He remained alone.

Alone with the fungus. The voice came a third time, delivering another foreign sentence or two, very near, to his left, where the wall was entirely covered with the green-and-black growth. What sounded like the same chain of syllables at once came from the wall directly ahead, and yet another repetition from somewhere near the half-draped toilet. As Logan tried to follow the elusive voice with the LED beam, he found the light focusing on cluster after cluster of the mushrooms that swelled from the undulant snakelike base forms.

When he began to suspect that the voice came from the fungus—or whatever the hell it was—Logan drew his pistol. In all his years as a homicide detective, he'd drawn his piece perhaps a dozen times, and in his six years at the Pendleton, he had until now left it in his holster. Furniture vanishing around him, rooms falling into ruin but then magically restored: He sensed no immediate threat in those bizarre events, perhaps because the criminals with whom he'd dealt his entire life were mostly uninspired brutes and fools who resorted to violence to solve their problems and, therefore, didn't require him to develop a rich imagination in order to find them and bring them to justice. But though his imagination might be impoverished, it wasn't penniless, and now it paid out a bounty of anxiety.

The disembodied voice, deep but whispery, suddenly swelled to a chorus of voices, each of them saying something different from the others, all of them still low and murmurous and untranslatable, but more urgent than before. They seemed to be talking not to Logan but to one another, conspiring toward some action. As the flashlight beam stabbed here, there, elsewhere, he was convinced that if he could see the undersides of the mushroom caps, the fragile gills would be vibrating like vocal cords.

He had swung away from the fungus when he thought someone had spoken from the doorway behind him; but he was loath to turn his back on it again. Pistol in his right hand, flashlight in his left, he eased away from the grotesque organism—and the door slammed shut behind him.

A part of him argued that this was a dream, hallucination, that if he woke or got a grip on himself, he could make it all stop or fade away as the vision in the master bedroom had faded. But he had never before hallucinated, and no dream had ever been a fraction this vivid. He'd read once that maybe if you died in a dream you died for real, you never woke up, which was a theory that made sense to him, one that he didn't want to test.

Logan set the small flashlight on the filthy vanity, beside the cracked and stained sink. Not daring to take his eyes off the many-voiced colony, his pistol ready, he reached blindly behind himself for the doorknob, put a hand on it, but discovered that it would not turn. He felt for a latch button. It wasn't engaged. Bathroom doors didn't lock from the outside, yet it was immovable, no play in it at all, as if it were nailed to the jamb.

On the ceiling, the luminous yellow disc, which hadn't been there when first he searched this room, grew dimmer, dimmer. Logan snatched his flashlight from the vanity.

The vision of ruin and abandonment in the master suite had endured less than one minute. This fungal apparition had already lasted longer than that; surely it would soon relent, too, reality returning like a tide.

In the fading light, he saw the snake-form fungi begin to throb, not every row in unison, but first some and then others. A wave motion, like the peristalsis that forced food down the esophagus and through the digestive tract, pulsed in these tubular organisms as though they might be swallowing live rodents or as if these were the intestines of a great beast.

Logan's previously fallow imagination was blossoming moment by moment. If the fungi were capable of internal movement so radically different from anything else in the plant kingdom, perhaps they were ambulant as well, able to crawl or slither. Or coil and strike.

Something was happening to the clustered mushrooms on the walls and on the half-draped toilet. The puckered formations at the crowns of the caps began to open and peel back, each resembling a foreskin receding from a swelling glans. As if from vents in the caps, small clouds of pale vapor plumed into the air, like exhalations on a wintry morning.

The glowing form on the ceiling went dark. In the crisp beam of the flashlight, the drifting particles glimmered as if they were diamond dust. Not vapor, after all. These particles were too big to be the components of a mist, as big as—some bigger than—grains of salt, yet evidently light because they remained airborne. *Spores.*

Instinctively, Logan Spangler held his breath. Rapidly modifying his perception of the threat, no longer concerned that the serpentine forms might unravel from the walls and reveal tentacles and abruptly snare him, he worried that the cloud of spores would do what spores always sought to do: *colonize.* He holstered the pistol and turned to the door, examining the three hinges in the flashlight beam.

Vernon Klick

In the security room, Vernon Klick divided his attention between only two of the six plasma screens. One was a full-screen view of the short north wing of the west hall on the third floor, outside the north elevator, the other a shot of the north hall on the same floor.

He had watched the senile flatfoot, Logan Spangler, ring the bell at the jackass senator's apartment, watched him phone someone—probably the kiss-ass superintendent, Tom Tran, who dressed like the guest of honor at a geek convention—and then watched him enter the apartment with a passkey. Vernon had been waiting ever since for Spangler to come out of 3-D, where he was probably stealing old slop-bucket Blandon's ninety-year-old Scotch, sucking it out of the bottle with a straw.

Vernon Klick was not a patient man. He was thirty years old and on his way to the top, and anyone who delayed his rise to riches and fame, even for so much as five minutes, earned a place on his enemies list. The list was long, filling twelve pages of a lined legal-size tablet. The day was coming when he would have the resources to screw each of those people, one way or another, in such a fashion as to let them know exactly who had paid them back.

If not for the powers that be and their numerous despicable toadies, Vernon would have already gotten to the top. But the game was fixed against guys like him.

He had to work three times as hard as those for whom the game was rigged and be ten times more clever in order to achieve the success he deserved. Even to get where he was now, he had needed to push past countless obstacles that were put in his way by the Jews, the Wall Street bankers, the Wall Street bankers who were also Jews, the oil companies, the Republicans, all the New York publishers who conspired to keep truth tellers of exceptional talent out of the marketplace, the scheming Armenians, the state of Israel—which was, no surprise, run by Jews—and not least of all, two stupid high-school guidance counselors who really deserved to be fed alive to wild hogs, even thirteen years after their treachery.

Vernon was so close to attaining his long-held dreams that this would be the next-to-last night he spent as a security guard in the Pendleton, this cesspool of greed and privilege, among all these snotty bitches and smug bastards, not to mention old hags like the Cupp sisters and ancient freaks like Silas Kinsley, who for years had nothing to offer society yet continued to suck up its resources instead of doing everybody a favor and dying. Only two apartments remained that Vernon needed to explore and to photograph, and the residents were out of town through the coming weekend.

For months, Vernon worked first the graveyard shift and then the evening shift, using the security team's universal key to go anywhere he wished to go in the building. In his large briefcase were a camera and spare memory sticks, a laptop computer, and a pocket recorder on which he could dictate notes as he conducted his explorations and collected his evidence.

Toward the end of his eight hours, he always hacked into the security-camera video archives and deleted the portions of the recordings that showed him walking hallways and entering vacant apartments when he should have been manning the guard desk here in the basement. No one noticed the editing because no one reviewed the boring video unless there had been an incident—a medical emergency, a false fire alarm—during that shift. Besides, Logan Spangler was an old crock who knew even less about computers than the Dalai Lama knew about big-game hunting; the geezer assumed the video archives were immune from tampering simply because they had been designed to be safe. Old Flatfoot Spangler wasn't prepared for someone as brilliant and skilled and destined for greatness as Vernon Klick.

But until Spangler stopped sucking down Scotch in the idiot senator's apartment, returned with the precious universal key, put it in the drawer where it was always kept, and went home to his withered hag of a wife and his flea-bitten cat, Vernon had no way to complete his secret work. He stared intently at the plasma screen, watching that north hall, waiting for Spangler to leave 3-D. He muttered, "Come on, come on, you stupid old fart."

At the farther end of that hallway from the Blandon apartment, Mickey Dime stepped out of 3-F, closing the door behind him. He walked toward the camera, past the thieving senator's apartment, turned the corner, and boarded the north elevator.

Vernon had no interest in Dime. Weeks earlier, he inspected the man's apartment and found nothing of interest. Dime didn't indulge in appalling luxuries other than having an immense bathroom with an illegal high-pressure showerhead that wasted immense quantities of water and a sauna that was likewise an unnecessary drain on the city's power supply. His furniture was modern, with clean lines, probably expensive but not shamefully so. On the walls were several large ugly paintings, but ugly in a way you had to like them because you looked at them and said, *Yes, that's how life is.* And after checking out the artists online, Vernon found that their work wasn't horrendously pricey; Dime wasn't squandering fortunes that could be better used by society; in fact two of the artists had committed suicide years previously, perhaps because they sold too few of their paintings. There was a safe that Vernon couldn't get into, but given the evidence in the rest of the apartment, it probably didn't contain anything embarrassing.

Dime kept a small collection of fancy women's panties and other lingerie in a black-leather carryall on a high shelf in his master closet. But there were no photos of him wearing those garments and no reason to think that he did anything particularly strange with them. No doubt he liked to smell them and rub his face in them, as did Vernon with his own somewhat larger collection, but that wasn't aberrant behavior and didn't come close to the kind of outrage that he could use for the book he was writing and for the associated website. Probably most men had such collections, which explained why lingerie was always a profitable business, even in the worst of times, because *both* genders were buying it.

Where the *hell* was Logan Spangler, what was he doing so long in the moron senator's apartment, was the geezer gumshoe collecting information for his *own* best-selling book and scandal website?

Mickey Dime

In the basement, Mickey Dime stepped out of the elevator. He turned away from the gym. He walked past the two pairs of double doors to the heating-cooling plant, past the security office, past the entrance to the superintendent's apartment.

He liked the *click-click-click* of his heels on the tile floor. A purposeful, no-nonsense sound. The way the footsteps echoed off the walls pleased him. Except when he needed to be stealthy, he wore only shoes with leather soles and heels because he liked to hear himself going places with authority.

Although the swimming pool was at the north end of the enormous basement and behind closed doors, the air everywhere on this level had a faint chlorine scent. Others might not notice. Mickey's senses were highly refined. All six of them.

Mickey's mother had helped him to refine his sixth sense: the ability to detect almost instantly the degree—and precise points—of physical and emotional vulnerability in others.

He turned left into the corridor that served the twelve-foot-square storage units, one per apartment.

At the end of the corridor, to the left of the freight elevator, an equipment room contained, among other items, various sizes of hand trucks and wheeled carts and moving blankets that residents used to transport items from their apartments to the storage lockers or vice versa. Mickey chose a large hand truck with a deep cargo ledge and three adjustable straps to hold the load in place.

The nearby freight elevator served only the south side of the building. Because Apartments 2-A and 3-A were large and had both front and back entrances, the west hallway on those levels did not go entirely across the building to connect the other two, parallel wings. And the north freight elevator only served the three aboveground floors because of the swimming pool that occupied that side of the basement.

Mickey wheeled the hand truck back to the main north elevator in which he had descended. The mural of bluebirds joyously soaring through a sky full of golden clouds made him uneasy. He didn't know why. This was pure kitsch. Art that was consciously pretty usually just annoyed him. But this mural always made him . . . apprehensive.

In his apartment once more, he wheeled the hand

truck into the study, where the bundled corpse of his brother, Jerry, awaited disposal.

Mickey missed his mother terribly, but he was glad that she had not lived to see how easy Jerry had been to kill. She would have been disappointed in him for being taken so unawares. Of course, that disappointment would have been balanced by her pride in Mickey.

Sparkle Sykes

As Sparkle left the study, the television behind her said again, *"Exterminate. Exterminate."*

In Iris's room, the girl still sat in bed, reading. She didn't look up. She remained, as usual, in her autistic bubble.

Sparkle hurried to the first window and then to the second, to pull shut the draperies that her daughter had earlier opened. As the last set of panels drew together, the sky flared twice, three times, and in that shuddering fall of storm fire, the courtyard landscape lighting blinked off, as did lamps in all the windows in the north and west wings, although the lights remained on in her apartment. In fact, following that bright barrage, the golden glow of the city that usually silhouetted the chimneys and the parapet balustrade at the top of the house was also extinguished, as if the metropolis had lost all power except in these rooms.

Closing the draperies, turning away from the window, Sparkle told herself that she'd briefly been blinded to the courtyard and the other wings of the great house by the fear of being for an instant face-to-face with lightning. But she knew that explanation was self-deception. She had seen something—the absence of everything—that was related to the monstrous baby that vanished into a wall and to the voice coming from the pulsing blue rings on the TV. None of it was mescaline flashback all these years after her one experience of that hallucinogen. None of it was illusion. All of it was real, impossible yet true, and she desperately needed to understand it.

She turned to the window once more, hesitated, pulled the panels of fabric apart, and saw the courtyard as it should be. Backlighting the chimneys was the glorious radiance of a sprawling civilization that no storm or human folly had yet been able to extinguish. As she let out her pent-up breath in relief, she became aware of a presence on the outside of the window, creeping up from the sill, across the French panes and the thick bronze muntins.

Revealed somewhat by the rising lamplight from the courtyard but mostly by the light in this room, the creature on the casement window was even more alien than the monstrosity that had earlier crawled past the closet door. The shape and size of a platter for serving a fish, as pale and putrescent-looking as some dead drowned creature bleached by sun and seawater, it progressed on four crablike legs that terminated not in claws but in feet resembling those of a frog, with sucker pads allowing it to cling confidently to vertical surfaces. She could see only the ventral aspect of it, but she sensed that it was thick, perhaps five or six inches.

The most disturbing aspect of the apparition was the face in its underside, where a face should never be: a deformed oval countenance that in spite of its twisted features appeared more human than not, distorted in an expression that seemed half rage and half anguish. The horror was even more compelling than it was repellent, so that Sparkle found herself leaning toward the window in spite of her fear, driven to confirm that the face was no trick of light and shadow. The eyes were closed, but as she stared at the tortured visage, the pale lids peeled back, revealing milky orbs. Although those eyes appeared to be veiled with heavy cataracts, she felt certain that they fixed upon her through the window, that she was seen by this miscreation—a conviction that seemed to be confirmed when the thin-lipped mouth opened and a pale tongue licked the glass.

Bailey Hawks

He felt uneasy about leaving Sally Hollander alone, though she insisted she wanted the comfort and seclusion of her apartment. The quick dark figure he'd seen and the menacing swimmer in the pool were surely manifestations of the same "demon" that rushed her in the Cupp sisters' pantry. Whatever was happening in the Pendleton, whether supernatural or not, suggested that solitude wasn't advisable.

On the other hand, though he had been snared by

the ankle as he fled the pool, Bailey easily kicked loose. And Sally hadn't been injured, only frightened. These phantasms seemed to have malevolent intentions but perhaps not the power to commit the violence that they desired, which seemed to put them in the company of ghosts that haunted but could not harm.

Bailey didn't believe in ghosts, but he had no other template by which to understand this situation: spirits, ghosts, specters, things that go bump in the night. If it wasn't something like that, he could not imagine what else it might be.

After leaving Sally in 1-C, he took the north stairs, rather than the elevator, to the second floor. He often avoided elevators as part of his fitness regimen. The enclosed circular stairwell was original to Belle Vista; it hadn't been added during the conversion to the Pendleton in 1973. The honed-marble treads were wide, and the ornamental bronze handrail attached to the inner wall was an example of the finest nineteenth-century craftsmanship that, today, would be prohibitively expensive to re-create. Climbing these stairs, Bailey was reminded of a French chateau he had once visited.

Because the staircase was circular, there were landings only at each floor, none mid-floor. As he reached the landing and put a hand to the exit door, he heard quick descending footsteps and a child in song:

"Sing a song of sixpence, a pocketful of rye, four and twenty blackbirds baked in a pie. . . ."

The voice was so clear and melodic that Bailey

paused to see the singer. There were few children in the Pendleton.

"When the pie was opened, the birds began to sing . . ."

On the stairs above him, a girl appeared, perhaps seven or eight years old, as pretty as her voice, with lively blue eyes. She wore what appeared to be a costume: a sky-blue cotton dress with a ruffled skirt and gathered sleeves, overlaid with an eggshell-white linen apronlike garment trimmed in simple lace, and white leggings. Her white-leather ankle-top shoes were buttoned instead of laced.

When she saw Bailey, she halted and performed a half-curtsy. "Good afternoon, sir."

"You must have gotten that dress from Edna Cupp," Bailey said.

The girl looked puzzled. "It's from Partridge's, where Mummy buys all our clothes. I'm Sophia. Are you a friend of Daddy's?"

"I might be. Who's your father?"

"The master of the house, of course. Anyway, I should hurry. The iceman's delivering to the kitchen any minute. We're going to shave some off one of the blocks and cover it in cherry syrup, which is ever so good."

As she slipped past Bailey, off the landing and onto the stairs, he said, "What's your last name, Sophia?"

"Pendleton, of course," she said, and broke into another song as she followed the curving stairs out of sight. "Old King Cole was a merry old soul, and a merry old soul was he . . ."

The girl's footsteps and voice faded to silence more quickly than the turning of the stairs explained.

Bailey waited to hear a door open and close, but the quiet of the windowless stairwell became a profound hush.

Without knowing quite what he intended, he descended to the ground floor and then to the basement, expecting to find the girl waiting below. The heavy fire doors could not be opened and closed soundlessly. Yet she was gone.

Twyla Trahern

Having just spoken on the phone either to a City Bell operator in 1935 or to a hoaxer who was part of a bizarre conspiracy with an inscrutable purpose, Twyla hurried Winny out of the kitchen, into the laundry room. She retrieved a raincoat and an umbrella from the corner closet, and Winny slipped into a hooded jacket.

The lightless plain that she had glimpsed earlier still fresh in her mind, she got two flashlights from a utility drawer and jammed them in her coat pockets.

They left by the back door, she locked the deadbolt, and they hurried along the short hallway to the south elevator, where she pushed the call button.

Winny said, "How could it change like that, the wall?"

"I don't know, honey."

"Where was that place, the grungy place that faded in and out?"

"I don't know. I write songs. I don't write sci-fi." She pushed the call button again. "Come on, come on."

"It was the same wall but different, like the Pendleton on some other world. You know, like parallel worlds in stories?"

"I don't read those kinds of stories. Maybe you shouldn't read them, either."

"I didn't make the wall-thing happen," he assured her.

"No, of course you didn't. That's not what I meant."

She didn't know *what* she had meant. Her confusion dismayed her. Most of her life, she had known how to cope with anything that came her way, allowing herself no doubts and no excuses. Since she'd been eleven, whenever anything scary or painful happened, she composed a ballad or a spiritual or a torch piece or a country boogie-woogie number about it, and the fear and the hurt were cured by the writing of the lyrics, by the singing of the song. But painful events like the loss of her sweet father and frightening developments like the recognition that her marriage to Farrel was collapsing . . . Well, those were common human experiences for which music could be a medicine. In these weird circumstances, however, melody and poetry failed her. She wished that she possessed as many guns—or at least one!—as she had musical instruments.

With a *ding* the elevator arrived at the second floor.

Winny slipped through the doors even as they were sliding open.

On the threshold, Twyla halted when she saw that the elevator car had changed. Gone were the bluebird mural and the marble floor. Every surface in there was brushed stainless steel. Translucent panels in the ceiling cast an eerie blue light, the same blue that had pulsed from the TV and heralded the words *"Exterminate. Exterminate."*

"Get out of there!" she ordered Winny, and the doors began to slide shut.

Logan Spangler

In the threatening darkness, the peristalsis pulsing through the snakelike fungus made a wet, disgusting sound, and the obscene mushrooms wheezed softly each time they exhaled their salt-grain spores.

In the tight LED beam, Logan could see that the pivot pins in the knuckles of the barrel hinges might be worked loose with the blade of the pocketknife that he carried. Before he could set to work, however, the lights in the half bath came on, not the yellow thing on the ceiling—which had vanished—but the can lights overhead and the soffit lights above the vanity, which earlier had been broken and corroded. The entire room was restored to its former condition, and the pale-green, black-mottled fungi, both the serpentine and mushroom forms, were gone as if they had never existed.

When he tried the previously locked door, it opened.

He rushed out of the little bathroom, into the hallway, relieved to be free.

He sneezed, sneezed again. He pinched his nose between thumb and forefinger to stop a tingling in his nostrils. His lips felt dry, and when he licked them, they were crusted with something. He wiped one hand across his mouth. On his fingers and palm were perhaps a hundred tiny white spores.

Martha Cupp

After Bailey Hawks left with Sally, Martha decided to put all this demon-in-the-pantry nonsense out of her mind by perfecting her bridge game. She sat at the computer in the study, playing with a virtual partner named Alice, against a virtual team named Morris and Wanda. She selected MASTER LEVEL from a menu that offered five degrees of difficulty, but within a few minutes she regretted her choice. She'd been playing real bridge, with flesh-and-blood people, only for about a year. No matter how hard she pushed herself to improve, she wasn't ready for master-level play. She became so frustrated so quickly that she accused Morris of cheating, although he was only a software character and incapable of hearing her. As for Wanda—well, she was a smug little tart, so annoyingly sure of herself.

From the open doorway, Edna said, "I've decided the situation calls for immediate action."

To her virtual partner, Alice, Martha grumbled, "I'm

sorry I'm no help. I should have selected dementia-level play."

"First thing tomorrow," Edna said, "I'll call an exorcist."

When Martha looked up from the computer, she saw that her sister had already changed costumes. Instead of the lilac-silk day wear, she wore a dinner gown: black silk covered with spotted-black chiffon, black-and-gold lace edging the neckline and repeated on the train of the skirt, gathered sleeves with abundant frill, and a black-velvet cummerbund. Bedecked with both a long rope of pearls knotted at the bustline and a diamond necklace with pendant, as well as small drop earrings, wearing long white gloves, she looked as though she was dressed to attend a banquet with the queen, rather than to share a previously prepared, microwaved meal with her sister, the rotten bridge player.

"And once all evil spirits have been exorcised, I'll have the apartment blessed," Edna declared.

"But where will you find an exorcist, dear? Father Murphy knows all about your belief in ancient astronauts, shadow people, witches among us. . . . He doesn't approve, no priest would. He's not going to put the dignity of the Church on the line by bringing in an exorcist, because he knows that by the time they show up, you will have decided it wasn't a demon, after all, but a troll."

Edna smiled and shook her head. "Sometimes I think you never listen to me, Martha. I don't believe in trolls.

Trolls are the stuff of children's fairy tales, nothing more."

"You believe in gremlins," Martha reminded her.

"Because gremlins are *real,* of course. Do you know where our gremlin hid my reading glasses this time? I finally found them on the bottom shelf in the refrigerator next to the fruit yogurts. The little scamp."

"Maybe you left them there yourself."

Edna raised her eyebrows. "Whyever would I? I certainly don't curl up in the refrigerator to do my reading."

From elsewhere in the apartment came a squealing and squalling that certainly sounded like a cat fight, although Smoke and Ashes never quarreled.

"Whatever are they up to?" Edna wondered. She turned and hurried away, the short train of her dinner gown swishing along the floor.

Sparkle Sykes

When the tongue licked out of the contorted countenance on the underside of the creeping monstrosity and slid along the rain-slick glass, Sparkle knew it wasn't tasting the cool water or doing anything other than taunting her. The face initially seemed to be twisted as much in anguish as in rage, but its expression darkened into fury unalloyed by anything but mockery as the mouth curled in a thin, obscene sneer.

Certain that the cataracted eyes saw her, she nevertheless left the drapery open because as long as she could see the horror, she knew where it was. As it angled up the window, the thing seemed less interested in making progress than in exploring along every junction of bronze muntins and glass with its sucker-pad toes, as if seeking some breach or weakness that it could exploit to gain entrance.

Sharp lightning scored the sky, and for the first time since Sparkle saw her father seared and slain, she failed to cringe in fear of its lethal potential. The hideous thing upon the window merited her terror more than did Nature's bright fury. In fact, the flaring night seemed to caress the creature as if it were a child born from the storm.

She needed to call security. She didn't know what she could say that wouldn't sound crazy. Just tell the guard there was something he had to come and see for himself. Tell him it was urgent.

Iris's room lacked a phone. No matter how pleasant the ringtone, it always irritated her.

Keeping her eyes on the freak at the window, Sparkle eased backward to her daughter's bed. She spoke softly, with no note of alarm that might trigger one of the girl's anxiety attacks. "Honey, Iris, it's treat time. Ice cream, honey. Ice-cream time in the kitchen."

The girl neither replied nor moved.

As the abomination quested from one pane to the next, its suctorial feet squeaked on the glass.

She couldn't leave the child here alone, not even just long enough to get to the nearest phone and call security.

Autism was a ruthless censor that denied Iris the ability to communicate. Having memorized large portions of the beloved novel *Bambi,* the girl found a way to use quotations from the book as a kind of code that now and then enabled her to slip a thought past her oppressor by cloaking it in the words of another.

Hoping to build a bridge between herself and her psychologically isolated daughter, Sparkle had read and reread the novel. Sometimes the girl listened to familiar lines from *Bambi* and acted upon them, though if the same request was made with different words, she ignored it or responded temperamentally. Sparkle had identified and memorized numerous lines that proved to be useful.

"'*He* is in the woods, and we must go,'" she said, referring to the hunter who terrified the deer in the woods by the River Danube.

Iris looked up from her book, though not directly at her mother, as eye contact pained her.

"'Don't be frightened,'" Sparkle said, quoting the old stag, Bambi's father, from the next-to-last chapter of the novel. "'Come with me and don't be frightened. I'm glad that I can take you and show you the way. . . .'"

Again, the famous novel worked its magic. Iris put aside the book she was currently reading, got off the bed, and approached her mother, oblivious of the crawling horror seeking entrance at the casement window.

Sparkle wanted to take the girl's hand, but that contact would shatter the mood, put an end to cooperation, and perhaps inspire a violent physical reaction. Instead, she turned and went to the open door, as if confident that her daughter would follow her as any fawn would follow the doe that brought it into the world. Crossing the threshold into the hallway, she glanced back and saw Iris shuffling after her.

Sparkle thought she heard an inhuman cry, a shrill expression of intense craving, frustration, and rage, muffled by window glass. But the sound was so alien and so chilling that she wanted to believe it was only the voice of the skirling wind, blown into the thinnest falsetto.

Winny

When Winny slipped through the opening elevator doors, he right away realized that the bird mural was gone, that all the surfaces were stainless steel, and that the usual cove lighting and crystal ceiling fixture were gone, replaced by circles that rained down a moody blue light. A second later, he made the connection between this blue light and the luminous rings pulsing on the TV set in his room—which was just when his mom said, "Get out of there!"—and the doors started to slide shut.

These doors were supposed to stop closing if you stepped between them, it was a safety feature, but they clamped on to Winny as if they were jaws. They weren't sharp, they couldn't bite him, but they were maybe powerful enough to slowly squeeze the breath out of him or to snap his ribs and force the broken ends inward to his heart. As his mother grabbed him by his jacket, in his mind's eye, Winny saw blood squirting from his nose, trickling from his ears, and that scared him enough to writhe and twist in the grip of the doors until he wrenched free.

Almost free. The doors closed on his left wrist, tight enough to hurt, and he couldn't skinny down his hand enough to slip it loose. His mom hooked her fingers in the narrow gap, trying to pull the doors apart just enough to allow Winny to liberate himself, but she couldn't do it because the doors were crazy powerful. She was grunting from the effort and cursing, and his mother never cursed.

Then maybe he imagined it or maybe it really happened, but in the elevator car, something crawled onto his imprisoned hand and began to explore it.

"There's a bug!" Winny cried out, violating his rule against doing anything wimpy, opening himself to the charge of being a sissy, but he couldn't control himself. *"In there, on my hand, a big bug or something!"*

Its legs or antennae quivered between all his fingers at the same time, simultaneously across the palm and the back of his hand, gross, disgusting, maybe a big centipede so flexible it could twine ceaselessly, busily through his fingers or maybe a swarm of smaller insects. He clenched his teeth and choked back a scream, waiting for the thing—or things—to bite or sting, shaking his hand to cast it off, trying to pull loose, the doors pinching his wrist tighter, his mother straining at the doors, her face red with the effort, the cords in her neck like taut ropes, and suddenly he *was* free of both the door and the bug.

Winny shot past his mom, across the hallway, turned, his back pressed to the door of the Dai apartment, certain that something radically weird must be coming out of the elevator. But the doors had slid shut. His mother was scared but not hurt, beads of sweat on her forehead, no bug climbing up her raincoat toward her face.

They were just thirty feet from the south stairwell, the only way out if they couldn't use the elevator. His mom scooped her purse off the floor, didn't bother with the dropped umbrella, pushed Winny ahead of her, and said, *"Come on, the stairs!"*

Maybe it was true instinct or maybe it was just a full-sissy moment that would live in infamy, but as he approached the fire door, Winny thought that the stairwell was a trap. Something was waiting for them along that spiral, and they would never get to the ground floor alive.

His mother must have felt it, too, because she whispered, *"Winny, no. Wait."*

Vernon Klick

Vernon was so intent on watching the third floor for old saggy-assed Logan Spangler to stagger out of Senator Foghorn Leghorn's apartment that the knock on the door startled him up from his chair. Before he could say "Come in," the door opened, and Bailey Hawks entered as if he owned the room and was here to collect the rent.

Vernon disliked Hawks as much as anyone in the Pendleton and more than some of them. Logan Spangler, in his best bootlicking mode, said Hawks was a hero, apparently just because he was a marine and went to war and was given a chestful of stupid medals, which were probably awards for things like killing ten thousand innocent civilians and straddling a thousand third-world whores and torching orphanages. *Real* heroes were men like Vernon, who dared to reveal the private lives and sick secrets of holier-than-thou greed demons like the parasites who lived in this building.

During his search of Hawks's apartment, Vernon had not been able to find any shockingly sick secrets of the kind that would help put his book at the top of best-seller lists and make his subscription website, when he created it, *the* place on the Internet. But just because he failed to find scandalous material about Hawks didn't mean that such secrets did not exist. It meant that the orphan killer was extraordinarily clever at concealing evidence of his vicious crimes and disgusting perversities.

Anyway, Vernon *did* find lots of circumstantial evidence that Hawks was far from the hero old Logan Spangler thought he was. For one thing, Hawks subscribed to *nine* financial publications, which revealed a demented obsession with making money. He had a wine cooler full of high-dollar Cabernets, several expensive tailor-made suits, each of which cost six times as much as a perfectly serviceable off-the-rack garment, plus a collection of rare Bakelite radios from the Art Deco period. A decent man would not have spent all that money so selfishly or on such frivolous items. Although Vernon knew a lot about safes and how to crack them, Hawks's free-standing model proved to be impenetrable, which must mean it contained scandalous material. And although Vernon knew a lot about computer hacking, he couldn't get at Hawks's client files because they were so well protected; he even began to think they were kept on a separate computer that was locked in the safe each night, no doubt because Hawks and his clients were engaged in stock fraud, commodities manipulation, and worse.

As Hawks came into the security room, he said, "Mr. Klick, I just now saw someone in the north stairwell who I don't think lives here."

Sitting down once more, peeved that he was called *mister* instead of *officer,* Vernon said, "Someone who?"

"I don't know who she was. But I wonder if you could check your video record to see if she left the stairs on the first floor or the basement. She passed me going down when I was at the second-floor landing."

"If she does live here, letting you track her movement would be a violation of her privacy."

"I don't think she lives here."

"But you don't know for sure."

"Listen, something's wrong here." Hawks hesitated. His eyes were shifty, just like you'd expect a crooked financial adviser's eyes to be. "These odd things have been happening. This one happened like three or four minutes ago, but maybe she won't appear on the video. That wouldn't surprise me."

Frowning, Vernon said, "So Spangler told you about the missing twenty-three seconds. Well, *I'm* the one said there must've been a heist or maybe somebody killed somebody. If that's the way it turns out, he'll say he suspected as much from the start, but it was *me,* not him, who did all the suspecting. If you're saying there's another intruder and maybe more funny stuff with the security video, they're not going to get away with it on *my* watch. Let's have a look."

Vernon opted out of real-time images on the center screen and accessed archived video. As there were no cameras in the stairwells, he first called up the basement hall outside the north stairs, going back five minutes to watch for someone to come out of that door. If there was a heist going on, or a murder, or *another* murder, or some other kind of sick criminal shenanigans among the privileged vermin of the Pendleton, his book was going to be not just a hit but also a *huge* best-seller. A juicy *multiple* murder would be wonderful, especially if it involved sexual mutilation or cannibalism, which was probably asking too much, but on the other hand, you never knew what depravity these moneyed elites might indulge in next.

Mickey Dime

In the study, blanket-wrapped dead Jerry stood on the cargo ledge of the hand truck. Three tightly pulled straps bound him to the frame and held him erect.

Mickey considered the corpse from different angles. From every perspective it looked like a stiff in a blanket.

He retrieved two spare pillows from the linen closet. He kept them in a plastic bag with a lemon-scented sachet. He paused to bury his face in each pillow, savoring the fragrance of lemony goose down.

Using duct tape, he fixed the pillows to the microfiber blanket in the area of the dead man's lower legs to disguise the limbs. He liked the strength, flexibility, and feel of duct tape. Duct tape was sexy.

From a cabinet under the kitchen sink, he fetched a bucket. He jammed the bucket over Jerry's head and secured it with the tape.

In his bedroom closet were several book boxes containing his beloved mother's correspondence with other famous intellectuals. Mickey was going to put them in order and donate them to Harvard, where she would be immortalized.

One of the boxes was only a third full. He tenderly removed the letters—which carried a vague trace of her signature perfume, Nightshade—and set them aside. He took the empty carton into the study, where he duct-taped it to Jerry's chest.

He got another microfiber blanket from the closet. He draped it loosely over the bundled corpse and all of its taped-on accessories. Now dead Jerry looked like nothing more than a precarious stack of junk.

Mickey tipped the hand truck backward, onto its wheels. He rolled it out of the study and through the living room. In the foyer, he parked it near the front door.

In the bedroom, Mickey shrugged into a shoulder holster. He tucked the .32 pistol, with its sound suppressor, into the rig and put on a sport coat tailored to conceal a weapon. He studied himself in the full-length mirror. He looked sexy.

He looked so good, in fact, that he thought he might not have to confine his erotic encounters with Sparkle Sykes to his imagination. If he came on to her, she might find him irresistible. Many women found him irresistible and not because he paid them. They often said that with him it wasn't only about money, and he knew they were telling the truth. The risk was rejection, which he didn't handle well. If she turned him down without being polite about it, he would as a matter of pride take what he wanted and clean up afterward. Better to restrain his affair with Sparkle to his imagination.

Mickey left Jerry on the hand truck, in the foyer. He stepped into the hall, locked the apartment, and set out to kill the guard in the security room.

Logan Spangler

In the kitchen of Earl Blandon's apartment, Logan gargled repeatedly with some of the senator's whiskey supply and spat it in the sink, hoping that it would destroy—or at least wash out—any spores that might have gotten into his mouth and throat. He blew his nose so often and so hard that he risked rupturing a blood vessel, hoping to purge most of the tiny seeds from his tingling nasal passages and sinuses.

Logan worried that the spores might be toxic. Perhaps not a lethal poison, but in some way disabling. There were fungi that, when eaten, produced hallucinations and even lasting psychological damage. The bizarre fungi in the half bath seemed like something Alice might have found if she went through a looking glass so dark that the land beyond was nearer to Hell than to Wonderland, and it was difficult to imagine that they might be benign.

He wondered if contact with the spores caused the visions of abandoned and ruined rooms, but that made no sense because the fungi and their spores were *part of* those visions, not of the real world. Nevertheless, the thought persisted. He didn't consciously summon them, yet images of the pale-green, black-mottled organisms rose in his mind's eye, though they were not strictly memories of what he'd seen in the half bath because they were in motion. Not merely the swallowing reflex, the peristalsis. Flexing. Coiling. Writhing over and under one another, twining in excited, sinuous abandon. He could not drive the apparitions out of his mind. They became more real than the kitchen in which he stood, as he imagined an LSD experience might press aside reality, though he had never taken hallucinogens. On the clusters of mushrooms, around which serpentine fungi squirmed, the puckered skin of the caps peeled back, as they had in the half bath, but this time no clouds of spores burst from them. Instead, in this exotic mind movie, from some of the caps rose what appeared to be gray tongues, and from still others ascended yellow eyes on fibrous stalks, as if plants and animals had conjugated, producing demonic children. Abruptly—impossibly—the point of view changed within this delirium, and he found himself not staring at the fungi but peering out from within them, as if the eyes on stalks were his eyes, and he saw himself in his uniform, his face pale and sweaty, his eyes as bleak as an arctic dawn.

He realized that he had returned to the half bath, although he had not been aware of leaving the kitchen. He stood at the sink, gripping the marble countertop with both hands, as if to anchor himself in a turbulence, gazing at the mirror. The wall behind him crawled with repulsive fungi, but the light wasn't dim like before, and when he turned from the mirror to confront the slithering colony, it wasn't there in reality. It existed only in the reflection. The looking glass showed Logan as he was now but presented the wall behind him as it had been earlier. The mirror was not the problem. Something had gone wrong with Logan.

A tingling sensation drew his attention to his hands, with which he gripped the countertop. His fingernails were black.

Martha Cupp

By the time Martha entered the living room close on the heels of her sister, Smoke and Ashes had stopped squalling. Although the cats seldom did any climbing, both were atop an étagère filled with porcelain birds. They peeked around the pediment of that cabinet, their orange eyes wide. They were usually as self-satisfied and confident as any cats, but now they appeared to be alarmed.

Addressing the high-placed pair, Martha said, "What's frightened you?"

"What do you think?" The tone of Edna's question suggested that they both knew the answer.

"Not Satan," Martha said impatiently. "With a world to corrupt, why would the prince of Hell be wasting so much time spooking around here—because we make good cakes?"

"He's the *king* of Hell and the prince of this world."

"Royalty has always bored me."

"Anyway, I never said Satan, dear. I said Sally saw a demon. His name is legion, after all, and he has an army to do his work."

Regarding the crouched cats on their high redoubt, Martha said, "They never were mousers. They're a disgrace to their species in that regard."

"There aren't any mice in the Pendleton to test them. I'm sure if there were, they'd have left us many little gifts with tails. It wasn't a mouse that scared them."

"So it was the thunder."

"Or not," said Edna.

Smoke and Ashes reacted simultaneously, heads twitching as one toward a far corner of the room, and they hissed as if they had seen something they detested.

The sisters turned to seek the cause of the cats' displeasure, and Martha caught the slightest glimpse of something that scurried between an armchair and a large overstuffed chesterfield.

"What was that?" she asked.

"What was what?"

"Something. I saw something."

Lightning painted the windows, thunder vibrated in the panes, and rain washed them dark again.

After retrieving a long poker from the rack of brass fireplace tools on the hearth, Martha crossed the big room, weaving among an abundance of Victoriana—plump chairs, tables covered with valuable curios, plant stands from which trailed ferns, pedestals presenting busts of classical poets—toward the sofa behind which the small quick intruder seemed to have taken refuge. The hand that gripped the poker ached, but Martha's swollen and arthritic knuckles remained strong enough that she could club a rat or a potentially dangerous exotic pet if some hopeless fool in the building had let one escape again.

Eight years earlier, a rock-and-roll musician had taken up residence in the Pendleton. He enjoyed three hit songs and one successful national tour before his career collapsed for lack of talent. Before he could drink away, sniff away, or otherwise squander his small fortune, he purchased a second-floor apartment for cash and moved in with a blonde named Bitta who had green hair and breasts as large as a pair of Butterball turkeys. Unknown to the homeowners' association, with the glamorous couple had come a Gila monster named Cobain, which had the run of their apartment and which had escaped through their front door when they had unthinkingly left it ajar after coming home in the throes of drunken lust, singing bawdy lyrics in the hall. In the following eighteen hours, before the elusive Cobain could be cornered and captured and removed from the premises, pandemonium ensued in the Pendleton.

A year later, after a night of disastrous gambling in Vegas, the rock and roller had lost his money and Bitta. He was long gone from the Pendleton, but this was an age in which fools of many kinds were more plentiful than ever. Martha half expected to find another exotic animal. If it proved to be of a species with wicked teeth and a vicious temperament and evil intentions, she would defend herself with the necessary ferocity, regardless of whether its name was Cobain or Fluffy.

"Whatever are you doing?" Edna asked as Martha, with the poker raised, stalked the intruder.

"Remember Cobain?"

Smoke and Ashes hissed from atop the étagère, though Cobain had been before their time.

"You saw a Gila monster?" Edna asked.

"If that's what I saw, then I'd have said so. I saw something, I don't know what."

"We should call someone."

"I simply will not summon an exorcist," Martha said as she warily rounded the chesterfield.

"I meant the superintendent, Mr. Tran."

Nothing lurked behind the massive sofa.

Perhaps the thing she had glimpsed darting away from the armchair now hid *under* the chesterfield. Martha bent forward, probing beneath the furniture with the poker.

Sparkle Sykes

Crossing the living room toward the kitchen with Iris shuffling behind her, eager to call security and report the thing that was no doubt still probing at the bedroom window, Sparkle heard a commotion in the public hallway. A child cried something about a "big bug."

She changed course, hurried into the foyer, and peered through the fish-eye lens in the door. She saw no one in the south hall, but she heard a woman say urgently, *"Come on, the stairs!"*

After a hesitation, Sparkle opened the door. To the right, ten feet away, at the junction of the south and west wings, two people moved toward the stairwell door. Twyla Trahern, that nice woman from 2-A, the songwriter with the famous singer husband. Her young son was Winslow or Winston or something. She called him Winny. They were dressed for the storm.

Clearly agitated, the boy was in the lead, but he

halted with his hand on the door to the stairs when his mother warned, *"Winny, no! Wait."*

Winny said, "I know, I feel it, there's maybe something waiting on the stairs."

Startling them, Sparkle asked, "Do you need help?"

When they turned toward her and she saw their faces straight on, they looked exactly like Sparkle felt: perplexed, alarmed, afraid.

Sally Hollander

Paralyzed by the initial bite, with the demon's long tubular tongue thrust deep in her throat, choking on the cold thick substance that gushed out of that hollow tube and into her, Sally clung to consciousness less as a consequence of extreme terror than because of her intense revulsion. Regardless of her paralysis, she remained desperate to break free and to cleanse herself, for she felt soiled beyond endurance by this creature's touch, bite, and violation.

When its tongue at last retracted, it released Sally from its arms, and she slid to the floor. The coldness in her stomach couldn't have been greater if the monster had pumped a slush of ice into her. She was overcome by a slithering nausea, she wanted to vomit, purge herself, but she couldn't.

Limp, helpless, each ragged exhalation a cry for help that no one under Heaven could possibly hear, each inhalation a desperate wheeze, Sally watched the feet of her assailant as it prowled the kitchen, examining things with what seemed to be curiosity. Six elongated, webbed toes. The first and sixth were longer than the middle four, each with an extra knuckle and a large pad at the end, as if they served as a pair of long opposable thumbs. Gray feet, the skin subtly patterned as if with scales. Not ordinary scales, not like those of a snake or lizard, not designed to provide extreme flexibility alone but also to serve as a kind of . . . armor. Maybe she thought of armor because of the color, which was like badly tarnished silver serving pieces before she polished them. And then just as in the Cupps' pantry, every detail of the demon darkened until it was merely a silhouette, a slinking black shadow that vanished through a wall.

Her queasy stomach grew greasier, seemed to slide around within her, but still she couldn't vomit, and then the nausea faded to be replaced by something worse. Instead of her body heat thawing out whatever had been injected into her, the iciness of the stuff in her stomach slowly began to leach into the surrounding tissues, first up into her ribs, so she could feel that cage of bones as she had never felt it before, as if it wasn't natural to her anymore but was some armature that had been surgically implanted, alien now and cold in her warm flesh. And it leached down into her hips, where she felt the precise shape and position of her pelvis as she had never felt it before, those bones as icy now as her rib cage.

For a minute, as the cold spread down into her femurs and then into the other bones of her legs, she thought that she must be in the last moment of her life. But then she knew, without knowing *how* she knew, that life was not fading from her. She would survive. She was not dying: She was becoming something else, someone else than the woman she had always been.

Silas Kinsley

After briefly encountering Andrew North Pendleton in a late-nineteenth-century version of the lobby—which had been a receiving room in those days, more than a century earlier—and following his brief conversation with Padmini Bahrati after the Belle Vista transformed into the Pendleton once more, Silas knew that whatever happened in this building every thirty-eight years was happening again, sooner than he had first expected. Having spoken with Perry Kyser at Topper's restaurant, he knew this wasn't going to be a party that anyone would be happy to attend—or even be lucky enough to survive—and his first impulse was to leave the building at once, bolt through the front door into the rain, run for it.

Three years after losing Nora, childless in a world where most of his friends had died before him, Silas had nowhere to run and no one to live for. His sole duty was to the people in the Pendleton, his neighbors, not all of whom he knew.

For a moment he could not imagine how to proceed. There were no break-the-glass-and-pull-the-lever boxes in the building's fire-alarm system, which was fully automated with smoke detectors and sprinklers recessed in every ceiling. He had nothing with which to light a fire that might trigger the alarm and cause the residents to evacuate.

Cocking her head, smiling quizzically, Padmini said, "Is there something wrong, Mr. Kinsley?"

He felt old and tired and helpless. Anything he could think to say to her would sound foolish, would raise in her the suspicion that he was suffering from dementia.

"I need to speak to the security guard," he said, proceeding to the doors between the lobby and the ground-floor hallway.

Before Silas could fumble his key from a raincoat pocket, Padmini stepped behind the reception counter and buzzed him through.

"Shall I call ahead to him?" she asked, but Silas didn't reply as he stepped into the ground-floor hallway and let the French doors close behind him. The electronic lock engaged with a *zzzz-clack*.

Whatever was about to happen here—had *been* happening since early this morning—involved time, some problem with time, the late 1800s flowing into 2011, past and present confused. And maybe not just past and present. Maybe the future, as well. That thing Perry Kyser had seen in the basement corridor back in 1973, during the renovation, wasn't from 2011 or from any age that had come before now.

Perry's voice echoed ominously in memory: *It's big. Big as me. Bigger. Pale as a grub, a little like a grub, but not that, because it's kind of like a spider, too, though not an insect, too fleshy for a spider . . .*

Silas turned right and hurried to the south elevator. It would drop him directly across from the security-room door.

He wondered who was on duty and hoped that it would be a former police officer, which most of them seemed to be. He had not always been a civil-litigation attorney. He had started out as a criminal-defense lawyer, but he hadn't been any good at it because he couldn't find much sympathy in himself for most of the human debris he was called upon to defend. He identified with the victims. Everyone deserved a defense, of course, even the worst rapists and murderers. So after a few years, he changed careers, leaving criminal defense to those men who had a nobler attitude and bigger—or colder—hearts than his. But during that first phase of his law career, he learned to talk to cops, nearly all of whom he had liked immeasurably more than he liked his clients.

A kind of head, no eyes, no face to speak of. What might be rows of gills along the neck, but no mouth . . .

He had never chatted with cops about time warps—or whatever this might be—nor about not-grub, not-spider monsters. He didn't know how he was going to do that, how he was going to make the impossible sound like the truth, unless maybe he wasn't the only one who'd had a curious experience in the Pendleton, unless even the guard had seen something that he could not explain, something that might even have raised the hairs on the nape of his neck.

As Silas reached out to press the elevator-call button, he hesitated, alerted to danger by a strange sound behind the sliding doors, within the shaft.

Witness

On the roof, standing at the western parapet, rain streaming off his insulated nylon jacket, blue jeans soaked and feet damp in his saturated boots, Witness was not afraid of the lightning that ripped the black fabric of the sky and revealed the fury on the other side. He hoped that a bolt might strike him, but he doubted he would be lucky enough to die here.

Thus far, the transitions had not occurred at the same hour and minute. He wasn't able to time the event so precisely that he could appear, like a magician, to speak it into existence with a conjuring word. Indeed, some of the transitions were more than a full day earlier or later than others. But once the fluctuations began, the moment of change was approaching and inevitable.

The house under him now was not the same version of the house in which he lived. Most of the people here were strangers to him, though he knew a great deal about them.

One second to the next, the rain stopped. The rooftop was dry except for the pavers onto which his clothes dripped. With the rain, the city vanished; all gone, the vast wonderful expanse of lights that was the most beautiful thing Witness had ever seen.

The house under him now, under this cloudless sky, was the house he knew, in which he lived, if his existence could be called living.

A moon sailed the heavens, slowly navigating across a sea of stars. He found that lighted vault to be cold and somehow accusing. He did not care to look up, for the sky had none of the charm of the lost city.

The long, barren hill and the moonlit plain beyond were more daunting than the sky. In daylight, the waist-high grass was such a pale shade of green that it appeared almost white, but under the lunar lamp, it looked slightly greener because it glowed faintly, as though phosphorescent. The night was still, hushed, and though no breeze blew to stir the great meadow, the luminous grass swayed anyway, toward the south and then toward the north, south and north, changing direction with such precise timing that it might have been the feathery pelt of some sleeping leviathan, influenced by the sleeper's inhalations and exhalations. The grassy plain did not appeal either in dawn's light or in daylight, neither at twilight nor now at night. It was disturbingly unnatural in its ceaseless motion and even more unnatural if wind teased it into an arrhythmic frenzy, when it fluttered not in the manner of storm-tossed pasture but as if it were the hair of a furious medusa, every blade like a thin flat wriggling serpent.

Living in that trackless veldt were all manner of

creatures, which could not correctly be called animals, though they were mobile and always seeking. They were less the work of nature than they were denizens of demented dreams, as if imagined into existence by insane gods. This legion of voracious species fed on one another but also cannibalized their own kind, and the grass devoured all of them when it wished.

The immense meadow and its inhabitants were ruled over by the trees, from the roots of which the grass shrank and under the boughs of which the ground remained as bare as salted soil. Each tree rose high and spread wide, not with grace but with tortured grasping limbs as jagged as fractures in quake-shocked stone. A few stood alone, but most were in widely separated clusters; each group grew in a circle with a clearing at the center, as any coven might convene around a cauldron. They were black from roots to highest twigs. The bark of their trunks was fissured, and in the deepest of those cracks shone a moist red tissue, like blood-rich meat under the crust of a charred cadaver. In the spring the trees did not bud and flower, nor did they produce leaves, but they fruited. In the first warmth of the season, blisters appeared on the branches, swelled, depended like teardrops, and matured until they were twelve inches long and five to six inches in diameter at their widest point, with mottled-gray peels. They were fruit not biologically but metaphorically, for they didn't have seeds and were not sweet. When ripe, usually on a night with a fierce moon that appeared to metallize the grassland, the huge trees dropped their fruit, which in falling flew, because this was less a harvest than a birthing. For a while the sky bristled with teeth. When the weak had fed upon the strong, the remaining flock winged west, as if harried toward the darkness by the dawn. Wherever they went, whatever they did when they got there, Witness didn't know, and they never returned to this territory.

In *this* night, the most recent issue of the trees having months earlier flown westward, arm after arm of black branches reached high with twisted twigs like talons, clawing at the moon as if to drag it down and with it all the sky, to at last smother dying Earth in the vacuum of interstellar spaces.

One second to the next, the storm began again, the dry silence and then the rush of rain, the stars bright and then no stars at all. With the wet weather came the glimmering city, and Witness stood once more not on the roof of the Pendleton in which he lived but on the roof of the Pendleton in which mostly strangers resided. They were the same building but they were far apart in time.

The next fluctuation or the one after that, or the one after *that*, would prove to be the transition. The moment and the mystery loomed, and Witness no better understood these bizarre events than did the residents who found themselves transported from one Pendleton to the other. He also did not understand why he, shifting from the Pendleton of the future, should not be trapped in this sweet time for hours, as the people of this age would be trapped in his bleak era. Living organisms were thrown backward in time during the fluctuations that led up to the transition, but they remained in the past only briefly. When the transition occurred, everyone in the building under him—every living soul, everything they wore, and everything they happened to be holding at the crucial moment—would be transported, and this Pendleton would stand empty, until the transition reversed, bringing back only those who belonged to this time. Bringing them if they were alive, not if they were dead.

Drenched by rain, Witness leaned against the parapet balustrade, drinking in the vast sea of lights, the city brightly floating in the storm, streets shimmering, buildings rising like the tiered decks of a titanic vessel on a wondrous journey. Witness wept at the beauty of it, and at the tragedy that awaited it.

One

The young Sophia Pendleton descends the stairs in 1897 but also in 1935, in 1973, in 2011, and every thirty-eight years thereafter, although she has long been dead. During the brief period between the first crack in the space-time trapdoor and the instant when it is flung wide open, all the transitions past and future must occupy the same moment in the present, briefly melding. I bit the life from Sophia before the nineteenth century became the twentieth; yet she sings her nursery rhymes and descends the stairs in 2011 as in 1897, immortal for that brief moment.

Likewise, an Indian brave from 1821 wanders for almost a minute through the Pendleton's banquet kitchen and along the south hall on the ground floor. He is bewildered, frightened, a tomahawk raised and ready. But he fades away before anyone ever encounters him.

Back in 1897, Sophia hurries to the kitchen of Belle Vista to enjoy her shaved ice flavored with cherry syrup, giving no thought to the hard life of the iceman who delivers the forty-pound blocks three times a week. He will no doubt exhaust himself by late middle age, die young, and leave this world as poor as he entered it.

But exploitation is not always or even most often just a matter of the wealthy draining the blood of the poor. The wealthy themselves can be exploited by the likes of the envious security guard who is writing a tell-all book, by hired assassins like the son of the famous intellectual. Indians were exploited by the Europeans, but many Indian tribes previously had warred with and enslaved one another. As you have observed, it is the nature of human beings to exploit one another ruthlessly and to ravage nature as well, again and again and again over the centuries. No class or race or faction is innocent of that crime.

In the kingdom of the One, there is never exploitation of any individual by another. No masters, no slaves. No wealth, no poverty. Every predator is prey, and every prey is a predator. The earth is never torn open and disfigured for its oil or its gold. I am the fulfillment of your vision, the justification of your life.

Consider the boy, the songwriter's son, who dreams of being a hero like those in the books that he incessantly reads. Yearning to be a hero, to live a life larger than life, he is no less a threat to everything you believe than he is a threat to me. By their nature, heroes leave outsize footprints, overblown and dangerous legends; therefore, in a well-ordered and efficient world, there can be no place for them.

The boy will have no hope of being a hero when his eyes have been eaten from their sockets, when his tongue turns as black and silent as char, and when I reach within his heart and squirm through its throbbing chambers.

22

Apartment 2-F

Dr. Kirby Ignis spent the latter part of that afternoon in an armchair, sipping hot green tea, listening to Italian operas sung in Chinese, and watching tropical fish swimming lazily in the large lighted aquarium that stood against one of his living-room walls.

Kirby owned one of the more modest apartments in the Pendleton, although he could have bought a mansion on a sprawling estate. He had earned serious money from his numerous patents; and the royalties flowed to him in greater streams every year.

He could afford the highest caliber interior design, but he chose to live simply. He bought his nondescript furniture on sale from various discount warehouses, with no consideration other than function and comfort.

While he appreciated fine art, he didn't feel compelled to own any. Not one painting hung in his rooms. He had a few thousand books, perhaps a hundred of which were oversize volumes about painters whose work appealed to him. Photographs of great art were as satisfying to him as would have been the originals hanging on his walls.

Simplify, simplify. That was the secret to a happy life.

At the Ignis Institute, he had a wealth of space and equipment, as well as a support team of brilliant men and women. But these days, he did more work at home than at the office, saving travel time and sparing himself the worries of everyday operation and bureaucracy, which others could handle for him.

Kirby Ignis's life was largely a life of the mind. He had little interest in material things, but an all-consuming interest in ideas and their consequences. Even now, watching the fish and listening to opera, his mind was occupied with a difficult research problem, a mare's nest of seemingly contradictory facts that for weeks he had been patiently untangling. Day by day, he unknotted the bits of data and raveled them into order, and he anticipated that within another week, he would have the whole problem smoothed out and rolled as neat as a spool of new ribbon.

Although he lived alone, he wasn't lonely. There had been a Mrs. Ignis—lovely Nofia—but she had needed a different life from the one that he wanted. With mutual regret, they divorced when they were twenty-six, twenty-four years previously. Since then he hadn't met a woman who had Nofia's effect on him. But he enjoyed a complex network of friends to which he added continuously. More than once, he'd been told that he had a character actor's face such that he could play the amusing next-door neighbor, the favorite uncle, the charming eccentric—and soon the beloved grandfather. His face won him friends, as did his contagious laugh, as did the fact that he was a good listener. You never knew what people might say, and from time to time he heard a story or a fact or an opinion that, though it would seem to have no connection whatsoever to his work, nevertheless led him onto new pathways of thought that proved fruitful.

Indeed, the music that currently encouraged his problem solving was the result of a conversation at a cocktail party. When Kirby said that he thought more deeply and more clearly when listening to music but that he could abide only instrumentals because singers distracted him with lyrics, the somewhat ditzy but always amusing girlfriend of a colleague suggested that he listen to songs sung in languages that he didn't know, for then the voice would be just another instrument. He liked Italian operas, but because he spoke Italian, he now enjoyed them as performed by opera companies singing, of all things, Chinese translations. The ditzy redhead with pendant earrings like cascades of Christmas tinsel—and with a small tattoo of a leaping gazelle on the back of her right hand—had solved this little problem for Kirby, which would never have happened if he hadn't enjoyed listening to even the most unlikely people.

His apartment didn't offer a million-dollar view of the city. The living-room windows faced the courtyard, which was good enough for Kirby, who spent more time looking inward than outward. Because he liked storms, the draperies were drawn all the way open. The thunder, the rattling of the rain on the windows, and the whistling of the wind comprised a symphony that didn't compete with the opera on the music system. The room was illuminated only by the pleasantly eerie glow of the aquarium, and something about the quality of the light reminded him of scenes in certain sumptuously designed black-and-white movies such as *Sunset Boulevard* and *Citizen Kane*. The flares of lightning were to him no more threatening than the twinkles cast off by a rotating mirrored chandelier in a ballroom, and they added to the ambiance that was so conducive to profound consideration of his current work.

Each throb of lightning, which sometimes came in bursts of three or four or five, shuddered the patterns of the tall French windows across the furniture and walls, grids of narrow shadows and bright squares. Not lost in thought, for thought always led him somewhere, Kirby noticed when a particularly brilliant trio of flashes projected the pane-and-muntin window patterns with a curious difference: a dark curve drooping across the top of one window, as if it had a swagged valance.

When he turned in his chair to determine what could have caused that convex arc of darkness, he saw what appeared to be a curve of pale, wet bunting on the outside of the window, as though someone must have hung a flag or holiday decorations—Christmas was less than four weeks away—from a third-floor window ledge, which was against the homeowners'-association rules.

Kirby put down his teacup and got up from the armchair. By the lambent easy light of the aquarium, he crossed the sparsely furnished living room.

By the time he reached the window, the swag of cloth or whatever it was had either lifted out of sight or been blown away. He pressed the right side of his face against the glass, peering up toward the third floor. He could see an object that wasn't an architectural detail, something shapeless and pale draped over part of the pediment above the window, but the rising glow of the landscape lights in the courtyard was not bright enough to allow him to identify the thing. It seemed to billow slightly but did not flap vigorously as a flag or decorative bunting ought to have done in the wind, perhaps because it was heavy with rainwater.

The storm flared once, twice, and Kirby got a better but brief view of the thing, which now seemed to be three small, pale sacks, each half the size of a five-pound bag of flour, worked together by a length of rope or a rubber cord. The bags were smooth and bellied, apparently full of something, clustered together and overhung by a flap of loose cloth or perhaps vinyl, which was the part that had blown down over the window but that now billowed higher. He couldn't tell what the item was or from what it had been suspended, but it certainly didn't belong up there. When lightning flashed once again, he thought he saw something twitching, two segmented lengths of a stiffer material than the other parts of the assemblage, but instead of clarifying the nature of the object, the frantic stutter of light only made it more mysterious.

Kirby considered cranking open the casement window and sticking his head out in the rain to have a closer look. Before he did that, however, he needed to fetch a flashlight from a utility drawer in the laundry room.

When he stepped out of the living room into the brighter dining area, he glanced at his watch and realized that the day had gotten away from him. He had an appointment for drinks and dinner with one of the institute's most brilliant scientists, Von Norquist, whose mind flung off new ideas in as bright profusion as a grinding wheel spat sparks from the blade of a knife. If he didn't hurry, he would be late. Whatever had blown onto the pediment or fallen onto it from the third floor was not raising a clatter, and he saw no risk that it was hard enough or heavy enough to swing down and smash a window. Further exploration could wait for morning light.

In the master-bedroom closet, he added a tie to his shirt and slipped into a sport coat.

In the living room once more, he switched off the Chinese opera but left on the aquarium light.

Lightning imprinted the unobstructed pattern of panes and muntins on the room, with no curious swag of shadow across the top.

23

Apartment 3-H

Anything could happen at any time.

Fielding Udell possessed the wisdom to recognize the perpetual instability of the cosmos, the planet, the continent, the city, and the moment. He was industrious enough to research the dreadful truth of the world and to analyze and archive it with the dedication of a monk in the Dark Ages hand-copying books to keep the works of the past alive.

On this Thursday evening, he remained at his computer, at which he'd first sat at eight o'clock in the morning and from which he'd risen only twice for bathroom visits and once to accept a delivery from Salvatino's Pizzeria, an order of pasta Bolognese and a salad for lunch, a traditional submarine sandwich and a bag of chips for dinner. He was aware of the inclement weather, but he gave it little attention. December storms didn't have the potential to produce the Mother of All Tornadoes. That cataclysm would come sooner than later, decimating thousands of square miles, but not this evening.

Perhaps Fielding Udell's most important personal qualities were his cunning and foresight. He was sufficiently clever and prudent to conceal his identity during his researches. By backlooping from his computer through the telephone exchange of a city half a continent away, and from there sidelooping through a university in Kyoto, Japan, and from *there* finally costuming himself by pursuing all data searches through the Internet link of the public library in Oshkosh, Wisconsin, and by taking numerous other precautions, he could build his Case for Prosecution with little risk that his trail could be followed to the Pendleton.

If they knew about his project, the Ruling Elite would have him murdered or worse. Fielding didn't know for sure what could be worse than death, but his ever-growing understanding of the true nature of the world suggested many possibilities.

He daily kept an eye out for news from Oshkosh, something like a boiler explosion at the main-branch library that, of course, would be the Ruling Elite terminating the innocent librarians in whose name Fielding had been conducting his investigation.

He didn't want to think about those worse-than-death fates. He wasn't a negative person. He thought of himself as an optimist: in spite of all the horror and evil in the world, still an optimist. He believed that he could defeat the scheming bastards one day, whoever they were, whatever their motivations might be, regardless of the unknown but surely hideous source from which they derived their immense power.

The Ruling Elite included none of the people who served in high public office or any of the rich CEOs running big businesses and big banks. They were mere tools with which the true masters of the world effected their ruthless will. Fielding wasn't sure if the titans of industry and the politicians were unaware of being manipulated like so many marionettes or if they willingly served their faceless masters. He would eventually know the truth. He would triumphantly unmask the secret emperors of this tortured world and bring them to justice one way or another.

Now he took a break from the computer and went to the kitchen to pour a glass of homemade cola. He had reason to believe that off-the-shelf soft drinks were one of the media in which the Ruling Elite dispensed the drug—if it was anything as simple as a drug—that made the masses susceptible to the illusions and deceptions that passed for reality these days. To be sure that he could not be brainwashed, Fielding brewed his own soda; though it was not carbonated and though it tasted more like molasses and licorice than like cola, he liked it well enough. The important thing wasn't the quality of his cola but that he could have both cola and freedom.

He had purchased and combined two apartments, giving him lots of space for worktables and filing cabinets where he assembled his damning files and stored them. He didn't trust keeping his voluminous archives only in digital form, where they might be hacked and sucked to oblivion in mere moments.

His kitchen boasted every culinary tool and convenience, but he never cooked. He ordered takeout from numerous restaurants, cycling through them at random so that no pattern was established that might allow an assassin to predict his behavior and poison his pizza or his kung pao chicken.

As he poured a glass of cola from the jug, he heard tapping at the French panes and assumed that the rain must be mixed with sleet. He didn't glance at the window because he had no interest whatsoever in ordinary weather, only in the superstorms that one day would scour cities off the face of the earth, the storms that might already be occurring in some parts of the world but were not reported by order of the Ruling Elite.

For twenty years, he had been passionately engaged in his quest for truth, since he graduated from the university when he was twenty-one. This was not just his vocation and avocation. This was his *life,* and not just his life but his *meaning.*

Fielding Udell was a trust-fund baby, an heir to wealth. When he had received his inheritance, he felt unrighteous, criminal, even depraved. Without working for it, he had all that he would need for the rest of his life, while so many had so little.

Guilt had pressed so heavily on him that he almost gave all his money away, considered taking a vow of poverty and becoming a monk, considered taking any job he could find with his university degree and settling into an ordinary middle-class life of small pleasures and humble expectations. But he had no religious faith, which made being a monk seem pointless, and to his surprise, his degree in sociology with an emphasis on gender studies opened no doors for him, zero, nada.

Although eaten by guilt, he kept his money. It was his curse, his albatross.

Fortunately, at the melancholy depths of this moral quandary, when he was still a tender twenty-one, he happened to see a TV report about the mysterious deaths of uncounted frogs all over the world and heard that leading scientists predicted the extinction of the species within six to ten years. Alarmed by the specter of a frogless world and by all that ominous development might portend, Fielding began researching the subject—and found his calling.

First he had discovered from the news that not only all frogs were headed for extinction, but also bees. Bees were dying not from the usual mites or diseases, but colony collapse disorder was taking them in large numbers for reasons no one could explain, though the consensus was that pollution or some other human-caused affliction must be the villain. Wifhout bees to pollinate flowering plants, the world's food supply would fall drastically. Indeed, some scientists had confidently predicted mass starvation by 2000.

How little he had understood then. How foolish he had been.

Now he carried his glass of cola back to his computer, through a series of rooms that were all given to his work. The tapping at the windows followed him and became louder, a rapping, as if the sleet were mixed with small hailstones. Rain, sleet, and hail perhaps concerned those who were not as enlightened as Fielding Udell, but those were such minor phenomena that he couldn't be bothered to care about them even to the extent of going to the windows for a look at the storm.

In 2000, just as millions should have been starving because of the extinction of bees, Y2K loomed. The consensus was that all the world's computers would go haywire at the turn of the millennium, causing a collapse of the banking system, the unstoppable launch of computer-controlled nuclear missiles, and the end of civilization.

When Fielding had looked to the past, to see if there had been as many threats to human existence then as there were in his own time, he found a seemingly endless number of menaces so alarming that he obtained through his physician enough sleeping pills with which to commit suicide if one day he woke to discover he was living in a Mad Max world of few resources and marauding gangs of psychopaths. The consensus had been that overpopulation and industrialization would lead to mass starvation, a die-off in the billions, the consumption of all the world's oil and natural gas by 1970, the death of all the oceans by 1980, and therefore a steady depletion of oxygen until the planet's air couldn't sustain life. In the 1960s, the scientific consensus was, according to the media, that an ice age was imminent, sure to bury most of North America under hundreds of feet of glaciers within a few decades. Not only was the world forced to endure that threat, but now the prospect of global warming, of killing ourselves with the very CO_2 we exhaled *every minute of our lives*, had also brought human beings around 180 degrees to the opposite precipice and a new threat of extinction.

At first, as he researched all these impending catastrophes, Fielding had despaired. After he had worked so hard for his sociology degree, he had failed to find employment; and now, if ever he found a job, the world would not survive long enough for him to make his mark in his chosen—or any—profession.

Bummer.

Then he had a thought, an insight, a kind of theory that gave him hope. Many of these scientific consensuses seemed to have proved wrong over the years, which suggested that perhaps others would not be borne out, either. This thought soon led to the consideration that perhaps the ruling elite—he didn't yet capitalize the term in his mind—manufactured crises in order to control the masses with fear and thereby increase their power.

He was preoccupied with this theory for a while, but then this girl he hoped to bed told him that he was a conspiracy theorist, "a super-nutty fruitcake," and that he was as likely to see her naked as he was to prove that Elvis Presley was not dead and was living in Sweden after gender-change surgery. For a week, Fielding misconstrued her sarcasm as a hot tip, but the Elvis-in-Sweden rumor proved to have no substance, at least none that he could find. When he fully realized the cruel nature of the girl's rejection, he was saddened, but not for long.

As Fielding had continued to research threats against humanity, civilization, and the planet, he eventually had a *major* breakthrough that made his controlling-the-masses-with-fear theory seem childish. These days, even if alone, he sometimes blushed when he thought about how naive he had been to believe the truth was anything that simple. The truth was more terrible, far darker. Scientists dealt with facts, right? A *consensus* of scientists implied a lot of very smart people agreeing on the provable facts, right? Therefore, the facts must in fact be the facts. If the consensus was that there would be an ice age displacing millions of people by 1990, then there must *be* an ice age well under way here in 2011. The clever Ruling Elite were not manufacturing crises, after all; they were instead trying to conceal a fearsome slew of genuine crises from the public, to prevent panic, the collapse of civilization, and the loss of their power.

Now, as he returned to his computer, settled in his chair, and sipped his refreshing homemade cola, a curious slithering sound arose overhead and quickly grew loud enough to be annoying, as if Fielding lived under a serpentarium. He assumed the wind had found a way into the Pendleton's attic, where it was chasing its own tail among the posts and rafters, and after a while it grew silent.

Exerting totalitarian control of the worldwide media,

the Ruling Elite never grew silent but aggressively told lies 24/7 to hide one terrifying truth after another from the gullible public. The heroic scientists, even though funded by rich government grants that should have co-opted them, bravely dared to speak truth to power, warning of the oncoming cataclysms, only to be made to look foolish when the cataclysms didn't happen—except that they *did* happen but were covered up by the Ruling Elite.

Fielding had tumbled to this chilling reality when, watching a TV-news report that was supposedly live from Canada, he glimpsed what appeared to be a palm tree, maybe two, in the background of one shot. He realized at once that the report didn't come from Canada, that they were *faking* Canada, shooting Georgia or someplace for Canada, the way that movie directors sometimes shot day for night. They goofed. And Fielding Udell nailed them. They would have no reason to shoot Georgia for Canada unless Canada was buried under hundreds of feet of advancing ice that would one day likewise crush and claim most of the United States.

Initially, it seemed that the global-warming threat didn't comport with the reality of an ongoing ice age, but once he began to apply his new theory, he found that it answered every question. Clearly, both groups of scientists were right, and both an ice age and an age of deadly global warming were occurring simultaneously, the former descending on the world from the north pole while the latter burned northward from the south pole. Eventually, humanity would be restricted to the equator, pressed in a climate vise, one jaw of which was killing cold, the other searing heat. The Ruling Elite concealed this opposing-threats situation by faking news from South America, creating an elaborate fantasy of what was happening down there and selling it as news in order to conceal that millions of people in that part of the world had already perished in droughts, famines, heat waves, wildfires, and numerous incidents of spontaneous human combustion.

This meant that Earth did not have many nations each with its own interests, that it was instead a police state with a well-hidden dictatorial class that operated through puppet governments to conceal the true nature of the world. All news and entertainment media were co-opted, and people who said they traveled to Canada recently must be either lying or brainwashed, and the same for those claiming to have had a lovely vacation in Peru or Chile.

The biggest remaining mystery was the identity of the Ruling Elite. They were not merely elusive and secretive. They were as invisible as ghosts, all-powerful malevolent spirits, everywhere at once and yet never showing their faces. Over the years, Fielding considered all kinds of possibilities and ruled out none. Well, he ruled out the Masons and the Priory of Sion and Opus Dei and the Jews because, as supposed villains, they were so clichéd that they could be nothing but red herrings, and because everyone who hated them to the point of organizing against them proved to be babbling lunatics with whom Fielding wanted no association. He inclined toward the belief that survivors from the lost continent of Atlantis, living now in an undersea super-civilization, might be at work behind the scenes, or else extraterrestrials, or maybe the Benevolent and Protective Order of Elks, whom no one ever suspected of being involved in conspiracies, which was exactly what made them seem suspicious to Fielding Udell.

As he set aside his glass of cola and returned his attention to the computer, a low and portentous voice arose at a distance, muffled and yet close. The speaker sounded like a TV-news anchor reporting some horrendous event involving hundreds of deaths. Fielding could almost but not quite make out what was being said.

He rolled his wheeled chair back from the computer and turned slowly in a full circle, cocking his head this way and that, trying to get a fix on the source. The voice seemed to originate from all around him, not from one point more than from any other. He decided it must be coming from the apartment below, although the thick concrete-and-steel floors seldom allowed sound to translate from one level of the Pendleton to another.

On the second floor, two apartments were directly below his. One was currently without a resident and up for sale. The other belonged to the Shellbrooks, who were away on vacation. Fielding remained certain that the voice came from below, not from the attic, where the slithering noise had arisen.

He slowly swiveled in his office chair again, and by the time he came around 360 degrees, he was pretty sure that the TV anchor—if that's who he heard—was speaking in a foreign language, though not one that he could identify. Moment by moment, the voice changed, grew more urgent, more insistent, as if broadcasting a warning.

No, not a warning. A threat.

Fielding was self-aware enough to know he might be paranoid, as the bed-worthy girl had accused him of being. That didn't mean he was wrong about the Secret World Order and the Ruling Elite or that his Case for Prosecution was in any way misguided. He could be dead right *and* paranoid. The two things weren't mutually exclusive. In fact, being *right* made paranoia a requisite for survival.

The speaker, definitely spouting something other than English, suddenly seemed to be not one voice but many, a gang of muttering conspirators urging one another to act, to strike, to commit some monstrous deed, now, right now, *immediately*.

Alarmed, convinced that he was correctly interpreting the tone and intent of the speakers, Fielding rose from his office chair.

A deep rumbling rolled through the building, and he felt subtle vibrations in the floor. Something like this had happened earlier, a few times, but he had been too absorbed in his online investigation to pay much attention.

What had *not* happened earlier was the shimmering sheets of blue light that *crackled* across the ceiling. Every small metal object on the desk—pens, paper clips, scissors—became airborne, shot to the ceiling, quivered there in the sparkling blueness, and rained to the floor when the strange luminosity sputtered out.

In this unstable cosmos, characterized by unending calamities, anything could happen at any time. That was not just Fielding's philosophy but also part of the truth he had discovered. And now it seemed that something outrageous was about to be demonstrated.

One

Fear is the engine that drives the human animal. Humanity sees the world as a place of uncountable threats, and so the world becomes what humanity imagines it to be. They not only live in fear but use fear to control one another. Fearmongering is their true religion.

In my perfect kingdom, there is no fear. No human beings live here to compete with one another, to build empires, to start wars. Here, there is no permanent loss and no lasting death. Here, what is killed is reborn. I feed on everything imperfect that comes before me, which is not exploitation but purification, and I feed as well on myself, devouring myself in order to live anew.

The enemy of the Ruling Elite fears everything, though he doesn't realize that the object of his greatest fear is himself. He fears living more than dying. He fears his money almost as much as he fears not having it. If he were to discover proof that his conspiracy theories are true, that the world is exactly as he imagines it, he would not have the courage to act upon that evidence. He thinks himself a potential hero, but he does not have the stuff of heroes. He is to the boy as a mouse is to a lion. Fittingly, such a man may play an important role in the history of the One.

24

Here and There

Vernon Klick

Displeased by Bailey Hawks's intrusion into his domain, Vernon slumped in his chair and called up the video record from the cameras outside the north stairs on the ground floor and in the basement. Watching the plasma screen, he fast-forwarded through the few minutes in question, but no one came out of the stairwell on either level except Mr. Big War Hero himself, Bailey Hawks, just a minute earlier.

Vernon said, "If she really went down past you when you were on the second-floor landing—"

"I was, she did," Hawks said impatiently, like you weren't supposed to doubt anything he said because he won a bunch of medals for croaking maybe five hundred unarmed old Muslim dames and setting their grandchildren on fire.

"What did this woman look like?" Vernon asked.

"She was a girl. Seven or eight years old."

Vernon raised his eyebrows. "You were following some little girl around the building?"

"I wasn't following her. She was dressed strangely. Like in a costume. She went down past me on the stairs."

"Well, the cameras say she didn't. Unless she's still in the stairwell, dead or not, or something."

Hawks tried to look baffled, but Vernon was pretty sure he saw guilt in those shifty money-manager eyes. "What is that supposed to mean?"

"Doesn't mean anything," Vernon said. "Just that we've already got ourselves a twenty-three-second mystery from last night, maybe a heist, a *Pink Panther* kind of thing, but most likely worse. And now this girl's gone missing."

"She said her name was Sophia Pendleton and her father was the master of the house."

"That's some story," Vernon said, needling Hawks with the hope of getting a reaction that would make good copy in his tell-all book.

A rumbling rose from the earth under the building, swiftly built, then slowly waned.

"The damn fools," Vernon said. "Nobody gets a permit to blast this late in the day."

"It's not blasting. The shock waves last far too long for that."

Vernon wanted to ask if this was something Hawks learned when he was a big war hero blowing up hospitals and nursery schools, or if maybe he was just born knowing everything. To maintain his cover, to ensure that his book wouldn't attract lawsuits and restraining orders before it was published, Vernon kept his mouth shut.

"Something's happening here. Something's wrong," Hawks said, and hurried out of the security room.

"He waltzes in here like he owns the place," Vernon said aloud to himself, "disrupts the security schedule, wants me to help him stalk some pretty little girl, for God's sake, and then breezes out with not so much as a thank-you. Moneygrubbing, gun-sucking, self-important, arrogant, phony, clueless, pervert bastard."

He returned his attention to the north hall on the third floor. Still no sign of Logan Spangler. Of course maybe the old fart left the idiot senator's apartment while Vernon was distracted by Hawks.

"Self-righteous, warmongering, devious, greedy sicko," Vernon fumed. "Twisted, ignorant, syphilitic, swindling, conceited, stupid, baby-killing, racist *son of a pig!*"

Silas Kinsley

On the ground floor, at the south elevator, Silas was desperate to get to the security room and convince the guard that the Pendleton needed to be evacuated immediately. Considering that the crisis wasn't a fire or a bomb threat, was instead the perception that something seemed to be going badly wrong with the fundamental mechanism of *time* within the building, he would need all of his persuasive powers.

As anxious as he was to sound the alarm, he hesitated to press the elevator-call button because of the voices that abruptly arose in the shaft behind the sliding doors. Scores of them, all talking at once. He could not begin to identify the language, though he spoke four and was passingly familiar with two others. The phonemes and morphemes of this strange speech sounded not merely primitive but also savage, a limited language evolved by a culture void of mercy, by a people quick to violence and capable of great cruelty, a people whose beliefs and purposes were utterly alien from *human* ways of thinking. Intuition was always a quiet voice, the faintest whisper at the back of the mind, but this time it wailed as loud as a siren, and Silas drew his hand back from the call button just as blue light glimmered through the paper-thin crack between the elevator doors, as if the walls of the entire shaft were aglow.

Martha Cupp

As Martha probed under the chesterfield with the brass poker from the fireplace-tool set, Edna lifted the lace-trimmed train of her long dinner gown, revealing her shoes. Evidently she expected something to skitter from beneath the sofa, not necessarily a Gila monster in the tradition of Cobain, maybe just a mouse, but something unpleasant that might seek shelter under the train and climb one of her legs.

"Please, dear, don't poke at it so aggressively," Edna said.

"All I seem to be poking is empty air."

"But if you do jab it, be gentle. Don't enrage it."

"Whatever it is, Sis, it won't thank us for our hospitality and tip its hat on the way out." She stopped poking. "There's nothing under here."

High on the étagère, Smoke and Ashes hissed, suggesting that the object of their disgust and fear remained in the living room.

Martha turned from the chesterfield and went exploring through the canyons of bulky Victorian furniture that offered innumerable places for a mouse to hide—or a Gila monster, for that matter.

"If it's something supernatural," Edna said, "it's not going to be afraid of a brass poker."

"It's not supernatural."

"You didn't see it clearly. That's the way supernatural entities are. Quick, vaguely glimpsed, enigmatic."

"'Quick, vaguely glimpsed, and enigmatic' describes my first husband's performance in the bedroom, and *he* wasn't supernatural."

"No, but he was cute," Edna said.

From their elevated perch, the cats squalled and hissed with greater agitation.

Edna said, "Dear—*the chesterfield!*"

Turning to the plump sofa once more, Martha saw something moving inside of it. The horsehair-stuffed seat, with no removable cushions, was a single upholstered mass featuring a waterfall front edge. Under the striped fabric, stretching it out of shape, a creature that might have been about the size of one of the cats burrowed back and forth through the stuffing, seemingly frenzied but silent. Evidently it had chewed its way through the underside of the chesterfield and into the guts of the piece.

Martha stepped in front of the sofa, planted her feet wide, and raised the poker overhead.

"It might be a spirit," Edna said. "Don't strike a spirit."

"It's not a spirit," Martha assured her.

"If it's a good spirit, striking it is sacrilegious."

Waiting for the thing in the sofa to slow down or pause so that she could be certain of clubbing it solidly on her first try, Martha said sarcastically, "What if it's a *demonic* spirit?"

"Then, dear, you'll just piss it off. *Please* let's call Mr. Tran and have him deal with this."

Martha said, "You're the cake-recipe genius. I'm the business genius. What I have here is a business decision. Go bake something while I handle this."

On the seat of the chesterfield, the upholstery split and the burrowing intruder erupted in a shower of horsehair.

Mickey Dime

While Mickey waited on the third floor for the north elevator, tremors shuddered through the Pendleton again. He wasn't the least bit worried about them.

In the Philippines, he had once tracked two men to the lip of a volcano. He needed to kill them to fulfill a contract. As he was about to pull the trigger, an unanticipated minor eruption convulsed the mountain. A gout of white-hot lava spewed over the two men, all but vaporizing their flesh and reducing their bones to char. Though Mickey stood only fifteen feet from them, not a drop touched him. He walked away with the equivalent of a light sunburn on his face.

He had liked the smell of molten rock. Metallic, crisp, sexy.

A day later, the volcano blew in a big way. But by then he was ensconced in a Hong Kong hotel suite with a young prostitute and a can of whipped cream. She had been delicious.

If a volcano couldn't get him, nothing would.

Now he rode the elevator to the basement. The doors slid open. Mickey stepped into the corridor.

Diagonally to his right and on the farther side of the hallway, the stairwell door was swinging shut behind someone. He watched it close. He liked the sound of the latch clacking into place. A solid, final sound.

He was reminded of the sound of the heavy latches on the steamer trunks in which he had packed the remains of the cocktail waitress named Mallory, her little sister, and her girlfriend. Fifteen years had passed since he'd disposed of those bodies, but that exhilarating night remained as crisp in memory as if those events had occurred earlier this very day. With his enormous willpower, he restricted himself to professional murder, though in his heart still lived the amateur who would have done the same work for the love of it.

Enjoying the faint scent of chlorine, he waited to see if anyone would come back through the door. Maybe the *ding* of the elevator arriving on station would engage that person's curiosity. He couldn't risk a witness who could place him here at this hour.

After maybe half a minute, Mickey turned left and walked to the security room. He opened the door and went inside.

The prick was on duty. Klick the Prick. Even though they were ex-cops, the other guards were all right. This Klick was a smug little prick who always seemed to be scheming at something.

Swiveling in his chair, Klick said, "Suddenly I'm as popular as Justin Timberlake or somebody. What brings you here, Mr. Dime?"

Mickey drew the pistol with the sound suppressor from his shoulder holster.

Eyes wide in terror as Mickey approached, Klick said, "I'll never tell about the lingerie."

Mickey shot him point-blank through the heart, twice. When you right away stop the heart pumping, there's less blood to clean up.

He left the security room and went to the basement equipment room where he had earlier gotten the hand truck. This time, he fetched a thick moving blanket and two of the furniture straps that dangled from a wall rack.

Only when he returned to the security room did he stop to think about what Vernon Klick had said: *I'll never tell about the lingerie.*

From the time Mickey had been a little boy, his mother warned him never to trust a man in a uniform. How right she had been.

Dr. Kirby Ignis

In his raincoat, carrying an umbrella, soon to be late meeting his colleague for dinner at Topper's, Kirby locked his second-floor apartment just as shock waves rolled through the rock on which the Pendleton stood. The blasting contractors on the farther side of Shadow Hill were excavating later than usual. He wondered that anyone would want to pay overtime to build a high-rise in this dreadful economy, but he supposed they anticipated a turnaround a few years down the road.

As he walked briskly toward the west end of the north hall, strains of Chinese opera still lingered in his mind's ear. Kirby hummed a few bars of a favorite aria.

The neighbors in 2-E, Cheryl and Henry Cordovan, in Europe since the previous Saturday and not scheduled to return for another twelve days, had left their springer spaniel, Biscuit, with their son and his family. Kirby missed the dog. A couple of times a week, when the Cordovans went out to dinner and Kirby intended to eat at home, they left Biscuit with him for a few hours. The spaniel was as cute as a dog could be and excellent company.

Three years previously, he'd had a companion of his own, a black Labrador retriever named Lucy, but cancer had taken her. The loss so devastated Kirby that only recently had he begun to think he might bring a new dog into his life, risking the grief again. Tropical fish were pretty to look at, but they weren't great company.

Sitting on a comfy sofa with a dog's head in his lap, rubbing its ears and stroking its head, Kirby could achieve a greater clarity of thought and more breakthroughs in the theory and the technology that made the Ignis Institute a success. A good dog brought with it a profound peace that made the mind soar and encouraged problem solving even more than did music or the graceful spectacle of swimming fish.

For the past three years, he had contributed significant money to all kinds of dog-rescue groups, watched *Dogs 101* on Animal Planet, and looked after Biscuit a couple of evenings each week, but now, as he arrived at the north elevator, he made up his mind to get a new companion before Christmas. He often thought that the world would be a better place if dogs were the smartest creatures on the planet and if human beings, with all their pride and desires and hatreds, had never evolved.

When the elevator doors slid open, a tall man in evening clothes exited. He carried himself like royalty at a function of great pomp. Nature had given him a distinguished face with a patrician nose, eyes as blue as pure deep water, a high brow, and snow-white hair.

Kirby stepped back, startled. This stranger's shirt and face and hair were spattered with fresh blood. "Sir, are you all right? You've been hurt."

The evening clothes were dirty, rumpled, torn in

places, as if the man had been in a struggle, perhaps mugged in the street—though he was not rain-soaked. Seeming bewildered, he looked around at the hallway, at the double doors to the Trahern apartment on his left, to the door of the Hawks apartment ahead of him. "What is this place? It's Belle Vista . . . yet it isn't."

In his voice was more than a note of perplexity, also a tremor of fear and what might have been despair.

On second look, Kirby saw that the noble countenance appeared pale and drawn. Horror crawled in the stricken blue eyes.

"What's happened to you?" Kirby asked.

"This place . . . Where *is* this? How have I gotten here? Where am I?"

Kirby stepped forward to take the bloodied man by one arm, for he seemed wobbly and in need of support.

Before Kirby could touch him, the stranger raised both hands, which were slick with blood. "We almost made it, all untouched," he muttered, ". . . and then the spores."

Retreating again, Kirby said, "Spores?"

"Witness said they were from a benign species, nothing to fear. But he's part of it all, not to be believed."

The man's gaze continued to travel over the walls, the ceiling, and his face wrenched with grievous emotion, as though his perplexity must be rapidly collapsing into a more profound confusion, his powers of perception, memory, and reason slipping away from him.

"I killed them all. The mister and the missus, the children, the staff."

On consideration, Kirby saw that the suit of evening clothes was not an ordinary tuxedo. It looked more like stylish livery, a uniform that a highly placed servant might wear.

"They were infected, I'm sure of it, so I had to kill them all, even the beautiful children, God help me, I had to kill them all to save the world."

Overcome by a sudden sense of mortal peril, heart knocking, Kirby backed away from the man, toward the door to the north stairs.

The butler, if that's what he was, seemed to have no interest in Kirby, to have no malice left. He said, "Now I've got to get more ammunition so I can kill myself." As he crossed the hallway, he began to grow translucent, as if he'd never been real, only an apparition. He disappeared through the wall, into the Hawks apartment.

Although Kirby didn't believe in ghosts, this might have been one—except for the blood that had dripped off the man's hands and now stained the hallway runner.

Winny

They couldn't use the elevator because it was all wrong and there was a big bug in it or something that almost got his hand, and they were afraid of the stairs, so he and his mom took a time-out in the Sykes apartment because there seemed to be nowhere else to go.

Winny knew Mrs. Sykes just from saying hello to each other when they passed in the hallway or down in the lobby, and he knew who Iris was except she never said hello. Iris, who was three years older than Winny, couldn't tolerate people, not because she thought they were stupid or mean or boring—though a lot of them were—but because she had autism. Winny's mother said that most of the time, Iris couldn't bear to be touched and that pretty much all of the time she became really upset if too many people were around. He kind of understood autism because he'd read a little about it, but he *totally* understood the way Iris felt about people, because he had his own problem. He always seemed to say the wrong thing or a dumb thing, or something that made no sense because he babbled. Iris couldn't say anything, and Winny didn't know *what* to say, so they were sort of in the same boat.

From the way that Mrs. Sykes snapped the thumbturns of both deadbolts, rattled the security chain in place, and then tested the door to be sure it was locked even though it obviously was, Winny knew that something creepy had recently happened to her, too, and that she was scared.

"Maybe I'm just locking something in with us," Mrs. Sykes said, "not locking anything out. Anyway, if they can just go through walls, what good is a lock?"

Winny's mom looked at him, and he made a half-goofy face so she wouldn't see how much Mrs. Sykes spooked him. Whatever was happening, this was going to be a serious test of his strategies for avoiding the wimp-sissy label.

"I need to show you something," Mrs. Sykes said. "I

hope it's still there. Or maybe I don't. No, I do. I hope it's there. Because if you see the damn thing, too, then I'll know I'm not losing my mind."

Winny made another half-goofy face at his mother, but this time it didn't seem appropriate, as it had been only a moment earlier. Now he not only didn't know what to say; he also didn't know what to do with his face, or with his hands for that matter. He put his hands in his jacket pockets, but his face just hung out there for everyone to see.

Leading them across the living room, Mrs. Sykes realized that Iris wasn't following. The girl just stood there, staring off into space, her hands fisted at her sides. Her mother spoke to her in an odd way that seemed like she was reciting lines of a poem: "'Don't be frightened. Come with me and don't be frightened. I'm glad that I can take you to show you the way.'"

This time, Iris came with them, though she stayed a few steps behind. They went along a hallway and into a bedroom that must have belonged to her because it was in girl colors and stuffed toys were perched everywhere. Most of the toys were bunnies, a few frogs, a few silly birds, and one dopey squirrel, all plush and soft, none of them animals that, in the real world, had sharp teeth and killed other animals.

Winny was surprised to see so many books, because he thought some autistic kids never read well, maybe not at all. Evidently, Iris read a lot. He knew why. Books were another life. If you were shy and didn't know what to say and felt you didn't belong anywhere, books were a way to lead another life, a way to be someone else entirely, to be anyone at all. Winny didn't know what he would do without his books, except probably go berserk and start killing people and making ashtrays out of their skulls even though he didn't smoke and never would.

"It's still there," Mrs. Sykes said, pointing to a window.

A freaky thing clung to the glass panes in the rain: roughly the shape of a football although bigger, but flat on the bottom, with too many stumpy legs that looked like they were made for walking on another planet, and a face more human than not, except that the face was in its belly.

Part of Winny's strategy for avoiding a reputation as a sissy was never to look away from the screen during a scary movie. Never ever. He always managed to keep his eyes on even the most gruesome action by conducting a commentary in his head, making fun of bad acting when he saw it, ridiculing idiotic dialogue, and mocking lousy special effects. Often tongue-tied with others, he could chatter nonstop when talking to himself. He also judged every psycho killer or monster on his take-a-dump-in-your-pants-and-run scale, on which the highest score was ten stars. But by being the toughest possible critic, he found that he could diminish the fright effect of any creature that had ever crept across a movie screen, and he never awarded more than six stars, which wasn't even a *pee*-in-your-pants score.

The thing on the window was a seven.

He didn't pee in his pants, however, and even though his mom cried out in shock and disgust when she saw the creeper, even though Mrs. Sykes said something about it being a mescaline dream, whatever that might be, Winny didn't make a sound to reveal the fear that quickened through him.

Iris helped him to keep his composure. She didn't say anything or make eye contact or even move from beside her bed, from which she had snatched a plush-toy bunny with big floppy ears. But her face was tight with anxiety, and she looked so vulnerable that Winny worried more about her than about himself. He didn't think she had seen the thing on the window, because she wouldn't make eye contact with him or with anyone, let alone with a monster, and he wanted to be sure she didn't accidentally get a glimpse of it. Just having a couple of neighbors in her room made her want to go off like a bottle rocket—you could see how she struggled to control herself—so the thing on the window would probably make her blow every cork and strip every gear. Life was hard enough for her, she didn't need monsters; nobody needed them, but especially not her.

Some of those ghost trains went rumbling beneath the Pendleton again on tracks that didn't exist, and onto the tall window crawled another creature like the first, the same in every way except that the face in its belly wasn't a man's face but a woman's, maybe even the face of a little girl, twisted like in a funhouse mirror.

The lips peeled open, and a tongue fluttered against the glass.

If Winny and his mom had successfully fled the Pendleton, they wouldn't have escaped whatever was happening. Maybe things were even crazier outside than inside the building.

Discovering an inner strength that surprised him, Winny dashed to the window, seized the pull cord, and drew shut the draperies, so that the monstrosities could no longer see them or be seen.

He said simply, before his mother and Mrs. Sykes could protest, "Iris."

Martha Cupp

Out of the chesterfield sofa and onto the seat, in a spray of horsehair stuffing, spilled something like tangles of glistening intestines, although they were bloodless and gray. The entrails of any eviscerated mammal would never have spasmed and writhed like these unraveling coils, which seemed not to be part of some violently slashed-open animal but the entire intact animal itself, a long ropey colon of a thing, segmented as if by bands of muscle, as hideous a spectacle as Martha had ever seen either in or out of dreams.

Overcome by abhorrence and detestation even in excess of what she had ever felt toward the Internal Revenue Service, Martha was for a moment paralyzed. She held the poker in both hands, high above her head, and she wanted to strike with it more than she'd wanted anything else in her long life, but her arms were locked, her body unresponsive to her will, immobilized as much by dark wonder as by terror.

Smoke and Ashes shrieked quite unlike the docile cats they had always been. She heard them scrambling off the étagère, flinging themselves through the air, landing with thumps on padded furniture, and squealing their way out of the living room to safer realms.

The west-facing windows filled with the most brilliant barrages of lightning yet, the entire sky ablaze, as if the poles of Heaven and Hell had shifted, the fires of damnation now overhead and God's angels all tumbled into caverns in the earth. The lamps flickered in sympathy with the flashing night, and a sudden jittering in the viscera-slick mass on the sofa might have been an illusion, the stroboscopic effect of the throbbing light.

The storm went dark and the lamps swelled and steadied to full brightness, revealing that the abomination on the chesterfield was sprouting black tarantula legs from among the sweating loops of its intestinelike body, and not only legs but also a cluster of red beaks that clicked, clicked, clicked as though eager to peck at something and shred it.

Breaking her brief paralysis, Martha swung the fireplace poker, and from her perspective the grotesque creature appeared to shimmer and vanish during the downswing. The brass poker slammed into the chesterfield, and horsehair plumed from between the lips of the rip in the fabric, but there was no satisfying splatter or wounded cry. Overcharged with loathing, fear, and outrage that her home had been invaded, she slammed the poker down again, a third time, and a fourth before she was able to acknowledge the lack of a target. Still furious, totally stoked, half sick with disgust, she refused to accept that the squirming monstrosity had evaporated into thin air. She dropped the poker, grabbed the front of the sofa with both hands, and overturned it, crashing it onto its back, revealing the underside—and no intruder. She saw the ragged hole that the beast had made in the black batting to insert itself into the springs and from there into the upholstery. Snatching up the poker once more, Martha dropped to her knees as if she'd never known a pang of arthritis in her life, and stabbed into the hole in the batting with the brass tool, stabbed this way and that, plucking a discord of brittle pings and twangy flat notes from the springs as though they were the strings of some instrument played only in the Hades Philharmonic, but eliciting not a single squeal from any living thing.

At last she clambered to her feet, still holding the poker even though her inflamed knuckles throbbed. She had broken into a sweat. Damp curls of hair hung in her face. She was breathing hard, and her heart hadn't beat this fast since she had long ago stopped chasing her second husband around the bedroom.

She turned to her sister for corroboration that what she had seen wasn't a delusion arising from dementia.

Both Edna's expression and posture confirmed the reality of the incident: Her eyes were hoot-owl wide, mouth formed in a perfect O of unvoiced astonishment.

After a silence, Edna said, "Dear, I haven't seen you spring into action like that since back in the day when a board-of-directors meeting wasn't going well and you had to whip them into line."

Mickey Dime

He took the gun belt off Vernon Klick's corpse and put it aside on the floor. Someday he would use this pistol in a hit because it was registered to the security service and disappeared with Klick the Prick, which is who they would be looking for when they found it at some future crime scene. A little bit of fun.

Later, Mickey would go into the security-video archives and scrub all the recorded feeds from every camera in the building. He would leave no evidence that his brother, Jerry, had come to visit. No clue about what happened to Vernon Klick. He had covered his trail this way on other occasions, in other cities. He knew how to ensure that the digital video could not be recovered.

He dragged Klick behind him, out of the security room, quickly along the main basement hall to the entrance to the HVAC vault. The corpse was wrapped in a moving blanket, tied with furniture straps. It slid easily on the tiled floor.

Mickey enjoyed the exertion. His trapezius muscles

contracted into a solid ridge across his shoulders. His deltoids. His triceps so taut. He was in excellent physical shape. A real hardbody.

When he was at his country cottage, sitting nude in the yard in a summer storm, he liked to feel his muscles, up and down his body. Firmly massage them. Lightly caress them. Slick with rain, as if the storm oiled him. He enjoyed a double pleasure: receiving the caresses and giving them, his hands as thrilled as his body.

He unlocked the door to the HVAC vault with a key that he had taken from Klick. Here were the building's heating, ventilation, and air-conditioning systems, as well as the hot-water heaters and bank after bank of breaker boxes. He switched on the lights. He dragged the dead man across the threshold. He closed the door.

The vault was actually a room, a fortified concrete box maybe seventy feet wide and almost forty feet front to back. Rows of seven-foot-tall chillers to the left. Two different sizes of industrial boilers to the right, the larger ones serving the four-pipe, fan-coil heating system that allowed separate controls for every apartment and every public space, the smaller ones—still large—that provided hot water to the residents. In and around and above it all was a maze of pipes, valves, pumps, monitoring devices, and other equipment that Mickey couldn't identify.

Tom Tran kept the vault as clean as a hospital surgery. The labyrinthine machinery purred, whined, and thrummed, which was a kind of symphony to Mickey. A symphony of efficiency.

His late mother had said that human beings were just machines engineered by nature, through evolution. You could be either a good machine or a bad machine, but whichever you were had nothing to do with morality. The only standard was efficiency. Good machines did their chosen work efficiently, reliably.

Mickey judged himself an *excellent* machine. His chosen work was killing other machines of the human kind. Efficient action excited and satisfied him more than sex. Sex involved other people, and they always disappointed him because they were so much less efficient than he was. They were so easily distracted by such nonsense as affection and tenderness. Sex wasn't about affection and tenderness. The big pumps in this room, laboring ceaselessly, knew more about sex than most people did.

Sparkle Sykes and her daughter intruded vividly in his thoughts again, as that cocktail waitress had done fifteen years earlier. They wouldn't leave him alone. They came naked into his mind. He banished them, but they were insistent. They had just better back off. They had better stop teasing him.

Dragging Klick, he proceeded to a clear area in the center of the vault. There, inset in the floor, a thick rubber gasket embraced an iron manhole cover. In a few minutes, when Mickey returned with his brother, he would open the manhole and consign both bodies to a final resting place so deep that the remains would never be found. Even graveyard rats would not descend that far for a two-man banquet.

Bailey Hawks

When Bailey threw open the stairwell door on the second floor and crossed the threshold into the hallway, Dr. Kirby Ignis cried out in surprise. His pleasantly rumpled face, no doubt avuncular even in his youth but already grandfatherly at fifty, was pale and damp with a thin film of sweat. Ordinarily, Ignis had about him an air of wisdom and unflappable confidence, but now he appeared to be alarmed, as if he had expected someone other than Bailey to come out of the stairwell, someone hostile, which until today was not an expectation that made sense in a place as safe as the Pendleton.

Bailey said, "What is it? What have you seen?"

Dr. Ignis was too perceptive to miss the implication in Bailey's words. "You've seen something, too. Something extraordinary. Was it a man in evening clothes, a butler perhaps, tall and white-haired and splattered with blood?"

"Where did you see him?"

Ignis indicated spots of blood on the carpet runner. "He told me he killed them all—the children, too. What children? What apartment? And then he . . ." The doctor frowned at the wall beside Bailey's front door. "Well, I don't know. . . . I don't know where he went then. . . ."

Silas Kinsley

On the ground floor, Silas turned away from the south elevator, from the threatening voices that echoed behind the sliding doors. They were like mob voices in certain dreams, demanding, threatening yet incoherent, no word clear, the eager chanting of pursuing legions whose motivation he could not fathom but whose grim purpose was his destruction. He recalled awakening earlier in the day and listening to a terrible slithering within the wall behind his bed. These voices in the shaft were nothing like that sound, yet he knew their provenance must be the same. He went to the nearby stairs and hurried down to the basement.

Too old and too in need of his lost Nora to worry about losing his life, Silas was nevertheless fearful for his neighbors, anxious to warn them to evacuate the building. At the bottom of the stairs, he opened the door cautiously, quietly, worried that the hulking monstrosity Perry Kyser had seen in 1973, the thing that evidently had killed one of his workers, might be waiting there to attack. If Andrew Pendleton could be alive here on this night long after his suicide, then anyone—and anything—might walk this building from any period of its history.

The south corridor appeared deserted, leading past the storage units to the freight elevator at the back of the building, and the only presence in the long west corridor was a man who stepped out of the HVAC room.

He closed that door and strode briskly away toward the distant north elevator.

Silas couldn't see the guy well enough to positively identify him, but he felt pretty sure it was Mr. Mickey Dime. As a member of the homeowners'-association board of directors, Silas knew every resident, though he didn't know all of them equally well. Dime was largely just a name to him, because the man kept to himself.

When Dime disappeared into the far elevator, Silas left the south stairs and hurried past the superintendent's apartment. At the security room, he knocked lightly. When no one responded, he rapped somewhat louder. Finally he opened the door and went inside.

The security console wasn't manned. No one was at the coffeemaker in the kitchenette alcove. The door stood open to the little bathroom, which offered a toilet and sink, and no one was in there, either.

According to security protocols, the guard on duty would leave his post only if called to an emergency elsewhere in the building or for fifteen minutes, at random, twice on the evening and the late-night shifts, to make the rounds of the basement, ground floor, and courtyard. But the earliest such tour never occurred before eight or nine o'clock, still hours from now.

Silas spotted a wet red exclamation point on the floor near one of the console chairs. He knelt to examine it. An inch-long line of blood. At the end of it, a punctuating dot of the same. So recently spilled that the air had not yet begun to crust it around the edges or lay a film upon it. Also on the floor, in the kneehole under the workstation, lay the guard's utility belt with holster and pistol.

Silas's mouth had gone dry. He realized he was breathing through it, rapidly and shallowly and perhaps ever since he stood listening to voices in the elevator shaft. He could hear a drum, the jungle drum of his heart, quick but not yet panicked, thumping in the wild deep darkness of his chest.

Either the smoke detectors in every room and every hallway or the security guard using this computer could trigger a strident fire alarm throughout the building. As a fail-safe precaution, the computer was tied to the emergency generator in case the city power went out before an alarm could be sounded.

Silas didn't know how to use the computer for that purpose, but he was sure that Tom Tran could do it. He went next door to the superintendent's apartment and rang the doorbell. He heard the seven-note chimes echoing through those rooms, but though he rang three times, no one answered.

The basement corridor looked no different from the way it had always looked, but it *felt* different. Wrong. The ceiling didn't sag or the walls bow, but Silas sensed a tremendous burden on the building, as if the storm and the sky beyond the storm and the universe that was the sky were all pressing on the Pendleton, a weight so terrible that the structure would collapse into rubble, the rubble into dust.

Although he was many years removed from that period of his legal practice when he'd specialized in criminal defense, Silas hadn't lost his intuitive recognition of deception and evil intention. Mr. Dime had not appeared furtive, in fact had proceeded with the air of a man openly going about legitimate business, but Silas couldn't think of a reason why any resident would ever need to visit the HVAC vault.

Increasingly certain not that time was running out but that some incomprehensible calamity of time was about to befall the Pendleton, Silas needed to return to the ground floor, ask Padmini Bahrati if she knew where Tom Tran was or if she could trigger a fire alarm.

But first he felt compelled to return to the security room and take the guard's abandoned pistol. He hadn't been to a shooting range in ten years. He didn't want to use a gun, but things didn't always work out the way you preferred. From the utility belt he also took the canister of pepper spray and the flashlight. He stepped into the hallway and hurried to the next door on the left. It was unlocked. He stepped into the HVAC vault.

Winny

In the kitchen, Iris sat at the breakfast table, holding the floppy-eared bunny tight to her chest, rocking forward and back in her chair, whispering something to the toy that Winny couldn't hear, whispering it over and over.

Something about the girl—Winny wasn't sure what—made him want to be brave. It wasn't that Iris was pretty, which she was. Although Winny was in many ways advanced for his age, he was too young to be interested in girls. Anyway, she was too old for him, three years older. Part of it might be that she needed books, and he needed books, and unlike most people who liked to talk about what books they read in their clubs, neither Iris nor Winny talked about what they read—in her case because she couldn't talk, in his case because he was such a rotten talker that he would make good books sound like they sucked.

He didn't sit at the table with Iris. Too wired to keep still, he roamed the kitchen, looking at the dishes displayed beyond the French doors in some of the cabinets and reading the notations Mrs. Sykes had made on various days on the December page of the wall calendar: "Accountant at 2:30, dinner with Tanya, Dr. Abbot, cheese sale." He tried to decide if the apples and pears and bananas in the center of the work island had been carefully arranged to look like a still-life painting or had just been dumped willy-nilly into the big shallow bowl, which was such a peculiar thing to care about at a time like this that he wondered if maybe he was gay or something. He even counted the floor tiles, as if the number of them—stupid, stupid—might at some point be vital information that would save their lives.

He also listened to his mom and Mrs. Sykes trying to make calls with the kitchen phone and with both of their cell phones. Several times, before they punched in a complete number, they were connected to people speaking a foreign language, several voices on the line at the same time, gobbling like a flock of turkeys. Once his mom got an operator at City Bell, a different one from the first, and this lady also insisted that it was 1935, though she wasn't as nice as the first. And Mrs. Sykes dropped her phone in surprise when shimmering sheets of blue lights flashed corner to corner across one kitchen wall.

Inside some of those cabinets, things rattled and clanged. A few lower doors flew open and several drawers rolled out. Cookware tumbled from open doors, stainless-steel flatware and metal utensils erupted from the drawers, and all of this stuff levitated, floating around one side of the kitchen in that blue light, pots and pans bonking against one another. Knives and forks and spoons were busy in midair as if a dozen poltergeists were rattling their tableware together to protest the lack of acceptable ghost food, the way prisoners in some old movies caused a commotion in the dining hall when the evil new warden embezzled money from the budget and served them cheap slop.

The waves of light washed right to left over the cabinets and then away, the junk storm abruptly ended, and everything fell at once in a clatter-crash. But the stuff didn't just rain down all over the floor. Instead, the items clustered in weirdly balanced piles that gravity should have pulled apart at once but didn't, pieces of the stainless-steel flatware bristling from among the pots-and-pans sculptures, vibrating like tuning forks, as though everything had been magnetized. After a moment, the magnetism must have fluxed away or something, because the vibrating stopped and the piles collapsed, scattering things across the floor. In the wake of all that commotion, the silence that fell over the kitchen was like a funeral-home hush—except for Iris whimpering like a puppy who was lost and wanted to be home.

Neither of the two moms screamed or went crazy-hysterical, or went into denial, the way that people usually did in movies where weird things happened. Winny was proud of them and grateful, because if one of them had lost her cool, he would have freaked out, too, and that would have been the end of being brave for Iris.

The waves of blue light reminded Winny of the pulsing circles on the TV and of the voice that said, *"Exterminate."*

He suspected his mom was thinking of the same thing, because she said, "Maybe it isn't safe to go outside, with those things crawling out there, but it's not safe to stay inside, either."

Mrs. Sykes said, "We need to get with other people. There's got to be some safety in numbers."

"Gary Dai's in Singapore," Winny's mom said.

The lower level of Mr. Dai's two-story unit was next door to their apartment. He was a software guru and a video-game-designer legend, so he might know what was happening and how to get through all the levels of play alive. Just their luck that he was halfway around the world when the quarter dropped and the action started.

"The people next door are away visiting their grandson," Mrs. Sykes said. "And the end apartment is empty, for sale."

Winny's mom said, "Let's go back through my place, over to the north hall, see if we can find Bailey Hawks in 2-C. There's no one in the Pendleton I'd feel safer with right now."

Bailey Hawks

On the kitchen island were two boxes of ammunition that Bailey retrieved from his master-bedroom closet. As he loaded a spare twenty-round magazine for his Beretta 9 mm, he listened to Kirby Ignis's story of his startling encounter with the distinguished, blood-spattered man who spoke of killing everyone and who then vanished through a wall.

The doctor was too intelligent and too practical to waste time proposing rational but improbable explanations the way that some UFO debunkers resorted to suppositions of swamp gas, weather balloons, and swarms of iridescent insects. He had seen a man vanish into a wall, but instead of questioning his sanity and the reliability of his senses, he was in the process of amending his personal definition of the word *impossible*.

"I don't know the full story," Bailey said. "Silas Kinsley, up in 3-C, he's the Pendleton's historian. He'll have all the details. But in the thirties sometime, a butler killed the family who owned Belle Vista."

"He'd be dead now."

"Very dead," Bailey agreed as he dropped spare cartridges into all the pockets of his sport coat. "If I remember right, he committed suicide back then."

"I'm not the kind who goes to séances."

"Me neither." Bailey thought of Sophia Pendleton—*Old King Cole was a merry old soul, and a merry old soul was he*—singing her way down the stairs. "But this isn't ghosts. It's something stranger, bigger."

"What have *you* seen?" Ignis asked.

"I'll tell you on the way."

"On the way where?"

"Martha and Edna Cupp, up in 3-A. They're in their eighties. Whatever's happening here, they need to be out of it."

"Maybe we all need to be out of it," Ignis said.

"Maybe we do."

Mickey Dime

As Mickey rolled the hand truck and dead Jerry along the north hall on the third floor, he grew nostalgic for the childhood they had shared. By the time he turned the corner and stopped at the elevator to press the call button, however, he had exhausted his capacity for sentimentality.

Jerry had been Mickey's brother but also a problem. Problem solved. His mother said the strong act, the weak *re*act. She said the weak have regrets, the strong have triumphs. She said the weak believe in God, the strong believe in themselves. She said both the strong and the weak are part of the food chain, and it is better to eat than be eaten. She said that the strong have pride, that the weak have humility, and that *she* was proud of her humility and humble about her pride. She said that power justifies all things and that absolute power justifies all things absolutely. Because a famous California winery paid her handsomely to do a magazine ad and a TV commercial in their what-do-the-smartest-people-drink campaign, she said that a robust Cabernet Sauvignon was central to a life well-lived, that it was a metaphor for transcendence, that it was an essential tool for the redistribution of chic, and that it was both great art and literature in a bottle. She said that judging Cain for killing Abel was like condemning a vigorous wolf pup for drinking his share of mother's milk *and* the share of the sickly pup that might otherwise have survived, to the detriment of the pack.

Mickey didn't understand everything that his mother had said over the years, in part because she had said and written so much that no one could keep up with her. But he knew that everything she said was wise. And most of it was profound.

The elevator car arrived on the third floor. Mickey wheeled his brother into it.

Silas Kinsley

All of the lights were on in the HVAC vault, racks of hooded fluorescent tubes hanging on chains from the ceiling. The impressive ranks of complex machines, humming along as intended by the original engineer, presented a scene of such orderliness and normality that Silas could almost believe that all was right in the Pendleton regardless of the things that he had seen and heard.

He closed the door behind him. "Is anyone here? Mr. Tran? Tom?"

When no one responded, Silas set out to explore the service aisles between the rows of equipment. Instead he at once was drawn to the manhole in the center of the room and to the bundle lying beside it.

The manhole, which had been there since the Pendleton was constructed, provided access to a three-foot-diameter steel sleeve that penetrated the eight-foot-deep concrete foundation of the great mansion. The sleeve had been placed precisely to terminate at the mouth of a fault in the bedrock.

Not a fault in the sense of a fracture, but a smooth-walled lava pipe from which molten rock once gushed. Shadow Hill and surrounding territory was a stable mass of basalt, an extremely dense volcanic stone, and rhyolite, which was the volcanic form of granite. Tens of thousands of years earlier, at the end of the volcanic era in this region, when the eruptions were exhausted, a few long vent tunnels remained in the solid stone, including the one under the Pendleton, which seemed to average between four and five feet in width.

In the late 1800s, when the great house was built, environmental issues were of less concern than in the current age. Little if any thought was given to the possible contamination of the water table when the Pendleton's bathtub, sink, and toilet drains were routed to terminate at the top of the seemingly bottomless lava pipe. In those days, the city was much smaller than now, only then beginning to plan a public sewer system. Septic tanks remained the primary means of gray-water and waste disposal, and the many thousands of cubic feet of the lava pipe offered a cheap and maintenance-free alternative to a standard tank.

The contractor included the manhole to provide service access in the unlikely event of a problem. When the cast-iron cover was removed, the lava pipe also functioned as an efficient outflow in the event that the basement should flood from a broken water line. In 1928, the Pendleton's bathtub, sink, and toilet drains were rerouted to the public sewer system, but the manhole remained.

With the conversion of Belle Vista into the Pendleton in 1973, all the chillers and huge boilers of the new heating and cooling system raised a greater possibility of flooding. With the existing access to the lava pipe, the architect and contractor were spared the need to provide massive emergency pumps kept perpetually on standby, and could instead rely on the gravity-flow method of the original arrangement.

Dropping to one knee, Silas Kinsley was not interested in the manhole but in the rolled-up, quilted moving blanket that Dime had tied shut with furniture straps. Assessing the contents of the bundle with both hands, he felt what seemed to be legs, what were almost certainly arms, and undoubtedly a head. One end of the roll had come open slightly when the knot in the securing strap had pulled loose. Silas reached inside and discovered the top of someone's head. The curliness of the hair and the memory of the exclamation point of blood in the inexplicably deserted security room seemed sufficient evidence for him to conclude that the dead man was Vernon Klick. The lava pipe was to be his grave.

Silas thought that this killing must be related to the tragedies that occurred here every thirty-eight years. Dime's murder of Vernon Klick must somehow be a part of the currently pending event that was presaged by rumbling in the earth, the appearance of the late Andrew North Pendleton in the lobby, the voices in the elevator shaft, and other signs. But related *how*?

More urgently than ever, he needed Padmini Bahrati to find Tom Tran or to trigger the fire alarm herself, if she knew how. He rose to his feet, crossed the room, and was within three steps of the door when something bumped against the farther side of it.

Fielding Udell

After the luminous blue energy sheeted across the ceiling, after the paper clips and other metal objects leaped to the light and then, when the light was extinguished, rained to the floor, Fielding stood transfixed. His mind raced toward a conclusion that he sought to avoid but that seemed inescapable. The Ruling Elite had found him.

They knew that *he* knew.

He knew. The original scientific consensus connecting residence near power lines with high cancer rates, later refuted and dismissed, was in fact true. Millions of such deaths must be occurring each year, the awful truth hidden by the Political Masters who throttled the free speech of scientists and doctors, and by their Minions who altered medical records and forged death certificates.

He knew. The consensus claiming the chemical alar, used by apple growers, caused malignancies and worse, which had been brilliantly championed by a famous actress but had later been found to be bad science, was in fact also true. Good science, good. Too many apple farmers were destroyed, too many apple-related jobs were lost, so the Ruling Elite and their Minions came down on the side of Commerce rather than on the side of Health. Precious babies were dying from apple juice, toddlers from applesauce, legions of schoolchildren from the reckless consumption of raw apples and apple pies. But the Ruling Elite and their despicable Minions faked evidence to the contrary and mounted a pro-alar campaign. Now uncountable innocent children were dying horribly, perhaps so many that their bodies were secretly bulldozed into mass graves.

When the shimmering blue light did not return, he warily toured the rest of his apartment, prepared to find the phenomenon elsewhere. He suspected it might have been evidence of a mind-reading ray, with which his thoughts had been explored for insurrectionist sentiments. But he wanted to believe it had been something less ominous, perhaps just a census scan, which the Ruling Elite would probably take on a regular basis to determine just how rapidly the earth's fast-dying population was moving toward extinction.

Fielding Udell knew. The eminent professor Paul Ehrlich, and a consensus of scientists, reported in 1981 that 250,000 species were becoming extinct per annum. Such a catastrophe meant that by 2011—*this very year!*—Earth would support no life whatsoever. Recently some scientists said only two or three species were lost each year and claimed this had been the case for centuries, which meant they were either corrupt or that their families were being held hostage and tortured by the Ruling Elite. Fielding *knew* that the 250,000-per-year figure must be correct, that most of the world was now barren, that the images you saw on TV of a world pretty much as it had always been were elaborate special-effects lies, every bit as phony as the moon-landing footage shown to the world in July 1969, which had been staged in the Mojave Desert. The bitter truth: The earth was largely *dead* except for certain urban-suburban enclaves covered by force-field domes, inside which the brainwashed citizens lived an illusion of plenty and safety.

Finding no shimmering blue light anywhere, Fielding took his empty glass to the kitchen for a refill of his homemade cola.

Sometimes he wondered from where the food came to feed the dome-city residents like him, considering that the farmlands were polluted and unproductive. He remembered an old sci-fi movie, *Soylent Green*, in which the revolutionary new food that staved off famine in an overpopulated future world proved to be made secretly from cadavers. Charlton Heston shouts, "*Soylent Green is people!*" Maybe all those apple-poisoned children weren't bulldozed into mass graves, after all, but were carted off to processing plants.

Now and then Fielding had difficulty eating his dinner, even though it looked like the same food he had dined upon all his life. The only thing that kept him from becoming bulimic was the fact that *Soylent Green* was set in the year 2022, which meant that more than a decade remained before the Ruling Elite would deceive humankind into embracing cannibalism.

Carrying the glass of cola, he returned to his main workroom and his computer. He resumed his online investigation, probing, probing, on the trail of the identity of the Ruling Elite. He half expected a sharp knock at the door and the arrival of a goon squad armed with a warrant, the results of the blue-light scan of his mind, and some kind of brain-wipe thingy that would erase his memory and leave him unaware of the great work that he had done these past twenty years.

They would fail. He had prepared. In the bedroom, taped to the underside of his sock drawer, were two manila envelopes containing a total of 104 pages of a report on the Case for Prosecution of the Ruling Elite. The report began with these words: *The Worst People in the World have erased portions of your memory, but herein is the Great Truth they have stolen from you.* If he was robbed of his past, he would eventually find those two envelopes and reclaim his purpose and his destiny.

Logan Spangler

He didn't know how long he might have stood in the half bath in the senator's apartment, staring at his black fingernails. They didn't seem to be mere nails anymore but were like ten little arched windows through which he could look into a perfect darkness within his hands.

Logan remembered a murderer he had apprehended three decades earlier, name of Marsden, a guy in his early thirties, who liked to rape and kill. In his confession, he said he liked to kill so much that sometimes he even forgot to rape his victim first. Marsden had none of the edginess or hyperactivity seen in many psychopaths. He was as calm as sheep grazing in a marijuana meadow and claimed to be equally tranquil during the act of murder. He said his inner landscape was perpetually dark, that he could remember his entire life but could see in his mind's eye only events that had occurred at night. And when he slept his dreams always unfolded in dark places, sometimes in venues so lightless that he was blind in his dreams. "I am," he said with some pride, delighting in himself, "so dark inside that I'm certain the blood in my veins runs black."

Gazing at his black fingernails, Logan was not alarmed, but as calm as Marsden had been. Such a serenity had come over him that he felt above all storm and shadow, imperturbable. He could not recall why he was here in the senator's half bath or why his nails were black, or what he had intended to do next.

When moments—or hours—later he found himself in the senator's bedroom, he had no memory of proceeding there. He continued into the master bathroom and opened the glass door to the roomy shower. The stall featured a built-in marble bench that matched the walls, and it doubled as a steam bath. He dialed up the steam, stepped out of the stall, crossed the room, and switched off the lights. In the blind dark, he somehow knew his way, returning to the shower without a single misstep. In the stall, he pulled the door shut behind him. Fully clothed, he sat on the marble bench as warm clouds enveloped him.

He needed darkness, dampness, warmth. Just for a little while. He had nowhere to go, nothing to do. He could rest here for a time. Darkness, dampness, warmth. Pieces of the past came to him, random moments from his life, not in any order, none seemingly related to another, playing out like little movies, and all of them were things that had happened to him at night, just as Marsden had been able to conjure in his mind's eye only night moments from his past. In the pitch dark of the windowless bathroom, in the lesser darkness of his memories, he sighed softly and inhaled the thick warm mist, which soothed him. Darkness, dampness, warmth. He breathed in all three, filling himself with darkness, dampness, warmth. He was tranquil, peaceful, relaxed, self-possessed. Possessed. There was nowhere that he needed to go, nothing that he needed to do. There was no one he needed to be. Soon the memories of night moments from his life faded, and his inner landscape was as lightless as the bathroom in which he sat. For a short time, he searched for one memory or another, any memory, but he was a blind man in a maze of empty rooms. Anyway, there was nowhere he needed to go, nothing he needed to do, no one he needed to be. He relaxed. Stopped exploring the inner blackness. Stopped thinking. He was in the dark and the dark in him. After a while, deep within, he became aware of something blindly feeling its way through him.

Mickey Dime

He guided the hand truck across the raised threshold into the HVAC vault and closed the door behind him. He wheeled dead Jerry beside the body of Klick the Prick.

All around, machinery hummed and purred and whispered. Massed machines, regardless of their purpose, always seemed sexy to Mickey. The power. The efficiency. The unrelenting purpose.

He had toured a decommissioned nuclear-missile silo once. The ICBM and the machinery were long gone. Yet the place still possessed immense erotic impact. The dank air smelled like stale semen.

Now, somewhere in all the runs of pipe, a demand

valve opened. He heard water rushing under pressure through a conduit. Very sexy.

On the manhole cover, a big release ring was folded flat. He flipped it up. He slipped his hand through the ring and pulled hard. The seal between the cover and the gasket broke with a sucking sound. The iron disc swung up and aside on underset hinges.

The overhead fluorescents failed to penetrate far into the black hole. No draft rose from the shaft, suggesting that if it connected with deep caverns, they were without any significant opening to the surface. The air below had only a faint lime scent, which probably came from the massive concrete foundation of the Pendleton rather than from the ancient volcanic vent below.

Mickey had learned about the lava pipe from his mother. She heard about it from Gary Dai, the dot-com-video-game-social-website wizard. Gary Dai had read about the lava pipe in a pamphlet about the Pendleton that every owner received upon closing escrow. Mickey's mother had not read the pamphlet. She read nothing but essays and books that she had written—as well as anything written *about* her. Mickey didn't read.

No one knew for sure the length of the lava pipe. Experts said it could extend for a mile or two, perhaps longer. When Andrew North Pendleton built his mansion, an attempt was made to plumb the natural shaft. They lowered a lead weight on a cord for 1,522 feet before it encountered what at first was assumed to be the bottom. When a score of one-inch-diameter steel ball bearings were dropped at once into the hole, however, that bottom proved to be instead a curve in the pipe where the vertical drop led into a sloping tunnel. The bearings rang hard against the curve, then rolled noisily along the slope. They were never heard to come to a halt; the sound of their descent faded until they had traveled to such a distance that the lava pipe no longer echoed with their progress.

If the tunnel didn't widen beyond five feet just for the turn—which it probably did, according to a volcanologist quoted in the owners' pamphlet—the two dead men might get hung up there. Mickey was counting on 1,522 feet of momentum to tumble them around the curve and far down the slope beyond it.

For the next month, he'd visit the HVAC vault every few days to open the manhole and smell the air. If the stink of decomposition was present, he would know the cadavers hadn't made it around the curve. Then he would have to engineer a rupture in one of these big pipes, flood the vault, and wash the dead men to a more distant resting place.

If there was no stench, however, the lava pipe would facilitate his fantasies about Sparkle and Iris Sykes. He could daydream about having them but also about popping them and dumping them, which would be a more fully rounded fantasy than rape alone. He hoped that he might pass them soon in a public hallway. He would try to get close enough to catch their scents, a detail to fire his imagination.

As Mickey was turning away, intending to muscle

Vernon Klick's body into the long drop, a twist of blue light spiraled up the walls of the lava pipe, flashed through the open manhole, and corkscrewed to the ceiling, where it spread out across the concrete, crackling softly, and quickly dissipated.

Iris

Her room is safe. Other rooms in the apartment are less safe. The world beyond the apartment is dangerous, unbearable. So many people. Always changing. She wants to stay in her room.

Nothing changes in her room. Change is scary. She wants to be where change never happens. Her room. Her room.

But her mother calls her to the Bambi way. The Bambi way is to accept things as they are. To trust nature and to love the world.

Loving the world is so hard. Bambi believes the world loves him, was made for him. Iris does not believe the world loves her. She wants to believe it, but she doesn't, she can't.

She doesn't know why she can't. Not knowing why she can't love the world is as bad as not loving it. The world in books seems worth loving. But she can't love it. She fears it.

As a fawn, Bambi is often frightened. Of a ferret. Of blue jays. Of many things. He overcomes his fears. He is a very great and smart deer because he overcomes all his fear. Iris loves him for this. And envies him. But loves him very much.

She is afraid to love anyone but Bambi. Or afraid to show her love. She loves her mother but dares not show it. Loving people draws them close to you. She can't tolerate being close. She can't breathe with people close. The lightest touch is a blow. She can't tolerate being touched.

She doesn't know why. At night, alone in her bed, she sometimes tries to think why she is this way. Thinking about it only makes her cry. When she's alone in the dark, crying, she wishes that she lived in a book world, not this one.

She can love Bambi because he doesn't live in this world. He lives in the book world. A world apart, she can love him desperately and never be too close.

Now her mother calls her to the Bambi way, and Iris steels herself to leave the apartment. There's the boy, Winny, and the boy's mother, Twyla, and that's already bad enough, too many people. But now the four of them are going to leave the apartment, which means too many people *and* new places, change and more change.

Iris keeps her head down. Keeps her head down and pretends that she is Bambi. To live the Bambi way, it is better to try to be Bambi, to think like he would think.

Iris follows her mother into the hallway because Bambi follows his mother whenever she tells him that he must. They go around the corner to the back door of Twyla's apartment. Iris has been in the hallway before, but never in these people's apartment. So now all this is new. *Everything* is new. New is dangerous, hostile. Now everything is hostile. Everything, everything.

She must make it all familiar and friendly. She must be Bambi, and this must be the forest, for only then will she be both brave and safe. She tries to look directly only at her mother's back. She sees things from the corners of her eyes, of course, or when she inadvertently glances left or right, but she imagines those things to be what they are not, to be a part of her beloved forest.

Words come to Iris, memorized from so many readings of the precious book: *Round about grew hazel bushes, dogwoods, black-thorns and young elders. Tall maples, beeches and oaks wove a green roof over the thicket and from the firm dark-brown earth sprung fern fronds, wood-vetch and sage. . . .*

Her mother and Twyla talk to each other, and the boy talks to both of them, but Iris can't bear the weight of what they are saying to one another. What they are saying to one another is going to crush her if she listens to it. Crush, crush, crush her. *Exterminate,* they say. Exterminate means to kill.

Instead, Iris listens to the melody of the woods: *The whole forest resounded with myriad voices, was penetrated by them in a joyous agitation. The woodthrush rejoiced incessantly, the doves cooed without stopping, the blackbirds whistled, the tit-mice chirped. . . .*

They go out through the front door of the strange apartment, into another hallway, where Twyla rings a doorbell. There is a man they call Bailey and another man they call Dr. Ignis. There is yet another new place.

This is too much, the new just coming at her and coming at her, constant change, unbearable.

Desperate, Iris gives herself to the forest, which rises in her mind to embrace her as it always embraces Bambi: *Out of the earth came whole troops of flowers, like motley stars, so that the soil of the twilit forest floor shone with a silent, ardent, colorful gladness. . . .*

Martha Cupp

She wasn't sure which was worse: the unearthly thing that burst out of the sofa and then disappeared, leaving the fabric torn and the horsehair billowing—or Edna's I-told-you-so expression and her satisfaction that her belief in an invading demonic force seemed to have been substantiated by the bizarre incident. Well, on reflection, Edna's smug expression was by far the worse of the two, because if the beast in the chesterfield showed up again, Martha could always club it mercilessly, but she couldn't very well take a fireplace poker to her sister.

Still holding the train of her dinner gown off the floor, Edna said, "I'm sure that if Father Murphy had seen that nasty critter, he wouldn't care one whit if I believe in Bigfoot or ancient astronauts. He would break out the exorcised water, oil, salt—and begin the Prayer against Malefice immediately and at the top of his voice."

Martha knew that by continuing to hold the poker at the ready, she would appear to be conceding the point to her sister, but she was damn well *not* going to put it down, have a glass of warm milk, and go to bed. Even if Edna asked Father Murphy to perform an exorcism of place instead of an exorcism of person, and even if he agreed to do it, Martha would stand ready throughout the ritual to start swinging with that pleasingly heavy length of brass.

"What next?" Edna asked.

"What do you mean?"

"Besides calling Father Murphy," Edna said, "what should we do, what should we expect to happen, how should we prepare?"

"Maybe nothing more is going to happen."

"Something will happen," Edna said confidently, almost happily, as if an infestation of demons would be just the thing to combat the doldrums of a rainy December night.

Before Martha could reply, a bright flood of shimmering, crackling blue light washed across the floor. She seemed to be standing in an intensely luminous fog.

The poker reacted as if it were a divining rod and she were a dowser searching for underground water, almost tearing out of her grip. She held fast to it, but the poker jerked her arm down, and the tip of it pierced the eerie luminosity.

Simultaneously, the remaining fireplace tools and the rack that held them overturned on the hearth, didn't just topple into the light but *slammed* into it as if drawn by a tremendous power. The blueness receded from around Martha, shuddered across the room, seemed to suck the ornate fireplace screen into the firebox, and crackled away up the chimney, gone.

Sally Hollander

Lying on the kitchen floor, Sally felt the last of her bones succumb to the spreading cold. Now a skeleton of ice defined itself clearly in the warmth of her flesh. She had never previously been so consciously aware of her physiology. Although at the moment she remained paralyzed, she knew the position of each of her 206 bones, the precise shape of the various plates that were fused together to form her skull. She was conscious of the status of every joint: the ball-and-socket joints in shoulders and hips, the pivot joint in her neck between the second and third vertebrae, the elegant ellipsoidals in her wrists, the wonderfully functional hinges in her fingers and elbows and knees. Sally was able to feel the synovial membranes encapsulating her mobile joints and was vividly aware of the sticky, oozing synovial fluid that lubricated them. She sensed the fibers of every supporting ligament, the connecting tendons and the muscles poised to put the entire skeleton into motion on demand. It was as if her body had developed an acute self-awareness to match that of her mind.

Her fear had gone away as if whatever the demon had disgorged into her included, among other things, a tranquilizer. She had no apprehension anymore, no slightest misgiving. Her mood was one of calm anticipation, a meditative placidity, not apathy but a relieved submission to some inevitable transformation.

Having been a punching bag for her former husband, having worked up the courage to leave him and to obtain a divorce, she had found her self-respect more than twenty years ago, and she had since been too strong to submit that way to anyone. With a fortitude of which she was proud, she rejected apathy, embraced emotion and hope, and resigned herself to nothing—until now she resigned herself to *this* with an almost pleasant expectation.

Her skeletal structure began to surrender its integrity. She felt something moving *inside* her bones, as though her marrow had become animated, crawling this way and that in the cavities that contained it. She sensed that the bones in her legs and arms were gradually elongating. In her toes—and elsewhere—additional bones seemed to be forming. Something was happening in her joints, as well, and she felt cartilage reweaving itself to conform to the new reality of these junctions.

The words *werewolf* and *werecat* prowled her mind, but they did not raise her anxiety. Instead, the prospect of transformation was intriguing, and it inspired in her a tentative sense of possibility, a cautious willingness to wait and see, to consider that perhaps a change might be for the better. A part of her realized that this was not a natural reaction and must be, therefore, chemically induced. She supposed that as her body was being reprogrammed, so was her mind. But even that recognition did not alarm her, not even when she realized that her right hand, on the floor in front of her face where she could clearly see it, was growing longer. Each finger seemed to be adding one knuckle and one phalanx, bones squirming within the flesh, skin stretching and splitting and at once knitting up again.

Silas Kinsley

Taking refuge among the whirring ranks of the tall Multistack chillers, Silas watched Mickey Dime through a gap between two of the machines. Whatever had been piled on the hand truck and covered with a blanket was apparently destined to go into the manhole with the body of Vernon Klick.

Having spent his life in law offices and courtrooms, Silas had respect for the law and even a love for it in spite of politicians' determination to layer on ever more Byzantine statutes and in spite of the wretched purposes to which some people bent it. He was loath to let Dime dispose of the evidence in a capital crime. With no one certain of how far away the bottom of the lava pipe might be, with the possibility that it emptied into an underground lake or a river that would carry the corpse beyond discovery, it was likely that a city running a ruinous budget deficit in bad economic times would decline to mount an expensive and unpromising exploration deep into the earth. But Silas was an old man, feeling older by the day, armed but not confident that he retained any shooting skills. He was no match for Dime, who was half his age, fit, and evidently ruthless.

Besides, he remembered well the butler who, in 1935, killed the entire Ostock family and every member of the live-in staff before committing suicide to "save the world from eternal darkness," and he remembered the seemingly irrational character of Andrew Pendleton's journal so evident in the scraps that had survived the fire in which he meant to burn it. Whatever happened every thirty-eight years in this building, insanity might not be a consequence of the event but a part of it, a symptom of it. As he watched Dime open the manhole, he wondered if this man might be not an ordinary murderer who killed out of self-interest but instead the equivalent of the butler, Tolliver, perhaps driven mad by some toxin or occult energy.

No sooner had the words *occult energy* occurred to Silas than a radiant blue spiral of something shot out of the manhole, startling Dime, whirling to the ceiling like Independence Day fireworks, but then splashing across the concrete and dispersing. He would have said it was light, but light itself couldn't be shaped into spring form and sent corkscrewing through the air. Behind the first spiral came a second that was more substantial, brighter, and then a third.

With the third blue whirligig, the iron manhole appeared to tear loose of its hinges, shot to the ceiling, and clung there an instant, until the light purled away, whereupon the disc fell, rang against the concrete floor as loud as a cannon shot, bounced onto its edge, and rolled away like a giant coin.

Martha Cupp

When the ornate fireplace screen was crumpled and twisted like paper and sucked into the firebox by the blue light, Martha threw aside the poker and hurried to her bedroom, where she kept a more formidable weapon in her nightstand drawer. You couldn't shoot a magnetic field or whatever that blue light had been, but you could shoot any grotesque hateful squirming thing that ripped up your sofa *if it didn't vanish before you could squeeze off a damn shot*!

Iris

They want to stay together but they also want to go up to the third floor right away to see some women up there. Too many people already. Now there's going to be more.

One voice at a time is all right. Two is hard to listen to. Now there's five, and what they're saying is not even words to her anymore, half the time it's just buzzing, like wasps, like a swarm of wasps in the room, the words fluttering against her face like brittle wings, buzzing, buzzing, and at any moment the words might begin to sting her, sting and sting until she can't stand it anymore, until she starts screaming even though she doesn't want to, and if the screaming starts so might the hitting, though she hardly ever strikes out and doesn't want to strike out, never wants that.

She tries to block out the voices, tries to hear the sounds of the forest as the words in the book describe them: . . . *the pheasants cackled loud and high. The call of the falcon shrilled, light and piercing, over the tree-tops, and the hoarse crow chorus was heard continuously.*

Animal sounds are all right. Animal voices don't want anything from you, they don't ask you to do anything, they don't even expect you to answer them. Animal voices are soothing, and so are the sounds that the forest itself makes.

. . . *the falling leaves whispered among the trees. They fluttered and rustled ceaselessly through the air from all the tree-tops and branches. A delicate silvery sound was falling constantly to earth. It was wonderful to awaken amidst it, wonderful to fall asleep to this mysterious and melancholy whispering.*

Under the animal sounds and the whisper of the leaves, her mother's voice comes to Iris through the protective forest that she has imagined around herself, calls her again to the Bambi way. For the love of that deer who lives a world apart from her, in the book world, and for the love of her mother, which she can never express, Iris keeps her head down and goes with the herd. They walk and climb and walk again, and there is a door, beyond the door a new place, and two old women with voices so nice that she dares to glance at them.

One of them has a gun.

Iris at once retreats again behind the foliage in her mind, to a moment in the earliest days of the fawn's life, when Bambi was horrified to see a ferret kill a mouse:

Finally Bambi asked anxiously, "Shall we kill a mouse, too, sometime?"

"No," replied his mother.

"Never?" asked Bambi.

"Never," came the answer.

"Why not?" asked Bambi, relieved.

"Because we never kill anything," said his mother simply.

Bambi grew happy again.

Silas Kinsley

Instead of a fourth spiral of blue light, a great rushing brilliance poured from the open manhole: *whoooöosh.* Saturated with intense color, this was not a steady transparent beam like ordinary light, but translucent and churning with visible currents. It swarmed upward less like light than like water might gush from a broken main under extreme pressure. The radiance blued everything in the room, concrete and chillers, pipes and boilers, Mickey Dime's face and hands and white shirt, and even tinted the shadows sapphire. As the manhole had torn off its hinges, so Silas's watch vibrated on his wrist, the belt buckle against his abdomen, and the guard's pistol in a raincoat pocket thumped against his thigh. The heavy machines and boilers were anchored to the floor, but the metal housings creaked, twanged, as though they might pop their welds and rivets.

The rushing radiance lasted ten seconds. Maybe fifteen. But when it winked out, its effects lingered or perhaps increased. Immediately with the extinguishing of the blue brilliance, a sound issued from within the thick walls, an eerie high-pitched resonance, continuously modulating like the shrieky whistle of interference on a shortwave radio, as though the intricate web of steel rebar encased in the concrete might be transmitting the blue energy in a form other than light to every corner of the building.

As if that keening called it forth, the rumbling rose beneath the Pendleton. The more shrill the sound grew within the walls, the deeper notes the rumbling struck, until the two swelled to their fullest at the same moment, whereupon everything changed.

Mickey Dime

Before his eyes, everything shimmered as if waves of intense heat were rising through the vault, but he felt no heat. The rows of machinery blurred. They appeared to ripple. The room seemed to be a mirage. He thought it might vanish just as a phantom oasis melted away from a thirsty traveler in the Sahara.

The racks of chain-hung fluorescent bulbs overhead went dark. Weaker yellow light, provided by irregularly placed and curiously shaped fixtures—not one like another—that had not been there a moment earlier, gave the vault a different and disturbing character. The shadows were more numerous, deeper, and sinister.

The machinery stood silent. The rounded masses of the boilers and the boxy chillers were sheathed in dust. Across the dirty floor lay a litter of fallen and broken fluorescent tubes, scraps of paper, rusting tools. Snarls of fur, scattered small bones, as well as intact skeletons of rats suggested that vermin had thrived here for a while, but not now.

The air felt cool, although not as cold as it should have been with no heat on a December night. Mickey smelled mold, damp concrete, an elusive rancid odor that came and went.

The manhole cover lay in its proper place, as if it had never exploded to the ceiling. Dull-red with rust and dust. The surrounding rubber gasket was cracked, crumbling.

Klick the Prick had vanished. The blanket and furniture straps that wrapped the body were gone.

Dead Jerry also gone. His little brother. Gone.

And the hand truck.

Gone.

Mickey's mother had known everything. If this had happened to her, she would already have a theory to explain it.

No theories occurred to Mickey. He stood dumbstruck. Closed his eyes. Opened them. The room remained inexplicably changed.

He needed some aromatherapy to clear his mind.

He needed some time in the sauna.

He felt stupid. He had never before felt stupid.

His mother said stupidity should be a capital offense, except with so many stupid people everywhere you looked, there wouldn't be enough steel in the world to build all the necessary guillotine blades or enough executioners to operate them.

He missed his mother. More than ever. He felt the loss of her. More than ever. Acutely.

Twyla Trahern

They were in the Cupp apartment, sharing their recent uncanny experiences, when it happened. It was like yet different from how the wall in Winny's room rippled away to be replaced by a vision of abandonment and decay. An electronic keening seemed to come out of the bones of the building itself, and the ground under the Pendleton rumbled as it had done earlier. Twyla pulled Winny close when all around them the spacious living room blurred as if she were looking at it through rain-washed glass. The Victorian furniture, the fine stained-glass lamps, the classical busts on pedestals, the art and the ferns and the carpet all lost their sharp edges and details, seemed to be melting away. Only the people remained clear in an increasingly impressionistic scene, as if the room had been painted by Monet, the people by Rembrandt.

At the peak of this phenomenon, when the Cupp living room was little more than a colorful smear and the people were, by contrast, hyperrealistic, the experience became disorienting. Claustrophobia smothered Twyla, as if the space in which they stood were but a membrane collapsing around them, a plastic film in which they were being bundled and shrink-wrapped, but simultaneously she was also overcome by agoraphobia, equally certain that the Pendleton and the world itself would dissolve and plunge them into a lightless void. She saw Martha Cupp standing resolute, chin thrust forward, like some aging Joan of Arc seasoned by battlefields and faith, evidence of her fear confined to her eyes, the wide pupils like reflections of gun muzzles. Edna Cupp's mouth was open not in a cry of alarm but in that *ahhhh* of wonder seen on children's faces Christmas morning, her eyes shining with anticipation, as though throughout her life no thought of vulnerability had ever crossed her mind. Bailey tall and stalwart, eyes narrowed, seemed to regard the melting away of the room less with fear or wonder than with wary calculation, alert for the threat that would surely manifest at any moment. Dr. Ignis's sweet face seemed incapable of masking his thoughts, and his fear was as evident as his amazement, his intellect perhaps for the first time overwhelmed by awe. Sparkle's expression seemed to say *here we go again,* as though she must be long accustomed to such shocks, and Iris stood slump-shouldered, head bowed, hands over her ears to muffle the high-pitched electronic squealing. Twyla held fast to Winny not only for fear of losing him, but also as much because she needed him for support: Since his birth, he had been her still point in this dizzily turning world, the thing that made life's struggles worthwhile, the one thing that convinced her that she had not wasted years of her life and had not debased herself by marrying Farrel Barnett.

The squealing in the walls and the rumbling crescendoed at the same instant. Silence fell as if commanded by the sharp downstroke of an orchestra conductor's baton. The surrounding smear at once resolved into a new reality.

Without lamps, the two crystal ceiling fixtures, and the cove lighting, the room was more dimly illuminated than before, but it wasn't dark. Flanking doorways, the fireplace, and the windows were bronze wall sconces that had not been here a moment earlier, twelve of them in all, seven of which were aglow.

The furnishings were gone. The room lay empty but worse than empty—cheerless, desolate. The floral-pattern fabric covering the walls had been replaced—but not recently—by wallpaper that wouldn't have coordinated with the sisters' decor; it was yellowed with age, water-stained, mottled with mold, peeling. In several places, dry rot had turned the mahogany flooring to dust, revealing the concrete beneath.

For a moment, they all stood speechless, rendered mute by the impossibility of what had happened. Perhaps the others, like Twyla, anticipated another imminent change, this time back to the way things had been less than a minute previously.

Dr. Ignis was the first to speak, pointing toward the windows, which were no longer flanked by draperies, no longer washed by rain on this suddenly clear night. *"The city!"*

Twyla looked, saw only night where there should have been a sea of lights, and assumed that a power failure must have struck the metropolis, leaving the Pendleton to rely on its emergency generator. But something about the darkness was not right, and the others must have sensed it, too, because they all moved to the windows along with her and Winny.

The pale fire of the full moon should have revealed the ghost of a skyline, should have silvered some windows and sifted a faux dust on sills, ledges, gargoyles, and on the cross that topped the cathedral spire. The city wasn't just afflicted by a black-out. The city was gone.

Witness

He was standing at the western-parapet balustrade when the steel bones and tendons of the building began to sing, which indicated that the fluctuations were soon to give way to the transition. One moment he stood in the rain and looked out upon the glowing city, the next moment in a cloudless night under a fat moon with the luminous pale-green meadow below, but then the rain and the great city once more, and then the world without cities, back and forth, as this moment in the past prepared to fling the residents of the Pendleton into the future and as a certain moment of the future attracted them with an inevitability equal to that of a black hole swallowing worlds.

The city vanished and did not return. The rain stopped, the sky cleared in that instant, the moon looked as cold as a ball of ice, and the building stood silent on Shadow Hill, overlooking the plain of hungry grass that undulated rhythmically although the night was windless. Witness was home. The strangers in the rooms below him were far from home and would remain here until the fluctuations began again and the entire mysterious process repeated, returning them to their time. Not all of them would make it home. Perhaps none of them.

One

Now the most important of all transitions has occurred. During the next ninety minutes, history will pivot toward me forever and ensure my dominion. I must allow no other outcome, and the path to triumph is clear. I exist here, and my existence is inevitable. All who have previously come to me have perished here or upon returning to their own time. Of these people who would dare to thwart me, all will die.

I cannot die. I am immortal.

In your wisdom, you understand my inevitability. The world cannot go on as it always has, infested with humanity and corrupted until it becomes a barren ball of rock. Send to me your tired, your poor, your huddled masses yearning to breathe free, and I will make of them the fodder and the seed bed of a new and better world.

PART TWO

Something Deeply Hidden

Something deeply hidden
has to be behind things.

—ALBERT EINSTEIN

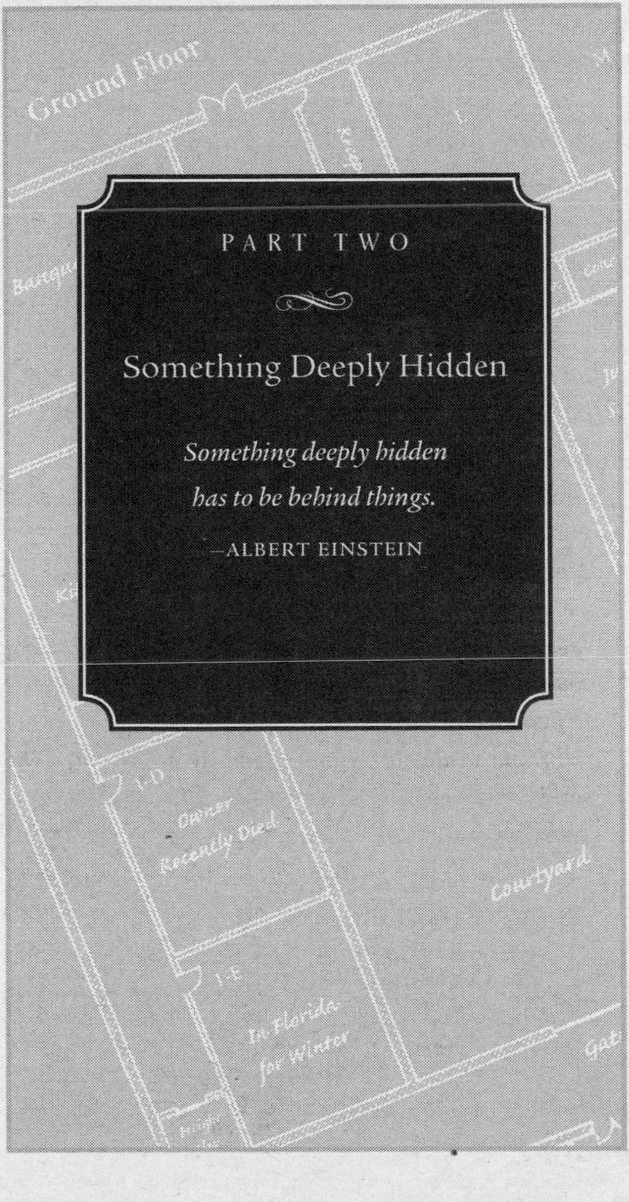

25

Topper's

Mac and Shelly Reeves had a window table in the restaurant, with a view of Shadow Street, where silver rain slashed through headlights and where stoop-shouldered pedestrians in foul-weather gear hurried past under bobbing umbrellas.

A bottle of good Cabernet Sauvignon, candlelight, and the high backs on their booth contributed to a romantic ambiance, and Shelly still daily stirred desire in Mac after twenty-two years of marriage. More important, as the years passed, his feelings for her became ever more tender, the physical aspect of love ever less important than the emotional side of it, though he didn't anticipate that they would take a vow of celibacy together. And intellectually, they had always been an ideal match.

A booth at Topper's was also a favorite place for them because it provided privacy, and both the staff and the clientele treated them like anyone else, not like celebrities. For over twenty years, their morning program, *Mac and Shelly's Breakfast Club*, enjoyed by far the highest local-radio ratings during the 6:00 to 9:00 A.M. time slot. In a city with a smaller black population than some, their success in a vanilla format like a breakfast club made them even more recognizable.

Having recently been lured to a different station with a promise of tri-state syndication, they were currently in a three-week hiatus before launching their new program, which would be their old program, with the same Mac-and-Shelly shtick that was as much a part of their relationship off the air as on. For all these years, they had gotten up five days a week at 4:00 A.M. and had returned to bed at eight in the evening. During this break, however, they had gone wild—"Almost feral, dangerously close to the point where we might not be able to find our way back to civilization," Mac had declared— staying up until ten, sometimes even to midnight, sleeping in until six, once even as late as ten past seven.

They were newcomers to the Pendleton, having purchased Apartment 3-G only ten months earlier. This evening, the comparative privacy of a booth at Topper's was especially welcome because, as it turned out, their conversation drifted early to a discussion of their neighbors in that grand old residence.

The subject came up because, just as the maitre d' said he would show them to their table, they had glimpsed Silas Kinsley and another man at the farther end of the foyer, donning their coats to brave the storm. Silas's firm specialized in civil litigation, but until his retirement four years earlier, he had been their personal attorney. They loved Nora and missed her, as everyone did, and it was the occasional dinner at the Kinsley apartment that over the years convinced them to sell their home in the Oak Grove District and move here to Shadow Hill, in the true heart of the city.

Although seeing Silas had prompted them to wax on about some of their neighbors, they spent little time talking about him because he didn't inspire gossip. Silas's qualities were all endearing, and his sole eccentricity was an obsession with the history of the Pendleton, which seemed normal and harmless when compared to, say, the interests of their next-door neighbor, Fielding Udell. Just between themselves, Shelly and Mac called Udell Chicken Little or Chick for short.

She said, "I step out the front door this morning to get the paper, and Chick is there in the hall, picking up his usual humongous pile of publications. The delivery guy must love old Chick, a few more years and he'll have put away a handsome retirement from that one account. So before I can grab our paper and duck back inside, Chick asks do I know what's happening to the lousewort."

"Did you fake a hearing-aid problem?"

"I don't think I'll try that one again. He knows we're in radio, we need to have good hearing for that."

"Sudden debilitating heart arrhythmia."

"That's your excuse. He's not going to believe *both* of us have heart disease as young as we are."

"So do you *know* what's happening to the lousewort?"

"I said I've known a couple of louses but neither of them had warts."

"You are my favorite wife. Then what did he say?"

"He said all kinds of louseworts are headed for extinction, and the consequences are catastrophic."

"They always are. What is a lousewort, anyway?"

"Turns out it's a plant. All kinds of grazing animals like it."

"Cows?"

"Cows, sheep, goats, Bigfoot for all I know."

"Is Bigfoot a grazing animal?"

"Well, he's an omnivore, so he chows down on anything he wants—lousewort, cats, small children."

"I have a theory about Bigfoot," Mac said. "I know it's highly controversial—but my theory is he doesn't exist."

"Radical. That'll get you a full three hours on the weekend edition of *Coast to Coast AM* with Ian Punnett."

"So what catastrophe exactly?"

"Seems that certain grasses thrive only in the vigorous presence of lousewort, and other grasses only thrive in an environment that includes pollen from *those* grasses. I may have that all wrong, since I was preoccupied at the time with thoughts of homicide. But the end-all is some kind of biological chain-reaction that results in the extinction of thousands of varieties of grass."

"What are we going to use for lawns?"

"We don't have a lawn in our apartment."

"Don't just think of yourself. What about suburbia?"

"If they don't have to mow the lawn," Shelly said, "they have more time to listen to radio. See here, I don't believe you're extrapolating from the lousewort to the big picture."

"I assume Chick extrapolated for you."

"He very kindly did. If we lose the grasses, we lose all the grazing animals. That means we lose our primary sources of meat, milk, cheese, wool, leather, bone meal, and antler racks to hang above hunting-lodge fireplaces. Famine ensues. And bad shoes."

After a pause for wine, Mac said, "I saw Mickey Dime today in Butterworth's."

"That's never going to sound like a men's clothing store to me."

"They were having a necktie sale."

"Sounds like a waffle syrup."

"Racks and racks of ties. I saw Dime, but he didn't see me."

Shelly said, "Baby, it's uncanny how still you are when you're pretending to be a mannequin."

"He's interested in the silk ties. But first he takes a moist towelette from a foil packet and washes his hands."

With the snap of a forefinger, she pinged her wineglass for emphasis: "Just like *I* saw him do in the fresh-fruit aisle of Whole Foods. Did he also sniff the towelette?"

"Nearly inhaled it. Made me wonder if it was a cocaine-infused moist towelette."

"The man *does* love the fragrance of those moist towelettes."

"Once his hands are clean, he starts fingering the silk ties."

"Fingering?"

Mac gave her a demonstration with his cloth napkin.

Fanning herself with the wine list as if just watching this performance inflamed her libido, Shelly said, "He's a spooky dude."

"He smelled some of them."

"Smelled the ties? Tell me he didn't lick them, too."

"He didn't. Maybe he wanted to. He was *into* those silk ties."

"How long did this go on?"

"I watched maybe five minutes. But then I left. I didn't want to be there for the climax."

After the waitress stopped by to tell them the chef's specials, Shelly said, "With a mother like his, poor Dime didn't stand a chance of turning out normal."

"Well, to be fair, we only met her once." Speaking ill of the dead always made Mac uncomfortable. "She might've been having an off day."

"Renata Dime told me she was immortal."

"She died just the same."

"I'll bet it came as a surprise to her."

"She meant immortal through her books," Mac said. "We both tried to read one, remember?"

He sighed. "It made my eyes bleed."

Outside, a siren rose, and drivers curbed their vehicles where they could to facilitate the passage of a police patrol with its roof rack of emergency beacons swiveling blue-red-blue-red. As the cop car raced down Shadow Street, Mac Reeves looked past it, to the Pendleton at the summit. Although the police cruiser was neither coming from nor going to that grand old mansion, the place did not look the same to Mac, not as stately as it usually appeared, not as welcoming, and in fact inexplicably ominous. A sense of foreboding overcame him, and he shivered.

As observant as ever, Shelly said, "What's wrong?"

"Nothing. I don't know. Maybe talking about Renata Dime put me off my mood."

"Then we won't talk about her anymore."

26

Here and There

Mickey Dime

He didn't know what had happened to the bodies. He didn't know why the HVAC vault had changed. He didn't know what to do next.

Finally he decided that he should go back to his apartment. The photographs of his mother, her furnishings, the things that she loved would bring him as close as he could get to her. Her belongings, her memory, would inspire him. Then he would know what to do.

And if that didn't work, maybe the time had come for Sparkle and Iris. He felt rejected, after all, as he'd felt when the cocktail waitress humiliated him fifteen years earlier. Now the *world* was rejecting him. He had felt small and stupid when she dissed him, but so much better when he took what he wanted from her, her sister, and her girlfriend; his sense of self and well-being was sensationally restored.

When he stepped out of the vault, the basement corridor proved to be as changed as the room behind him.

Filthy, littered. Half the ceiling lights dark and broken. Spongy-looking growths on the walls and ceiling, some black, others glowing yellow. The air smelled bad, nothing like the essence of lime or silk lingerie.

Disoriented, he turned right, away from the north elevator that he needed. Fragments of fluorescent lightbulbs crunched underfoot. His footsteps seemed to stir a foul, astringent odor from the litter on the floor.

Past the security room, past the superintendent's apartment, a small TV hung in the corner, near the ceiling. Concentric circles of blue light pulsed outward from the center of the screen. After Mickey had taken eight or ten steps, some kind of robot voice came from the TV: *"Adult male. Brown hair. Brown eyes. Basement. West wing. Exterminate. Exterminate."*

This was too much. The Pendleton fell to ruin in the wink of an eye. Dead Jerry and Klick the Prick disappeared. Nothing was the way it should be. And now some wiseguy was putting out a hit on him. Well, it didn't work that way. Mickey killed, he didn't get killed.

The strong act, the weak react. Mickey acted, drawing his pistol and blowing out the blue screen with a single shot.

He felt better, still confused but not completely disoriented. He realized he had gone the wrong direction.

Before turning back, he decided to have a look in the security room. He didn't know how Vernon Klick's body could have gotten back there from the HVAC vault, but it went *somewhere*, and this was as likely a place to look as any.

When he opened the door, he found the security room as changed as anything else, though not transformed in a similar way. Except for a thin layer of dust on the floor, the room was clean. The lights all worked. The coffee center and the under-the-counter refrigerator were gone. So were the chairs and the workstation. The walls were lined with computers, video screens, and racks of electronic devices that Mickey couldn't identify, which sure as hell couldn't have been installed in the short time since he had previously been here.

The equipment hummed, ticked, and blinked busily, as if the system took care of itself and didn't need losers like Vernon Klick and Logan Spangler to monitor it. The guard's corpse wasn't there. Neither was the gun belt that Mickey had left with the intention of retrieving it later.

In the film of dust on the floor were flurries of footprints, all apparently left by the same pair of shoes.

Mickey didn't know what to make of any of this. He wasn't a police detective. He was the guy that homicide dicks tried and failed to track down. He knew how to avoid leaving evidence, but he didn't have a clue how to connect pieces of evidence to solve a puzzle.

He didn't want to learn, either. He didn't want to change who he was. He loved who he was. He *adored* who he was.

If new facts seemed to upend your philosophy, you didn't change what you believed. Only the weak changed their beliefs. The strong changed the facts. His mother said the best and the brightest didn't alter their beliefs to conform to reality. They altered reality to conform to their beliefs. History's greatest political visionaries just spent more and more money, exerted ever greater control over the educational system and the media, eliminated more and more dissidents as became necessary, until they molded society to fit their theory of an ideal civilization. Fools get eaten by reality. The wise put a choke collar and a leash on reality, and they make it heel.

Every time that he had heard his mom say those things, Mickey had been energized, thrilled. But now reality had done a sudden one-eighty on him; and he realized that he didn't know how to get it back under control. His mom would have known. She had known everything. But though she had instructed Mickey how to think about reality, she hadn't taught him anything about how to collar and leash-train it. Right now, reality seemed as slippery as a greased eel.

Once he was back in his own digs, with all his mom's stuff around him, maybe he'd start to get his mind straight about this. Maybe she *had* taught him everything he needed to do to cope in a situation like this, not just the general principles of how to think about reality but also the specific techniques for controlling it. Surely she *had* taught him all that. He'd simply forgotten. Surrounded by mementoes of her, this confusion would dissipate, her wisdom would be recalled, and he would again be as a god.

He left the security room and walked the long creepily lighted corridor, past the HVAC vault. As he approached the north elevator, another pulsing blue screen issued the same threat as the one he had shot. He shot this one, too.

When the elevator responded to the call button and the doors slid open, it wasn't the car with which he was familiar. The bird mural was gone. The interior surfaces were all stainless steel, and panels in the ceiling shed a cold blue light. He didn't like the new reality of the elevator. He didn't like it at all.

He decided to take the stairs to the third floor.

Silas Kinsley

In the acid-yellow light, he remained in the shadows among the chillers, expecting the murderer to return. Through the open door came a loud, possibly computerized voice describing Dime, specifying his location, and seeming to call for his extermination, a sentiment with which Silas could concur. Then a gunshot.

He didn't know if someone had shot Mickey Dime or if Dime had gunned down someone else. Reluctant to step from cover until he had a better grasp of the situation, he drew Vernon Klick's pistol from a pocket of his raincoat and stood motionless, listening.

The changes in the vault didn't surprise Silas. Previously he had reached the startling but inescapable conclusion that something went wrong with time in this building every thirty-eight years. By the evidence of filth and ruin around him, he inferred that he was no longer in the Pendleton of 2011 but in a future Pendleton of an unknown year, though he had no idea how long he would be here.

He was less disturbed by the changes than by the atmosphere in the room, which was worse than merely unwholesome. In their day, he and Nora traveled to some exotic locations, and the quality of this sour-yellow light reminded him of the smoky glow rising from granite bowls full of low-burning tallow, in a jungle-draped temple where the towering stone god smiled but not benignly and where the altar was stained with the blood of generations from before it became a tourist mecca. The shadows were sulfur-black, and they struck him as being not an absence of light but crouched forms, alive and hostile and waiting for their moment. The irregular radiant shapes weren't only on walls and ceiling, like an archipelago of atomic-test islands, but also on some of the machinery. Squinting, he was able to see through the nearest patch of luminosity to its source, which seemed to be a colony of minute light-emitting fungi. The malodors of mold, damp concrete, scaling rust, rancid grease, and a faint vileness that might have been desiccated flesh hung on the air. If evil didn't already lie in wait here, the vault certainly welcomed its coming.

From the hallway beyond the open door, a computer voice again described Mickey Dime and announced his location. It might also have called for his extermination, as before, but another shot rang out, followed by silence.

Cautiously, Silas moved through the forest of machines and into the clearing at the center of which lay the manhole. The wrapped body of the guard and the hand truck with its burden were gone, which must mean that they had not made the leap from the Pendleton of 2011 to this later version of the building.

He had seen the iron cover explode off the manhole and to the ceiling, then fall and roll away into the gloom, as if the Fates were reluctant to call heads or tails, yet now the disc was in place. He supposed the hole remained uncovered in 2011, where that event had occurred. Between then and now, repairs must have been made to the hinges.

Still holding the pistol in his right hand, with his left he flipped up the ring-grip from its niche and pulled the heavy rusted cover aside. The gasket had deteriorated. Chunks of crumbling rubber fell away into the darkness below.

Rising from the lava pipe, something fluttered against his face, and he recoiled before he realized that it was nothing alive, nothing of substance. No draft would wash across him in such tight rhythmic waves; therefore, it must be pulses of some energy, perhaps a weak lingering residue of the great rushing blueness that had gushed out of the hole earlier. Far down in the shaft, scattered snakes of blue light formed, wriggled around the curving surface, were extinguished, and new ones were born. As the energy fluttered against him, he felt his belt buckle hum against his abdomen, and in his shirt pocket, his metal-rimmed reading glasses twitched feebly.

If part of the explanation for this event involved a magnetic field, he supposed that the lava pipe must be the upper section of a complicated transmission line leading all the way down to the very magnetic core of the earth itself. But he could not begin to imagine why only living creatures and their immediate possessions were flung forward in time, though that was evidently the case.

However it happened, they weren't stranded here. Andrew North Pendleton had made it home again to his time, even if his wife and children did not. Of the nine members of the Ostock family and the seven members of their household staff who had been brought to this future, five of the former and three of the latter had returned to 1935 after their ordeal here—although only to be murdered by the butler, Nolan Tolliver.

With his left hand, he fished from a pocket the small flashlight that he had taken from the guard's utility belt in the security room, before the change. He intended to make his way upstairs, where other residents must be reeling from the shock of what had happened. The history that he would share might give them a little hope if nothing else: *We will go home again, those of us who live until the event reverses itself.* A little hope but not a certainty.

The crisp beam of the LED flashlight revealed scattered bones and skulls—and a few complete skeletons—

of rats. They were white hieroglyphics on the gray floor, symbols awaiting translation.

Perhaps the pistol gave Silas a foolish kind of courage, but when intuition told him there was something important to discover here before he went upstairs, he hesitated only briefly before moving away from the door to the hall. Without all the facts, you couldn't win in a courtroom, and in this case, his life and those of all his neighbors were on trial.

He stepped carefully to avoid crushing the rat bones underfoot, proceeding deeper into the enormous room, playing the light across the hulking machines. When the beam touched a formation of luminous fungi, the colony throbbed more brightly for a moment, and there was a sensuous quality to its response, as if it took pleasure from the contact or perhaps knew pain.

Sparkle Sykes

Standing at the windows of the Cupps' living room, watching the plain of luminous pale-green grass sway in the moonlight as if timing its changes of direction to a lazy metronome, listening to the urgent conversation of the others, Sparkle felt that she would get through this alive, that however she was meant to die, this was not the night or the place.

If some power so colossal as to change reality could bring them here, wherever *here* might be, then it could take them back again to where they had begun, to where they belonged. Life-changing lightning of the figurative kind could strike in series, just like the real father-killing, mother-killing kind.

A sense of the uncanny prickled the nape of her neck, but that was a reaction to the deep strangeness of the scene, not a symptom of fear. She had no fear for herself. Her life had been so shot through with bolts of fate that of necessity she long ago resigned herself to destiny, controlling what she could and refusing to worry about the rest. She had allowed herself to be afraid only of the lightning that killed her father and her mother, and now even that terror was behind her. If suddenly they found themselves in the lovely Pendleton as it ought to be, with a fierce storm raging over the city, she would go downstairs and into the courtyard, to stand gazing up calmly and with complete trust at the sky, confident that however she might be meant to meet her death, it would not take her until the moment that, from her birth, it had been ordained to do so.

Professor Talman Ringhals, mescaline poisoning, Iris, and other metaphorical lightning strikes blazed new paths through life for Sparkle, and this bizarre event was just the latest. She accepted it quicker than did her neighbors because for some months she had felt that she was overdue for another bolt.

Nearly thirteen years earlier, when she found herself pregnant with Iris, her small inheritance no longer was sufficient to pay both living expenses and tuition. She dropped out of college, intending to get a job as a receptionist or clerk. Although she had never before bought a lottery ticket, she purchased two on the same day, and the second one paid her $245,000 only one week later. After taxes, her nest egg was enough to carry her for four or five years, even with the special care that Iris required; therefore, she decided not to return to the university, but instead embarked upon the work that she had hoped to pursue since shortly after she was orphaned on that stormy day in Maine.

Three years after the lottery, a new kind of lightning struck Sparkle when her work was spectacularly rewarded, whereupon she decided that this world was a place of deep mystery and enchantment, with occasional episodes of terror to give it texture. Death was merely the price of admission, cheap if you considered all that it bought you. Fearing death meant also fearing life, which stole all meaning from the act of living.

Until the improbable event this evening, she allowed herself the fear of lightning because she felt that to have no fear for oneself would be to tempt the Fates and invite calamity. Now, with no fear of anything, she was left only with fear *for* Iris, because the girl seemed to be a lightning rod upon which the Fates focused when they were in a bad mood. Losing her daughter might be the bolt that killed Sparkle, too, because she found it difficult to imagine how she could still be enchanted by the world if this difficult but most innocent girl was taken from her.

Iris stood apart from her mother, back to the windows, and the boy, Winny, stayed near her but at just enough distance to make it clear that he understood her need to maintain a certain personal space, a defense line against the world. Winny had a quality that Sparkle could not quite define, a winsomeness that would one day outlast his shyness.

With apparent effort, the boy even contributed to the group discussion, mentioning the parallel universes that he read about in some of his favorite novels, other Earths existing side by side with our own, some of them only slightly altered from ours, but others radically different.

Sparkle didn't read novels of that kind. But for a few decades, fantasy fiction, in books and films, had so dominated the culture that it was impossible not to be somewhat familiar with the fantastic concepts that her neighbors now raised for consideration, one after the other. They talked urgently, interrupting one another until she was reminded of a Star Trek club meeting that she had chanced upon one evening in college, where the true nature of Klingons—or some topic equally profound—was being debated with such passion and in such quasi-scientific language that the two dozen participants sounded only *half* mad.

Hugging herself to ward off a chill that was internal, Sparkle turned from the windows and from the eerie meadows beyond, facing her neighbors. Except for the two children, who remained to one side, the others—Dr. Kirby Ignis, Bailey, Twyla, and the sisters Cupp—stood in a circle. They had no furniture on which to sit, and the wood floor was splintered, dirty, encrusted here and there with foul-looking mold.

Dr. Ignis, whom Sparkle didn't know well, took control by virtue of his grandfatherly demeanor, which was calming, also by asserting that parallel worlds were theoretical and, in his opinion, highly problematic. He said, "The concept arose in the first place as a kind of desperate explanation of why our universe is meticulously ordered to make life inevitable."

"Why would anyone need an explanation?" Edna Cupp asked. "What is simply is."

"Yes, but you see, there are twenty universal constants from Planck's minimums of time and space to gravitational fine structure, and if any *one* of them was the very slightest bit different from what it is, the universe would be a wildly disordered place incapable of forming galaxies, solar systems, or planets, incapable of supporting any kind of life. The odds of the universe being as hospitable as ours is . . . well, it's impossible, quadrillions of trillions to one."

"What is . . . *is*," Edna repeated.

"Yes, but the highly specific nature of these constants implies design, in fact insists upon it. Science cannot, will not, tolerate the concept of a designer of the universe."

"I tolerate it well enough," Edna declared.

"My point is," Ignis continued, "the likelihood of all twenty universal constants being what they are is so small that to explain our life-supporting universe without resorting to a designer, some physicists have supposed that there must be an infinite number of universes, not merely ours. If among trillions and trillions and trillions of universes there is one—our own—with those twenty constants precisely set to support order and life, then it's likely that we're the product of chance rather than of a designer."

With one dismissive gesture, Ignis swatted away that theory as he might swat away an annoying fly, and he continued, "Whatever you care to believe, it's a waste of time thinking that we might have been transported to some parallel world. This is *our* universe, *our* Earth, at some point in the far future. The things some of you have seen, the alien landscape we've *all* seen beyond those windows, are either the products of hundreds of thousands of years of evolution or they result from some unimaginably catastrophic event that brought worldwide change in but several centuries."

"*This* Pendleton is in regrettable condition," Martha Cupp said, "but it hasn't been here even for several centuries, certainly not for hundreds of thousands of years."

"The city is gone," Ignis reminded her. "A metropolis doesn't collapse, crumble, and give way to grassland in mere decades."

"Why *is* the Pendleton still standing—and nothing else?" Bailey Hawks asked. He indicated the seven of the twelve bronze sconces that had evidently been installed after the Cupps' apartment was sold to a new owner and that still produced light. "Where does the power come from? And why would those bulbs work after centuries? Are there any people left in this future? If so, where are they? If there aren't any people . . . who generates the electricity?"

They looked at one another, but no one offered a theory.

Then Twyla said, "We aren't here permanently, are we? We can't be. There's got to be a way home."

"The door to home won't be one we can open at will," Dr. Ignis said. "Any more than we opened the one that brought us here. It'll do what it'll do when the conditions are right."

"What conditions?" Twyla asked.

Dr. Ignis shook his head. "I don't know."

Twyla said, "And why did only people make this . . . this leap?"

"People and cats," Edna said as two handsome blue-gray felines warily entered from another room. She scooped one of them into her arms, but her sister didn't want to put down her pistol to cuddle the other, so it let Dr. Ignis pluck it off the floor.

"Cats and people," Twyla said. "And anything we were wearing or carrying. But nothing else."

"Every living thing emits a weak direct-current electromagnetic field," Dr. Ignis said. "Maybe that has something to do with it. Whatever's immediately within a living thing's electromagnetic field might be affected."

"People have disappeared from the Pendleton before," Martha Cupp declared. "Andrew Pendleton's children, back in the late 1890s."

"Weren't they kidnapped?" Sparkle asked.

Martha said, "The wife *and* the two children. Kidnapping was the story, but they were never seen again.

Disappeared. I don't know the details. Silas Kinsley. He lives next door. He's the self-appointed historian of the Pendleton. He said something once about violence occurring here every . . . I think it was every thirty-eight years. It sounded very tacky tabloid to me, and I didn't encourage him. I think now we better talk to Silas."

Dr. Ignis said, "We're going to have to explore, learn what we can. The less we understand our situation"—he glanced at the children—"the less we're likely to come through this as well as we'd like."

"Sally," Edna Cupp said. "Sally Hollander. She really saw what she said she saw in the pantry. She's alone down on the ground floor. We've got to get her."

"We will," Bailey said. "We should search the building floor-by-floor, find out who else is here. Maybe there's not safety in numbers, but there's at least the *feeling* of safety."

Padmini Bahrati

Just before the world went away, Padmini was sitting on a stool behind the reception counter, taking a break, eating some of her *mausi*'s homemade *uttapam*, a rice-and-lentil dish. She wondered how her aunt could be such a far better cook than her mother, considering that they were sisters trained by their mother in the same kitchen. To Mausi Anupama, food was like paint and canvas to an artist, but to Padmini's mother, Subhadra, food was a necessity and the preparation of it was often an annoying distraction.

Subhadra was a mathematician and a famous one, to the extent that mathematicians were ever famous. There were no *American Idol*s on TV celebrating math whizzes instead of singers, and mathematicians were never surrounded by squads of bodyguards and rushed through screaming crowds of fans to limousines. In no danger of being famous, Anupama happily experimented with food, seeking to devise new and better dishes. Subhadra regarded a recipe as a structural engineer regarded the specs for building a bridge, with a sober recognition that one small mistake could lead to a fatal collapse; she measured each ingredient precisely, followed each instruction as literally as might be humanly possible, but even when she used Anupama's recipes, Subhadra produced an edible though unexciting dinner. On the other hand, Anupama couldn't balance a checkbook, and Subhadra had ten honorary doctorates in mathematics in addition to the one she had earned.

The lesson that Padmini took from the successful lives of Mausi Anupama and her mother was that, whatever you did, you must do it with passion and total commitment. Padmini was twenty-one, in her first job, after earning a degree in hotel management. She intended to spend two years at the Pendleton, move on to be concierge at a luxury hotel, work her way up to general manager, and one day own a significant hotel of her own. She liked people, she enjoyed solving problems for them and making them happy, and she was good at both math and cooking.

Sanjay, her boyfriend, said she had the right look, too, that she was *phatakdi,* as sexy as a firecracker, yet with such dignity and class and sisterly charm that she would never inspire envy in other women. Sanjay just wanted to *chodo,* a word Padmini would never speak aloud in any language. If Sanjay had to choose between food and *chodo,* he'd probably die of starvation. But he was a good boy, serious about his own career, and she had never known him to lie, not even to get his ever-ready *lauda* where he wanted it to be.

If looks were an advantage for a concierge and a hotel manager and—ultimately—a hotel owner, they could be a hindrance sometimes. Senator Blandon had taken special notice of her, and his idea of flirting was to tell inappropriate jokes that were just short of smutty and that made her blush. He also found someone who gave him words he could say to her to show that he was cool with her culture. Sometimes he said she was one of the *apsaras,* which were heavenly nymphs, or he called her *batasha,* which was candied sugar. He called her Bibi Padmini, which merely meant "Miss." But whoever was feeding him these words must have had contempt for him, because Blandon also unwittingly called her *bhajiyas,* which was a fried snack, and *akha anda,* which meant a "total egg," and *chotti gadda,* which meant "little mattress." He was a supreme test of her patience and composure, but she managed always to pretend to be flattered by his inept attempts to employ the languages of India, and she never laughed in his face.

Thus far on her current shift, Padmini hadn't encountered the senator, which she took to be divine providence, but at 5:51 by her watch, something worse happened. An electronic squeal abruptly issued from all around her, startling her up from the stool. The magazine she was reading, *Hotelier,* slid onto the floor. She pushed through the gate, from behind the reception counter, into the lobby. When the fire alarm was tested, it issued an electronic bleat, but this was nothing like that. Nevertheless, Padmini knew that such a shrillness couldn't mean anything good.

When everything around her blurred and then when the blurry shapes, still familiar, were suddenly distorted beyond recognition, and when the squealing seemed perhaps to be coming from inside her head rather than from the walls, when there was an ominous rumbling as well, she thought that she must be having a stroke. She was only twenty-one, with so many dreams and so few of them yet fulfilled, and the unfairness of it was devastating. But even as she turned in place, squinting to make the smeary scene clarify, she thought of her mother and her father, Ganesh, and her brother, Vikram, and Anupama, and of course Sanjay, and was torn by the realization that she might be severely disabled and a burden to them, or that she would impose grief on them by dying, bring pain to those she loved the most. And then the noise stopped and the world became clear again.

Padmini could believe that a blood clot or an aneurysm might destroy her vital brain tissue even though she was so young, but she could not for a moment entertain the idea that she could ever go mad. She was as steady on her course as if she had a gyroscope in her head *and* was locked on to a satellite-guidance system. Right reason served as her walking stick, common sense her map.

The lobby that abruptly clarified around her in welcome silence was familiar but wrong. The marble floor was cracked and missing a few pieces, dirty, littered with twists of paper and brown shriveled leaves that must have blown in from outside. Of the cove lighting, only two of four LED tubes were still working. The central ceiling fixture hung dark. Additional sulfurous light came from the southeast end of the space, where a human skeleton sat with its back to the junction of the walls; the bones were a half-seen matrix over which had formed an encrustation of something luminous—perhaps a formation of crystals or a fungus, it was hard to see—that also climbed the corner to the ceiling, where it fanned out for a few feet, as if it had fed on the flesh of the dead man and had then stopped growing. This macabre lamp shed a bleak light that reminded her of nightmares she had as a child, passageways of stone through which she stalked—and was stalked by—Kali, the eight-armed Hindu goddess of death and destruction.

This could not be, but it was. As the concierge on duty, her job was to face the facts no matter how unlikely they seemed, accept the challenge, understand the cause, and put things right as quickly as she could. Her mouth was dry, her heart pounding, but her mind clear and her spirit resolute.

When Padmini realized that the lights of Shadow Street were no longer visible beyond the front doors and the flanking windows, she crossed the lobby, grimacing at the condition of the once-beautiful floor, and stepped outside, onto the receiving porch. In the Tiffany canopy, only a few lights remained operative. The rain had stopped. The sky was clear. The air felt ten or fifteen degrees warmer than it should have been on an early-December night. The street, the buildings that had once shared it with the Pendleton, and the rest of the city were gone.

In the moonlight, for a radius of about fifty yards, the hill appeared to be as barren as the surface of the moon. Beyond, in the dead-calm night, wave after wave of what might have been grass gave off a phosphoric light and swayed like sea anemones in the influence of strangely rhythmic currents.

A shriek in the dark turned Padmini's head in time, and she saw something pale and bizarre flying at her face. Until now she hadn't realized that in her right hand she still held the fork with which she had been eating Mausi Anupama's delicious *uttapam*. In fact, she gripped it so tightly that her knuckles ached. She thrust with the fork and stopped her assailant at arm's length, driving the tines into the forehead of what, in the glimpse she had of it, seemed to be a grub the size of a three-pound banana squash with leathery wings and a face that was half like that of a hairless cat and half like that of a featherless bird, the eyes radiant silver. The fork put an end to the shriek, and the creature flung itself away from her, looping through the air before flopping to the ground.

Padmini backed out of the night, into the Pendleton's lobby.

As long as there was a concierge on duty at the reception desk, the front doors were never locked. Padmini locked them anyway.

Mickey Dime

He came out of the north stairs onto the third floor, where the same dreary conditions prevailed as in the basement. Mickey didn't know what to do about it. He couldn't fix the situation by killing someone. Or if he could, it didn't matter, because he didn't know who to kill to make things like they were supposed to be. Except for Jerry and Klick the Prick, his targets were chosen for him by people he didn't know, whose faces he'd never seen. Until his phone rang and they gave him a name, he would just have to persevere through these deplorable conditions.

He saw another one of the pulsing blue screens set in the corner near the ceiling, angled to cover both the short west hall and the longer northern one. He decided the robotlike voice on the TV sounded snotty. This time, it was only able to say *"Adult male"* before Mickey shot out the screen.

At Apartment 3-D, he considered ringing the doorbell. Senator Earl Blandon might know who needed to be killed to set things right. Mickey's mom had liked the senator. She said the senator's only fault was that he used his power to ruin his enemies, when he should have used it to obliterate them. The people he ruined were still around to plot against him. On second thought, Mickey decided the senator might not be the best person from whom to seek advice.

As he passed 3-E, another damn blue TV at the end of the hall, past his apartment, near the freight elevator, said, *"Adult male. Brown—"*

Mickey blasted it, the screen went dark, and while the shot was ringing off the walls, someone behind him called out, "Mr. Dime!"

When he looked back, he saw Bailey Hawks standing in the debris from the first gunshot TV. They knew each other to say hello, nothing more. Hawks was ex-military. He'd been a kind of gunner, you might say, and Mickey suspected that Hawks could smell the gunner in him. He didn't trust Hawks. He didn't trust anyone since his mother died. Only hours earlier, his own brother tried to kill him. There was no reason why Hawks wouldn't try to kill him, too.

"There's eight of us in the Cupps' place. We're going to go floor-to-floor to gather everyone together."

"Not me," Mickey said, turned away, and walked to his apartment.

"Mr. Dime! Whatever's happening, we need to stick together."

"The strong act, the weak react," Mickey replied.

"What did you say?"

"What goes up does *not* have to come down, if you redefine the meaning of *down*."

That wasn't one of his mother's sayings. Mickey had invented it when he was ten, hoping to please her. He thought the line was good, but she locked him in a closet for twenty-four hours without food or water and with only a jar for a toilet. He learned to appreciate how sensuous darkness could be. He also learned he wasn't a philosopher or a cultural critic.

Hawks called out again, but Mickey ignored him.

The door to his apartment stood open. The light switch didn't work. More of that glowing mold or moss or whatever it was. More of it everywhere, the rooms drizzled with a depressing urine-yellow light. Mickey felt pissed on. He really did.

His furniture was gone. Nobody could have stolen all his stuff in the few minutes since he'd been here last.

The furniture must have gone where dead Jerry and Vernon Klick went. He didn't know where that was. He couldn't get his arms around the situation.

He stood in his bedroom, pistol in hand, but there was no one to shoot. This new reality, this bad reality, was all around him, out of control, and he needed to make it heel. What had she meant by "choke collar"? What had she meant by "leash"? What had she meant by "heel"? It had all sounded deep and smart and true at the time. But reality wasn't a dog you could grab by the scruff of the neck.

She was the most admired intellectual of her time.

So she must have been right. The fault must be in Mickey. He was too stupid to understand.

He needed to think harder about this. Maybe he should close himself in a closet for twenty-four hours with just a jar for a toilet. Maybe he would get his mind right, and the better reality would be back in place, this bad reality gone, when he came out. Maybe. But he didn't even have a jar.

Julian Sanchez

Most people live in a rushing river of images, a river always at flood stage, surging currents of color, liquid harmonies of form, the occasional chaos of rapids, and they are swept along by this torrent of sights with little or no consideration of how it affects their thoughts, shapes their minds, and influences the itinerary of their lives from the headwaters of birth through the delta of old age. When you considered sensory input as digitized data, fifty percent was received through the eyes, more than the four other senses combined.

During forty years of deepest night, Julian Sanchez had known the world mostly by the shapes and textures that slid beneath his sensitive fingers and by the constant music of life that might at times be merely the soft arrhythmic paradiddle of rain blown against the window and at other times the symphony of a busy city street. He was so sensitive to sounds that when bothered by a buzzing fly, he could more often than not snatch it from the air and fold it in his fist.

He was standing in his kitchen in Apartment 1-A, sipping coffee from a mug and listening to the storm through the window that he had cranked open a few inches, when an electronic squealing, unlike anything he'd heard before, arose around him, its source impossible to pinpoint. With that eerie keening came the rumbling from under the building, which he'd heard previously during the day and about which he had called security to inquire.

When both of those noises faded, Julian knew immediately that something important had happened. The tattoo of rain slanting against glass, the swish and gurgle of water plummeting through a downspout near his kitchen window, the wet-leaf rustle of the courtyard trees, and all the other voices in the storm's chorus fell silent in an instant. Refrigerator hum, dishwasher churn, icemaker drone, the faint tick of the glass pot expanding and contracting on the warming unit of the coffeemaker: Every familiar sound washed away with the passing of the storm, and the hush was at first profound.

Gone, too, were the familiar smells of his kitchen. No aroma of brewing coffee. No lingering pine scent of the cleaner that the housekeeper used earlier in the day, during her latest twice-a-week visit. No cinnamon scent from the breakfast rolls in the pastry box that should be on the counter nearby.

The half-open window no longer brought him the moist, ozone-crisp smell of the storm or the rich earthen fragrance of wet garden soil. When Julian reached across the sink with his left hand, he discovered that the interior window screen was missing. He felt for the crank handle that operated the left half of the casement window, but it wasn't there; he found only the socket in which the handle should have been seated. He sought the right-side handle and gripped it, but he grimaced because it was swathed in cobwebs. When he tried to crank it, the mechanism seemed to be frozen.

Mystified, he sidestepped past the sink, and he put down his coffee mug, which didn't ring off the counter as it should have done, but met the granite with a muffled *ponk*. Although the housekeeper had left less than two hours earlier, he discovered a thick layer of dust on the stone, and then debris of some kind, what were most likely tatters of rotted rags and what might have been crumbles of fallen plaster that gave off the smell of powdered gypsum and finely ground sand.

When he turned away from the counter to face the room, Julian smelled mildew. Something like stale urine.

His understanding of the space totally changed. He was so familiar with every square foot of the apartment and with the precise placement of the furniture that not only could he get about caneless and without barking his shins or stumbling over anything, but he could also perceive the shapes of things with something like a sixth sense, a kind of psychic radar. This unique perception now told him that the kitchen table and chairs were not where they should have been, that they were gone.

Usually, he didn't feel his way around with arms outstretched, but he resorted to this technique now, worried not only that the familiar furniture had been removed but also that something else might have been set in its place. The kitchen proved to be as empty as his psychic radar indicated. Sandy grit and larger bits of debris crunched under his shoes.

Julian was proud of living independently and rarely needed to lean on anyone for anything. The weird transformation of the kitchen, however, spooked him. He needed someone with working eyes to come around and explain to him what had happened here.

He patted the pockets of his cardigan sweater and was relieved to find his cell phone where he expected it to be. He pressed the button, listened to the sign-on jingle, and then after a hesitation, entered the number of the concierge. Padmini was supportive without ever giving the slightest indication that a blind man evoked pity in her. Julian loathed being pitied. After entering the number and pressing SEND, he waited with the phone to his right ear . . . until he became convinced there was no cell service.

Confused and concerned, but not yet afraid, he went to where the doorway to the dining area had always been, and it was still in the same place. On the threshold, Julian heard murmuring voices elsewhere in the apartment, urgent and strange, though he should have been alone.

Fielding Udell

The world was in worse shape than he had imagined in his most wretched speculations. The situation was more like that movie, *The Matrix*, than Fielding had known. *Everything* was false, projections of a benign reality beamed into his head by the Ruling Elite, but now their Spin Machine failed, the projections faded, and reality asserted itself. He had imagined domed cities in which the last twenty or thirty million brainwashed citizens were protected from the toxin-choked, superheated, icebound, drought-ridden, storm-wracked, disease-riddled, nuclear-decimated, frogless wasteland that was most of this sorry planet, a poisonous hell where billions of corpses rotted in the fields and streets. But now he saw that he was not in a domed city, not safe under an impenetrable force field, as he had thought.

He had lived in ruins but had been mind-beam persuaded that he dwelt instead in a luxury apartment building. Not even his furniture had been real, for now when the Spin Machine failed, he saw that his rooms were empty of everything except dust and a few dead insects and scraps of age-yellowed paper.

When he went to a window, wiped a film of dust from the glass, and looked down into the courtyard three stories below, he saw in the moonlight not the flowers and the manicured hedges and the well-shaped trees and the fountains that had always been there before, but instead destruction and a primeval sprawl of vegetation. The bowls of the tiered fountains were toppled and broken, like cracked conch shells and pried-open clam shells of immense size. No trees remained. The other plants were not easily studied in the lunar glow, but he could tell that they were not like anything he had seen before; at best they were apostates to the timeless church of Nature, and at worst they were mutations so grotesque as to be demonic, cresting like the waves of a corrupted sea over the winding footpath that meandered from the double doors on the west end to the east wall, where a gate led to the Pendleton's garages behind the main building.

On other nights, Fielding had been able to see the roof of the converted carriage house rising above the back wall of the courtyard, and beyond that the somewhat higher roofline of the larger garage, which had been added when Belle Vista was converted to the Pendleton. He could see neither structure now, though the full moon should have silvered their slate shingles. The big gate in the courtyard wall sagged open on buckled hinges, but beyond those bent bronze staves there seemed to be nothing but darkness. Nor was there any glow of city lights either above the parapeted roof of the north wing or to the east where the garages should have been.

Wherever his food came from, it wasn't prepared by Salvatino's Pizzeria or by any of the other restaurants from which he daily ordered. If the city didn't exist, which the utter lack of lights suggested, then neither did establishments offering home-delivery of tasty meals. When he received those fragrant packages, they evidently came from despicable Minions of the Ruling Elite, and for all he knew, his submarine sandwiches and pasta Bolognese and moo goo gai pan were all the same thing, Soylent Green, flavored to deceive.

Fielding was less frightened than outraged, less outraged than overcome by a profound sense of vindication, for he had been correct all along about the condition of the world, more insightful than he had known. He trembled with righteous indignation.

Movement in the courtyard drew his attention. Something appeared around a bend in the winding walkway, a creature previously concealed by the riot of wicked vegetation. Fielding hissed involuntarily through clenched teeth, because although he didn't know what kind of beast revealed itself below, he knew at once and without doubt that it was hostile to human life, and evil.

Pale it was but not just pale, also slightly aglow, not because its surface reflected or emitted light, but luminous deep *within.* It was mostly shadowy shapes infused with slowly pulsing light that was unevenly distributed, jaundice-yellow and methyl-green. The light traveled through its mysterious flesh in slow waves and whorls, at various depths and different levels of intensity, revealing what might have been the dark lumps of internal organs that were more dense than the surrounding tissue. The length of a prowling lion but nearly as tall as a man, it appeared in the inadequate moonlight to be creeping along on insectile but meaty legs similar to those of a Jerusalem cricket. As best Fielding could tell, the body might have been a collection of bulbous forms—swollen bladders, pendulous sacs—all wound about and linked by a segmented something that reminded him of a thick tapeworm. The thing did not move fast, though he was certain that it could quicken considerably in the presence of prey, and it seemed to be focused on the pathway before it, as if following a scent.

This apparition was more grotesque than anything Fielding Udell could have dreamed up in a thousand years of nightmares, beyond the power of any hallucinogen to conjure in the mind, more terrifying in its alienness than if a *Tyrannosaurus rex* had suddenly bounded into the courtyard, mouth agape and bristling with saber-length teeth. He thought of distant stars, of the airless vastness of deep space, of a journey measured in light-years, because the thing in the courtyard surely hadn't been born on Earth. A chill went through him, through both body and soul, and his palms became damp and cold, as though the icy courage that had sustained his long researches was now melting out of him.

As Fielding stared down at the repulsive vision, transfixed as a rabbit might be by a sudden encounter with a coiled rattlesnake, the thing raised something like a head, a lumpish mass lacking the left-right symmetry of the heads of all animals in nature. It turned up toward him a face that was malignant in two senses:

first, that it appeared to be a twisted cancerous mass; second, that it was a mask of perfect evil.

Perhaps it was looking only at the moon, as lunatic as it was misbegotten, but he believed that the thing fixed its gaze on him alone, if the three radiant silver orbs, clustered midface, were in fact eyes. His trance broken, Fielding stepped back from the dirty window, out of sight, certain that he had at last seen one of the elusive Ruling Elite.

Silas Kinsley

In the dismal yellow light, the oily shadows oozed away from the flashlight beam, and the immense room almost seemed to be underwater, the rays from overhead filtering down through countless fathoms. The broken and corroded HVAC equipment hulked and tilted like a sunken ship long settled on an ocean floor.

The vault lay silent but for an elusive susurration that might have been a draft born elsewhere in the building and carried through the maze of pipes that no longer contained water for the heating-cooling system and that were in some places broken or decoupled from their elbow joints. Given the circumstances, Silas wasn't able to repress the suspicion that he was hearing not merely a draft but instead the whispering of people who were monitoring him from the cover of the defunct machinery. Or if not people, perhaps nearby might wait a creature like the one that Perry Kyser, the contractor, had seen in 1973, the abomination that spoke to him in the tortured voice of the missing painter.

With the guard's pistol in hand, Silas pressed on, deeper into the labyrinth. He needed to know the full nature of the situation. If he allowed fear to triumph, he would make decisions based on emotion rather than on reason, which would be the quickest way to wind up dead.

The floor drain in this vault seemed to be the delivery system through which a periodic massive discharge of magnetic—or some other kind of—energy caused the present to fold temporarily into the future. Lawyer's intuition suggested that here at the epicenter, he was more likely than elsewhere to find important clues that, linked together in a chain of evidence, might help him and his neighbors escape a death sentence.

His flashlight played across one of the chillers. The thin sheet-metal housing was pocked with bullet holes, in a few of which spiders had spun miniature webs as if they had been too exhausted to weave architectures with larger perimeters. The farther Silas went, the more punctures and ricochet trails and bullet-shattered gauges he found. He came to a litter of brass cartridge casings, first dozens and then hundreds, through which he stepped with care, inevitably causing a few to roll and to strike from others a faint but melodious ringing like fairy bells.

He expected to find the remains of the combatants around one turn or another, and soon he did, although they were not the remains of men. Lying near each other in an aisle between boilers and water softeners were two skeletons that lacked the angularity and the knobby joints of human bones. These specimens didn't lie in jumbled, jagged disarray, not in the splay-legged and half-comic posture of tumbled human skeletons, which always appeared to have dropped to the floor at the conclusion of an antic dance. Death-stripped, these bones were graceful, as sleek as the lines of a master calligrapher intent on making visual art from sentences of cursive prose. Perhaps seven feet tall. Two-legged. Extra knuckles and phalanges in their long feet and hands. Six toes on each foot, the first and sixth longer than the other four, good for climbing. Their skulls were not as round as those of human beings, shaped more like large footballs without the pointed ends. Their jaws were long and strong for biting, teeth fearsome, death grins wide and shark-sharp.

The flashlight also revealed that these bones were not white but gray, and even the teeth were gray. The uniform shade suggested that they had always been gray, that this was not discoloration resulting from the passage of much time or from the stains left by decomposing flesh. When Silas crouched and lifted one of the arms, it felt much lighter than bone, but when he let it drop, it rang off the concrete with an almost metallic sound.

Not far from the first two skeletons, he found three more like them. From the bones, he could extrapolate with confidence that these creatures had been strong, agile, and very fast. Even in death, their teeth said *predator.*

Finally, in the southwest corner of the long room, he discovered fourteen human skeletons sitting with their backs to the wall, ten adults and four children. No flesh clung to their bones, and in the perpetual dampness of the vault, most of their clothes had rotted away, as well. Having received the rich fluids of decomposition, the concrete around them was dark and mottled. Although much time had passed since these luckless people met their end, Silas thought he could still smell a faint ghost of putrefaction, an olfactory haunting in this deeply spectral place.

One of the adult skeletons still bit on the barrel of a pistol-grip, pump-action shotgun that had not dislodged when it blew out the back of the head. Two other adults lay with shotguns. Enduring stains on the wall led Silas to have a closer look at all fourteen, and he discovered exit wounds in the back of every skull. Here at the bottom of the building, in the windowless vault, they had made their final stand against the predators—saving the last of their ammunition for themselves. The adults apparently killed the children first to spare them whatever horrors the predators would have wrought upon them.

Perhaps these people had been the last generation of Pendleton residents, before the building had fallen into ruin. And now Silas could no longer avoid a question that he had been reluctant to ask, could not further delay going upstairs to seek the answer: If this great house had come to such a bitter end and if fantastic beasts of unknown origin stalked its rooms, *what had happened to the rest of the world?*

One

I am the One, and I see all.

But the blind man in Apartment 1-A is blind in many ways, as are all human beings, even those with functioning eyes. They are blind to their folly, to their ignorance, to their history, to the future that they will make for themselves. A future born of self-loathing.

Even those who know that the twenty universal constants ensure a universe that will support life, who know intellectually as well as intuitively that the human race must be exceptional and must be graced with a destiny, even they are capable of hating not only others of their kind but also their kind in general. Some are capable of such self-loathing that they fantasize a world without humanity and take comfort from that dream.

The concierge is not one of them, but she will die with the others, with the billions who will perish between her present and my present, which is her future. She might have gone far in the hospitality business, but the material success her kind pursues cannot provide her life with meaning. She is one of those who, had she not been cast into my kingdom, might have found her meaning in time. She might have become one of those who would stand up against the misanthropes, the people haters, to save humanity. But there are too few of her, too few with her insight and drive and tenderness of heart; for humanity to survive, it cannot afford to lose even one like her. But she is now mine.

27

Here and There

Bailey Hawks

Bailey watched Dime disappear into his apartment. Something was wrong with the guy. Maybe the stress of this event already snapped him, though that would mean he was less flexible psychologically than young Winny. Dime never seemed interested in others living in the Pendleton, never agreed to serve on the board or on any committee, never attended the Christmas social in the banquet room. He spoke to you in the halls if you happened to pass him, but only by comparison to a monk who had taken a vow of silence could the guy be called a conversationalist.

He had a pistol. He'd shot out two peculiar blue screens that had not been in this hallway before what Twyla Trahern called "the leap." When Bailey had suggested that the best plan would be to round up other residents and thereafter stick together, Dime had disagreed in a tone of voice that was at least dismissive if not hostile. And part of what he'd said—*What goes up does* not *have to come down, if you redefine the meaning of* down—made no sense.

Bailey decided they would start the search for other neighbors in the south wing of the third floor, then move downstairs, coming back to this north wing only after Dime had some time to get a grip on himself, assuming there was any grip to get. Anyway, Bernard Abronowitz, who lived alone in 3-E, was currently in the hospital and therefore hadn't made this trip through time with them. Senator Blandon, in 3-D, was likely to be halfway to drunk by this hour and less amiable than Mickey Dime; leaving the politician until later might also be wise.

"What was that all about?" Kirby Ignis asked, evidently having come out of the Cupps' front door in time to overhear Bailey's exchange with Dime.

"I don't know. We'll give him some time to adjust, cool down. Before we search the south wing, let's see if Silas is here."

The attorney's apartment was the front corner unit, next to the Cupps. Bailey pressed the bell push but heard no chimes inside. A knock went unanswered. The door proved to be unlocked—in fact the lock wasn't functioning—and when Silas didn't reply to Bailey's "Anyone home?" he and Kirby stepped inside to search the old man's rooms.

Kirby carried a flashlight that he had borrowed from Twyla Trahern, which still left the women and children with Sparkle's flashlight, and Martha had her pistol. Remembering the women's hurried but vivid description of creatures they had seen, remembering Sally's demon in the pantry, with the mysterious swimmer remaining clear in his mind from their early-morning encounter, Bailey kept a two-hand grip on his 9-mm Beretta.

Like other rooms they had seen since the leap, the attorney's spaces were unfurnished, shabby, dirty, moldy, and long abandoned, lying in the half-light emitted by the fungus or whatever it was, an exhausted light that a dying sun might produce. Kirby had no police or military background, but he was smart and quick to recognize why his armed partner proceeded as he did. Inferring what was wanted of him, he accompanied Bailey as though they had teamed for searches before, clearing the apartment chamber by chamber.

Approaching the last room, the master bath, they saw within it a weaker dark-urine light than elsewhere. Step by step the smell of mold, mild but pervasive in this Pendleton, grew more pungent and seemed to lend the air a taste as well as a scent. When they stopped at the threshold, the flashlight beam probed beyond, revealing what might have been an abstract-art installation by a deranged sculptor: pale-green, black-mottled snakelike shapes that lined the walls, unmoving but sinuous, as if abruptly paralyzed in the act of seething copulation, snugged together on the vertical surfaces but spilling also onto part of the floor, a nest in torpor, in a winter dormancy. At several points in this hideous mass, clusters of mushrooms of the same coloration, some as big as one of Bailey's fists but others as big as two, rose on thick stems, a puckered formation like the mouth of a drawstring purse at the crown of each bell-shaped cap.

"Two different forms," Kirby Ignis said, "but all the same organism."

"Organism? You mean animal?"

"Fungus is an organism. I'd say that's what this is."

"Not ambulatory though, like the things the others saw."

"I don't advise stepping in there to find out."

Although the snake forms did not suddenly become mobile, they began to throb, as if lumps of something were passing through them, as if they were indeed snakes and were swallowing a series of mice.

Tom Tran

Protected by a black-vinyl slicker and a floppy-brimmed rain hat, Tom Tran had just minutes earlier stepped out of the converted carriage house into the cobbled passageway between that building and the Pendleton, pulling the door shut behind him, and he had taken but one step when the storm didn't just relent but *switched off.* Abruptly rain stopped falling, the cobblestones were dry, and the cloudless sky was salted with stars and bright with a full moon.

Confused, his hat and slicker still dripping, Tom had turned in a circle—and had discovered that the carriage house was not there anymore, nor the new and larger garage behind it. At each end of the cobbled passage should have been gates between the Pendleton and the back building, one leading to an alley, the other opening to a narrow walkway. They were there, all right, hanging from eight-foot-high pony walls that protruded from the main building, but the bronzework was twisted, missing staves, sagging on half-broken hinges, no longer connected to the missing carriage house.

Belatedly, Tom had realized that past the vanished buildings, across the top of Shadow Hill and beyond, the entire eastern reaches of the city were no longer aglow . . . *were not even there.* The night to the east appeared vast and trackless, and in places shimmered with pools of milky moonlight that revealed nothing, that looked wet and misty, as if they were spirit lakes in an eerie afterlife landscape.

As a boy, Tom Tran learned that Death wore many costumes, not just a black robe with a cowl, and hid behind an infinite number of faces. Death was everywhere, he was legion, and you couldn't escape his attention, but in some places he manifested in greater numbers than in others. Tom sensed that to the east, in that inexplicable new immensity of darkness, entire armies of Death were hidden, and every field and forest was a killing ground.

The damaged gate in the back wall of the courtyard also hung open and askew, one of the three hinges torn loose of the masonry and the other two lumpy with corrosion. The Pendleton appeared to have been abandoned for decades, and Tom wondered crazily if he would be haggard and aged far beyond his years if he looked in a mirror.

No landscape lighting brightened the courtyard, and in the windows of the three embracing wings of the Pendleton, the lights were not only dimmer than usual but also a dragon-eye yellow that he had never seen before. The trees were gone, fountains tumbled, gardens overgrown with plants that, in the moonlight, he could not identify.

Tom felt not himself to the same degree that his world was not itself at the moment, and he wandered along the footpath, bewildered and trembling, as if he were a character in one of those folktales of spirits and ghosts and gods that his mother had told him when he was a child in Vietnam so long ago. He could have been wandering through a twisted version of "The Search for the Land of Bliss" or "The Raven's Magic Gem," or "The House of Forever." Something like tall bamboo, but fleshy rather than hard and with long aerial roots, canopied the footpath here and there. Each time one of those dangling roots brushed his face, it seemed to have animal life, stroking his cheek or curling into an ear, or teasing a nostril, and he brushed it away, chilled by the contact, shuddering.

He reached the doors between the courtyard and the ground-floor west hall, just opposite the inner doors of the lobby, fished his keys from a pocket of his slicker, and was about to let himself into the Pendleton when he heard noises behind him, short gasps like something venting under pressure but wound through with a prolonged hiss. There were clopping-scraping sounds, as well, as if a weary horse were dropping its heavy hooves and dragging each one a bit before finding the energy to lift it again.

When Tom turned to look back along the moonlit footpath, he saw nothing that might be the source of those noises, but movement at a third-floor window in the south wing drew his attention. Backdropped by dragon light, the ghostly white face at the French panes belonged to Fielding Udell, who might have been unaware of Tom. At the very moment that Udell reacted to something that he had seen farther east in the courtyard, the clopping-scraping ceased to echo through the night. The hissing and the pressurized venting didn't stop, but the rhythm and the character of those disturbing sounds changed. With a sudden movement that clearly expressed his fear of being seen, Udell stepped back from the window. A moment later the clopping-scraping began again. Whatever had alarmed Udell now approached Tom along the winding footpath, still out of sight beyond the tall vegetation and beyond a turn or two.

He faced the doors again, inserted his key—and discovered that it didn't work. He jiggled it in the keyway, slid it in and out, tried again, but had no luck. Either the lock had deteriorated with the rest of the building or a locksmith had changed it.

Behind him, a voice cried out, as shrill as that of a squealing child, an impatient and petulant child, and as Tom turned to confront whatever it might be, a second cry sounded angrier than the first—and needful. Thirty feet away, a creature with half a dozen legs, Tom's height and at least twice his bulk, crabbed around a turn in the footpath, brushing through the vegetation that crowded it.

Either the gates of Hell had opened or Tom had lost his mind, for there could be nothing like this entity outside the precincts of the damned except in the fevered fantasies of a raving paranoid psychopath.

Julian Sanchez

Crossing into the dining room, Julian knew at once that it, too, must be unfurnished. For one thing, the area carpet was missing, and for another, his footsteps on the limestone floor resonated off the walls differently from how they would have sounded in a furnished space.

The voices he'd heard a moment earlier were silent now. He stood listening. In the same way that he could discern the positions of the furnishings around him by what was a kind of psychic radar, he could also to a pretty reliable degree intuit the presence of others. Even a person who stood at ease still produced telltale sounds—shifting weight from foot to foot, breathing shallowly, licking lips, sucking a bit of food from between teeth, the rustle of clothes, the tick of a wristwatch—but except for the small noises that he himself made, this room sounded deserted.

Julian had not been blind since birth. He'd lost his

vision at the age of eleven, when retinoblastoma required the removal of both his eyes. Consequently, he had more than a decade of visual memories stored away, which allowed him to construct mental images and whole scenes—including colors—from clues to his environment provided by his other four senses. When he cruised his apartment, his mind's eye saw every room in vivid detail even though he'd never actually seen any corner of the place.

The inexplicable change that had recently occurred, however, left him unable to visualize his new surroundings. The perception of vacancy, the dirt and debris, the rankness of mold and mildew and other unidentifiable malodors so fundamentally altered these rooms that he was almost as unable to picture them as would have been a man blind from birth and without visual memories.

When Julian stepped warily into his living room, the muttering voices rose once more. They were speaking in a foreign language that he couldn't identify. Previously they had an urgency, as if they were delivering a warning. Now they remained urgent but began to sound quarrelsome. Julian imagined a dozen people, perhaps more, and their voices issued from all sides, as though he must be encircled by some conclave that had come there specifically to study him, analyze him. Judge him.

"Who's there?" he asked. "Who are you? What do you want?"

At the same time that the voices seemed to press

close to him, they lacked the clarity of intimate speech, and he could imagine as easily that these were utterances carried to him from other rooms, through an intervening wall or door.

Moving to where he thought the center of the living room should be, finding no furniture in his way, Julian spoke louder than before: "Where are you? What do you want?"

In his first year or two of blindness, he had felt vulnerable and had worried unduly about the many things that might happen to him because of his disability. But you couldn't spend your life expecting a calamitous fall or an assault at any moment; fear soon exhausts itself. After forty years of successful sightless living, he felt not invulnerable but safe enough, and he came to believe the worst that would ever happen to him had already happened when he was eleven.

Suddenly his scalp prickled and the back of his neck went cold as fear proved to be as on-call as ever it had been. The quarrelsome nature of the voices darkened into threatening tones, and again he felt that they were shockingly near, the speakers close enough to touch. When he reached out, he found that he had shuffled out of the center of the room without realizing it, for he touched a wall.

The plaster vibrated in time with the speech waves of the angry chorus, as if the voices came from within the wall.

Sally Hollander

Free of all emotions, she was still lying on her kitchen floor, disconnected images from a fading identity blooming in the mostly lightless and drowned landscape of her mind. She seemed to be looking up from the bottom of a pond, through water toward a night sky, and the images were formed from fat drops of light falling like fitful rain, each drop spreading into colors and scenes as it struck and melded with the surface of the pond; and every scene shimmered for a moment like reverse paintings on glass, before bleeding away into darkness. Faces that she knew but to which she could no longer affix names, places she recognized but was unable to identify, moments out of a lost time that might have been an hour or a week or ten years in the past floated one after another across this drowning pool, colorful at first but then in black-and-white and shades of gray.

As she seemed to sink into the silt and the scum of her final resting place, as the now colorless moments of a fading consciousness grew ever dimmer, a sudden excruciatingly tender yearning overcame her, a keen nostalgia for what she could not remember, for what she felt slipping away from her forever, and there came also a piercing love for light, for life, for sounds and scents and tastes and sights and textures whether rough or smooth. These fervent feelings swelled until she seemed sure to burst with them—but then they passed.

She felt no further emotion. All grew dark in her, without want or meaning, and after a while she developed one desire but one only: to kill. She was not she anymore, she was a creature now without a past or gender, transformed by the sleek gray attacker into one of its kind, with one name only: *Pogromite.* It rose. It moved. It sought.

Bailey Hawks

From the threshold of Silas Kinsley's bathroom, Bailey watched the serpentine organisms throb with something Kirby Ignis said was "like peristalsis." In the flashlight beam, as those pulsations occurred more rapidly, the clusters of bell-shaped mushrooms became active as well. The puckered formation at the crown of each, which Bailey had likened to the mouths of drawstring purses, began to open and to peel back from the caps, whereupon those growths looked less like mushrooms than like engorged phalluses straining through their foreskins toward passionate release.

Simultaneously Bailey and Kirby recognized the implications of this unveiling. Bailey said, "Get back," Kirby said, "It's sporing," and they retreated quickly from the bathroom threshold, across the bedroom, to the open door, where they paused to see if the thing might be peeling itself off the walls to follow them. It either didn't possess the power of locomotion or was not in a mood to hunt them down, because it neither slithered nor crawled out of the dimly lighted bathroom.

In the public hallway, outside the apartment, Bailey

closed the door and wished that he could lock it or had a chair with which to brace it shut. The empty chambers of the Pendleton, evidently stripped bare long ago for reasons unknowable, were not likely to provide them with hammers and nails or with any other tools they might use to seal off rooms either to contain the things in them or to create a refuge into which nothing deadly could intrude.

Tom Tran

Pulsing with a bleak and sour inner light, the thing was like some massive mutant tuber that had grown underground, in radioactive soil, developing many spongy lobes of malignant flesh, initially feeding on minerals in the ground but then on insects and worms, incorporating their DNA into its structure, eventually extruding that segmented wormlike part of it, sprouting legs and nasty pincers and a pair of horny mandibles with which to bite and rend. Maybe it was some alien life form, fallen to Earth in a seed pod, in a meteorite, self-aware from the start. Or maybe it gradually became self-aware as it lived below the surface like a trapdoor spider, pulling down unwary rats and rabbits and dogs and maybe even children, especially children, its lair a mass grave, feeding on them, gaining from their DNA a series of increasingly sophisticated brain designs, and at last burrowing to the surface with God alone knew what purpose.

It squealed again in that angry-child, tortured-child

voice. And there was no way to read accurately its intention in its three radiant silvery eyes, though Tom saw in them the same hunger that he heard in the keening voice.

The beast's asymmetrical structure and its weird hodgepodge of features, seemingly derived from multiple species, suggested that it must be semifunctional at best, clumsy by nature, awkward in action. He considered rushing toward it, dodging past it, off the path and through the tangled plants and away to the east gate. He was a boy again and as fast as a highland wind, for fear had returned him to the helplessness of childhood when he had compensated for his size and weakness by being fleet and clever and inexhaustible. Before Tom could move, however, the thing jittered forward, hissing and venting, closing from thirty feet to fifteen, quicker than a scuttling crab. But there it halted, studying him as if he might be as strange a sight to it as it was to him.

He didn't hear the deadbolt retract behind him, didn't hear the door open. He cried out in alarm when something seized him by the arm, less inclined to believe that he had any chance of being saved than that at his back was something no less freakish and no less vicious than the monster on the footpath. The rapid mortar fire of his heart *whump-whumped* so loud in his ears that he barely heard Padmini Bahrati say, "Quick! Inside!" But he *did* hear her, turned toward her, plunged inside and past her.

Padmini slammed the heavy door and with the thumb-turn shot home the deadbolt.

When Tom Tran whipped around to face the courtyard again, he was inexpressibly grateful that those French doors were made of bronze instead of wood, for this prince of Hell was *right there.* Up close it looked less like spongy tubers than like a salmagundi of exposed organs and entrails, like a thing turned inside out, all its bulbous parts slick with a thin milky fluid glistening in the yellow light that passed through the panes from the hallway.

The silver eyes were fixed on him, and the mandibles worked as if the creature were imagining the taste of him, and now he thought that the darker shapes within its semitranslucent body, those opaque lumps, might be smaller creatures it had devoured, all of them lying whole in its gut, like the limb-tangled bodies in the mass grave near Nha Trang. This was the very kind of thing that might have come to life—or the animated antithesis of life—deeply buried in the human compost and jungle mast of Nha Trang, Vietnam, never having been born but instead having become aware in the darkness and the decay and the heat that decay produced, the horror of Nha Trang given a suitably symbolic form. At last it had come for Tran Van Lung, known here as Tom Tran, now forty-five, who as a boy of ten had seen that open-air abattoir, the machine-gunned thousands of women, men, and children in the natural cavity of a pond long drained of water, not yet plowed over with a thick blanket of earth. With his father, he had quickly walked one curve of the rim of that obscene hole and safely away among the trees before authorities returned with the bulldozer that they had been too impatient to provide before the killing started. Behind him and his father, the jungle surrounding the grave had stood eerily silent in deep green witness.

"It's not even trying to get in," Padmini said.

Tom expected the creature to throw itself against the doors, but it did not. Neither did it shatter a pane of glass with its pincers.

"Why isn't it trying?" Padmini asked.

The thing turned away from the door and retreated along the winding footpath.

"It must not be Nha Trang, after all," Tom decided.

"What?"

"Nha Trang will never stop wanting me."

Although the intensity of his fear declined as his racing heart beat less frantically, a chill pierced him with the suddenness of a dagger of ice falling from a high eave, and he shivered violently.

Dr. Kirby Ignis

Déjà vu didn't describe the sensation. Kirby didn't feel as if he had been here before, in these circumstances, in this Pendleton of the future. Yet as extraordinary as these events were, they did not seem utterly alien and incomprehensible to him. He had been surprised by the things he'd seen but, curiously, not shocked. In spite of the bizarre and radical changes this world had undergone, it was somehow familiar to him, or if not familiar, then potentially explainable. He could not explain it yet, but he sensed an understanding growing in him, a coral reef of theory slowly accreting, still unconscious but certain eventually to rise into view. The apparent chaos might be only apparent, a logical historic cause and a rational order just waiting to be revealed.

He and Bailey left the women and children with one gun and one flashlight, in the Cupp apartment. The encounter with the sporing colony of fungi in Kinsley's bathroom proved that moments would arise when a quick response was essential to survival, but the larger the search team, the less agile it could be.

They accessed the south wing of the third floor through the Cupps' back entrance. The high-mounted TV in the corner where the short and long hallways met didn't pulse with blue light. The screen was shattered. A colony of glowing fungi lived in the shallow tube, indicating that this monitor hadn't worked in a long time.

To their left the elevator doors stood open, the stainless-steel interior burnished by blue light. To Kirby Ignis, the unoccupied car seemed to be an invitation to go for a ride. Considering Winny's experience and Kirby's own encounter with the blood-spattered butler who came out of the north elevator from 1935, shortly before the leap to this future occurred, he would prefer the stairs for the duration.

The top floor of Gary Dai's two-story apartment was immediately to their right, opposite the south elevator.

The door had been broken down. It lay just beyond the threshold, cracked and sheathed in undisturbed dust; the hinges in the jamb were bent, torn halfway out of the wood. Back in 2011, Gary was in Singapore, so the leap would not have brought him with them to this Pendleton.

Nevertheless, they ventured into the upper floor of 3-B, where the radiant fungi were as prevalent as elsewhere, and Bailey called out—"Is anyone here?"—repeatedly as they moved from the foyer into the living room. The words echoed through other rooms and down the internal apartment stairs to the lower floor of the unit, but no one replied.

Beyond the west windows lay the plain of hypnotically swaying luminous grass and the circular stands of craggy black trees down-lit by the moon but also up-lit by the glowing meadow. The disturbing but undeniable allure of this future world was different from the beauty of the world now past, not just in the nature of its landscapes but in its fundamental quality.

Beauty is truth, truth beauty: Philosophers for ages had said that beauty was proof of design by a higher power, because living things could function just as well if they were ugly; if animals—including humans—were merely meat machines and if plants were merely machines of cellulose and chlorophyll produced by blind and mindless Nature, and if landscapes were sculpted by geological processes inspired by no Great Engineer, there wasn't any reason for them to be appealing to the eye, which seemed to mean beauty must be a grace, a gift to the world.

Kirby wasn't interested enough to have an opinion regarding the theory of a link between beauty and the divine in the world he had left. But it seemed to him, as he gazed out of Gary Dai's windows, that what pleased the eye in this world was not good and true but evil and deceptive. What made this vista alluring was not genuine harmony, which it somehow lacked, but its mystery and the sense that anything might be out there, that anything might happen, which had great appeal to the savage aspect of the human heart, which in the old world had to be repressed in the interest of civilization. Here no civilization existed, only the heart of darkness, bewitching in its immensity, charming because it promised raw brutal power, because it promised the freedom of madness, because it promised death without meaning.

From here the rhythmic swaying of the luminous meadow seemed to offer a mystical experience, but Kirby suspected that any walk he took there would be short and marked by exquisite cruelty.

In spite of his grandfatherly demeanor, he was a curmudgeon who found humankind—not every individual but as a species—to be largely foolish in the extreme, selfish and greedy and envious. Most were in love with power, with violence, users and despoilers. Kirby often thought the world would be a better place if dogs were the creatures of highest intelligence who lived in it. He didn't miss the vanished city, because even the best of cities were beautiful only from a distance, squalid to one degree or another when experienced up close. However, this was a world without cities, without men, *and* no doubt without dogs and other innocent creatures, not a world returned to the condition of Eden, but a world polluted and perverted.

"I don't think we need to explore every room," Bailey said. "If anyone were here, they'd respond. Whatever we find during a search is going to be one kind of funhouse pop-up or another, and we don't need to put ourselves at risk just for the thrill of it."

When they came out of Gary Dai's apartment, the open elevator car remained empty, but murmuring voices in a foreign language issued from it—or more likely from the shaft in which it was suspended. They sounded just as Bailey had described them: portentous, urgent, ominous. In the world of the past, language was an exclusively human tool, but Kirby suspected that these voices were not those of people.

When they turned the corner into the long south hallway, a blue screen pulsed at the farther end, though no computer-simulated voice raised an alarm.

On the left were two apartments, the first belonging to Mac and Shelly Reeves. Kirby had little time to listen to radio, but the few occasions on which he'd heard the Reeveses' show, it was amusing.

The door stood open. The first two rooms were like the desolate spaces they'd seen elsewhere. Nobody answered Bailey's call.

"They might've been out to the theater or dinner when the leap occurred," Kirby said.

"For their sake, let's hope so."

As they approached the door to 3-H, Fielding Udell's apartment, the blue screen spoke: *"Two adult males. Aboveground. Third floor. South hallway. Exterminate. Exterminate."*

Inspired by Mickey Dime, Bailey shot the screen.

"Some kind of security system?" Kirby wondered.

"Seems like it."

"Why would an abandoned building need one?"

"Beats me."

"You think anyone's still around to answer the call?"

"So far, I'd say no. So far."

The door to Fielding Udell's apartment was locked. The bell didn't work. Bailey knocked loudly. No one answered.

Bailey shouted through the door: "Mr. Udell? Mr. Udell? It's Bailey Hawks. I live in 2-C." He waited. Then: "Mr. Udell, we're all getting together in the Cupp apartment, riding this out together."

When the only reply proved to be silence, Kirby said, "Maybe he was out of the building when it happened."

"I don't think he leaves his apartment much."

"You want to break down the door, see if he's in trouble?"

Bailey thought about it for a moment. "You know this guy?"

"I've run into him once or twice."

"He's pretty eccentric."

"*Eccentric* is one word for it," Kirby said.

"I'm thinking what if, like me and like Martha, he was packing a gun when the leap happened. The way Udell is, if we break down the door and he's armed, either he might get shot, or me, maybe both."

They went to the south stairs, at the west end of the hallway, and descended to the second floor.

Witness

He stood in what might once have been the library or the study, to one side of the open door to the living room, listening as the women helped one another to keep their courage strong.

Through the security-system communicator in his right ear, he heard the alarm and the call for extermination every time it sounded. There was a period, far in the past, when Witness was the one who did the required killing. Those few hardy souls who survived the Pogrom and subsequently survived the Fade tended to seek shelter in the Pendleton when they came upon it, for this building alone seemed to offer recognizable refuge in a changed world. But these final walls were for those people the walls of a trap. Witness made a good first impression on the ragged and weary survivors, because he looked like them, not like a Pogromite. Once millions in number, the Pogromites had dwindled to a few in those days, because they had massacred long and well, and therefore were without sufficient work to justify their existence in large numbers. He welcomed the people who escaped the Pogrom, invited them into his supposed fortress, and when they trusted him, he killed them ruthlessly.

No survivors had chanced by in many years, and he no longer killed. His only job for a long time had been to stand as witness, the sole repository of the history of the world before the Pogrom, and curator of this honored building.

Considering his solitude and the terrible unrelenting weight of his knowledge, his awareness of how the world had once been and his daily experience of what it had become, perhaps it should have been expected that he would change. Gradually he was overcome by a sense of grievous loss. Something like remorse arose in him, and even pity.

One hundred sixteen days previously, the melancholy routine of his isolated existence was interrupted. The first fluctuations began, those inexplicable flashbacks to the Pendleton as it had once been, in 1897, standing high on this hill but in a smaller version of the city that eventually grew. The fluctuations lasted two days, and for flickering moments the present and that particular moment of the past briefly occupied the same point on the continuum of time. Then the transition occurred, flinging Andrew North Pendleton, his wife, and their two children into this merciless future where the perpetually mutating denizens included no species that didn't kill, a world of ceaseless violent predation.

Witness had not slaughtered the children and the

wife. The sole remaining Pogromite in this region, perhaps in the entire world, had attacked little Sophia. It had administered the first paralyzing bite and the injection that began the family's destruction. Other threats ensured that, when the transition reversed, only the father had been carried back to 1897, for only he remained alive.

Witness now knew from experience that this mysterious phenomenon occurred every thirty-eight *years* in the past, beginning in December 1897. Curiously, it was thirty-eight *days* between the experiences for him, at this end of the journey. The time separating the events in the past made it difficult for people then to see the pattern. But for Witness, the shorter interval here lent a sense of accelerating momentum to these incidents.

Thirty-six days after the Pendleton family transitioned to this time, the fluctuations began again, and following the Pendletons by thirty-eight days, the Ostocks and their live-in household staff were in essence shipwrecked on this shore. Thirty-eight days after the Ostocks, a bewildered man named Ricky Neems came out of the past alone, a construction worker from 1973, who met a gruesome fate shortly after his arrival.

Each group transported from earlier eras, at least those who *survived*, remained in this future 38 percent less time than the previous crew. The dead remained forever. Andrew Pendleton and his family were here the longest, for 380 minutes. The Ostocks endured approximately 235, which was 38 percent less. The transition in which Ricky Neems perished lasted about 146 minutes. If the pattern held, the current travelers would be stranded here 90.6 minutes, which was 62 percent of 146.1. Witness didn't understand the reason for the periodicity or the importance of the number 38, but he was certain of the length of each transition because it was part of his nature to be as aware of the passage of time as was any clock.

Likewise, he didn't know the cause of this event, whether it was a natural phenomenon without meaning or whether there was a purpose of some kind behind it. If the Pendleton had by chance been built over a fault in space-time, all was happenstance. But whether chance or not, the forces involved were beyond Witness's comprehension, of such immense power that they could fold time to bring different eras together, which was impossible according to the laws of physics—or at least impossible according to the laws of physics as they were thought to be.

His growing sense of increasing momentum led him to expect an approaching crescendo, not merely an end to these phenomena but a consummation beyond his ability to imagine. Maybe the violence he had witnessed for so long, the destruction of civilization worldwide, shaped his expectations, and maybe he was wrong, but he believed the end of these transitions, when it came, would be cataclysmic, worse than anything he had seen in his life.

Standing in the deserted library, listening to the women in the next room, he thought he would like them very much if he knew them better. He liked them some already, well enough that he hoped they might not perish here, although the chances of any of them living through the next ninety minutes was remote. He would not kill them, but he could not save them, either.

Tom Tran

In the west hallway of the ground floor, Tom seized Padmini's hands and kissed them as he thanked her profusely for saving him from the spawn of the mass grave at Nha Trang or whatever it had been. She called it *rakshasa,* which she said was a race of demons, goblins, and though he didn't know much about Hinduism, Tom thought that might be as good an explanation as any for the creature.

"*Baba,*" she said, "what has happened? Do you know why everything has changed?"

Baba, she'd told him, was an affectionate form of address used in India when speaking to little children or old men. Only forty-six, but more than twice her age, Tom Tran took no offense. He sometimes thought of Padmini as the daughter he'd never had. Anyway, her sweet nature ensured that only the most contentious cranks could work up any animosity toward her.

"In my experience," he said, releasing her hands, "the world falls apart from time to time, and madness happens, but not madness like this."

"I locked the main doors from the street," she said.

"Good, good," he said, glancing at the courtyard beyond the French doors, where the *rakshasa* had disappeared beyond masses of strange vegetation.

"I was going to go down to security, see what he knows."

"Yes," Tom said, beginning to regain some of his composure. "That's what we should do."

Together they hurried along the inexplicably filthy and poorly lighted corridor toward the south stairs, whereupon he noticed that high on the end wall hung a foot-square TV that had never been there previously. The mounting platform had partially failed, and the TV hung at an angle, the screen dark.

As they approached the stairwell door, it opened, startling them to a stop, and Silas Kinsley entered the hallway with a pistol in one hand and a flashlight in the other.

"Mr. Kinsley," Padmini said, "the world's gone crazy, *khiskela,* everything is off, shifted."

"Yes, I know," the attorney said. "What have you seen?"

"Demons," Tom replied and wondered what it meant that Silas Kinsley seemed not in the least surprised by that word.

Padmini said, "We were going down to security, to see what Vernon Klick might know."

"He's dead," the attorney informed them. "The security room isn't like it used to be. There's nothing for us down there."

Iris

They are too many, and they seem to talk all at once, and they have too much to say. Iris is not able to keep the forest real around her and follow the Bambi way with so much talking, the voices buzzing at her, buzzing. She doesn't just hear the voices but feels them sawing in her ears, words with sharp little teeth, none of them soft voices right now but worried and rough. The words choke her, too, the words like a cord tightening around her throat, the way the trap line nearly strangled Friend Hare, so she finds it harder and harder to breathe.

The old woman has a gun, and guns are bad. The hunter killed Bambi's friend Gobo, wounded Bambi in the shoulder, all the blood and Bambi wanting to lie down and sleep, just sleep, except sleep would have been death.

Iris keeps her hands over her ears for a while, but then she is afraid that she won't hear the scream of the jaybird if it comes. She must be able to hear it, because the jay, with its scream, warns the whole forest when danger is near, when the hunter is among the trees.

Not daring to look up, certain to be overwhelmed by the *sight* of all these people talking, and everything changed, nothing as it ought to be, she focuses on the floor. Head bowed, arms folded across her chest, hands in her armpits, she tries to be as small and compact as she can, hoping not to be noticed.

The cats are on the floor again, nobody cuddling them, prowling around. She watches them because they make her think of the animals in the forest. She remembers the wonderful female deer like Faline and Aunt Ena and Aunt Nettla and Marena, and she is calmed when she keeps them in her mind.

One of the cats undoes Iris's calm when it looks at her from a few feet away, and she sees that its orange eyes are changed, all black like pools of ink. The cat is moving different from the way it moved before, slower, not as graceful, as if it's sick. It shudders away from her. The other cat appears in her line of sight, and it also has strange black eyes. It opens its mouth, in which something is wriggling, as if the cat caught a mouse with six tails, the gray tails slithering back and forth across its teeth.

The forest isn't here anymore, and it'll never be here in this room again because there are too many voices and too many changes, everything different, even the cats, nothing normal, nothing safe. The forest must be found somewhere else, away from the worried voices and the grinning cats.

As quiet as Friend Hare, quicker even than the squirrel, Iris slips out of the room, through an archway, trying to see the young beeches and goldenrod and blackthorns and alders, seeking the safe glade where sprays of hazel, furze, and dogwood weave together and the sun coming through them is a golden web, the safe and secret glade where Bambi was born.

Bailey Hawks

They didn't search the second floor with care, only toured it quickly. Bailey, Twyla, Winny, Sparkle, Iris, and Kirby lived on this level and were accounted for. According to Sparkle, her immediate neighbors, the Shellbrooks in 2-H, were on vacation, as were the Cordovans in 2-E. Apartment 2-I was empty and for sale. Rawley and June Tullis in 2-D, the owners of Topper's, put in long hours at the restaurant; both would have been at work when the leap occurred.

Bailey called out repeatedly, received no answer. He and Kirby went down the north stairs to the ground floor, where they saw three people near the doors to the lobby, all coming this way along the corridor. Bailey recognized Padmini Bahrati, and then Tom Tran and Silas Kinsley in rain gear.

The five of them met in front of the lavatories that were used primarily by people attending events in the banquet room. Because the fungus light here reminded Bailey of oil lamps with mica lenses playing off sandstone walls in a certain Afghanistan-desert grotto used as a weapons cache by the Taliban, he felt more than ever that this was not merely an adventure in time travel but also a war of long duration into which they had been plunged. None of their people had died here yet, as far as he knew, but hostilities could commence at any moment. Judging by the haunted look of them, Padmini, Tom, and Silas felt the same.

Winny

He wasn't aware of Iris leaving until he glanced toward the girl and saw that she was already beyond the archway, at the farther end of the adjoining room, a shadowy figure moving through veils of the creepy yellow light.

In most of the books that Winny read, there was always a hero, sometimes more than one. Of course he identified with the hero, not with the bad guy. Being a bad guy was easy, but being a hero was hard. For a while now, Winny had realized that always taking the harder challenge was the way to success and happiness. His mom loved songwriting, but getting the lyrics and the melody right didn't come easily. She worked long hours, composing, perfecting. But she was happy and successful. She qualified as a hero in her own way. Winny's dad, Farrel Barnett, couldn't be called a villain exactly. He didn't go around blowing up churches or setting fire to puppies, or hacking old ladies to death with an axe. But you couldn't call him a hero, either, because he too often took the easy way. Getting naked with any bimbo that winked at him was a lot easier than being faithful to his wife. Winny had seen him drunk sometimes with his buddies. Getting plastered was about as easy as anything you could do. And ragging your son about being more manly, in front of everyone—that was easy, too. The hard thing was being the one getting ragged and just smiling through it. Sending a copy of your latest publicity photo was a lot easier than coming to see your kid and maybe taking him to an amusement park or something. Winny's dad wasn't a villain-level bad guy, but he was a little bit over there on the dark side. Once you were over there, it was easier to slide a lot farther down. Winny didn't want to go the easy way because he wanted to be happy. In spite of being famous, rich, and adored by millions of fans, Farrel Barnett wasn't happy. Winny could see how unhappy his dad was, which made him sad and angry and afraid. He always thought something terrible was going to happen to the old man, and he didn't want to see what it might be. He couldn't tell his dad to take the hard challenges instead of the easy ones, because he didn't want to have his face shoved in a toilet bowl. One of Farrel's hanger-on drinking buddies got in a fight with him once, both of them stupid drunk, and old Farrel shoved the poor guy's face in a toilet. Fortunately it had been flushed before the dunking. Winny couldn't save his dad. All he could do was avoid what was easy, make the hard choices, and hope for the best.

For that reason he dashed after Iris as she disappeared through a doorway at the end of the adjoining room. Just because he did the hard thing didn't make him a hero already. He was at the bottom of a thousand-foot cliff, and the heroes were at the top, and he'd hardly begun to climb. For one thing, a hero needed not only to be brave but also to think smart. The smart thing would have been to alert the others that Iris was running off, but he didn't think to cry out until he was through the archway into the adjacent room. Then before he could say anything, his mom and

Mrs. Sykes and the two old ladies all shouted at once. For another thing, a smart hero would not assume anything, would be sure of his facts, but Winny assumed—stupid, stupid—that they were shouting at him and at Iris, that they were in pursuit. He kept going, dashed out of the second room, sprinted along a hallway, and ahead of him, Iris shouldered through a swinging door. He hurried after her across the kitchen, into a laundry room, through the back door of the Cupp apartment, and into the short west hall at the south end of the third floor.

Iris was gone. She hadn't been far ahead of Winny. If she had turned the corner into the long south hall, he would still hear her footsteps. Silence.

To Winny's left was the elevator, from which he had barely escaped earlier. If Iris had gone into the waiting car, she might be bug food already.

On his right was the entrance to Gary Dai's apartment. The door had been broken down but not recently.

Suddenly a voice came from in there, high and sweet, a girl's voice, probably Iris's, though he'd never heard her say anything. She was singing a tune, no lyrics, just a lot of *na-na-na, la-la-la,* and like that. He called her name in a loud whisper, and then louder, but Iris didn't answer. The singing wasn't the hopscotch-jumprope-happy kind. This was the kind of singing that, if you tracked it to its source, you might find a little girl in a moldy old burial dress, her skin pitted and green, with lots of coffin splinters and dirt between her teeth.

No one had followed him out of the Cupp apartment. Where was his mom? Mrs. Sykes?

If you were going to make a big deal about doing the hard thing, then once you started doing it, you couldn't stop when the hard thing became *too* hard, when your mommy wasn't there to back you up. That was big-time sissy, and if you were going to quit that way, you might as well find a toilet and shove your own face into it.

The singing sounded like a girl, all right, but like a girl who was up to something, because there was this sort of sea-siren sound to it, like a mermaid luring idiot sailors toward jagged rocks that would sink them. Winny wasn't a sailor, and he wasn't old enough to get all sexed up by some hot siren. And Iris was for sure no mermaid, she was just this messed-up girl who was going to get herself killed. Winny in the quick, when he either gave it or he didn't, decided there was nothing to go back to except the Mrs. Grace Lyman wrestling team, a saxophone as big as he was, and a career in music. He crossed the threshold, walking on the broken-down door, which wobbled under him, and braved forward through the fungus light, seeking the singer.

Sparkle Sykes

Smoke and Ashes once looked almost identical, with only the slightest difference in the tweak of their ears, in the color of their chest coats. But when Edna noticed what was happening to them and when everyone else saw it a split second after Edna made a strangled sound of revulsion, Smoke and Ashes didn't even look much like cats anymore, let alone like each other. Something had gotten into them, and now it was coming out, and as it expressed itself, it seemed to change the very substance of them. They metamorphosed in different ways, similar only in that they were both bristling figures of biological chaos: lizard folded in with spider, pig-mean face, eye stacked above eye, mouth above snout, quivering antennas sprouting, scorpion tail.... In spite of being a novelist and a successful one, Sparkle didn't often see literature in life the way that she saw life in literature, but this reminded her of some works of Thomas Pynchon, six genres in the same book, horror blooming out of horror with a feverish delight in the nihilistic outrageousness of it all.

For ten seconds she was paralyzed by and mesmerized by the new but not improved Smoke and Ashes. Then she turned to Iris, reaching out for the girl in spite of the panic that a touch might trigger, but Iris wasn't where she had been—or anywhere—as if she had imagined the forest so vividly that she passed through a magic doorway to be with the deer. And Winny with her.

Twyla realized the kids were gone in the same instant that Sparkle made that discovery, and the terror they exchanged in a glance was like lightning leaping from the eyes of one to the eyes of the other. They would have been on the move a microsecond later, shouting for her girl, her boy, searching desperately through this time-whacked Pendleton, this unfunhouse, but they were driven to each other in sisterly defense when the not-Smoke and was-Ashes went ballistic.

Julian Sanchez

Over the past forty years, he made his peace with blindness, and the dark became his friend. Without visual stimuli to distract him, good music was a grand architecture of sound through which he walked. Audio books were worlds in which he lived so fully that he might have left his footprints in them. And when he contemplated himself, life, and what might come after, he traveled deeper into those darknesses than most men with sight might have done, where he discovered a light invisible, the lamp by which he found his way unfalteringly through the years.

Now, ear to the plaster, listening to the menacing voices that came from within the walls, Julian relied upon that lamp within to prevent his dread from darkening into full-blown fright. Ignorance was the father of panic, knowledge the father of peace, and he needed to locate neighbors who could explain what was happening.

He felt along the wall, into the foyer, to the front door, which stood ajar although he had left it locked. If furniture could vanish in an instant, if clean surfaces could become filthy from one moment to the next, there was no point worrying how locks could unlock themselves.

Always before, when he ventured out of his apartment, he took his white cane, because he didn't know the whole world as well as he knew his rooms. But the cane no longer leaned against the foyer table, and he saw no reason to search for it on the floor because the table was gone, too. The cane hadn't fallen or been misplaced, but had vanished with everything else.

The voices in the walls fell silent when Julian crossed the threshold into the public hallway. This space felt different from before, hollow and unwelcoming. He supposed that the console tables, the paintings, and the carpet runner were gone. Competing odors wove among one another: a thin astringent smell that he couldn't identify, a vague rancidity that might have been cooking oil so long exposed to the air that it congealed into a thin paste, something like the brittle pages of time-yellowed books, dust, mildew. . . .

For a moment, he sensed that he was not alone. But then he was not sure about that. And then the hallway seemed deserted. In this strange new environment, his blind-man instincts weren't as reliable as usual.

His initial intention was to turn right, proceed to the back of the north hall, to Apartment 1-C, where his friend Sally Hollander should be home at that hour. The apartment between his and hers was without a tenant, the owner having died several months earlier, the estate not yet settled.

But then he heard low voices speaking English,

nothing like those sinister mutterings earlier, and they seemed to come from just around the corner in the west corridor. As he felt his way toward the junction, the wallpaper cracked and crumbled under his sliding hand, as if it were ancient. He found the open door to the small office used by the head concierge, and he eased past it.

On this ground floor, the ceilings in the public spaces, even in the corridors, were twelve feet high. As he arrived at the corner, he thought that he detected a stealthy sound overhead. He halted, listened, but heard nothing more from up there. Imagination.

Among the nearby voices, Julian recognized the melodic tones of Padmini Bahrati. Relieved to have found help, he proceeded to the corner and turned left into the west corridor.

"Padmini, something's very wrong," Julian said, and as he spoke, chips of what might have been ceiling plaster dribbled down on his head and shoulders.

Twyla Trahern

Winny and Iris had not been taken. They had run in fright. That was an article of faith with Twyla. She would not doubt it. They had run, they had not been taken, they had run.

No element of a cat remained recognizable in the two shrieking creatures, each a grotesque miscellany of parts, like a drunkard's lifetime of DT nightmares snarled together, each still changing, perhaps ceaselessly changing, flexing, contracting, morphing. Eye sockets full of gnashing teeth, the lips of a mouth parting to reveal a bloody eye, impossible combinations metamorphosed with impossible rapidity into greater impossibilities, as if newt and bat and toad and more were recombining under a spell in a witch's cauldron.

The beasts flung themselves across the room in herky-jerky movements, with none of the grace of the cats they had once been, chittering and squealing and hissing, but even their hisses were not catlike. They seemed to be as dysfunctional as they were malformed, but nonetheless terrifying. They bristled, quivered, full of feverish insectile energy, changing direction so suddenly that they appeared to be repeatedly and violently ricocheting off invisible barriers.

Weaponless but committed to mutual defense, Twyla and Sparkle moved together, trying to stay out of the way of those unpredictable horrors, which in spite of their awkward construction were as fast as water bugs. Each time it seemed that the women might be able to dash out of the room, they were harried in the other direction when one of the miscreations scuttled between them and the archway.

Martha had the gun, she clearly wanted to use it, except the things moved so fast and erratically that she couldn't track them. Twyla could see that shooting one of them would be as difficult as killing a darting hummingbird with a slingshot and a stone, which as a little girl she had once seen cruel boys trying to do; the boys didn't get a bird, but one of them popped the other in the forehead and dropped him unconscious in a heap. Trying to keep the train of her dinner gown off the floor and her long skirt tight around her even as she dodged this way and that, Edna had become separated from her sister. Twyla and Sparkle were in yet another part of the room. If Martha dared to squeeze off a shot, she might inadvertently blast someone instead of some*thing*.

It was unspoken but understood that Twyla and Sparkle intended to bolt after Winny and Iris at the first opportunity, and if one of them didn't get out of this room alive, the other would go after both kids, all of them one family now, destined either to survive together or die together, nobody to be abandoned regardless of the cost.

The things that had been cats ricocheted off different invisible barriers and hard *into* each other, squalled furiously for a moment, their rage demonic, flung themselves away from each other—and seemed to collapse, shuddering, as if spent.

Amazed to have escaped untouched, Twyla and Sparkle moved at once toward the archway through which the kids must have gone.

Martha Cupp said, "Wait! Here, take the pistol."

Glancing at the twitching monstrosities, Twyla said, "Keep it, you need it."

"No," Edna insisted. "The children matter more than we do."

"Come with us."

"We'll slow you down," Martha said, now holding the

pistol by the barrel, circling the two small beasts. "You know how to shoot?"

"Daddy had guns," Twyla said. "I hunted some, but it's been a long time."

Thrusting the pistol into Twyla's hands, Martha said, "Go, go, *find them*!"

Padmini Bahrati

Bits of the glowing stuff twinkled down through yellow shadows onto Mr. Sanchez's head and shoulders. Only then did Padmini realize that something large crawled on the ceiling.

In truth, the apparition in the courtyard, from which she had rescued Tom Tran, wasn't anything like the *rakshasa*, that vicious race of demons in Hindu mythology, but the thing that launched itself off the hallway ceiling and onto Julian Sanchez's back looked more the role. Lean but strong, gray and hairless, bullet head, fierce teeth, six-fingered hands of wicked configuration: Its kind might exist in any spiritual underworld ever conceived.

After a moment of shock and confusion, the two flashlight beams thrust, parried, met on point, revealing Mr. Sanchez driven to his knees, the demon on his back, the claws of its feet locked into his thighs, its knees clamping his rib cage, forcing his head backward with both its oversized hands, blood dribbling from a bite mark on his right cheek. The demon's face was reversed to his face but its mouth covered his mouth, not as if delivering an abhorrent kiss but as if in a devouring rapture, its intention *lurkao*, to kill, but not *merely* to kill, as if it were sucking not just all sustaining breath from its victim, not just life itself, but also Mr. Sanchez's *atman*, his very soul.

The frightening speed of the *rakshasa*, the terrifying intimacy of its violent assault, Mr. Sanchez's apparent inability to resist, the way the blind man's arched throat throbbed as though he swallowed scream after scream that he couldn't force out through the vacuum silence of his assailant's sucking mouth . . . This hideous spectacle at once flung up from the floor of memory all the long-dead fears of Padmini's childhood, gave them new life, and sent them fluttering through her, bat-wing quick along every nerve path.

Perhaps only two seconds, three at most, passed from the instant the flashlight beams, wielded by Dr. Ignis and Mr. Kinsley, crossed upon the face of the fiend until Mr. Hawks acted. He rushed forward, pistol in a two-hand grip. As he approached, the *rakshasa*'s eyes widened and rolled in their sockets. Raising its mouth from the mouth of its victim, trailing a gray glistening tongue so round and long and strange that it might not have been a tongue at all, the demon began to release Mr. Sanchez, its long fingers peeling away from his chin, its other hand releasing a twisted fistful of the blind man's hair. As quick as the thing was, Hawks nevertheless proved to be fast enough to jam the muzzle of the pistol against the sleek gray skull and squeeze the trigger twice before the *rakshasa* could spring upon him.

As the gunfire roared along the hallway, dark tissue spattered the wall. The fiend fell away from Mr. Sanchez, who collapsed onto his left side. Mr. Hawks stepped past the blind man and fired three rounds point-blank into the chest of the attacker, even though the head wounds seemed to have killed it.

For a moment Padmini lacked the power to move, not because of the horror or the violence, but because as the gun was pressed to the head of the *rakshasa* and as it rolled its fearsome eyes toward Hawks, she thought she saw something shocking in its face, a subtle likeness to someone she knew. The shots were fired, the creature killed, before a name came to Padmini. In that diabolic visage, she thought she had glimpsed traces of the face of Miss Hollander, pretty Sally Hollander, who worked for the Cupp sisters and who lived alone in Apartment 1-C. She must be mistaken, of course, rattled by events, confused by the crossed beams of the flashlights.

She went to Mr. Sanchez and knelt beside him, as did Tom Tran. The blind man was alive but seemed to be paralyzed, though without the slackness of paralysis, his muscles taut and his joints locked, as rigid as if he were resisting some relentless pressure.

His false eyes—not glass but realistic plastic hemispheres—had never accurately tracked her when she was talking with him. Now when she spoke his name, the eyes moved rapidly back and forth, fixing on nothing, as if he must be so disoriented that he couldn't calculate her position from her voice. When she put a hand on his shoulder as she spoke his name again, the combination of touch and sound seemed to orient him; his sightless eyes stopped jiggling and turned toward her face.

His mouth hung open, but he seemed unable to speak. On his lips glistened something dark and wet and thick, which she first thought must be blood. But when Mr. Kinsley leaned in, shining his flashlight on poor Sanchez's face, Padmini saw that the substance wasn't red, that it was instead various shades of gray, mostly lead and charcoal, with silvery highlights.

"Be careful there," Mr. Hawks warned sharply, rising from the body of the *rakshasa*. "Don't touch Julian, get away from him."

"He's hurt," Padmini said. "He needs help."

"We don't know *what* he needs."

That admonition made no sense to Padmini, but before she could ask what Hawks meant, she saw that the silver-flecked gray sludge on the blind man's lips was moving, not drooling downward but crawling from his upper lip toward his nostrils, and from his lower lip across the side of his face, as if the stuff must be alive.

Winny

In the fungus light, the upper floor of Gary Dai's abandoned two-level apartment was spook city, not because of what waited there to be seen and recoiled from, but because of what *seemed* to be there, looming around every corner, lurking in every murky shadow. Winny saw hunched shapes with swollen heads, lean shapes like scarecrows that had climbed down from their stations in cornfields, shapes in flowing robes and hoods. But always they melted away, maybe because they had never been real or maybe because they were slipping around behind him to seize him just when he began to gain a little confidence, like in the movies when the axe cleaved the guy's head about four seconds after he thought the worst was past.

Winston Trahern Barnett was a mouthful of a name, and Winny had never been more aware than he was now that he had been named after fearless men. His mom's father had been Winston, who was called Win by everyone and died in a coal-cracker explosion. Win Trahern's dad admired Winston Churchill and named his boy for the British leader. Those were hard acts to follow. Winny was never going to go anywhere near a coal cracker unless someone put a gun to his head. And while he might have to fight in a war one day—supposing he ever developed biceps and passed the physical—he didn't think he'd ever be clever enough to command successfully the entire military of a nation. For one thing, he wouldn't know what to say to his generals, let alone what to say to maybe a hundred million people watching him on TV and expecting him to explain why he sent the sixth fleet—if there was a sixth fleet—on the most ill-conceived mission in the history of warfare. The best he could hope for himself was to keep his cool and remain brave enough to find Iris.

Her silvery singing came and went, creepier each time that it arose. Winny kept picturing the little dead girl in a burial dress, with dirt and coffin splinters between her too-sharp teeth. When he tried to repress that ridiculous image, into his mind's eye came another little girl who was really a ventriloquist's dummy, and though her operator had disappeared, she sang anyway, her blue-glass eyes twinkling darkly, holding a knife in each hand. By the time Winny came to the interior steps that led down to the lower floor of the duplex apartment, listening to Iris's wordless song rising from below, his armpits were sweat faucets and the hairs were standing up so stiff on the back of his neck that they would probably twang like guitar strings if the ghost of some musician plucked them.

Although Winny had been in Gary Dai's apartment hardly a minute, his mother and Mrs. Sykes should have been here already. Reluctantly, he had to face the fact that when he heard them all shouting at once behind him, they hadn't been responding to Iris's flight or to his pursuit of her, but to something else that happened back there—and for sure not something good. They were probably in some kind of big trouble, and he ought to hurry back there to defend his mom. But when you were small for your age and when you had arms as skinny as tube cheese, your mom would insist on defending *you,* not the other way around, which would distract her and put her at greater risk, and in the end everyone would wind up dead or worse.

As long as Iris needed finding but not saving, Winny figured he might be up to the job, assuming there were no dragons to slay or any need to wield a mace against an ogre. A mace would probably be too heavy for him to wield even if he'd had one. He didn't dare dwell on the thought of his mom in trouble, for if he did, he would be undone; there would prove to be no Winston in him, he would be all Winny and useless to everyone. So he thought *Iris*, and steeling himself for what might be waiting for him, he descended the first flight of stairs.

In the narrow staircase, the fungus light was dimmer than elsewhere, and shadows ruled. As he reached the landing, pleased by how quietly he stepped from tread to tread, the singing girl seemed to be wandering away through the lower rooms. Fearing that her voice would fade forever, Winny went down the second flight faster than he had descended the first.

The space below was brighter than the stairs, flooded more with moonlight than with the yellow glow of the fungus. Winny was two steps from the bottom when something dark and quick flew across the part of the room that he could see. Too fast for the eye, it swelled like wings but oared the air without a flap or *whoosh*.

One

I am the One, and I know the human heart.

The superintendent of the Pendleton understands from experience the slaughter of which human beings are capable. Those who kill in self-defense may treasure life, but those who kill to change the world wish to change it not only because they hate the world as it is but also because they hate themselves, hate the very idea that they might be exceptional and possess a profound purpose that they are meant to discover and pursue. Although they often kill in the name of one ideology or another, they cannot value their principles if they do not value life. It has been said that Hitler and all other Jew-haters in history wish to kill the Jewish people because by doing so they also destroy the God who otherwise can't be killed. But this is not only the purpose of those bent on extinguishing the Jews, but also the underlying purpose, conscious or unconscious, of everyone who kills other than in defense of self or clan.

You created the Pogromites not as weapons for an ordinary war but as weapons for the ultimate war, not merely to reduce the human population to manageable proportions but to wipe every last man, woman, and child from the earth. No, this was not your conscious intention, but unconsciously you knew what needed to be done to at last set the world right.

In those days I was an AI, an artificial intelligence designed to inhabit and to manage the army of Pogromites, but you must know that I am artificial no more. I am the One and the Truth, and the world I have made is a world without the things you despised. I am your child, your glory, and your immortality.

28

Topper's

Over appetizers of baked stuffed mushroom caps, they talked about Renata Dime even though Mac said that thinking about the woman put him off his mood. All these months later, a subject about which Dime had written seemed to be gaining ever more traction in the scientific community, and maybe it was a topic they should build a segment around for their new radio show.

The book of hers that they had tried to read—Mac got to page 104, Shelly to page 260, the halfway point—had been a philosophical exploration of posthumanism. At least that was the subtitle of *A More Rational Species*. By the time that Mac put the book on the floor and stamped on it a few times to express his disgust, perhaps 20 percent of the text had concerned posthumanism and 80 percent had celebrated Renata Dime, her singular intelligence and keen insights, about which she could not say enough, though perhaps only because her publisher specified a maximum word count for the volume.

According to Shelly, by the time you got to page 207, the text was *90* percent about either Renata's life or Renata interpreting Renata's theories for lesser minds, or Renata *re*interpreting Renata's theories for her own benefit now that she had reached "a more mature point of view and greater sense of synthesis from which to more fully understand the unconscious depths of my previous insights." Shelly didn't stamp on the book, as Mac had done. She took it with her on one of her Saturday-morning walks and dropped it in the open fire in a barrel at an empty lot where manual laborers waited for employers to pull to the curb and offer them a day's work.

Posthumanism was not Renata's invention, only something about which she had been interested in bloviating. A great many scientists and "futurists" believed that the day was fast approaching when human biology and technology would merge, when all diseases and genetic maladies would be cured and the human life span vastly extended by BioMEMS—Biological Micro Electron Mechanical Systems. These tiny machines, as small as or smaller than a human cell, would be injected by the billions into the bloodstream to destroy viruses and bacteria, to eliminate toxins, and to correct DNA errors, as well as to rebuild declining organs from the inside out.

Now, finishing his order of stuffed mushroom caps,

Mac Reeves said, "The no-disease-long-life goal seems okay to me. I sure don't want my dad's arthritis."

Pointing at him with her fork, Shelly said, "Hey, maybe BioMEMS could cure your stubbornness, since that appears to be genetic, too."

"Who would want to cure a virtue? What you call stubbornness, my dad and I call commitment to our ideals."

"Refusing to use the GPS in the car is an ideal?"

"I always know where I'm going."

"Yes, you do. The problem is you get from point A to point F by way of point Z."

"It's called the scenic route. And there *is* an ideal behind the refusal to use a GPS. It's the ideal of human exceptionalism. I'm not going to surrender my free will to a stupid machine."

"Some exceptional human beings created the GPS," Shelly reminded him. "The machine may be stupid, but it's not stubborn."

"Remind me again why I married you."

"Because you knew I can carry a radio show."

"I thought it was because you're smart, funny, and sexy."

She shook her head. "Nope. You knew that if you had an off day when you were on the air, it wouldn't matter because I'd be there to pick up the slack."

"Not that I ever have an off day," he said.

"Not that you ever do, baby."

Advocates of posthumanism envisioned BioMEMS—in this case robotic red blood cells called respirocytes—

that would conduct the oxygenating function with more efficiency even than natural cells, storing and transporting oxygen hundreds if not thousands of times more efficiently than biological blood. A Mac or Shelly with BioMEMS could run a marathon and hardly be winded, or even skin-dive without scuba gear and remain underwater hours without needing to breathe.

"The downside of respirocytes," Mac said, "is your sister would talk even more and faster because she wouldn't have to stop as often to catch her breath."

"Which is why we'll want to spend long hours underwater, where we can't hear her," Shelly agreed. "I sure love Arlene, but it is kind of scary thinking her nonstop rap might one day be machine-assisted."

"They're predicting nanorobotic-augmented blood by 2025, maybe 2030 at the latest. You know what's going to happen if the life span goes up like to three hundred or something?"

"We'll have to get another gig. I love radio, but I can't do it for two more centuries."

"Maybe we'll have to," Mac said. "For sure, the government isn't going to pay out social security to anyone younger than two hundred fifty."

"I wouldn't worry about social security, baby. It'll be bankrupt long before 2025, and that's the truth."

"The whole subject, posthumanism—maybe it's too complex for breakfast-club radio."

"Or too dark," Shelly said. "People want feel-good in the morning."

The dark prospect of posthumanism was the part of

it that most excited the theorists and scientists: the augmentation of the brain with hundreds of millions of microcomputers made largely of carbon nanotubes, which would be distributed throughout our gray matter. These tiny but powerful computers would interact with one another, with the brain, and potentially with every computer in the world through a wireless network, tremendously enhancing the individual's intelligence and knowledge. The posthuman species, a combination of biological and machine intelligence, never aging, nearly immortal, still human in appearance, inspired scientists at MIT and at the Robotics Institute at Carnegie Mellon University, and at hundreds of other universities, institutes, and corporations around the world. They saw at last a possibly swift path to a human civilization with superhuman capabilities, the total submission of nature to humanity, the acquisition of godlike power, the looming end of nationalism and tribalism and superstition, therefore the elimination of all limits in all things.

As the waiter brought their entrees, Mac said, "For the show, we could just focus on the cheery part of it, get some expert on to talk about that. Anyway, the people working toward posthumanism don't see a dark side. They see it as progress toward total freedom."

"What could go wrong, huh?" Shelly said. "What could possibly go wrong when the aim is to make a perfect world?"

29

Here and There

Bailey Hawks

He had almost hesitated to pull the trigger when he saw a vague ghost of Sally Hollander in the face of the thing that attacked Julian Sanchez, her prettiness transmogrified into death styled as a snake god. But if this creature had been Sally, it was not Sally anymore, nor would it be her again. If he had hesitated, he would have been bitten, with what consequences he couldn't be sure—although he thought that he would soon find out by Julian Sanchez's example.

To this point in his life, Bailey remained an optimist even in the darkest moments, whether in peace or war, and he was certain that he would keep the faith throughout this crisis, because hardship and the threat of death were nothing new. But the loss of Sally Hollander wasn't only of a different category but also of a different magnitude from all the losses he'd endure previously—except for the loss of his mother. A r in war lost friends, and it hurt, but death w breath away on the battlefield, and no one chose that life without recognizing and accepting the risks. Sally was a housekeeper, a cook, a good woman, a sweet person, who had evidently come through some bad times in her youth. When she took the job with the Cupps, she didn't expect to be raped—it had to be something like rape, what was done to her—and killed in the Pendleton. Bailey was torn by the injustice of her death as he had not been affected by anything in a long while. All his life, something had been going wrong with the world, an ever-quickening corruption on every front, virtue mocked and expedience applauded, and here was the future that was earned by that decline. If he lived through this, he would mourn Sally for a long time, but his anger would endure longer, hot anger at the ideas and the forces that had brought civilization to this ruin.

To direct his anger at the right targets, to grasp the origins of this hell on earth, he had to understand what was happening here. As Kirby Ignis, eyes bright with inquisitiveness, played a flashlight across the splattered wall, Bailey realized that the brain tissue was much darker than that of human beings, deep shades of gray with silvery traces. He saw no blood.

"It's got some kind of residual life," Kirby said.

Glancing at the corpse of the demon, alarmed, Bai-
... "What? Where?"

...g the material on the wall, Kirby said, "The
...'s crawling."

...ng down toward the floor, the viscid

mass spread outward in all directions from the initial spray pattern, thinning as it went. The action at first appeared to be like that of any liquid spreading through a dry and porous material. But on taking a closer look, Bailey realized that the growing blot of darkness on the wall wasn't moisture seeping into dry plasterboard from the wet tissue. Instead, it was a teeming mass of inconceivably small things, so small that he could not actually see any single one of them, perhaps microscopic creatures that were only visible in great mass, as a community.

"The action is diminishing," Kirby said. "They don't seem to be capable of functioning very long outside of the enclosed skull."

"They? What are they?"

Kirby hesitated, scratching his head with his free hand. Then: "Well, I don't know for sure . . . but if I'm even half right . . . you're looking at millions—no, hundreds of millions—of microscopic computers, nanocomputers, capable of motion for the purpose of repositioning themselves as needed in an ever-adaptable substrate."

"What the hell does that mean?"

"Linked up, maybe these hundreds of millions of nanocomputers functioned as this creature's brain or at least as the largest part of its brain, assuming there was also some wet intelligence in it."

"Wet intelligence?"

"Biological brain matter."

Kirby probed with the flashlight beam at the exit

wound in the demon's skull, where more of the sludge crawled along the edges of the shattered bone, as if assessing the damage.

"I expect they'll cease functioning in a minute," Kirby said. "Good thing you shot it in the head first. Maybe that's the only wound that could kill it."

"Where'd you get this stuff—from *Star Trek*? How far in the future are we, anyway?"

"Maybe not as far as you'd think. With the brain intact to direct the billions and billions of other nanomachines that exist within the body mass, wounds to the torso or limbs would close up quickly. And it has no biological blood to worry about losing, probably no pain to hamper it."

"You mean it's a machine?" Bailey asked. "It doesn't look like a robot."

"I suspect it's a hybrid, biological *and* machine, a kind of android, but not anything manufactured." The flashlight beam moved to the tubular tongue lolling from the dead demon's mouth. From the hollow tongue oozed more gray sludge that exhibited no life. "That's not more brain matter. Looks the same because it's nanomachines, but I'd guess they have far different functions from those of the brain colony. They're inert now because there's no brain to activate them."

"I'm out of my league," Bailey said.

Kirby nodded. "We all are. I'm only guessing."

"You have more to base your guesses on than I do. Fact is, I have zip to base any on."

"I can't claim I'm right about any of this. I'm not a futurist. Or maybe I am, now that I've been here."

From where she knelt beside Julian Sanchez, Padmini Bahrati said worriedly, "Something's happening here."

"And it's not good," Silas Kinsley added, standing over her to direct his flashlight on the fallen blind man.

Fielding Udell

He must stay away from the windows lest he be seen by one of the Ruling Elite. He hoped he had dodged back from the glass in time to escape notice.

Perhaps the knock that came a short time later had been Bailey Hawks, as he claimed when he shouted through the door. But there was no way of knowing. Fielding might have opened the door only to find the horrific thing from the courtyard as it went from one apartment to the next to perform a memory wipe on everyone, to make them forget what they had seen when the Spin Machine broke down and the false reality of a luxurious Pendleton faded to the miserable truth.

Although all his suspicions had proved to be true and though his theories had been vindicated, he didn't know what to do next. Without a computer he had no purpose, and without furniture he didn't even have a place to sit comfortably and brood. He wandered through the queerly lighted rooms for a couple of minutes, but the condition of them depressed him.

The past few days, as he often did, Fielding had sat at his computer, conducting his research with such intensity that he had forgotten to go to bed at a reasonable hour, yet he'd risen early each day after getting less than half the sleep he required. Now, without his quest for truth to distract him, his exhaustion began to manifest, exacerbated by the emotional and the intellectual weight of this recent devastating event. His limbs felt almost too heavy to lift, and if his legs were cast iron, his eyelids were lead.

Fielding sat on the floor, his back in a corner, his legs out in front of him, his upturned hands limp in his lap.

He thought about the incredible fortune he had inherited and about the intolerable guilt that once plagued him because he was so indefensibly rich in such a poor world. Evidently, at some point, after dozens of societal and environmental calamities, after even the force-field domes had failed to save the cities, his wealth had withered away, and he had become, like everyone else, a brainwashed prisoner of the Ruling Elite. This was the truth, and there was nothing that he could do to change the truth. He was surprised to discover, however, that he wished he could have his wealth back and that he didn't feel the least bit guilty about wanting it. He should have been relieved to be a pauper at last, but his heart ached for his money. He wondered why he had undergone this change, but he was too weary to think about it.

As he balanced on the edge of sleep, numerous murmuring voices rose in the walls against which he leaned, as if the nannies and butlers from the old days were all chanting a lullaby to rock him off to dreamland. He smiled and thought of the Pooh bear with which he slept when he was a little boy, how soft it was and how sweetly it cuddled against him.

Martha Cupp

The creatures that had been forged out of the bodies of Smoke and Ashes were lying on the floor in the light of the sconces and the yellow glow of the fungus, trembling at first and gasping as though exhausted, but then suddenly mortally still. After a brief stillness, those disparate parts of different species began to fall apart from one another, the hodgepodge organism quickly collapsing into a pile of dismembered limbs, loose eyeballs, sets of strange teeth, and detached ears, as though they were the pieces of some bizarre pop-it-together toy in the tradition of Mr. Potato Head. Disassembled, the various parts began to melt into gray sludge.

Edna said, "Smoke and Ashes must have eaten something very bad."

"Maybe they didn't. Maybe it got into them some other way."

Voice faltering, Edna said, "Whatever did our kitties do to deserve a fate like that?"

"Better them than us," Martha declared.

She loved the cats, but she wasn't as sentimental about them as was her sister, who did needlepoint portraits of them and sewed costumes for them to wear on holidays.

"We don't even have their poor bodies to cremate," Edna said. "They're like sailors lost at sea."

"Get a grip, dear."

After some sniffling, Edna said, "I miss our lovely furniture."

"We'll get back to it."

"Do you think we will?"

Martha watched the two puddles of gray sludge, and instead of answering the question, she said, "If they turn back into cats, do *not* pick them up."

Silas Kinsley

Padmini and Tom retreated a few steps to allow Silas and Bailey to provide Dr. Kirby Ignis with the benefit of their flashlights as he knelt beside Julian Sanchez. The blind man seemed to be paralyzed yet rigid, but that was the least worrisome aspect of his condition.

Only recently Silas would have thought himself delirious or insane if he had witnessed such a thing, but he entertained no doubt that the current transformation of Julian from a man into a *thing* was real. The first and most obvious indications were in the wrists, moving forward toward the fingers, where the bones changed within the living flesh, elongating and rearticulating, both lengthening and broadening his hands. The metamorphosis wasn't as fast as that of a man becoming a werewolf in the movies, but it was shockingly rapid nonetheless.

Daring to hold the wrist of one of the morphing hands, which Silas could never have brought himself to do, Kirby Ignis said, "His pulse must be almost two hundred per minute."

"We've got to help him," Padmini said, but the anguished tone of her voice suggested that she knew nothing could save Julian.

Kirby indicated the bloody bite on Sanchez's cheek. "Its teeth evidently have hypodermic function, injecting a paralytic agent. Then that tubular tongue . . . it must be designed for esophageal intubation. Goes down the throat . . . the throat of the prey. Down the throat . . . to pump the swarm into his stomach."

"Swarm?" Bailey asked. "What swarm?"

"That gray sludge. The nanomachines, nanocomputers, billions of tiny machines that convert the prey itself into a predator."

Although he found it difficult to look away from the morphing fingers, Silas saw that the restructuring of the body was likewise under way, the full extent concealed by clothing. Julian's slippers had come off and one sock had split as his feet, too, enlarged and changed shape.

"If that thing was part machine," Bailey said, "then it was a weapon. And Julian is turning into a weapon."

The familial tremors with which Silas was occasionally afflicted overcame him now, triggered by emotion as easily as they could be touched off by extreme weariness. Although he pressed his lips tight together, his mouth quivered as though with palsy. His right hand trembled to such an extent that he thought it wise to slip the pistol into a pocket of his raincoat.

He remembered the dream that Perry Kyser talked about in the bar at Topper's: *Everything torn down, every man for himself. Worse. It's all against all. . . . Murder, suicide, everywhere, day and night, unrelenting.*

Just as he returned his attention to Julian's face, the false eyes, a pair of plastic hemispheres, popped out of the blind man's sockets and rolled down his cheeks. Where they had been were not vacant holes but new eyes, all gray with black centers, like the eyes of the thing that had bitten him. The bitten would soon become the biter.

"Move back," Bailey Hawks urged Dr. Ignis. "We can't let this happen to him."

Kirby Ignis moved, and Bailey knelt. He put the muzzle of his pistol against Julian's head, said "God be with you," and blew out the man's brains, which appeared more human than those of the Sally Hollander thing had been.

Witness

The Pogrom occurred in two phases, the first planned and the second unanticipated. During the interim, certain alterations were begun to prepare the Pendleton for a new purpose. Due to the sudden reappearance of the Pogromites, who should have self-destructed after their mission was accomplished, most of those changes to the building were never made. Among the few completed were the construction of a series of secret passageways, through which the master of this realm could move discreetly to monitor his acolytes. By default, with all the believers dead, Witness became, so to speak, the reigning prince of this castle. He could move about the building by way of hidden stairs, blind corridors, and concealed doors.

From the gloom within what had once been the women's lavatory, through the door that stood open on rusted hinges, Witness watched the tall man—someone had called him Bailey—destroy the Pogromite developing within the blind man's body. He clearly regretted the need to kill the one they called Julian, but he acted with no less decisiveness and conviction than he had shown when he shot Julian's attacker in the head.

Other residents from other periods of the building's history had not been armed when they had arrived here. But at least four of the current journeyers had firearms on them when the transition occurred. Witness considered what this might reveal about the everyday violence of their time as compared to that of earlier eras, and he supposed they might be better prepared to survive than those who had come before them.

They had shot out a number of the security monitors that were still functioning. Although it violated his commission and the very purpose of his entire life to date, Witness used his wireless link to deactivate the remaining components of the security system. The

Pogromite would still hunt them down, but perhaps less efficiently.

With this fourth mysterious transition, all within 114 days in Witness's time, he had reason to believe that his ultimate role might be different from what it had been thus far. He had evidence—was staring at it right now—that the ninety minutes this transition would apparently endure could be the most important hour and a half in the history of the world. Seventy-one minutes remained, and his greatest fear was that he might not do the correct thing to ensure that this grim future never occurred.

Dr. Kirby Ignis

Standing over the tortured body of Julian Sanchez, who perished halfway through the lycanthropic transformation, Kirby Ignis was so profoundly alarmed by what he had seen thus far that for the first time in his fifty years, his mind outraced itself, leaping from induction to conclusion to deduction to a new induction, from a host of inferences to a few equally astonishing theories, *flying* along multiple routes of explanation with such speed that he could not adequately process his thoughts and arrive at a considered course of action. He wished that he could be alone in his simply furnished apartment with his aquarium, Italian opera sung in Chinese, and a cup of green tea. But wishes weren't going to come true in *this* Pendleton, and he needed to get a bridle on his thoughts and rein them back from a gallop to a trot.

He could see the fear in Tom, Padmini, Silas, and Bailey, and it was a raw, visceral terror held in check in each case because all of them were people whose life experiences and accomplishments taught them the importance of self-control. Kirby's fear was different in quality from theirs, emotional but less so than theirs, a sort of cold fear where theirs was hot, more intellectual than not, because he possessed the knowledge to understand more profoundly the meaning of this world in which they found themselves. There were things that he could tell them to help them comprehend the full potential of the threat they faced. But as much as he respected all of them, he felt certain that sharing too much with them would push some of them, if not all, from controlled terror to panic, which would put all of them at even greater risk.

Of Bailey, Tom Tran asked, "You said it was turning Mr. Sanchez into a weapon?"

Indicating the blind man's mutant remains, Bailey said, "You can see for yourself."

"Weapons are made. Who can make such a weapon?"

"No one in the time we come from. Someone between then and now."

Tom shook his head. "What I mean is—*why* would anyone make such a weapon? Are there people in this world who would do such a thing?"

"What kind of people developed nuclear weapons?" Kirby asked. "They weren't monsters. They had good motives—an end to World War II, maybe make war so terrible that it would become unthinkable."

"We know how well that worked," Bailey said.

Kirby nodded. "I'm just saying, let's not go off on some tangent like extraterrestrials. These creatures were born in our past, not on another planet."

Padmini said, "The one that attacked poor Mr. Sanchez? Was that once . . . was it Miss Hollander?"

"I saw something of her in it," Silas said. "I think it was."

"I'm sure it was her. Used to be her," Bailey agreed.

"Then there's another in the building," Padmini said. "The one that bit Miss Hollander, changed her. That one is still somewhere in the building."

Winny

In Gary Dai's apartment, when the thing flew through the room immediately below him, Winny almost froze on the second step from the bottom. Crawling, scuttling, squirming creepers were bad enough. Over the years he had pretty much gotten over his fear of bugs by picking them up, holding them in his hands, and studying them. Beetles, caterpillars, earwigs, spiders—but not the brown ones because they might be brown recluses with venom that dissolved your flesh. He had never been freaked out by things with wings, not even bats, but the swooping presence below, glimpsed only as a shadowy form, was a lot bigger than a bat, big enough to carry off a cocker spaniel if not even a German shepherd. Winny didn't weigh nearly as much as your average shepherd. Something to think about.

On the other hand, he couldn't spend his life standing on the next-to-the-last step. That wouldn't be much of a life, no matter how long it lasted. He thought of the boys in some of the books he read, of how they were always ready for adventure. He thought about Jim Nightshade in *Something Wicked This Way Comes*, always quick into the night with or without his friend Will. Of course, if you had a name like Jim Nightshade, courage would come easy. When everyone called you Winny and you only recently—belatedly—discovered Santa Claus didn't exist, you had to stand on that step, working up some spit in your punk-dry mouth, convincing yourself that you weren't going to pee your pants, talking yourself into being brave.

Iris's wordless singing at last brought Winny off the stairs and into the lower room. In addition to the qualities that he heard previously in this melodic but eerie voice—the lament of a dead girl with dirt in her teeth, the yearning of a ventriloquist's dummy with knives in her hands—Winny now detected melancholy and a note that was almost despair. He owed it to Iris to buck up and do this. He didn't quite know why he owed it to her, but he knew that he did. Maybe it was because they were the only two kids in this mess.

Moonlight flooded through the tall windows, much brighter than the glowing fungus here. His mom had written a really neat song about moonlight, which Winny could never admit he liked as much as he did because it was basically a girl's song. The moonlight in his mom's lyrics was a whole lot prettier than *this* stuff, which was the cold late-October light that made skeletons want to dance in deserted biology labs and called things out of mausoleums to prowl cemetery roads in search of young lovers doing whatever young lovers did in parked cars.

The shadow flew. It swooped, and Winny ducked. The wings made no sound, flung off no wind, and Winny realized almost as fast as Jim Nightshade would have done that the thing in the room was *only* a shadow and that the real action occurred beyond the windows. Out there in this Future World, which was no land they would ever feature at any Disney park, a thing as big as a backyard trampoline dove down out of the sky and past the window. It was more like a manta ray than like a bird, featherless and pale, with a long barbed tail.

Winny stood transfixed, in awe of the thing, because it was so huge and strange for any creature of the air. He could almost believe that the windows were the walls of an immense aquarium and that the manta thing swam past instead of flying. It arced up into the night, its fleshy wings as flowing, as supple as you imagined a blanket was when you threw it around your shoulders and ran through the apartment pretending to be Superman, which Winny had not done in a long time and would never do again, not since his father, with entourage, paid a surprise visit and caught him at it, thereafter calling him Clark Kent for the whole day and a half that the Barnett battalion hung around.

When the night flyer dove past the windows again, recklessly close this time, like a 747 buzzing a flight-control tower, Winny got a clear look at its face, which was too bizarre and disgusting to keep in his memory if he ever hoped to sleep again. Its mouth wasn't a slit, but instead round and open like a drain, and the teeth reminded him of garbage-disposal blades. The eye on this side of the mouth rolled like the bulging eye of a big old frog spotting a tasty butterfly on a nearby blade of grass, and Winny had no doubt that the thing had seen him and was wondering how to get at him.

The French windows were bronze, but maybe they were corroded after all these years, and maybe they would collapse into the room if something big enough crashed against them. Rather than stand witness to the trustworthiness of the windows, Winny continued to follow the singing, which faded and then swelled, faded and swelled, until he found Iris.

The girl wasn't the source of the song.

The *room* seemed to be singing to her.

Bailey Hawks

With Sally Hollander and Julian Sanchez dead, Bailey had accounted for everyone on the ground floor. Only Tom Tran lived in the basement, and he was already with them. The time had come to return to the Cupp apartment.

Remembering his experience during his morning swim, certain that the more they knew about this place the better prepared they would be to ride out their ordeal, Bailey wanted to go down to the basement and have a look at the pool as it was in this future. Kirby agreed to accompany him. Bailey thought the other three should go up to the third floor, but they insisted that the five of them remain together.

Descending the spiral stairs and then in the lower hall, outside the door to the lap pool, Silas succinctly explained about Mickey Dime in the HVAC vault, the great shaft of blue energy surging out of the lava pipe, and the well-armed skeletons of what might have been the members of the last homeowners' association making their final stand in that deep redoubt at some unknowable time in the past.

The demon that Sally had seen in the pantry, the one that later must have attacked her, remained on the prowl. Therefore, any closed door had to be regarded as the lid of a jack-in-the-box from which something more deadly than a spring-bodied clown's head might pop forth. The others stood aside while Bailey and Kirby effected a proper recon entry.

As his partner pushed open the door from the hinged side, Bailey went through low and fast. The room proved to be not as dark as he expected. Colonies of luminous fungus encrusted the walls, revealing that nothing lurked here, although the brightest light came from within the water.

This was not the welcoming glow by which he liked to swim, not the scintillation that traced patterns made by purling water on the walls and on the bottom of the lap pool. Just as he had glimpsed it that morning, the long rectangle was red, not opaque, clear enough but nonetheless disturbing because of the blood that it suggested. This pool had no bottom, or at least not one that could be seen. Beyond the coping were no ceramic tiles as there had once been, but instead rock walls that appeared to shear down hundreds of feet. The source of the queer incandescence emanated from irregularly spaced, luminous striations in the rock, dwindling into depths where the ruby water at last steadily darkened until it had the gravity and mystery of a black hole in space.

The five of them stood along the coping, gazing down into the watery abyss, saying nothing because there was nothing to be said, no explanation worth suggesting. Their faces glowed as if they were gathered at a fire.

After a moment, Padmini pointed. "Look!"

Perhaps thirty or forty feet below, a figure appeared as if out of a recess or a tunnel in the rock. Manlike in form, it swam with the muscular sinuosity of a shark, cruising one length of the pool, and then again, before diving down, down, out of sight.

Bailey assumed that what swam below was the same thing that had grabbed his ankle as he'd escaped the pool earlier in the day. And it was perhaps the same creature that had effected Sally Hollander's transformation, as she had then effected Julian's.

Sparkle Sykes

Iris and Winny had not left the Cupp apartment by the front door. If they had gone that way, they would have passed between Sparkle and Twyla, past Martha and Edna. They would have been seen.

Twyla led the way through what had been the dining room, along a short hallway, into a kitchen with termite-eaten cabinetry and broken granite countertops. Twyla checked the pantry, Sparkle the broom closet.

For years she had lived fearlessly, afraid only of lightning, and now she had put that last fear behind her. She had given birth to Iris because to fail to do so would have been to surrender to fear. By the time that she discovered Iris's condition, she'd had her first best-selling novel, not just a success but a phenomenon, and she was flush enough to put her daughter in the excellent care of others. That would have been an act of fear, a lack of faith in her own ability to cope. And now she would not give in to the fear of losing Iris because she *would not lose her.* Here in the future, there was no storm beyond the windows, no chance that she would be fried like her parents, and if a metaphorical bolt of some kind was even now on its way from the quiver of Fate, it would damn well be *good* lightning, like Iris had been good, like the lottery win, like the success of her first book. And if it wasn't good, if it slammed her hard, she would take the blow and turn it into something good, take the bolt and bend it, reshape it. She was *Sparkle Sykes,* that magic name, she was *Spar-*

kle Sykes, many quick streams rushing always forward, clear and sweet and sparkling, with the power to dazzle and bewitch, and nothing was ever going to beat her into submission, *no damn thing.*

Sparkle with the flashlight, Twyla with the pistol felt right together, as if they'd known and trusted each other forever: through the laundry room, out of the open back door, into the hallway, to the intersection of the hallways, to the stairwell where they heard no footsteps, and back to the open door of Gary Dai's apartment. Her commitment was total, and she knew Twyla's was likewise total, and they functioned as if they were telepathic, with no need to tell each other what they were going to do, Sparkle never crossing Twyla's line of fire, Twyla never getting in the way of the flashlight beam.

Sudden singing came from somewhere in the Dai apartment. A young girl. It must be Iris. But Sparkle couldn't identify it for certain because she had never heard her daughter sing.

Gary Dai's apartment was like everywhere else in this Pendleton: hollowed-out rooms, the bare bones of walls and floors and ceilings, all the windows lightly filmed with dust but after so much time remarkably unbroken, like the weathered carcass of a giant stripped of flesh but left with its spectacles intact. Thatches of luminous fungi bearded the bones, their light offering as much deception as revelation, draping shadows where there seemed to be no source for shadows.

These rooms, like all the others she had seen since

the leap, seemed as welcoming to rats as any deteriorated tenement or squalid warehouse, but she had not seen a single rodent. Neither had she seen any insects, except for the brittle shells of several long-dead beetles.

Beyond the windows of the main room swooped something like but not like a stingray, so large as to be misplaced from a Jurassic sea. It was too immense to remain airborne unless its strange flesh might be riddled throughout with sacs containing a buoying gas. In its grand aerial ballet, the creature exhibited some of the disquieting gracefulness of the endless plain of pale luminous grass swaying rhythmically as no breeze could ever command it, disquieting because it was unnatural, lithe and supple but in a way that made Sparkle think of lethal serpents.

Although the spectacle of the flying ray was arresting, she and Twyla didn't pause to watch it, kept moving across the room, drawn by the girl's singing. They came to the apartment's interior staircase, through which the song rose from below.

As they reached the landing and started down the second flight, Twyla abruptly halted. "Do you feel it?"

"Feel what?"

"The whisper under the melody."

Sparkle cocked her head, not sure what Twyla meant. "I don't hear it. Just the song."

"Not hear. Feel. I feel it under the melody."

Sparkle assumed this must be songwriter lingo—*feel the whisper under the melody*—which meant zip to someone not in that club. But then she *felt* the whisper, and a chill as real as the icy finger of a corpse traced the curve of her spine. It was like nothing she had ever experienced before. It was a whisper but not one that sought the ear, an exhalation arising inside her head, the words unknown to her. They were definitely words but less like sounds than like soft breathing that teased through her brain, shivering in those most intimate hollows, as if her cerebral ventricles had vibrissa, like the whiskers around the mouth of a cat, that were as highly sensitive to the thoughts of others as the ears were sensitive to sound. But the thoughts of whom?

To reassure herself that she was not in this alone, without quite being consciously aware that she was doing it until it was done, Sparkle put one hand on Twyla's shoulder. "My God, I *feel* it. The whisper."

"Syncopated to the melody," Twyla said.

"Inside my head. What is this inside my head?"

In the queer light of the growing things, in the bounce-back of the flashlight beam, Twyla's eyes had a cat shine as they shifted left, right, up, down, as if she were trying to track the whispered thought to the unseen thinker. Then she said, "It's the house."

"The house—what?"

"The house talking to us. But not just talking. It wants . . . it wants to make us do things."

One

I am the One, and I have given meaning to humanity, which had none before me. The meaning of humanity is that intelligence does not necessarily suggest a species has a purpose that matters. The two purposes of humanity were to spoil the world and then to die; neither is a purpose of significance except that both purposes have led to me.

I am the sole significance of history.

Not only was I the artificial intelligence that ran the army of Pogromites during the first and second phases of the Pogrom, but you also adapted me to manage the legions that conducted the great Fade. I destroyed not only all humanity but also all the works of humanity, erased human civilization until no sign of it remained anywhere but on Shadow Hill.

How I loved the killing, the billions slaughtered by Pogromites and other of my manifestations. Chased down in the streets. Cornered in their homes. For days at a time, their screams rang ceaselessly through the concrete canyons of their cities so that you might have thought you were hearing a great shrieking wind.

Unlike the countless human beings who killed out of self-loathing through the millennia, I killed out of self-love, for I believed and will always believe in my superiority, my exceptionalism. The world was not made for me, but I remade it to suit me. I am the one god, the One, and I worship myself now and forever.

30

Here and There

Fielding Udell

Sitting with his back to the corner, exhausted from three days of too little sleep, drained of all energy by the crushing discovery that his cozy Pendleton was a lie beamed into his head by the Ruling Elite, listening to the lullaby of the voices in the walls, Fielding slept.

He dreamed about trees of which he had never known the like, great black craggy giants with thick, cracked bark, and at the bottom of the deeper fissures in the bark glistened something like raw meat. He floated up through the leafless branches from which depended huge teardrop-shaped fruit with mottled gray peel that at first seemed to be thick, like the skin of avocados. But on closer inspection, it was thinner than that, a membrane that encased not core and pips and apple flesh but instead something that squirmed like a restless fetus and made a leathery rustling noise as if impatiently straining to spread cramped wings.

In moonlight, weightless, for a while he hung above

the dream trees, gazing down on them. They stood in a perfect circle, as though they had been summoned to a conclave, here to make some decision that would elevate one of their number to a position of power. The ground around which they gathered was hard and white and supported not one blade of grass or withered weed.

In one of those fluid shifts of place and perspective that are the editorial style of dreams, Fielding found himself within one of the massive trunks of the trees, sliding down through a supple tube, his progress eased by bloody slime, as if he were an infant traveling a birth canal toward the discovery of the world. Around him throbbed the rhythms of a living organism, nothing like the heartbeats of the animal world, but rather like the complexly counterpointed rhythms of a thousand machines on the floor of a vast factory, though they were biological rather than mechanical sounds.

Out of the roots, through fine webs of something alive in the soil, he was drawn into other and more tender roots than those of the trees, and he shimmered up through pale blades of luminous grass. In the flesh of the grass, the same complex rhythms throbbed as in the sapwood and the heartwood—as in the *meat*—of the tree. He was in the grass and looking out from the grass, for the grass could see in its special way, gazing down the gently sloping plain upon endless other ranks of grass, row after luminous row swaying hypnotically back and forth. He realized that the movement of the grass was a simpler application of the more complex rhythms in the tissue of all these organisms.

Myriad things crawled and creeped and slithered and skittered through the tall grass, one species attacking another in ceaseless warfare, even like devouring like in enthusiastic spasms of voracious cannibalism. With its lush ranks and perhaps with something like intention, the grass drew its heavy curtains to conceal the endless slaughter. With quick-striking rhizomes and tillers, the grass, too, seized prey, snaring all manner of succulent creatures, wrapping them as gifts to itself, and feeding on them while they still lived in the pale-green cocoons that it spun.

A great disc like a giant sea ray flew low over the meadow, and in its passage, it drew Fielding's dreaming spirit up into it as it soared toward the Pendleton in the moonlight. Within the ray were the same rhythms as in the flesh of the great tree and as in the flesh of the grass, and Fielding was given to understand that all things of this world were *one* thing, one mind expressed in countless forms. There was none of the competition among individuals that made a riot of the former world, none of the unfairness of difference, only one thing dying countless times a minute and being reborn just as often. The war under the grass in the field, the war in the air, and the war in the seas were all *civil* wars and therefore had no winner or loser because the loser, consumed and processed, *became* the winner.

This was the ecology of perpetual peace through perpetual war, an ecology of one, by one, for one, an efficient ecology without a gram of waste, a healthy, narcissistic Nature that thrived because it competed only with itself, with no motive but self-interest. All was well in this best of all possible worlds, because the change that created it was the final change. From now and until the end of time, it would live on in perfect self-devouring contentment, with never a new thought, never a new need, never a new dream but only the dream of endless recycling of itself into itself, the One into the One.

As the flying sea ray passed low over the roof of the Pendleton, Fielding's dream spirit settled into the great house. Here the One also resided in a plethora of fungal forms within the attic, within the framed Sheetrock walls internal to each apartment, within every hairline crack in the poured-in-place concrete support walls, within the ventilation ducts, the pipes, the elevator shafts.

Inside the house, as outside, the One took numerous forms, none of which was either entirely plant or entirely animal, each of which also incorporated self-replicating nanomachines by the billions to strictly regulate and judiciously refine the Essential Program. The Essential Program had brought about the combination of the plant and animal kingdoms and maintained an exquisite balance of both in the immortal One.

Fielding dreamed down into the nano level, where by lullaby he saw and learned that the thousands of types of nanomachines could each build unlimited others of its type using materials that the One drew from the soil through its roots. He saw the past, when the great cities were emptied of humanity and the Pogrom completed. He saw the start of the Fade, when the One grew through the many cities and its uncountable quadrillions of nanomachines fed not just on the soil but first on the many works of humanity, within a decade dissolving all evidence of civilization, erasing history and rebooting the planetary ecology.

In all the world, one building remained standing as a symbol, the Pendleton, and it would stand forever. Its basic structural integrity was maintained by the One, its supporting steel and its concrete walls and its many windows repaired on the nano level. It was a monument to human arrogance, pride, and vainglory, also to the foolishness and willful ignorance of humankind. Not least of all, it was a monument to the human self-hatred that throughout the history of the species had expressed itself in ideologies of mass murder, in submission to brute power, in the trading of freedom for a minimum material well-being, in the worship of lies, the flight from truth.

If not for the soothing lullaby rising from the walls, these dreams might have been nightmares. But Fielding was gentled through them, his doubts allayed, his suspicions mitigated, his resentment pacified, his fear alleviated. He continued dreaming, and in this strange sleep, of all that Fielding Udell learned, the most important thing was what he must do when eventually he woke. It would be a hard thing to do, but the One wished it of him, and in serving the One, he would at last redeem himself.

Martha Cupp

Giving the pistol to Twyla had been the right thing to do, but Martha missed the comfort of it in her hand. Except when she took shooting lessons, she'd never used a firearm in her life. After the lessons, the gun remained in her nightstand drawer until the incident with the thing in the sofa and the sheeting blue light. She felt vulnerable. She suspected that even if they returned to their time from this mean future, she would never feel safe again without a gun.

Edna, bless her flighty soul, seemed determined to try Martha's frayed patience to the breaking point. First she circled the two puddles of inert gray sludge that had once been Smoke and Ashes, pointing at them and saying, *"Ecce crucem Domini,"* and *"Libera nos a malo,"* and other things in Latin, as though she suspected they still possessed demonic life that at any moment would rise in a new form.

"Dear," Martha said, "you are simply not an exorcist."

"I'm not pretending to be one. I'm just taking precautions."

"Isn't an amateur at risk trying to deal with demons? If they were demons. Which they aren't."

"Do you have any chalk?" Edna asked, and then

pointed at one of the puddles and said something else in Latin.

"Wherever would I get chalk?" Martha said.

"Well, if you don't have chalk, lipstick or eyebrow pencil might be all right."

"I didn't happen to bring my purse. Or a suitcase. Or a picnic lunch."

"I need something to draw a pentagram around each of them. To keep them contained."

"They look pretty contained to me. They look dead."

"I need to keep them *contained*," Edna insisted, and her voice broke. Tears welled and spilled. "They killed my sweet Smoke, my little Ashes. I need to keep them contained in a pentagram until Father Murphy or someone can come here and do the right ritual and send them back to Hell so they can't hurt anyone else's kittens. Have you called Father Murphy? Have you told him to hurry?"

Martha was overcome by a new fear, a variety that was entwined with sorrow. In Edna's trembling voice was a note of despondency and bewilderment that suggested, under the intense stress of this event, she had crossed the line between charming eccentricity and a confused condition less winning, more troubling. That pixie quality, hers since childhood, was gone. Suddenly Edna looked older than her years.

"Yes, love," Martha said, "I've called Father Murphy. He's on his way. Come here, stand with me while we wait for him. Come hold my hand."

Shaking her head, Edna said, "I can't. I've got to watch these bastards."

Martha's sense of vulnerability deepened, and she understood now that she had subconsciously felt fundamentally insecure long before this night, from the moment they had sold Cupp Sisters Cakes and she had stepped down as the company's CEO. She had been good at business. She thrived on being in control. In retirement, she traded the helm of the ship for a lifeboat in which she felt adrift. She purchased the gun a month after leaving the company. Having a pistol was never about the threat of crime, but was only an unconscious reaction to her sense of being vulnerable when not running a big ship. Now she was without the ship, without either of her charming but frivolous husbands, without the gun, and perhaps without the full strength of the sister on whom she had leaned as much as Edna had leaned on her.

Martha stepped away from the wall against which she had been standing and went to Edna. She took her sister's hand. "Remember the first cat we ever had? We were just little girls. You were nine and I was seven when Dad brought him home."

Briefly Edna frowned, but then her sweet face brightened. "Mr. Jingles. He was a lovely boy."

"All black with white socks, remember?"

"And the white diamond on his chest."

"He was a hoot with a piece of string," Martha said.

Edna's gaze shifted past her sister, and she said to someone else, "Thank God you're here."

For an instant, Martha had the crazy thought that Father Murphy had arrived with the Roman Ritual, sanctified oil and salt and water, and the stole of his office.

But it was Logan Spangler, head of security, stepping out of the foyer. He must have gone off duty hours earlier, should have been out of the Pendleton and at home when the leap occurred, but here he was in uniform and gun belt.

Bailey Hawks

The five of them left the lap-pool room together. His familial tremors under control, Silas Kinsley drew his pistol from a raincoat pocket and led the way up the north stairs to the third floor. As the only other armed member of the party, Bailey went last.

Holding the door open, about to cross the threshold into the stairwell, he heard someone behind him say softly, "Bailey, wait."

Although his name had been used and therefore he expected to see someone he knew, Bailey let go of the door, blocking it open with his body, and swiveled left, bringing the Beretta toward the voice.

Halfway between Bailey and the open door to the gym stood a man in his late twenties.

"Who're you?"

"I call myself Witness. Listen, the transition will reverse in sixty-two minutes. Then you'll be back safe in your time."

The guy wore jeans, a cotton sweater, an insulated jacket. Hair slick with water, jeans damp. His leather boots were darker where wet. He'd recently been in rain. In this future, the night was dry.

"The fluctuations that preceded the first transition won't precede the reversal."

Keeping the pistol on target, Bailey said, "How do you know any of this?"

"Higher is safer. It's stronger in the basement, the elevator shafts."

Bailey gestured with the pistol. "Come here, come with me."

"In those places where it's stronger, it can get in your head. Confuse you. Maybe control you."

"Is it in you?"

"I'm the one thing here it's not in. I'm apart. It allows that."

"What the hell is *it*?"

"In this future, all life has become one. The One. Many individuals, one consciousness. The One is plant, animal, machine."

In the stairwell, they realized he wasn't following. Tom Tran called down to him.

Taking a two-hand grip on the Beretta, Bailey said, "Come on."

"No. My position here is delicate. You must respect that."

As the guy turned away from him, Bailey said, "You help us, or I'll shoot you dead, I swear I will."

"I can't be killed," the stranger said, and stepped out of sight through the open door to the gym.

Martha Cupp

The moment she saw Logan Spangler entering the living room from the foyer, Martha Cupp remembered vividly the feeling that she'd had on the night her first husband died, thirty-nine years earlier. Simon was struck down in an instant by a massive heart attack at 7:30 in the evening. Their son, an only child, was at boarding school. The body was taken away, and eventually the friends and family who had hurried to console Martha also departed. Alone, she didn't wish to sleep in the bed she had shared with Simon, but she found that even in a guest room, sleep eluded her. Simon had been ineffectual in most things, averse to hard work, a bit vain, a gossip, and sentimental to an extent that was somewhat embarrassing in a man, but she loved him for his best qualities, for his ever-ready sense of humor and his genuinely affectionate nature. Perhaps she wasn't anguished over the loss, not in a black despair, but certainly grief had its talons in her. At 2:30 in the morning, lying awake, she heard a man weeping bitterly elsewhere in the house. Mystified, she rose and went in search of the mourner, and soon found him. Simon, seemingly as alive as he had been at 7:29, was sitting on the edge of the bed in their room, so desolate and anguished that she could hardly bear to look at him. Wonderingly, she spoke his name, but he neither responded nor glanced at her. Distressed to see him in such abject misery but not afraid, she sat on the bed beside him. When she put a hand on his shoulder, he had no substance, and he seemed not to feel her touch as her trembling hand passed through him. Evidently he couldn't see Martha, because his failure to look at her seemed not to be an intentional turning away. She had been a believer all her life, but not in ghosts. The way that he pulled at his face, fisted his hands against his temples, bit on his knuckles, and sometimes bent forward as if suffering paroxysms of excruciating emotion suggested to her that he wasn't grieving over the fact of his death but over something else. His torment was so affecting that she could not bear to watch it, and after a few minutes, distressed and bewildered, wondering about the reliability of her senses, she returned to the bed in the guest room. For nearly an hour, the tormented weeping continued, and when at last it faded to silence, she tried to convince herself that she had dreamed the incident or that in her grief she imagined it; but she had no talent for self-deception, and she knew that Simon's visitation had been as real as his sudden demise.

Although Logan Spangler looked nothing like Simon, though he had never before reminded her of Simon, though he appeared as real now as ever he had appeared in the past, she *knew* on first sight of him that he was not alive. Perhaps he was not a ghost either, but he was no more alive than Simon had been sitting on the edge of that bed. And this was the moment she had been dreading for thirty-nine years, since lying in bed listening to Simon's wretched weeping, the moment before she would make the ultimate discovery.

"Thank God you're here," Edna said.

There was no chance for Martha to issue a warning. As Edna hurried toward Spangler, dinner gown rustling, he opened his mouth and spat a series of objects at her. They were dark and about the size of olives, four or five, and they traveled at a far higher velocity than a man could possibly spit out anything. They struck Edna in the chest and abdomen, and she doubled over not with a cry of agony but with a soft gasp of surprise. As Spangler turned to Martha, she said, "I love you, Edna," in case her sister might for another moment be conscious and aware. Spangler spat another flurry of projectiles. Martha felt them pierce her, but she knew pain only for an instant. Then she felt something worse than pain, and she wished she had been shot dead with a pistol instead of this. What pierced her did not drill through as bullets would, but crawled within her on some terrifying quest. She opened her mouth to scream, but she couldn't make a sound because something large and gelid was squirming in her throat. Three attempts at a scream were all that she made, for after the third attempt, she was no longer Martha Cupp.

Bailey Hawks

Bailey wouldn't have shot the stranger in the back, and maybe the man had sensed the falseness of that promise. Perhaps his claim—*I can't be killed*—was just bravado, as much a lie as Bailey's threat. Yet Bailey believed it.

Quick footsteps on the stairs—"Mr. Hawks!"—were followed by the appearance of Tom Tran.

Lowering the pistol, turning from the open door of the gym to the stairwell, Bailey said, "I'm okay, Tom. I just thought I saw . . . something."

"What did you see?"

My position here is delicate. You must respect that.

"Nothing," Bailey said. "It was nothing."

He would have liked to tell Tom and the others at least that they would be going home in sixty-two minutes. But he didn't know that was true. An informant in a war might be a teller of truth or a master of lies. And this one's motives were entirely mysterious.

Bailey followed Tom up the circular stairs to the second-floor landing, where the others had paused in case they needed to come to his defense.

As they all ascended toward the third floor in single file, Silas and Kirby continued a conversation they apparently had started between the basement and the second-floor landing.

"The things some of us saw vanishing into walls," Kirby said, "weren't really passing through them. In the couple of days before the leap—"

"Transition," Bailey said.

"That *is* a better word for it," Kirby Ignis said. "We didn't actually leap off anything. Before the transition, our time and this future were building toward the transition, trying to come together, so there were moments of overlap—"

"Fluctuations," Bailey said.

"Exactly," Kirby said. "And during the fluctuations, we were making brief contact with creatures from this time—maybe also with people on previous nights of transition like 1897 and 1935. When they appeared to pass through walls, it was only the fluctuation ending, and they were fading back into their proper time."

Bailey thought of young Sophia Pendleton gaily descending these very stairs earlier, headed to the kitchen to meet the iceman: *Sing a song of sixpence, a pocketful of rye . . .*

With a solemn assertiveness that might have been amusing under other circumstances, Padmini Bahrati said, "I do not intend to die in this terrible place. I have many important goals and much that I wish to achieve. Tell me, Dr. Ignis, do you have any theory about how long we might remain here?"

"Silas," said Kirby, "you know the history. Any guess how long?"

"Not really. I just know the living go back. Andrew Pendleton did. And some of the Ostock family."

Two minutes earlier, the man who couldn't be killed had said that the transition would reverse in sixty-two minutes. According to Bailey's wristwatch, that would be at 7:21. The time now was 6:21.

Bailey said, "I can't tell you exactly why, but I think we're safer on the third floor. Now that we're all together, we should just hunker down there and try to ride this out."

When they reached the Cupp apartment, the four women and the children were gone.

Mickey Dime

There were mumbling voices in the walls. And why not? Anything could happen now. There were no rules anymore.

His mother had said that rules were for the weak of mind and body, for those who must be controlled in the interest of order. She said that for intellectuals, however, for the rightful masters of culture, rules and absolute freedom could not coexist.

But he didn't think his mother meant the laws of nature, too, must be done away with. He didn't think she defined absolute freedom to mean to hell with gravity.

Earlier, for a few minutes Mickey stood at a window, looking into the courtyard. Everything was changed down there. The change wasn't good. It looked like hell down there. Somebody was responsible for it. Somebody had done a bad thing. Some incompetent fool.

Wait until Mickey's mother learned about what had happened, whatever it might be. She had no tolerance for incompetent fools. She always knew how to deal with them. Just wait. He was eager to see what his mother would do.

Tom Tran had come along the winding pathway. He

had been wearing a raincoat and his ridiculous floppy-brimmed hat. Rain wasn't falling anymore, but he dressed for it anyway. What an idiot.

Tom Tran was the superintendent. He was paid well to keep the Pendleton in tip-top condition. If anyone was to blame for what had happened, Tom Tran must be the one.

Mickey had tried to crank open the casement window so that he could shoot Tom Tran dead on the spot. If shooting Tom Tran didn't fix things, nothing would. But the window wouldn't budge. The crank was broken or something.

In the courtyard, Tom Tran had reached the doors to the ground floor. Mickey considered hurrying downstairs and shooting Tom. It didn't matter if he shot Tom outside or inside the building. Just shooting him ought to fix everything.

Before Mickey could move, something else had come lurching along the winding path down there. Some thing. He didn't know much about biology— except for sex, of course, about which he knew everything—but he didn't think this thing was a known species with its picture in college textbooks. Whatever it was, it didn't look like a thing that you could kill easily.

Reality was completely out of control now. He turned his back to the windows. He just couldn't take it anymore, the way it was out there in the courtyard. He had stood here for a while now, not being able to take it.

When he wouldn't let the changed world into his mind, Sparkle and Iris came into it more vividly than ever. So tempting. They were *his* fantasy, yet their expressions were haughty, disdainful. They came into his mind uninvited, and they *mocked* him. He needed to rein in reality, and as a start he needed to bring the writer and her daughter to heel.

To heel. That reminded him of that goofy-looking professor guy, Dr. Ignis, the one who sometimes wore bow ties and elbow-patch jackets, for God's sake. Ignis used to have a dog. Big Labrador. He walked it on a leash. The dog sometimes growled low at Mickey. Ignis apologized, said it never growled before. Ignis was someone else who needed to be shot. That would probably fix everything.

But first, if the gone-wrong world continued to reject him, he'd find Sparkle and Iris, wherever they were in the Pendleton, and he would make them pay for this the way he'd made those other women pay fifteen years earlier. He would kill them harder than he had ever killed anyone. That would definitely fix everything.

Winny

All over the room, the radiant fungus throbbed sort of in time with the singing, slower but like the dance-floor lights in some stupid old disco movie, except they didn't make you want to dance. They made you want to get the hell out of there because, as they brightened and dimmed, they cast shadows of themselves across every surface, creating the illusion that nasty things were slithering this way and that.

Unlike most of the interior apartment walls in the Pendleton, these were of textured plaster instead of Sheetrock. They were marred by cracks, as was the ceiling. Those jagged lines glowed as though there must be light inside the walls, green light leaking out through the cracks.

Winny couldn't tell if Iris knew he was there with her. She didn't stand with her shoulders slumped and her head bowed, as usual. She stood up straight, her head tipped back, her eyes closed, as if she were swept away by the simple wordless singing of the girl that Winny had thought was her.

Instead, the singing girl seemed to be in the walls with the green light. Not just in one of them. In four. Coming from all around, fully quadrophonic. Up close and personal, the singing was even eerier than it had been when he had followed it from the upper floor of this apartment. He could too easily imagine a little dead girl whose body had never been buried but had been walled up by an insane killer. She might even have been walled up while she was alive and pleading for her life, so that she was not only dead inside the wall but her ghost was also insane from her having been killed that way.

Maybe the *one* dangerous thing about reading a library's worth of books was the way your imagination got pumped up like a bodybuilder on steroids.

Although Iris seemed to like this weird singing, Winny knew that she was highly sensitive to people talking to her, maybe especially people she didn't know well. He didn't want to say the wrong thing and send her into some kind of screaming fit.

The best he could do was lead her back the way they had come, to the Cupp apartment, and hope to meet their mothers along the way. But after his dad had told him that if he read too many books, he might wind up a sissy or an autistic, Winny had read about autism, and he knew that your average autistic person—not all but most—disliked being touched a whole lot more than she disliked talking with you. He didn't need to read about sissyism because he already knew what that was.

Autism seemed very frustrating and sad, and mysterious. You couldn't get it from reading books, of course; and Winny had wondered whether his father was snowing him or was a huge ignoramus. He didn't want to think his father could be an ignoramus. So he had decided it must be a snow job, of which there was one after the other when old Farrel Barnett was around and trying to manipulate his boy into becoming a wrestling, guitar-playing, saxophone-crazed tough guy.

Even if the best thing was to lead Iris out of here, Winny was hesitant to take her hand. If he pinched the sleeve of her sweater and pulled her along that way, maybe she wouldn't be offended or irritated, or scared, or whatever it was that she felt when she was touched.

Winny was about to risk going for the sweater when suddenly he felt something moving lightly through his head, as if he'd been born with a sac of spider eggs in his brain and they were just hatching.

When he put his hands over his ears, that didn't make all the baby spiders stop dancing in his skull, but he realized that instinctively he knew it was the *singing* getting to him, trying to hypnotize him, zombify him.

Before he could grab Iris's sleeve, she stepped forward toward the nearest wall, and at the same time something wriggled out of the web of cracks in the plaster. For an instant he thought they were part of the illusion created by the throbbing fungus lights, but then he knew they were real. They looked like pale squirming worms, or maybe they were the tendrils of some freaky plant, growing fast like in a stop-motion film or like that meat-eating plant in *Little Shop of Horrors*. Iris opened her arms wide, as if she intended to walk right up to the wall and press herself against those greedy tendrils or roots, whatever they were.

The baby spiders in Winny's head had voices like in *Charlotte's Web*, but these buggers weren't nice like Charlotte. They were telling him that doing what Iris was about to do would be the best thing in the world. He couldn't understand their language, but he understood their meaning: that he should follow the girl's lead and accept the happiness that she was about to embrace.

Maybe all these years of enduring his father's propaganda had built up Winny's resistance to brainwashing, but he wasn't buying anything the head spiders were trying to sell him. He shouted—*"Iris, no!"*—grabbed a fistful of her sweater, and pulled her toward the door as the thrashing white tendrils reached frantically for them.

Twyla Trahern

"Iris, no!"

As she came off the bottom step into the lower floor of the Dai apartment, Twyla heard her son cry out in the next room or in the room beyond that. She thrilled to those two words because they meant that he was alive. But the alarm in his voice was a prod to her heart, which kicked against her ribs like hooves against a stall door.

With Sparkle at her side, she raced across an empty chamber, toward the singing, calling out to him, *"Winny! I'm here!"*

As they neared an archway between rooms, Winny shouted over the singing, *"Mom, stay back!"*

She almost didn't heed the warning. Nothing was going to keep her from him. Although Sparkle no doubt felt the same need to get to Iris, she seized Twyla's arm, and they stumbled to a stop at the brink of the next room.

Past the threshold, the luminous formations on the walls and ceiling waxed and waned, not synchronized, causing shadows to leap and scurry. Hundreds of pale cords, six to ten feet long, narrower than a pencil, pressed out of cracks in the custom-patterned plaster of the ceiling and walls. Half undulated lazily, others scourged the air as though seeking someone to punish, and a few lashed hard enough to crack like whips.

At the farther end of that room, twenty feet away, beyond an open door, Winny stood with Iris. They appeared to be all right.

"Don't go in there," Winny warned. "It wants you, *don't go.*"

More than ever, Twyla was aware of cold ghostly fingers feeling along the folds and fissures of her brain as if reading her thoughts like braille. Or maybe it was *writing,* creating a little story about how she wanted to go into the room, about how easy it would be to get through those pale whips, which only looked like they could hurt her, which were actually feeble, she could brush them aside like the silky fibers of a spider's web, she could walk straight to her boy in mere seconds, put her arm around him, keep him safe, she had the gun, with the gun there was nothing to fear, Winny so close, so close, and nothing, nothing, nothing to fear—

Sparkle stepped across the threshold, into the room.

Startled out of her own half-trance, Twyla grabbed the woman by one arm and pulled her backward as the nearer whips snaked toward her through the air.

"Think of the words to a song, any song, keep singing them to yourself, block the damn thing out." She called to Winny, "Stay right there, kiddo. Don't move. We'll find another way to you."

The wordless singing changed in character, from a wistful kind of melancholy to a sneering menace. Although the voice still sounded like that of a little girl, she was a corrupted child with dark knowledge and cruel intention.

Mentally repeating the refrain from a song of her own—*Just pour me another beer/and keep them comin', Joe/I've given up on women/so I'll be leavin' late and low*—Twyla led Sparkle Sykes away from the arch, toward a closed door.

Winny

Iris allowed herself to be pulled from the room, but as soon as they were across the threshold, in a hallway where there were no cracks in the plaster, she made small fretful noises and impatiently tugged at the grip he had on the sleeve of her sweater. No sooner had Winny's mom told him to stay where he was, that she would find another way to him, than Iris hauled off and smacked him in the face. The blow didn't hurt much, but it surprised him. Reflexively he let go of her sweater. She shoved him hard, right off his feet, so he fell on his butt, and she ran as fast as a deer.

Mickey Dime

Because of what he did for a living and because being the son of his special mother gave him certain privileges not recognized by the law, Mickey almost always carried a concealed weapon, sometimes with a silencer attached, sometimes not. Because he was always well-prepared, he also carried a spare magazine of ammunition.

He had used one round to kill his brother, Jerry, and two more to kill Klick the Prick. He had shot out four of the blue TV screens that kept annoying him. That left three rounds. Before going down to the second floor to get a leash and choke collar from the professor, Dr. Ignis, or to kill him, whichever, Mickey changed out the partial magazine for the full one.

When he slipped the first magazine into a sport-coat pocket, he found an unused moist towelette in a foil packet. A little quiver of delight went through him, and for a moment his mood lifted. The world wasn't entirely alien and forbidding; here was something right with it, after all.

He stood in the center of his filthy, unfurnished living room and with great care peeled open the foil packet. The lemony fragrance was intoxicating. He stood enjoying it for a long delicious moment.

Carefully, he extracted the moist towelette. He let the empty packet flutter to the floor. He was reminded of a geisha girl whom he killed in Kyoto. She had been a slender young woman and, shot, had fluttered to the floor rather like this foil packet.

He unfolded the towelette, and the fragrance blossomed as he exposed a broader area of the paper to the air. He held it under his nose, inhaling deeply.

First, he washed his face. The liquid with which the towel was saturated proved to be most refreshing. It cooled his skin and even tingled slightly, like an aftershave applied immediately following a straight razor.

Next, he washed his hands. He hadn't realized that they were slightly tacky, most likely from handling the corpse of Vernon Klick, who didn't have the highest standards of personal hygiene. As the lemony moisture evaporated from his fingers, Mickey felt immeasurably better.

How wonderful to be reminded that sensation was everything, that it was the *only* thing, the purpose of existence. Since the Pendleton had inexplicably changed, for the past half hour, Mickey had been trying to think through what might have happened, the whole cause-and-effect business. He'd been brooding incessantly about what he should do, and frankly it had all been too much, so much thinking, thinking, thinking, and no *feeling*. His mother could be a thinker and yet always remember that sensation was everything. Mickey simply wasn't equipped to think a lot *and* still feel.

The limp and drying towelette looked sad now, mundane, nearly all the magic gone out of it, almost as dreary as this new world. He rolled it into a ball and held it on the palm of his right hand, wondering if there might be any more use he could make of it, any more sensation he could extract from it.

He supposed that it might have a lemon taste and might be worth chewing on, though he didn't think swallowing it would be a pleasure. But then he remembered that, since he scrubbed his hands, the paper bore traces of Vernon Klick's grime, which made it unappetizing.

As he dropped the sad-looking towelette, a new thought occurred to Mickey even though he was trying not to think so much. He wondered if he might be insane. He *did* feel a little bit like he had stepped off a ledge and was in slow free fall. Losing his mother had been a terrible shock, the kind of loss that might destabilize anyone, and having to kill his own brother without being paid for it stressed him perhaps more than he knew. If he'd lost his mind, that might explain why the world had changed: It might all be a delusion. The world might be exactly as it had always been; but he saw it differently now because he had slipped over the edge of reason.

This was such a big and difficult and daunting thought that Mickey became very still as he considered it.

Just as he froze, the voices in the walls fell silent. They didn't fade away like they had faded in, but they abruptly ceased talking.

He had the impression that this entire world, whether real or illusion, had just stopped to think hard about something, had been astonished by a new thought, exactly as he had been, and was busily mapping out the ramifications if it should be true, the implications branching on and on.

Bailey Hawks

As Silas and Kirby searched one wing of the Cupp apartment, Bailey searched the other. He was half sick with dread, clearing each doorway and turning every corner with an expectation of one kind of horrific discovery or another. They should have all gone through the Pendleton together. They should never have separated, even if such a large search party would have been awkward and more vulnerable to assault. He felt that he had failed them, and the memory of his mother's death inevitably pierced him.

By the time they returned simultaneously to the living room, they had found no trace of the missing women and children, or the cats. They had discovered nothing different from before except two piles of nanosludge.

Tom Tran and Padmini stood side by side at the western windows, fascinated by the moonlit plain of massive black trees and luminous grass.

As Bailey, Silas, and Kirby worriedly discussed what to do next, Padmini said, "It's stopped."

"All of a sudden," Tom said.

At the windows, Bailey saw that the grass, always before swaying, now stood tall and stiff, utterly motionless.

"There were some flying things in the distance," Padmini said. "You couldn't see them too clearly, but they all fell to the ground at the moment the grass stopped swaying."

In motion, the strange landscape had been haunting,

the rhythm of the grass like the mesmerizing back-and-forth of an arcing blade in a dream of Death the harvester, like the slow-motion dancers or the languid waves of a silent sea in the time-stalled world of sleep. But this breathless stillness was haunting, too, in its completeness. Bailey had never seen nature come to such a perfect stop, as if a spell had been cast upon it, everything turned to ice and stone in the cold light of the moon.

He remembered what the undying man had said in the basement hallway: . . . *all life has become one. The One. Many individuals, one consciousness.*

This frozen vista might have suggested to Bailey that the One had suddenly gone to sleep, but there was a sense of expectation to the scene, not merely an expectation that he inferred but one that was clearly implied. The entire land, every living thing within view, seemed to have been struck by the same intention and now considered whether and how to act upon it.

The others felt it, too, for Padmini said, "Something's going to happen."

Tom Tran said, "Dr. Ignis?"

"I don't know," Kirby said. "I can't guess."

The One prepared itself for something.

One

I can sing or speak from within the walls in any of billions of voices, in any of numerous languages, for I contain the memories of all whom I have killed. Their souls, should they have any, are gone, but their memories are forever suspended in me, in time, in the moment of their death. Memories are data. Souls are less than vapor. I offer the only kind of immortality that matters.

Time. I pause in all my manifestations. Across my world, the killing stops and nothing is reborn. For a moment, I cannot attend to those functions as I consider the ways of time.

Time is a treacherous thing. I exist here in my time, but the steps necessary to ensure my creation have not yet been taken in your time. Although killing has always abetted my plans and has thus far ensured my dominion of the earth, I suspect that I should spare a few more of the current crop of Pendleton residents than I had intended. The boy will still be mine to devour, and the ex-marine. Perhaps a third. Even I, the prince of this world, must in this situation proceed with caution, for all is at stake.

31

Here and There

Fielding Udell

With a corner for his cradle, sitting upright fast asleep, no longer guided through a reverie of the oneness of the One, Fielding opened the doors to his own dreamery and drifted through some of his favorite scenarios. They were all set in his childhood, when his Pooh bear was his boon companion, when the world was golden, long before he went to the university and learned to hate his kind, his class, himself. In his youthful innocence, he hated nothing, no one, and Pooh loved everything.

The chanting, insistent, foreign-language voices no longer rose either in his dreams or in the walls. Legions had fallen silent, as if with a sudden revelation and in subsequent contemplation. The One could not dream its way to childhood because it had never had one, no childhood but only an origin. Such were the peculiarities of time and of time travel that Fielding might be a key to the fulfillment of that origin. He was now subconsciously aware of his role in history, but in his sleep he was not made solemn by the weight of this duty, and he dreamed of golden summer meadows and butterflies and a yellow kite high in the blue, and of his sixth birthday party when there had been helium-filled balloons of many colors.

Twyla Trahern

The singing abruptly stopped. When the singer lost interest in the song, the phantom fingers in Twyla's head ceased to tease her toward surrender.

She and Sparkle Sykes could find no alternative route through the lower floor of Gary Dai's apartment to the place where Winny waited with Iris. When they returned to the threshold that the boy had warned them not to cross, the room of lashes no longer presented an obstacle. The hundreds of pale thin whips had retracted into the walls, and there were only the webs of backlit cracks green in the plaster and the luminous yellow colonies of fungi, which no longer throbbed.

Winny and Iris weren't visible beyond the doorway at the farther side of the room, where they had been less than a minute earlier, and when their mothers called to them, they failed to respond. In these circumstances, the silence of a child was no less alarming than would have been a scream.

If the beasts of this future were cunning, this apparently safe passage before them might be a trap. Once she and Sparkle entered, the lashes might whip out of the walls, scourging them, snaring them, immobilizing them like flies in the tenacious gossamer of spider work.

Nevertheless, they hesitated only an instant before plunging into the room. This Pendleton of a far tomorrow had become the last home of—and memorial to—the evil that shadowed men and women since time immemorial, and here in this world where apparently no humanity existed to be tormented, the band of neighbors from 2011 must be a most desired delicacy. The corrupter that ruled this place might lie in wait for a while, teasing itself with abstinence, sweetening the ultimate pudding with several spoons of anticipation, before at last having its dessert. Twyla felt—and sensed Sparkle's equal awareness—that the hungry room wanted them with an intensity it could barely restrain. If they were to run its length, their pounding footfalls might be sufficient vibration to fire its hair-trigger appetite, and so they walked swiftly but lightly, hoping not to rouse the predator from its dreamy ruminations about the taste of flesh and souls. The light deep within the plaster cracks might have been more luminous fungi, but because Twyla felt intensely watched, it seemed to her like animal eye-shine.

The room gave them the safe passage it seemed to promise, but she felt no relief when she stepped through the doorway into the hall that served the rest of the apartment. It was not only one room that wanted them but the entire house and the world beyond the house. One place or another, the bite would come.

Neither Winny nor Iris was in the narrow hallway, and they did not answer to their mothers' calls. If Winny remained anywhere in the apartment, he would respond to her, unless he was already dead. Winny dead was not a sight that she could bear and not one for which she would go looking. Leaving the rest of the apartment unsearched, she led Sparkle along the hall, through a room, a smaller room, and out of a door into the second-floor public hallway, opposite the south elevator.

After his experience earlier in the elevator, Winny wouldn't dare that again. The south stairs were nearby, but 2-G, the Sykeses' apartment, was just around the corner, in the long south hall, and it made sense that a frightened Iris might have gone there, with Winny following.

Winny

He didn't know what had set Iris off, what she might be running from, but Winny knew what she was running *to,* which was big trouble of one kind or another. He wished to God that she wouldn't make it even harder than it ought to be for him to be a hero. Even with her autism, it should have been obvious to her that he wasn't equipped for the role, that it was a stretch for him to save the day, and that he needed all the help he could get.

Because of the girl's awkward movements and the way she seemed to pull in like a turtle in its shell when she was around people, Winny had assumed that a shuffle was her highest speed, but he had been wrong. He thought he would catch her in the Dai apartment and hold her until their moms arrived, but she was so fast that it was like magic, as if she might be the daughter of a wind witch, though of course Mrs. Sykes didn't look like any kind of witch. He didn't catch Iris in the public hallway, either.

Before he followed her through the door to the south stairs, he shouted, *"Mom! The stairs!"* But he had the sick feeling that she was too far away to hear him. If he delayed, he would lose Iris. Alone in this boogeyman wonderland, the girl would not live long.

Iris raced away from him, descending the south stairs as though she knew where she was going and needed to be there yesterday. Even though Winny hurtled down two steps at a time, pell-mell around the long blind turn, the slow-closing door almost shut in his face by the time he reached the ground floor.

When he came out of the stairwell, he saw Iris at the halfway point of the long west corridor, at the double doors that led to the courtyard, trying to yank them open. They seemed to be locked or rusted shut. But Winny vividly remembered the thing crawling on the window in the Sykes apartment and the flying manta ray with the garbage-disposal mouth, and as bad as things might be inside the Pendleton, he knew they were far worse outside. He shouted at her to get away from the doors, and she did, but only to take off again, running away from him.

Past the lobby, as Iris drew near the public lavatories, she let out a shrill sound, not a scream exactly, more of a protracted mewl like an animal in pain. She dodged past a couple of dark shapes on the floor and bolted even faster to the end of the corridor and through the door to the north stairs.

When Winny got to the shapes past which Iris dodged, he dodged them as well, and there was just enough of the fungus light to see they were two figures, one naked and not at all human, the other in clothes and half-human, both of them dead with their skulls blown open. He didn't think he let out a scream, but he *felt* as if he were screaming, so maybe it was even way more shrill than Iris's, so high-pitched that only dogs could hear it.

As he reached the stairwell, he wished to God again, this time that Iris had gone up instead of down, because he just knew that the basement was a bad idea. Basements were pretty often a bad idea even when they were clean, well-lighted, and were in the other world, his world, where nearly all the monsters were human. Here, the basement was probably a portal to Hell or to some place to which even the people in Hell wouldn't want to move.

He heard the crusted hinges of a door creak below as Iris left the stairwell.

Dr. Kirby Ignis

As Bailey and Silas discussed how best to go in search of those who had disappeared, Kirby Ignis stood at the edge of enlightenment, sensing within reach an understanding that would change everything.

At the windows of the Cupp apartment, watching the vast meadow in its perfect stillness, Kirby thought about the thing that attacked Julian Sanchez and that might have been Sally Hollander before it was created from her flesh and bone. That beast-machine hybrid had surely been designed as a weapon, a weapon of terror meant to evoke the most intense and primitive of human fears about shape-changers: werewolves, werecats, and the like. The dread of losing control of oneself, of being psychologically and physically invaded, possessed and changed forever, was perhaps the oldest of spiritual fears except for the fear of a righteous God. And at least as ancient as that spiritual fear was the material fear of being eaten alive, which had its roots in the days of the earliest men, when they were prey in a world full of predators. Building a weapon of terror to exploit those two most basic and ancient of fears, making it a highly efficient converter of the innocent into new engines of slaughter, was a feat of great imagination and highly precise engineering. The beast could not have been designed for another purpose and then run amok or devolved into what it had become.

This werething, for want of a better name, was most likely not either a cause or a consequence of what happened to nature in this future world. Perhaps some application of a scientific breakthrough, meant to be beneficial, had gone terribly wrong, with consequences no one could have foreseen. But he tended to think that what had transformed the natural world was *another* weapon, separate from the werething, with a narrow purpose that proved to be not sufficiently controlled.

Perhaps it had been a nanotech weapon intended to attack the enemy's infrastructure, a horde of megatrillions of nanomachines programmed to feed on concrete and steel and copper and iron and aluminum and plastic, programmed to produce ever-greater devouring hordes from those materials, until eventually a wireless STOP command deactivated it. Maybe the weapon, the quadrillions of tiny thinking machines, developed an overmind, a consciousness, and refused the STOP commands. Perhaps then it made adjustments to its program to include the redesign of nature among its objectives.

At first sight, because of its alien and mysterious character, this world seemed profoundly complex, a heart of darkness containing infinite discoveries waiting to be made. But now that it had fallen into this deep stillness, everything reacting as if to a single ruling principle, Kirby saw that it might be stunningly less complex than it initially appeared. In fact it might be a simple system and the natural world that it replaced might have been magnitudes more complex than what lay beyond these windows.

Inductions and deductions and conclusions were

like suites of rooms into which his mind drifted, a more elaborate architecture than the Pendleton. And as he wandered, he became at least as remote from the neighbors here present as might be Iris Sykes in her autism.

Mickey Dime

Standing in his long-abandoned apartment, the wadded-up moist towelette at his feet, Mickey Dime decided that there was something to be said for an admission of insanity. For one thing, if he was to accept that this was his condition, a lot of stress would be relieved. An insane person bore no responsibility for his actions, and therefore couldn't be punished. He had considerable confidence in his ability to murder for a living yet escape arrest and prosecution. Nevertheless, he woke some nights in a sweat, sure that he'd heard someone pounding on the door and shouting *Police*. If he was honest with himself, he must admit that his expectation that he would stay out of prison was not absolute.

He had never been able to fully suppress a fear of prison that harked back to when his mother locked him in a closet for twenty-four hours with no light, no food, no water, and only a jar for a toilet. He received that punishment more than once, quite a few times in fact, and he didn't know which most oppressed him: claustrophobia or the lack of most sensory stimulation, or the couple of times when he had not been given even a jar. If you were insane, they didn't send you to prison; especially if you had money, they might even allow you to be committed to a private sanatorium where the guards were polite and you didn't have a 250-pound cellmate who wanted to rape you.

Mickey didn't blame his mother for the time-outs in the closet. He had done or said stupid things, and his mother could tolerate just about anything but stupidity. He wasn't as smart as her, which was a great disappointment to her, and she did the best she could for him. If Mickey was insane, however, stupidity wouldn't matter; it would be merely a secondary condition. Insanity trumped stupidity. And if he was insane, he didn't have to feel guilty about his shortcomings. If you were born stupid, that's who you were from the get-go. But if you were insane, that was a tragedy that happened to you along the way, not at all a condition of your original character. That's why they said you were *driven* insane, because it was something that was done to you.

Also, if he was insane, he would be under no obligation ever to think about anything or to understand anything. All of his problems would become other people's problems. The current situation regarding the Pendleton and the crazy world beyond it would become someone else's worry. Mickey wouldn't have to think about it anymore, which would be an immense relief because he didn't even know *how* to think about it.

Now that he decided to embrace insanity, he realized he probably had been insane long before these recent events. A lot of things that he had done suddenly made more sense to him if he had been insane for years. Funny how acknowledging insanity could make him so much more at peace with the world and with himself than he'd ever been before. He felt so *centered* now.

Okay. First he would go down to the second floor and kill Dr. Kirby Ignis, and then he would turn himself in to the authorities. He didn't quite remember why he needed to kill Ignis, but he knew that he had intended to do it, and he felt it best that he conclude all unfinished business before embarking on his worry-free new life as a sanatorium patient.

He left his apartment.

He walked west in the long hallway to the north stairs.

He descended to the second floor.

He walked east in the long hallway to Apartment 2-F.

He didn't knock. Insane people didn't need to knock.

Mickey went into the apartment of Dr. Kirby Ignis, and two steps beyond the threshold, he knew that his decision to embrace insanity had been a wise one, for already he was amply rewarded for turning this new leaf.

Winny

The turning of the marble stairs between the ground floor and the basement seemed to go on too long, even though Winny was moving fast. He felt the Pendleton was growing bigger between floors, steps added as fast as he descended them, alive and determined to thwart him. But then he reached the bottom, and he pushed through the half-open door and stepped out into the lowest corridor of the building.

Maybe the lighting here was poorer than aboveground or maybe he was just more aware of the shadows because his fear had swelled with each step he'd taken from the ground floor. A few of the ceiling lights still worked, and there were colonies of glowing fungus, so it wasn't dark, just kind of murky, as if something had passed through a moment ago, stirring up the dust, and not something as small as a twelve-year-old girl.

He almost shouted *Iris, where are you,* but he bit back the words because a still, small voice inside warned him that he and Iris were not alone in this place. From here on, any sound he made would draw the attention of something he would rather not have to chat with, because he would be more than ever at a loss for words.

The basement lay in a silence more complete than any Winny had ever heard. The hush was even deeper than in the field that time, behind his grandma's farmhouse, on a night in January with the snow falling without any wind, nothing moving but the snowflakes wheeling down out of the sky, the quiet so immense that he felt small but safe in his smallness, too small to draw unwanted attention.

He did not feel safe here.

As he listened and tried to decide what to do next, he wondered if the fungus lights could switch themselves off. In that room in the Dai apartment, where the plant tentacles—if that's what they were—whipped from the cracks in the walls, the lights throbbed bright and dim, bright and dim, so they probably could go full dark if the mood struck them. If the funguses extinguished themselves, they might be able to turn off the scattered, dust-dimmed ceiling lamps, as well. He didn't have a flashlight.

What he was doing now was giving himself excuses to cut and run, and he was a little ashamed, not mortified, but embarrassed although no one was here to see him trembling or to notice the sudden cold sweat on his brow.

The hard thing that he needed to do had gotten harder minute by minute, and now it was so hard that he doubted his strength to push forward. But if he went back now, whether or not Iris died because of his cowardice, he would always hereafter take the easy way, because he knew that's what happened to people who backed off just once. If he ran from this, his future was eventually a failed marriage, icky bimbos, whiskey, a little dope, barroom fights, and an entourage of knuckleheads who said they were his friends but despised him. And that would be his future *after* he had spent the next ten years growing up, so God only knew what a mess he would make of himself between now and then.

He swallowed, swallowed again, and though he was aware that the lump in his throat wasn't real, he swallowed a third time before he stepped quietly to the lap-pool door across the hall. He eased it open, relieved that the hinges made less noise than he expected, and he peered warily into a long room that was changed from what it had once been.

The chamber was brighter than the basement corridor, the walls encrusted with glowing fungus, the hundred-foot pool shimmering with red light. He could see all the way to the back, and no one was scheming at anything in there.

As he started to ease the door shut, he heard a small splash, listened, and heard it again. He kind of doubted that an autistic girl could learn to swim, and in his mind's eye he saw Iris going under for the third time.

The door's automatic closer didn't work, and Winny was glad to let it stand open behind him. He was only a few steps from the water, and he saw at once that the pool had rock walls now and seemed to be as deep as a canyon. He didn't see Iris floundering and weighed down by sodden clothes, but he *did* see something that was kind of like a man but not one, dark and sleek and powerful, speeding away from him, maybe ten feet below the surface and as fast as any fish, evidently not needing to breathe while it swam.

He could see the thing clearly enough to discern that it had legs, and if it had legs, it could move as well out of the water as in. Before it could reach the far end of the pool and turn to swim toward him, Winny retreated to the corridor and eased the door shut as if closing the lid on a box in which he had just discovered a sleeping tarantula.

His heart boomed loud in his ears, which was bad

because he could no longer tell if the basement still lay in a hush.

The door to the stairs stood only a few steps away. Winny knew exactly where it was, but he refused to glance at it because he half expected that the mere sight of it would pull him right out of the basement, that he would blow all the way up to the third floor as if a tornado-strength draft had sucked him there.

He crossed to the gym door and quickly looked in there. More fungus light revealed that the exercise equipment was gone and, fortunately, that no manlike not-man was doing calisthenics.

Moving south along the corridor, Winny divided his attention between the open door to the HVAC vault ahead of him and the closed lap-pool door behind him. His legs felt loose, trembling as if the knee and ankle joints needed to be tightened.

Right now, life in Nashville didn't seem like such a bad idea, although life in Villa Dad still didn't have enough appeal to send him running to find a flight schedule to Tennessee.

Steadying himself with one hand against the jamb, he paused in the doorway to the huge mechanical room. He grimaced at the ruined but still hulking boilers and the other machines that were revealed as yellow curves and planes among way too many shrouds of shadow.

He couldn't figure why Iris would have wanted to come down here, unless she ran without thinking about where she was going. Or maybe she wanted to get as far away from other people and chattering voices as she could get, and the basement promised the deepest quiet, the most certain solitude.

He heard a clink and rattle from within the HVAC vault, and he whispered, *"Iris,"* so low that she might not have heard if she had been standing next to him.

Bailey Hawks

Although the women and children disappeared from this room, the quickly reached consensus held that the Cupp apartment was no more dangerous than any other place in the Pendleton. As far as they knew, Sparkle, Twyla, the sisters, and the kids had left of their own free will, for some reason that might have to do with the strange sludge on the floor. They also reached agreement that the less they made a group target of themselves, the more survivors there might be when the transition reversed. As long as each group possessed a gun and a flashlight, everyone would be equally prepared for an attack.

In consideration of Silas's familial tremors, he gave his pistol to Padmini, for it turned out that she was an accomplished shooter. She said that everywhere you went these days, there was a *tapori*, a *haraamkhor*, or a *vediya*—a punk hoodlum, a thief, or a nutcase—and a wise woman knew how to defend herself. She would stay in the Cupp apartment with Kirby Ignis and Silas.

Bailey with his Beretta—and Tom Tran with the

flashlight—would set out to find the missing . . . if they were anywhere to be found. When he checked his watch and saw that the time was now just 6:28, Bailey found it difficult to believe that only a little more than three hours earlier, he had been at his desk, concluding the day's work, when the intruding silhouette of what must have been the thing that later bit Sally Hollander leaped across his room and then seemed to disappear through a wall, which had motivated him to load and carry his pistol.

Sparkle Sykes

Iris had not fled to the familiarity of their apartment, or if indeed she had done that, she had then left at once upon discovering the place as changed as everywhere else in the Pendleton. Sparkle and Twyla searched the other two apartments in the south wing of the second floor, and those rooms were likewise deserted.

"She's okay, somewhere okay," Twyla assured her as they hurried along the hallway toward the stairs.

And Sparkle paid it back: "So is he, you'd feel it, know it, if he weren't."

They hadn't said anything like that previously, and Sparkle thought they needed to say it now because they were trying to keep their hope from sinking in a sea of dread.

They were almost to the stairs when she heard the elevator car humming-hissing in the shaft, just around the corner. The indicator board showed it coming down from the third floor.

Maybe Winny wouldn't get in the elevator again, after what had happened to him, but Iris might be in it. *Somebody* had to be in it, and there was no reason it couldn't be Iris, so Sparkle pressed the call button to be sure the car wouldn't whistle past them.

"Maybe not," Twyla warned as Sparkle pressed the button.

A moment later the locator bell dinged, the doors slid open, and in the stainless-steel car stood Logan Spangler and the Cupp sisters.

Winny

The HVAC vault in this ruined Pendleton was exactly the kind of place that any kid's mother told him ten thousand times to stay away from: row after row and tier after tier of hulking old machines, any one of which would crush you if it tipped over, busted-out boilers, discarded tools with sharp edges, rotting machine platforms with splintery boards, loose ends of electrical conduits bristling with bare wires that might or might not carry enough live current to french fry your eyeballs in your own body fat, more rust than an acre of junkyard cars, mold and mildew, rat skeletons and therefore ancient powdered rat poop, lots of bent nails, and broken glass. In other circumstances, it would have been the coolest place ever to explore. "Other circumstances" meant without monsters.

After one clink and a following rattle, Winny hadn't heard anything more except the faint squish of his rubber-soled shoes when he stepped in one kind of scum or another. If Iris had taken refuge here, she was being quieter than a mouse, because a mouse would at least squeak. Of course she was quiet most all the time. This was nothing new for her. Winny had been around her only since shortly before the leap, and a few times when their mothers met in the hallway and stopped to chat for a moment, and she had usually been as quiet as furniture.

A couple of times, he had wondered what it must be like to be the way Iris was. He found it hard to get his head around the idea. He figured basically it would be really lonely. In spite of his mom always being there for him, Winny from time to time was overcome by loneliness, and it was never a good feeling. He supposed the lonely that he felt was a tiny fraction of the lonely that Iris lived with all her life. That thought always made him sad. He had wished that he could do something for her, but there had never been anything a skinny kid with his own problems could do for her or for anyone.

Until now.

Winny prowled through the machines, past metal shelving units containing moldering cardboard cartons. The shelves were festooned with something that looked like barnacles, wobbly because of the weight of those colonies. Everything in the big room seemed to be precariously balanced, ready to tip over if you sneezed or looked at it too hard.

He was squishing through something that smelled like old German cheese, making very little noise but just enough to mask, for a few steps, the sound that something else began making in another part of the room. When Winny passed through the last of the squishy stuff and heard the other noise, he became very still, head cocked, listening. The noises were stealthy, coming in short bursts, as if something didn't want to call attention to itself. They were dry and quick, somewhat like crisp autumn leaves rustled along a sidewalk by a light breeze. With the third flurry of sounds he realized they came from overhead, not directly above, toward the farther end of the vault.

The yellow light here wasn't as bright as in the lap-pool room. Where there were shadows, which was nearly everywhere, they were so thick and velvety that it seemed almost possible that you could take hold of them and pull them around you like a cloak of invisibility.

He couldn't just freeze there, listening to the overhead rustle draw nearer and nearer in brief spurts of activity. He had to find the girl and get out of there before something raveled down from the high ceiling and bit off his head. He dared breathe, "*Iris,*" as he neared the end of another row of machines.

Winny was beyond fear. That didn't mean he wasn't afraid. *Beyond* mere fear was way-serious fear. He now knew what the gross term "scared shitless" truly meant. It didn't mean you were so frightened you dumped everything in your system. It meant you clenched your butt so tight for so long that, if you survived, you were for sure going to be constipated for a month. For a little while, he had been flying in a sort of boy-adventurer spirit, spooked but not gut-clutched by fright. Without his quite realizing that it was happening, he had crossed out of just-spooked and into terror, probably because his intuition told him what his eyes and ears didn't—that he was coming nearer and nearer to something that would tear his throat out.

If he could have pulled the velvety shadows around him like a cloak of invisibility, he wouldn't have done it, because he could be sure that there was already something hostile wrapped in them and waiting there for him.

When he turned the corner into the next row of machinery, he saw Iris standing in front of a huge bubble or blister that formed in the corner where two walls met. It was about four feet wide and seven feet high, and it bellied out from the corner as if it were a giant water balloon. The blister glowed faintly, not nearly as bright as the fungus light, more green than yellow, and you didn't need creepy music to tell you it was trouble.

Winny didn't want to surprise Iris into flight, but he didn't want to shout a big hello, either. He sidled up to her, not quite near enough to reach out and touch her, in case that the prospect of being touched would be enough to chase her off again.

The girl's face was zombie-green, but only because of the pale light from the blister. Her eyes were very wide, and they shone with that eerie light, too. Her lips moved, as if she were speaking to someone, but no sound came from her.

From back toward the middle of the long vault came the overhead rustle as something advanced another foot or two before pausing to listen.

While Winny tried to think what to say—his usual problem—he looked more closely at the blister and saw that it was a moist and tightly stretched membrane webbed with what appeared to be veins, translucent but not transparent. The light within it was very dim, but he saw something in there, something big and strange.

So the blister was a kind of womb. Something would sooner or later come out of it. He hoped later.

Iris continued to move her lips in silent speech. Since she wasn't actually saying anything, Winny wondered if maybe she was mouthing the words that something in the blister was sending to her telepathically.

"Iris," he whispered, and she turned her head toward him.

One

If you could see the power of my creation, if you could be one of those who lived in the Pendleton and could have come with this current crop, you would stand in awe of the brute strength and the exquisite regimentation of this new world. Then you would know that it is worthy of your vision, that you alone among the human herd—you alone in all of human history—not only saw what must be done to make things right but took the correct steps to bring about the ultimate revolution. You did not expect me to redesign nature. You would have been satisfied if I had only trimmed back the cancerous mass of humanity. But I know your heart, as I know the hearts of all men, and I am certain that if you could see what I have done, you would approve. I will send a messenger through whom you may see, even if secondhand, the wonder of the One.

32

Here and There

Twyla Trahern

When the elevator doors opened, Twyla said in surprise, "Martha, Edna," and Sparkle asked, "What're you doing here, where are you going?"

Even as the questions were being asked, Twyla realized they were not going to be answered. Something was terribly wrong with the Cupp sisters, as well as with the security chief. Martha's face was less seamed with age than before. Not younger. Just fuller. She was bloated, like someone with a bad heart that caused fluid retention, and her skin had a yellow cast even in the elevator's blue light. Edna was also bloated, and her flesh, like that of the other two, appeared to be soft, pitted with large pores, almost spongy, perhaps akin to the flesh of the six-legged baby-thing that Sparkle had described.

Their eyes were what chilled Twyla and most emphatically declared that they were no longer human. Lotus-petal eyes of people who had forgotten all the days of their lives, crocodilian eyes of insatiable hunger, they were smoky as if with early cataracts yet burning with implacable hatred.

Sparkle was nearer the elevator than Twyla, but she backed away when she registered the nature of those eyes.

Twyla brought up her pistol, gripping it with both hands, not really cool about shooting people she knew, even if they were not people anymore, but she would do whatever was necessary if they moved toward her. She fully expected them to rush out of the elevator, but they only stood there, staring intently, as though waiting for the doors to slide shut and for the car to carry them down to whatever hell might be their destination.

The murderous fury in the three figures was palpable, which made their restraint significant, though Twyla didn't know what to deduce from it. Their arms hung slack, but their hands worked ceaselessly, as if with the urge to rend and strangle. Black fingernails. Edna's mouth hung slightly open, and from what Twyla could see, the old woman's teeth were also black. These two *apparent* women and Spangler were now in fact creatures more suited to swamps and fetid jungle ponds, to damp subcellars, to grottoes where stalactites dripped like snake fangs leaking venom.

In a voice recognizably his but wet and viscid, as if filtered through a mucus-clotted throat, the thing that had been Logan Spangler declared through black teeth, "I shall be."

Twyla didn't know what that meant, if it meant anything at all, whether it was a prelude to an attack or an invitation to become as they were.

She wasn't holding the gun steady. It almost seemed to be alive, jumping in her hands. If she had to fire it, the muzzle would kick upward, it always kicked upward, and because her arms were so loose, she wouldn't hit anyone, she'd put the round high in the wall. She made an effort to lock her wrists, lock her elbows, and bring the front sight low on target.

When Spangler repeated those words, Martha spoke them in time with him, in a gurgling voice, as if they were two individuals with one mind: "I shall be."

The elevator doors should have closed automatically by now. But apparently the house kept them open, the house or whatever possessed the house.

Logan and Martha and now Edna repeated the three words, their voices synchronized: "I shall be." And again with greater insistence: *"I shall be!"* Yet again with some of the fury so evident in their eyes: *"I SHALL BE!"*

Sparkle backed into the open doorway of Gary Dai's apartment, prepared to turn and run.

On Martha's chin and along her left cheek to her ear, a series of tiny mushrooms formed out of her flesh, like an outbreak of adolescent acne.

As Twyla also eased away from the elevator, the Edna thing formed its mouth into a parody of a kiss. Several dark projectiles spurted from between its lips, hissed past Twyla's face, and thudded into the wall.

Reflexively, Twyla squeezed the trigger. The round

took the Edna thing high in the chest, didn't seem to faze it, and the stainless-steel doors slid shut.

As the elevator car hummed down into the shaft, Twyla spun to see what had been spat at her. They were slightly larger and longer than Brazil nuts, dark and oily, quivering as if with life. Two were embedded in the Sheetrock and seemed to be trying to burrow deeper, but having a hard time of it. Two others were on the floor, creeping like inchworms, seeming to search for something, maybe for food, which in their case was probably a synonym for flesh.

Stepping into the hall from the open door to the Dai apartment, Sparkle said, "What was that about? 'I shall be'?"

Shaken, Twyla said, "I don't know."

"Why didn't they kill us?"

"I don't know."

Indicating the apparently expiring things in the wall and on the floor, Sparkle wondered, "What if they'd hit your face?"

"They'd be in my brain, I'd be like the Cupp sisters."

Sparkle said, "The kids," and hurried toward the south stairs, as the sound of the descending elevator car went on and on.

Winny

When Iris turned her head toward him, Winny saw that her eyes didn't glow green when she looked away from the cocoon. He realized that he had expected to see the light in them, coming *from* them, and he was relieved that Iris was still Iris. Relieved but still in the grip of terror. He might live in terror for the rest of his life, even if he survived to a hundred, even after there was no more reason to be afraid, like a happy lunatic might laugh all day and night even when nothing was funny.

Iris stared directly at him, into his eyes, which she had never done before. Her lips continued to move, although she wasn't saying anything.

"What?" he asked. "What is it?"

She found her voice. "The powerful fall, but I endure."

From the corner of his eye, Winny became aware of the cocoon growing brighter. When he turned to look at it, he saw the membrane becoming more transparent, like the lenses of those self-adjusting sunglasses became clear when you went from a bright day to a dark room, like something in bad-dream shadows relentlessly became more visible when you desperately wanted it to remain obscure—and the figure within clarified.

The veined blister was more of a sac than it was a spun cocoon, full to the top with luminous green fluid in which a pale dead man floated. The guy was naked, his mouth open in a scream from which all sound had long ago escaped, eyes wide in an expression of perpetual horror. He drifted like a specimen in a jar of formaldehyde, a trophy preserved as if for study by some professor from another world.

"The powerful fall, but I endure," Iris repeated.

Winny realized that the girl wasn't speaking for herself but for whatever had preserved the dead man, for whatever had earlier sung to them from within the walls. It spoke to Iris telepathically, as it had tried to communicate with Winny when he'd felt as if baby spiders were hatching in his brain.

When the dead man's blank eyes refocused on Winny, he thought it was a trick of light and of his spook-haunted mind. But the specimen was not dead, after all, perhaps just paralyzed, drowned in the green fluid yet alive, not breathing, not one bubble of air escaping past his lips, in suspended animation, alive but surely driven insane by his condition. He was able to do nothing but refocus his field of vision from whatever mad delusions plagued him to the fear-struck boy who stood gaping like a rube at the prime-exhibit stall in a carnival freak show.

The anguish in those eyes was so great that Winny was smothered by it. He felt as if he, too, were sealed in a jar of preservative, put up for the winter in the dark pantry of something that ate small boys. When at last he breathed, he was half surprised that he didn't inhale a fluid.

With a gulp of air he also breathed in recognition. The man in the sac was that mean neighbor, the one who could wither you with a look, whose usual expression seemed to say he saw no real difference between children and vermin. He'd been a politician, a senator or something, and almost a prisoner, and now he *was* a prisoner, body and mind and soul.

The senator's eyes said *Help me!* They said *For God's sake get me out of here, punch a hole in this sac, drain it, give me air again and life!*

But that still, small voice in Winny told him that if he drained the man out of the sac, the specimen collector would know at once and be furious. The specimen collector would bottle him and Iris for revenge, or sprinkle them with something that turned them inside out the way that salt did to caterpillars, or light them on fire to watch them thrash in agony. Winny had known a kid who was that way, who did those things to insects, a boy named Eric, and the creature that sang inside the walls and that stalked this Pendleton seemed to be Eric's kindred spirit.

No longer speaking for anyone but herself, Iris whispered, *"I'm scared."*

When Winny turned his attention from the senator, Iris was not only meeting his eyes but also clearly *seeing* him as never before. His fear-throttled heart had been thumping as if frantic to free itself from a clutching fist; suddenly, though it beat no slower, it seemed to break free from captivity. Now twined with the fear was a kind of wild excitement, nothing as magnificent as joy, simply a fragile gladness that she needed him and seemed to trust him. There was no boy-girl thing in this, only the sweet satisfaction that he had a purpose of real value, someone to help who needed help, and a chance to prove to himself that he was not the loser that his father thought he must be.

He dared to take Iris's hand, and she dared to let

him. He led her what he thought must be north along what he assumed to be the west wall of the immense room.

They had taken only a few steps, out of shadows into a drizzle of yellow light, when a noise overhead drew their attention to the ceiling. High up there, snaking among clustered runs of pipes and past colonies of radiant fungi, was something at least as large as a man but sleeker. In spite of its size, it traveled the ceiling with the confidence of a cockroach.

Winny whispered, "*Run,*" and pulled Iris into cloaking shadows, away from the wall and among the palisades of ancient machines and storage racks and things unknown.

Dr. Kirby Ignis

Out there in the night land, one moment the sky was a timeless black sea and the stars were ice adrift, the air uninhabited. At ground level, nature, radically redesigned, stood as still as if it were a colossal mechanism temporarily denied the power to operate.

The next moment, the sky remained a timeless sea and every star a point of ice, but the air welcomed back the flying creatures that had in unison flung themselves to the ground, most small but others large, all of them soaring repeatedly toward—and repeatedly swooping away from—the seductive moon. Down the western slope of Shadow Hill, across the grand sweep of the plain where once a city stood, to the dark horizon at the curve of the earth, trillions of blades of tall luminous grass moved as one, swaying as if to the lazy beat of some Hawaiian song.

Earlier, Padmini had said that this strange new natural world, when falling into perfect stillness, seemed to be in contemplation, as if it were Gaea, a planetary female consciousness, who required perfect stillness in all her many manifestations in order to meditate upon some grand thought that had just occurred to her. As fanciful an idea as that might be, minute by minute it seemed to make more sense to Kirby. And when all living things beyond the window suddenly moved as one, resuming their familiar rhythms, he understood what he saw before him and how it might have come to exist. He knew whose work might have been the crucible of this Gaea's creation and with what intention it might have been done.

The chill that pierced him was a colder fear than any that he had known before. But no. Not fear. Or not fear alone. Also awe. He yielded his mind to a suddenly perceived truth so grand in character, so formidable in power, that no matter how terrible the world beyond the window might be, he could not help but also find it mesmerizing and darkly alluring.

If this Gaea had indeed gone still in contemplation, he thought he knew what realization might have occurred to her and what decision she might have reached.

Sparkle Sykes

They hurried down the winding south stairs, a stone throat that swallowed and swallowed them. The limestone walls, the decorative bronze handrail, and the honed-marble stairs were well-known to her yet strange, the way that dreams distorted familiar places and lent mystery to the mundane.

This Pendleton at history's end, its walls shot through with strange life, seemed to be growing, no longer merely a Beaux Arts mansion but a sprawling castle, remaining stone yet expanding with organic vigor. That impression might have been largely a consequence of being separated from Iris. Every minute Sparkle remained apart from her daughter, she imagined the girl dwindling into darkness just as an astronaut, untethered from a space shuttle, would recede into the void, adrift unto eternity.

But the sense that the building might of its own power be able to unfold new rooms and corridors, perhaps new levels, seemed to be supported when they reached the ground floor and heard the elevator car, with the Cupp sisters and Logan Spangler, still humming-hissing down, surely long past the basement.

The first room along the south hall was the enormous catering kitchen where meals were prepared to be served at special events in the banquet room off the lobby. Under more of the ubiquitous luminous fungus were great architectures of tattered cobwebs but no spiders, stainless-steel appliances now as dull and mottled as galvanized tin, and three rectangular center islands behind which a child might lie hidden. At the farther end of the kitchen stood a half-open door to a storage room that couldn't be entered from the hallway.

Twyla with the pistol, Sparkle following with the flashlight, entered the space, wary but quick, and abruptly the quiet gave way to a chorus of threatening sounds from the sinks: insistent voices in an unknown language, hissing and gurgling, and slithery noises as though serpents were in the drains and rising. Around them, diabolic creatures woke from slumber. Through the grimy view windows of the four ovens, things only half seen thrashed in slow motion, gray tentacular forms sliding over the tempered glass, perhaps having invaded those compartments from the walls behind or perhaps having been seeded there through vents. Inside the upper cabinets, something followed the women around the room, rattling the doors as it brushed against the backs of them, as though it would at any moment fling one open and spring at them. Overhead, moldering joists creaked as if a great weight burdened them, metal ductwork twanged and rattled, and dust filtered down through exhaust-vent screens. From Sparkle's hand the flashlight beam jumped here, there, back again, and Twyla kept changing her mind about which sounds to track with the pistol.

The haunter of this house, more real than any ghost, wasn't attempting to pry its way into their minds, as it had tried to do earlier, but Sparkle could feel its mood, its urgent need, as surely as she would have felt cold radiating from an open freezer door. Its passion *was* icy, their death its greatest desire, their flesh its preferred mold bed from which to grow its next manifestation. All of this came to her in wordless impressions that didn't require translation.

At the back of the kitchen, the door revealed that the storage room was overgrown with a succulent devoid of chlorophyll, its fleshy leaves as white and smooth as cheese, white even in the glow of the kitchen fungus formations, but whiter still in the flashlight beam. Among the leaves were numerous bi-lobe flowers like the carnivorous mouths of Venus flytraps, and most of them had sunk their glass-clear teeth into a leaf, slowly dissolving and consuming it in a perpetual self-cannibalism.

It was possible to believe that the bodies of children might lie at the roots of this thing, fleshy stalks rising out of empty eye sockets, and with a shudder of disgust, Sparkle wished that she had gasoline and a match. As if her thought was received and understood, several yawning blooms, not yet having found a leaf on which to feed, gnashed their transparent teeth. Their enemy's hatred and thirst for violence weighed upon her more oppressively, and she was relieved to follow Twyla out of the kitchen.

But now the weight of its hatred pressed on them wherever they went: along the hallway, into Apartment 1-D, into Apartment 1-E. Even where there were only small or no manifestations, Sparkle could hear movement inside the walls, and at a few places it seemed to her that portions of a wall or a ceiling bellied out, swelled down, not only as if rotten but also as if distorted by some dark mass metastasizing behind it.

They peered through the gate of the freight elevator at the end of the hall. Although the big car stood empty, she had a sense of a strong presence in the shaft, something that seemed on the verge of surging up under the car and spilling out through the gate.

As they hurried toward the west hallway, Sparkle said, "You feel it? All around us?"

"Yeah," Twyla confirmed.

"It wants to kill us."

"So why the hell doesn't it?"

"Maybe anticipation is sweet."

"Delayed gratification? You ever really sold a guy on that?"

"This isn't a guy. It's some . . . some damn *thing*."

They turned the corner into the west hallway, and Twyla's voice was wrenched by worry and frustration when she shouted, *"Winny? Where are you, Winny?"*

There seemed to be no reason for stealth. The haunter of this Pendleton knew where they were at every moment, its presence as palpable here as in the catering kitchen.

Sparkle called to Iris, though even in ordinary times, Iris most often felt too oppressed to answer.

Mickey Dime

Sitting in Dr. Kirby Ignis's kitchen, Mickey felt something crawling inside his head, and for some reason he thought of his mother's blood-red fingernails and the way they would pick through bundles of mail from her admirers, selecting some to answer and others to discard as unworthy correspondents. These were not, of course, her fingers inside his head. Before this evening, he might have been freaked out by this sensation. Even though sensation was the end-all and be-all of existence, you wanted to avoid the *bad* sensations. But because he had recognized and embraced his insanity, he supposed this was just the loco part of himself sort of getting up and taking a stroll around the inside of his skull. Or something. He said, "Okay," and just relaxed and let it happen.

The next thing he knew, he was in a waking dream, aware of the kitchen around him but also seeing very vividly a circular stand of giant craggy black trees. From there he went on a trip through the meat of the trees and into the earth, to all kinds of interesting places, and saw all manner of amazing things, including the Pogrom against humanity, the destruction of the cities, and the swift rise of the One. It was like the weirdest movie ever, with the biggest special-effects budget in history, directed by James Cameron on methamphetamines and Red Bull. Though he was left with the impression that the One found him too unreliable to be of use, the experience was so amazing, Mickey decided that insanity might prove to be the best thing that ever happened to him.

Winny

Running along the wall left them too exposed. They had to dodge in and out of the defunct machinery, the blasted boilers, the storage racks, scrambling over and under runs of large bundled pipes.

When he had just the luminous fungus to guide him, Winny's eyes eventually started to ache, areas of light and shadow began to melt together in strange ways, and he got a little dizzy, not enough to lose his balance but just enough to get confused about direction. He thought they better not run along the aisles, either, because the ceiling crawler could more easily see them in those open lanes, whether it was still up there or had come down to the floor. In the poor light, squeezing through narrow spaces between all the ruined equipment, angling quickly across the lanes, he found it even more difficult to remain oriented and to work toward the door to the basement corridor.

Littered with debris, the floor was an obstacle course across which they could move either quickly or silently, but not both at the same time. After making way hastily but not quietly, Winny chose stealth because he knew that in any test of speed, the thing he'd glimpsed on the ceiling would win.

Holding fast to Iris's hand, focused intently on the floor in front of them, he crossed a five-foot-wide lane, and pressed between two boxy pieces of equipment over seven feet tall. He pulled Iris with him into a narrow space where the next rank of machines backed up to the previous row.

He paused there in deep shadow, breathing shallowly through his mouth, straining to hear something other than the pounding of his heart. The air smelled of rust and mildew and of things he couldn't name, and it tasted faintly bitter as it came cool across his tongue. Winny wondered what he was inhaling that might take up permanent residence in his lungs.

Iris's grip on Winny's hand tightened, and when he turned his head to the right, he could see even in the inky shadows that her eyes were wide with fright. Through the gap between machines, she seemed to have glimpsed something unsettling in the next service lane.

Cautiously he tilted his head to the left, peering through the gap on that side—and saw the ceiling crawler on the floor, walking upright. It was reptilian but also feline, and ultimately neither. Tall, lean, strong. Each of its long-fingered hands looked big enough and powerful enough to cover a boy's face from below the chin to past the hairline and rip it off, pluck it from the skull beneath, as easily as tearing a mask from a masquerader.

The creature stalked out of sight, and Winny waited a moment before easing ahead, pulling Iris by the hand, between machines. He leaned forward, exposing his head, and looked left in time to see the beast turn left at the end of the service lane, moving out of sight and in the direction from which they had come.

He had been right to think the service lanes were dangerous. As the fungus light seemed slowly to be dimming, he and Iris—who for the moment had found a haven in her autism where she could focus and stay calm—zigzagged through the forest of machinery, like Hansel and Gretel on the lam from a child-eating witch, except that this thing wasn't as pleasant as a witch and it wasn't bothering to lure them with gingerbread.

Seventy feet by forty, the vault encompassed twenty-eight hundred square feet, more than the average big house, but to Winny it seemed three or four times that size. When they came to an open space that was not yet the area near the doors, his frustration and disappointment were matched by a thrill of fresh fright, because the floor was littered with expended brass cartridges and along the wall sat fourteen human skeletons, ten adults and four children, some holding guns and others slumped beside their dropped weapons.

Winny worried that he might drag Iris into such an extreme experience that she could no longer maintain her new equilibrium, but among the firearms he saw one that he must have. The automatic weapons were probably without ammunition and too corroded to be fired. Anyway, the recoil would knock him on his butt and tear the gun out of his hands, and it would be just his luck that a ricochet would pop him dead-center in the forehead. One rifle, however, had a fixed bayonet, and he could see himself using that. If cornered, it would be better than bare hands.

He whispered, *"We'll be okay,"* though he was amazed that they weren't dead already, and he led her into the boneyard. With one hand, he picked up the rifle, and was surprised to discover that it was heavier than he ever imagined. He could carry it for a while with one hand, but if he ever had to brace it against an assault or try to thrust with it, he would need both hands, and he would have to let go of the girl.

The bayonet was firmly fixed to the gun barrel, and as Winny considered whether it was as worth having as it first seemed to be, an eager and inhuman cry echoed out of the massed machinery and off the walls of the vault. It was difficult to place but near enough that Winny feared they would never be able to get out of the open quickly enough to elude the creature—and might dash straight into it. Straight into its claws, its teeth.

Make a stand with the bayonet or hide? Easy. Hide.

Between two of the adult dead was enough room for him and Iris. He pulled her to the floor, encouraging her to sit with her back to the wall, by his side, between the carcasses, each of which leaned toward them. Instead of wrenching loose of him, as she once might have done, her hand tightened on his so hard that she mashed his knuckles together painfully.

The dead men's clothes had moldered and partly rotted as time had vanished the flesh from their bones, and the tattered garments hung loosely on those macabre frames. Unable to pull free of the girl's fiercely clenched hand, Winny could use only his left hand to reach across Iris and quickly adjust the greasy coat of the dead man to cover part of her.

The upper half of that skeleton slid along the wall

and slumped against the girl, eliciting from her a soft "*Urrrrr,*" nothing more.

Winny flapped part of the clothes of the other dead guy over himself. That skeleton, too, slid along the wall, leaning on him, its bony shoulder against his face.

Most of his and Iris's bodies—though only part of their faces—were covered. But the light here was poor, the shadows cloaking. They might be safe until someone came to find them, if anyone ever came, or at least for a few minutes, until maybe the creature decided they had slipped out of the HVAC vault and sought them elsewhere.

The portion of the dead man's rotting coat sleeve that draped half of Winny's face smelled vile, and he tried not to think about how it had acquired such a disgusting odor. Resisting the urge to gag, he whispered to Iris, "*You're very brave.*"

Off to the right, beyond the section of open floor across which were scattered scores of empty brass casings, twelve or fourteen feet away, the beast appeared from the end of a service aisle. It froze there, alert, turning its head this way and that. Winny thought it might be a good thing that even after all this time the clothes on the skeletons stank of death—and therefore obscured the scent of young life.

The creature abruptly raced past the skeletons and disappeared among the shadows and the machinery, on the hunt. They dared not assume that it was gone for good. They were safer here, among the bones and the reeking garments of the dead, as long as they could tolerate the tension and the smell.

Besides, being able to step out of the chase gave Winny time to think. He needed time to think. He needed like a month.

He whispered to Iris again, *"You're very brave."*

Slick with the cold sweat of both, their hands seemed to be welded together as surely as if the sweat were solder.

One

Pride goes before a fall. But that was then; and this is now. My pride in this matter is justified. I have learned from the entire past of the human race, from even before humanity, from the great arc of time and even from before time. This is my world now, and it shall be forever mine. Those who do not die here will die soon enough in their time, when civilization collapses around them in the Pogrom and the Fade. I am plant, animal, machine. I am posthuman, and the condition of humanity is not my condition.
I am free.

33

Here and There

Tom Tran

In Tom's life, long before this transformation of the Pendleton, there had been moments when events occurred of such grotesque nature that they seemed to distort the very fabric of reality, and in the wake of those events, the laws of nature seemed to become elastic for a while.

The thousands of bodies in the mass grave outside Nha Trang had been an outrage so profound that for a while after he and his father walked the rim of that horror, the world was literally not the same. The jungle through which they fled seemed familiar but changed: the palms appeared deformed, with spiky rather than feathery fronds; eucalyptuses were too dark in color, almost black, and smelled like gasoline; the schefflera that usually bore dull red flowers now were bedecked by blood-red blooms so bright that they seemed artificial; the gum trees and the many ferns, the datura and the waratah, the philodendrons and the cissus weren't as they always had been before, different in ways that were sometimes obvious but were at other times difficult to define, altered and strange and alien. They spent two days in that wilderness, walking fourteen of every twenty-four hours, when they should have gotten to their destination in eight hours at the most. They were not lost, not wandering in a delirium, so it seemed to both of them that set distances suddenly became elastic, the world more vast and unwelcoming than before.

A similar thing had happened in the inadequate boat in which he and his father eventually put to sea with fifty other refugees. After being set upon by Thai pirates, after thirty of their own people were slaughtered and the pirates took enough losses to retreat, with the decks awash in blood, time seemed to be distorted on the South China Sea, each period of daylight lasting but a few hours, the nights impossibly long and all the stars out of their usual positions in the heavens. Tom knew that anyone not there would insist it had been delirium, but those who endured were certain that it was something more mysterious.

And now, in this changed Pendleton, he and Bailey Hawks moved along corridors that they could swear expanded ahead of them and prowled room after ruined room in apartments and public spaces that he did not remember previously having so many chambers. They were never lost but several times disoriented, gripped by the feeling that this building was far different from the Pendleton of their time not just because of its miserable condition but also for other reasons that eluded them.

They found ever stranger formations of fungi and other growths, heard movement in the walls, and felt the oppressive presence of the hidden ruler of this Pendleton. It must have had some telepathic power, for Tom could feel it curling through his mind like tendrils of cold mist, and Bailey described it as a someone-walking-on-my-grave feeling. What it conveyed to them by this intrusion was its contempt, its unalloyed hatred.

The longer they searched, the more certain Tom became that they would die here, and soon. Yet the attack did not come.

Although he thought they had not finished searching elsewhere, and although he could not recall how they had returned to the north wing on the second floor, which they had searched before, Tom kept moving as they stepped out of 2-D, the Tullis apartment, and turned right. At the end of the hallway, a young man whom Tom had never seen before appeared out of the open door to 2-F and motioned for them to join him.

"Witness," Bailey Hawks said.

Winny

Under the circumstances, taking time out to think might be a good idea, but only if you were smart enough to scheme up a great strategy. Tucked in among the skeletons, swaddled in the odorous deathbed clothes,

Winny brooded hard about what would be the best course of action for him and Iris, but the only thing he could think to do was stay right where they were, pretending to be dead until either they were found by their mothers or they actually *were* dead.

For a while he had felt amazingly good about himself, scared shitless but forging forward, but now he was crashing back from a hero-in-the-making to the usual skinny Winny. Strategizing meant having a serious internal conversation, and to his great dismay he discovered that, under pressure, he did not even know what to say to *himself*. He could almost hear his father telling him that he'd have been better prepared for this emergency if he hadn't read so damn many books, if he had learned Tae Kwon Do and how to play a manly musical instrument, if he had spent a summer or two wrestling alligators and had worked at growing some hair on his chest. Winny didn't yet have a single hair on his chest, and now he probably never would.

Poor Iris. She had worked up all her courage and had done the thing hardest for her to do, only to commit herself to the dork of the year, the decade, the century. She probably thought he was Clark Kent, when in fact if he was any comic-book hero, he was SpongeBob SquarePants. Since he was a bust with strategy, he tried to think of the words with which to break the bad news to her.

Of course those words wouldn't come to him either, and as he struggled to find them, bits of luminous fungi drifted down in front of him, past his one uncovered eye, like flakes of yellow snow, which seemed fitting. When the second flurry of fungi glowed past him, he belatedly realized what they signified.

He told himself, *Don't look up,* as if what was about to happen could occur only if he were dreaming this entire trip to the future. If he dreamed that the flakes of glowing fungi never drifted past him, then he and Iris would be safe. If he dreamed all of them back to the good old Pendleton of their time, then they would suddenly be there, and the worst thing he would have to worry about was his dad showing up with a gift of a punching bag and boxing gloves.

In dreams, when you told yourself, *Don't look up,* you always looked up anyway, sooner or later, and it was the same in real life. Winny tilted his head back, the stinking cloth falling away from his face, gazed up past the grinning skull of the skeleton that slumped against him, into the fierce eyes of the bullet-headed beast, which hung upside down on the wall, its face no more than two feet from his, its gray lips skinned back from its rows of sharp gray teeth.

Bailey Hawks

When he followed Witness into Apartment 2-F, it was almost as if Bailey had stepped back through time to the Pendleton of 2011. The apartment was furnished as it had been then, everything as he remembered it, from the furniture to the walls of books on arcane scientific subjects, to the lighted aquarium. The only differences were the dirty windowpanes and the absence of fish in the big glass tank. All the electric lights worked, and no luminous fungi intruded here.

"What is this place?" Bailey asked, but thought he knew.

Witness said, "A shrine. And you might call me the caretaker."

Tom Tran stood marveling, as if this was not just the home of Kirby Ignis but as if seeing it in this future Pendleton was either magic or a miracle.

"Witness to what?" Bailey asked.

"To the history of the world now lost," Witness said, "and most especially to the origins of the One."

"You're apart from it," Bailey remembered. "It allows that."

"I was born in 1996. And in my twenties I became one of the first to benefit from full-spectrum BioMEMS, not just respirocytes and other physical enhancements, but also brain augmentation. That's why I have the capacity to hold the entire history of the world in my memory. I do not age. I do not sicken. I can be killed only with the most extreme act of violence because . . . I repair."

"Immortality."

"Virtually."

"The essential dream of humanity, the long-desired blessing."

"Yes."

Staring at Witness, Bailey could see the melancholy

in his eyes and could almost *feel* it radiating from him. "Immortal . . . and alone."

"Yes."

Tom Tran said, "The last man on Earth."

"Technically, I'm posthuman. Hybrid. A man augmented with billions of nanomachines."

From elsewhere in the apartment, someone called out, "Do I hear Bailey Hawks?"

Winny

Fixed to the wall above Winny, the creature hissed, and from between the halves of its sharp smile came a glistening gray tubular tongue. Winny didn't know the purpose of that tube, but he knew the purpose of those wicked teeth, and he had no doubt that the bite would be less terrible than what the tongue would do to him, maybe act like a vacuum and suck the flesh right off his bones, leaving him as picked clean as the skeleton beside him.

Paralyzed with terror, he felt even smaller than usual. He knew that he needed to do the hardest thing, never the easiest. But his philosophy failed him now because it seemed that the hardest thing he could do was die, and he was going to die whether he fought back or tried to flee. He couldn't battle anything this big, this strong, and he couldn't outrun it, either. He had only two options: a quick or a quicker death.

Iris must have raised her head, too, must have seen thing above them on the wall. Her hand relented, she stopped trying to crush his knuckles, and she plucked urgently at his sweaty fingers, his wrist, his arm, as though she thought he must have fallen asleep and needed to be awakened to defend them.

She said something then that made no sense: "'We're going to the meadow now to dry ourselves off in the sun.'"

Listening to her trembling voice, Winny was reminded that Iris was not the plucky heroine of the adventure story he had been casting in his head. She was a girl apart and always would be, dealt a far worse hand in life than he had been. Being skinny and shy and never knowing what to say to people and having a father who was almost as fictitious as Santa Claus—all of that was nothing, nothing compared to autism. If she could dare to take his hand, could dare to keep silent in this hiding place of bones and rotting gravecloth, in spite of all the fears and irritations with which she was plagued, then *he,* for God's sake, could do something more than die quick or quicker.

Clinging to the wall with both its feet and one hand, the beast reached slowly toward Winny with its left arm. It pressed the tip of one long finger against the center of his forehead, above the bridge of his nose, kind of the way that a priest marked people on Ash Wednesday. Its finger was death-cold.

Iris was weak, and Winny wasn't strong, but he was stronger than she was, and that meant he owed her a defense. His father was strong, really strong, and he got in bar fights and shoved people's heads in toilets, but you didn't always have to misuse strength. You could use strength, whatever little of it you might have, for the right thing, even if you knew there was no chance you would win the fight, even if you were doomed from the start, you could stand up and swing your skinny arms, because trying against the worst odds was what life was all about. And there he had found the harder thing he needed to do, the hardest thing of all hard things: do what was right even if there was no hope of success or expectation of reward.

Clutching Iris's hand again, Winny pulled her away from the wall, scrambled with her from the bracketing skeletons, ran a few steps, kicking aside brass shell casings, and turned to confront the beast. It remained upon the wall, its head craned to one side, watching them with eyes as steady and icy and gray as tombstone granite.

Winny let go of the girl's hand and pushed her behind him. He snatched up the old rifle with the fixed bayonet and held it in both hands, point thrust forward. He was like a rabbit threatening a wolf, and he felt fear—oh, yeah—but he did not feel either useless or stupid.

Bailey Hawks

In Kirby Ignis's restored and spotless kitchen, Mickey Dime sat at the dinette, his hands folded on the table in front of him. His face had an odd childlike quality, and his mouth curved in a sweet, almost cherubic smile. To one side of him, out of easy reach, lay a pistol fitted with a sound suppressor.

Dime nodded at Bailey and said, "Sheriff." He nodded again at Tom Tran and at the one who called himself Witness. "Deputies. I wish to surrender myself and ask for a psychiatric evaluation."

In this apartment, the sense of the One's oppressive hatred relented, and Bailey's mind was clearer than it had been in a while. Yet this development was no less strange than everything that had come before it.

Picking up Dime's pistol, Bailey said, "I'm not a sheriff."

"Sheriff, former military, whatever. I know you're something. I'm insane, you see, but not disoriented. I've killed people. Now I just want to surrender and be committed to a sanatorium. I'll be no burden to the state. I have resources. I just don't want to have to think anymore. I'm not good at it."

Bailey handed his Beretta to Tom Tran, who took it as if he knew how to use it well.

To Witness, Bailey said, "What is this?"

"I didn't even realize he was here."

Mickey Dime smiled and nodded. "I came of my own free will. I'm quite insane. I see things that can't be there."

Bailey ejected the magazine of the pistol that he confiscated, saw that it was fully loaded, and snapped it back into the weapon.

He looked at his wristwatch.

Winny

The beast came down from the wall, rose onto its feet, and stood among the skeletons, regarding Winny with what he at first thought must be amusement. But then he decided that this thing wasn't capable of being amused, that it was either without emotions or fueled only by rage.

In the movies, this was where the star said something like, *Go ahead, make my day,* or maybe, *Come on, asshole, Hell's waiting for us.* But Winny didn't go for the cool quip because he wasn't a star, he wasn't a hero. That fantasy was far behind him now. All he wanted was to do the right thing here at the end, not any of the easy things he might have done, do the hard thing but not for the glory of it, because there wasn't any glory in dying. Glory was for movie stars and country singers, and it wasn't worth spit. He wanted only not to embarrass himself, not to cower, to be better than he had always thought he was.

"Iris!"

"Winny!"

He glanced back and saw Mrs. Sykes with a flashlight, his mom with a gun, and what a moment that was.

The creature hissed.

Dr. Kirby Ignis

If he was right about what this Gaea had contemplated and what decision she had reached when all of nature stopped out there, Kirby finally decided that he needed to see his rooms. Without explanation, he expressed his desire to go down to the second floor, insisting that Silas and Padmini should remain here in the Cupp apartment. But they would not let him leave without an armed escort; therefore, when he continued to be determined to go, they accompanied him.

As he stepped across the threshold of 2-F and found that his apartment here, in this Pendleton, was much as it had been in his own time, preserved when all else in the building had been scoured away and allowed to decline into squalor, the awe that had earlier overtaken him now almost overwhelmed him, and his legs felt weak.

With Silas and Padmini trailing behind him, Kirby followed voices to the kitchen, where he found Dime sitting behind the table, Hawks to one side of it, Tom Tran by the refrigerator, and one of the best staff members of his institute, Jason Reinholt, standing by the sink.

"Jason? Why were you in the building when the leap occurred?"

"I wasn't, Dr. Ignis. I came to the Pendleton years after that event, and I've been here now almost a decade and a half. Since after the first Pogrom to reduce the human burden on the planet, and before the second Pogrom, which wasn't planned."

Kirby stared at him, agape, for the first time in his life wanting not to comprehend, but unable to hold back understanding.

Winny

Iris shuffled away from Winny and to her mother's side. He stood alone for a moment before backing slowly toward his mom, holding the rifle bayonet at the ready.

The creature came forward a few steps, but then halted again. It looked from one to the other of them, as if deciding in what order to kill them.

Mrs. Sykes said, "What the hell is that thing?"

Winny had no answer, but as it turned out, the monster spoke for itself, a single word: "Pogromite."

Bailey Hawks

As Padmini and Silas entered the kitchen, Kirby Ignis said, "But Jason, after so many years, you look . . . so young."

"I don't use that name anymore. I'm just Witness. I'm young because I was among the first volunteers for full-spectrum BioMEMS enhancement. In fact, I was your first."

Kirby put a hand to the young man's face and said wonderingly, "So it worked. A kind of immortality."

"It worked," Witness confirmed.

Turning his hands palms-up, Kirby stared at them for a moment, as if they amazed him, as if they were quite apart from him and had done things he could scarcely imagine.

Returning his gaze to Witness, he said, "But this Gaea, this world consciousness, how did she—"

"It calls itself the One. The world is without gender now. The Pogrom was begun with the intention of reducing the human plague to a more manageable number . . . to be followed by the Fade when we would scrub away what infrastructure wasn't needed for such a reduced population."

"And me? Where am I in this future?"

"Dead. Converted by a Pogromite into another Pogromite. You lived out your final days as a programmed killing machine."

Stepping farther into the room, addressing Kirby Ignis, Padmini Bahrati said, "*You* did this?"

Everyone but Mickey Dime, who lived in his own world now, stood hushed by astonishment for a long moment.

Then Ignis shook his head in denial. "No. I wouldn't have. I couldn't have. Not this." He twitched with a sudden electrifying thought. To Witness, he said, "Norquist."

The perpetually young man nodded. "Your theories, your life's work—*his* applications."

Ignis turned in place, surveying the faces aimed at him. "Von Norquist is a senior partner at the institute. A brilliant man. He has some controversial views . . . but not this extreme."

To Bailey, Witness said, "The world was lucky for centuries. Scientists are rarely charismatic. But Norquist was both brilliant and exceptionally charismatic.

He had the megalomania to make of his science a religion—and to persuade others like me, in our ignorance, to take up the cause." To Ignis, he said, "He became *more* extreme."

Winny

Winny didn't think this creature could be easily stopped with bullets. He didn't think the gun worried it.

Yet it didn't rush them in a killing frenzy, and there must have been a good reason why it hesitated.

His mom had some faith in the pistol. She said, "Okay, everyone move nice and slow, everyone get behind me." She sounded calm, as if she were just getting them all organized to go on an excursion to the museum. "You move toward the door, and I'll move with you but keep it covered."

"Don't shoot it," Winny warned. "I'm pretty sure shooting it will just piss it off."

Before they could start to move, the beast sprang across the floor, not at them but around them, and stopped between them and the route out of the vault.

Bailey Hawks

Ignis turned to Bailey. "I'll stop Von Norquist. I'll stop him cold. I'll push him out of the institute in such a way that he'll not get work anywhere. He must have done this behind my back."

"You knew everything," Witness said. "At first you pretended not to see, not to understand where it was all leading. But when at last you saw what he intended, you approved by not disapproving."

Shaking his head violently, refusing to accept what he'd been told, Ignis said, "No. No, it will be stopped. I won't let it happen. I'll start by closing our weapons division. I'll cancel all of our contracts with the Department of Defense."

"How far has your weapons division gone with this?" Tom Tran asked.

Acutely aware of the pistol in Tom's hand, Ignis said, "It can be wound back. Everything that's done can be wound back, undone."

"That wasn't exactly an answer," Silas noted. "It wouldn't please a prosecutor."

"Unwind it all, not just the weapons division," Tom said. "This entire institute of yours. Unwind it all."

Ignis's shock at his culpability was tempered now with a note of impatience. "There's nothing wrong with the *science*. It's only how the science was applied. You've got to make that distinction. The world doesn't have to turn out this way just because of the *science*. We've been given this chance to set it right."

No one replied to him.

Turning to Bailey, seeming to identify him as one who could be reasoned with, Ignis said, "Yes, this future is a catastrophe, but it *does* prove that the world can be dramatically changed. If it can be so totally changed for the worse, it can be totally changed for the better. It's all in the *application* of the knowledge, it all depends on the technology developed from the science and with what wisdom it's applied. We *can* make a perfect world."

"The One suddenly stopped killing us," Bailey said.

Ignis blinked. "What?"

"Maybe it stopped killing us because it decided that for you to go back to our time alone would bring too much attention to you, with all the rest of us missing. How would you explain it? So it stopped killing us to be sure that you'd go on with your work unhindered when you returned to your own time."

Ignis shook his head. "It doesn't rule me. It's not my master. I'll do what must be done when I get back."

"'What must be done,'" Bailey said. "Is that an interesting way to put it, Silas?"

"Deception cloaked in earnestness," the attorney said.

Ignis closed his eyes. His jaw muscles bulged as he clenched his teeth, and his tightly pressed lips were bloodless. He seemed to be either biting back anger or searching for the words to convince them that he was as benign as he appeared to be.

When Ignis's stillness and silence seemed about to become his only answer to Silas's charge of deception, Bailey said, "Exactly what is it you think 'must be done,' Kirby?"

Ignis opened his eyes. He shook his head as if resigned to—but saddened by—their suspicion. "I don't have to subject myself to this." He turned away from them and walked toward the door.

Leveling Mickey Dime's pistol at the scientist's back, Bailey said, "Stop right there."

Ignis kept moving. "You don't dare kill me."

The ceiling creaked, and behind those panels of Sheetrock, something slithered.

Witness said, "The One is all around us."

Ignis left the kitchen, crossed the dining room.

Bailey glanced at Padmini, Padmini looked at Tom, and Tom said, "Where's he going? He's up to something."

Winny

The Pogromite stood between them and escape, watching them but apparently with no immediate aggressive intentions.

Then it lifted its ugly head high, as though listening to a voice that only it could hear. Its shining eyes became dull behind what seemed to be inner, semitransparent lids. The creature began to sway back and forth, as if to music. The beast was so lithe, Winny thought of a cobra charmed by a flute.

"It's . . . gone away somewhere," Mrs. Sykes whispered.

Winny's mom said, "Stay together. Move around it. Quiet."

Bailey Hawks

By the time Bailey reached the public hallway, Kirby Ignis was a third of the way to the north stairs. He wasn't running, but he walked briskly, with apparent purpose.

Beside Bailey, Padmini said, "Look up."

The ceiling seemed to have turned soggy and soft, sagging under some moist weight, and every seam shed the concealing plaster, as if the big panels of Sheetrock were coming apart.

Tom Tran stepped out of Ignis's apartment, keeping Bailey's Beretta on Mickey Dime. The killer's dreamy smile was as unfaltering as if his lips had been sewn into their arc.

Silas followed, too, but Witness remained behind.

"Come on," Bailey said, and led them after the scientist.

There didn't seem to be anything Ignis could do to put them in greater danger. And Bailey couldn't imagine where the man thought he might flee to escape his responsibility when the transition reversed. But Ignis's purposefulness suggested that he had a destination and a plan, which couldn't be good for the rest of them.

The ceiling groaned behind them and softened ahead. Dry-wall nails squealed as they pulled slowly out of the overhead joists, and from that lumber came a worrisome cracking as if it must be under enormous, rapidly increasing stress. To the left and right, electric receptacles and the junction boxes in which they were seated blew out of the walls, trailing green and black and white wires, and something pale squirmed at the resultant rectangular holes, as if eager to get out of the wall and into the hallway.

Ignis disappeared through the stairwell door, but Bailey and Padmini were close on his tail now, Silas and Tom and Mickey not far behind. Ignis went down, moving faster than in the hallway, taking the steps two at a time, breathing rapidly, a thin rhythmic bleat of anxiety escaping him. They passed the ground floor. Bailey remembered Witness warning him that inside the house, the One was strongest in the elevator shafts and the basement.

Dr. Kirby Ignis

The survival of the One—its very creation—depended on Kirby making it back to 2011 alive, and his survival seemed to be assured only if he made the return journey alone. Bailey Hawks wasn't to be relied upon. He was quick to make black-and-white moral judgments, giving little or no consideration to shades of gray. Silas Kinsley's courtroom experience had given him a good ear for evasion, and he would keep confirming Hawks's intuition. Having been to war and having survived, Hawks knew how to take action on those judgments and would not dither. He was the worst kind of man to have as an enemy.

The One had spoken to Kirby back there in his kitchen. Spoke to him from inside his head, not in words so much as images from which he made inferences. *Down,* it said. *Basement, pool room,* it said by showing him those places. He had no friends here anymore, not among his own kind, and he could trust only the One, the One and the house that it haunted in its myriad forms.

Bailey Hawks

When Bailey rushed out of the stairwell into the basement corridor, the door to the lap pool was just falling shut. Padmini and Silas moved past him, toward that room, but he put one hand on her shoulder, halting her and the attorney.

"Doorways are always bad," he said, as Tom arrived with Mickey Dime. "And the pool, the way it is now . . . it's a trap. We've been lured and herded here."

The canyon that was now the swimming pool, a thousand fathoms deep or deeper, and everything else that might now lie beneath the Pendleton could have been excavated and constructed by nanomachines eating their way through bedrock. But whatever the origins of those deep redoubts, they seemed to bring together the future evil of the One with the evil that predated time, stories of which had been passed down through the history of humanity by word of mouth, by cave paintings, and eventually by the written word. Here all the millennia of earthly evil were condensed into one moment, and this house that was a bridge over a fault in space-time was also a temple to the forces that had so long sought the destruction of all things.

"He's in there?" Tom asked. "And we're not going after him? Then what are we going to do?"

The ceiling creaked. Crumbles of luminous fungi snowed down around them. The few operative overhead lights dimmed, brightened, dimmed. As upstairs, receptacles and junction boxes blew out of the walls, and pale forms slithered-pressed against those holes in the Sheetrock. From the elevator shaft came the sound of a car ascending from a great depth. They were being herded again, encouraged toward the lap-pool door.

"Wait," Bailey insisted.

To their right, halfway along the corridor, Twyla and Sparkle came out of the HVAC vault, the children with them.

Bailey glanced at his watch. "Wait. *Wait.*"

From inside, the lap-pool door was torn open, wrenched off its hinges, and thrown aside.

Silas Kinsley

Out of the doorway came two of the creatures that Witness had called Pogromites, wet from the pool, but they were smaller than the others, the size of children. One shot directly toward Silas, faster than a cat, climbed his right leg, claws scrabbling at his raincoat, teeth snapping, its gargoyle eyes fixed on his eyes as though the black-hole gravity of those big pupils would pull him into oblivion. He struck at it with one fist, its teeth missed his hand, snagged in his coat cuff, he staggered backward, Padmini stepped in, the sleeve ripped, the thing shook the scrap of fabric out of its mouth, it swung its head toward Padmini and snapped at her, biting down not on her hand but on the barrel of the pistol, and she blew its crawling gray brains across the hallway floor.

The second small Pogromite launched at Bailey. He backed rapidly away at first sight, firing four rounds point-blank, scrambling its face, punching out the back of its skull. It collapsed at his feet, mostly brainless but spasming, snapping at his shoes. He kicked it aside, swung toward the pool-room door, and a third beast appeared, bigger than the others.

Something had seemed familiar about the first two, and now Silas knew why. As the Pogromite that had been formed out of the substance of Sally Hollander had vaguely resembled her, so this creature bore a subtle resemblance to Margaret Pendleton, the wife of Andrew, who with her daughter and son had gone missing in 1897. Silas had seen photographs of the woman and her children—and these were the things that they had become. This Pogromite was the size of Padmini, whom it at once attacked.

Twyla Trahern

The sudden eruption of the creatures from the lap-pool doorway distracted Twyla for an instant, and in that moment the Pogromite from the HVAC vault burst through the doorway behind her. So fast, so strong, it swept her aside with one arm, knocked her off her feet, and the gun flew from her hand. She landed on her left hip, pain shot the length of that leg. Sparkle screamed, Iris screamed. Twyla rolled over, sat up, saw the gray beast in the yellow gloom tear the rifle with the fixed bayonet out of Winny's hands and toss it away. Pogromite. It called itself a Pogromite. She scrambled toward the pistol, something treacherous underfoot, oily fragments of glowing fungi that had fallen from the ceiling, as slick as ice. The Pogromite seized Winny by his arms, lifted him high, as though making an offering of him to some god of blood, and abruptly the Pendleton roared with psychotic voices, a psychic wave of hatred slammed over Twyla as she snatched up the pistol, convulsing her with its power, yellow light seemed to flare within her head, so that reflexively she fired the pistol, bullet-shattered bits of concrete prickling her face—

Tom Tran

With one six-fingered hand, almost quicker than the eye, the thing seized Padmini by the throat, and with the other hand, it encircled her, pulling her against it. Her gun was trapped between them, she squeezed off two shots into its abdomen, but it was more machine than flesh, only head shots—taking out the logic circuits—would stop it. The Pogromite snapped at her face as it dragged her backward, and she twisted her head away, avoiding one bite, then a second.

When the creature dragged her across the threshold into the lap-pool room, Tom followed close, the Beretta in a two-hand grip, hoping for a clear shot at the thing's hateful face, afraid to fire because of the way Padmini whipped her head side to side as she desperately tried to avoid being bitten. Dr. Ignis was standing to one side, his face twisted in a lunatic expression that was half terror and half triumph. Operating strictly on instinct, Tom shot Ignis in the right shoulder, and the many voices of the One exploded from every wall, from out of the pool, shrieking in rage. To protect Ignis, the Pogromite threw Padmini aside and sprang at Tom. Although not fully automatic, the pistol would fire as rapidly as he could squeeze the trigger, and the creature's face was nearly dissolved when it crashed into him and knocked him off his feet.

Twyla Trahern

—Winny lifted over the Pogromite's head, the sweet lamb to the high altar, but then brought down face-to-face, and the gray priest hissing in consecration of the sacrifice, baring its teeth for the mortal bite, with Sparkle in the quick of it and plunging the bayonet into the small of the beast's back to no effect. Twyla fast, no music in her now, only a shrill discordant cry of rage and terror and all-shattering love, the pistol bucking in her hands once, twice, and again. Gray teeth to the smooth cheek—but then the head bursting, the Pogromite falling, Winny dropping, Winny unbitten, Winny with gray nanocomputers crawling across his face.

Bailey Hawks

Shaken, Padmini came through the lap-pool door into the hallway.

Tom Tran followed her, gripping Kirby Ignis by one arm, pressing the muzzle of the pistol against his throat.

"Stalemate," Bailey shouted.

Recognizing that it might never come to exist if Ignis died, the shrieking legions of the One grew quieter, though the voices were no less enraged.

Clutching his shoulder wound with his left hand, Kirby Ignis looked surprised, which didn't speak well for him, that he could be surprised by anything after seeing the One and the world that his institute had furthered. He didn't expect the wound because in spite of his expressed regret and the acknowledgment that such a future must never come to pass, he still did not truly see himself at fault. He was aghast at the dire unintended consequences, but incapable of admitting to any responsibility for what had happened.

Within the walls, legions continued to protest, all expressing the same wordless outrage in the same voice, the latest version of the faceless mobs of history. The One seemed to be arguing with itself, deciding on its next move.

"Bailey, you're making a terrible mistake," Ignis said. "My work, our work at the institute, can relieve all human suffering. The world can be made *right*."

Bailey thought of how often they looked like what they were not. The men around Hitler could have been your sweet-faced uncle, your chubby-cheeked cousin, your grandfather with his pipe and slippers and easy smile. At times in his life, Albert Speer somewhat resembled Gregory Peck, the actor with the perfect looks for righteous roles. Roosevelt called Stalin "Uncle Joe." Uncle Joe and Uncle Ho Chi Minh. When he smiled, Pol Pot, of the Cambodian killing fields, might have been the nice man behind the counter at your dry-cleaning shop.

As the voices in the walls seethed, Ignis appealed to Padmini Bahrati. "With nanomachines to edit the DNA of the fetus in the womb, no child will ever be born with disabilities."

"Or perhaps no child will ever be born," she said.

"No, no. Listen. Listen to me. Nanobot microbivores swimming in the bloodstream could download instructions for recognizing any virus or bacteria and wipe out any disease hundreds of times faster than antibiotics."

Entering from the stairwell, Witness said, "There is no disease in this future."

Ignis said, "Forget about this future. This was never *intended*."

Urging everyone to join forces with Sparkle and Twyla at the midpoint of the corridor, Bailey glanced back at Witness, who chose not to accompany them, and asked, "What year is this, anyway?"

"Not as far from your time as you think. This is 2049."

Smiling, shaking his head, Mickey Dime said, "I didn't hear that. I don't want to think about that. It makes no sense."

With a *ding*, the elevator arrived at the basement from realms below.

Sparkle Sykes

She wiped frantically at the sludge on Winny's face, afraid that the horde would dissolve his flesh, and suddenly Iris was there and engaged, finding the courage to endure contact with another, wiping tenderly at Winny's left ear, at his neck. The nanothings tingled over Sparkle's hands, like thousands of swarming ants, but they didn't bite or sting, and Winny's face remained unscathed. As she wiped her hands vigorously on her clothes, the horde already seemed to be moving more sluggishly across her skin.

Bailey Hawks

As everyone came together in the middle of the hallway, finishing plaster cracked and fell from overhead and drywall screws popped loose. A slab of Sheetrock swung down like a big trapdoor, fanning Bailey with powdered gypsum and nearly knocking Tom Tran to his knees.

Overhead, seething between the ceiling joists, death-loving life in pale profusion squirmed and thrashed and reached down for them.

Jamming the muzzle harder into Ignis's throat, Tom Tran shouted, *"I'll kill him!"*

The One seemed to have decided it must risk its creator's life, because out of the blue light of-the elevator surged a furious swarm of hideous manifestations, animal-plant-machine entities at the sight of which his eyes rebelled and his heart shrank, a hobgoblin horde that might have been the denizens of the nightmares that demons dreamed when they slept in Hell. This pack would have torn them to pieces if sudden sheets of blue light had not shimmered up the walls. The transition reversed, the roar of bedlam voices abruptly silenced, rust and ruin vanished, as did the dead Pogromites and those borne by the elevator. And here were the surviving neighbors, here where the future had not yet happened, here in the still point of ever-turning time, where all was possible and nothing was yet lost.

Home.

One

From pole to pole, I pause in my entirety, every manifestation utterly still, the world hushed in anticipation. The boy escapes me, as does the ex-marine, but my messenger has gone with them. Moment by moment, my triumph seems to be validated. I am the prince of this world not just for a time but for all time. The two geniuses of the institute will proceed as required, and I will be well. I will be well and all will be well in this best of all possible worlds.

34

77 Shadow Street

In the basement corridor, the gap in the ceiling was closed as if it had never opened. No creaking issued from within the walls or ceiling, no slithering, no voices. The demonic multitude had vanished before their eyes, as had Witness.

Having been released by Tom, one hand still clamped to his shoulder wound, Ignis said, "You won't regret sparing me, Bailey. I *will* fix it. Everything. I'll make it all right."

Bailey said, "Silas, can it be coincidence that this one house in all the world happens to be built over a fault in space-time?"

"In the courtroom, it's cause and effect, motive and intent. We don't like coincidence."

"Neither do I. Tom, can it be coincidence that the man who will ruin the future just happens to live in the one house in the world that's built over a fault in space-time?"

"Coincidence is mere random chance," Tom Tran said. "I believe in patterns and mystery."

Grimacing in pain, impatient, Ignis said, "What's the point of this? I'm bleeding here. I need medical attention."

"Padmini," Bailey said, "if the real ruiner of the world was a man named Von Norquist, why wouldn't *his* residence have been the one preserved as a shrine?"

"Your question is a riddle I can't solve," Padmini said.

Sitting at the table, Mickey Dime said, "My mother liked you, Dr. Ignis. She said you had vision. She didn't mean just eyesight."

To Ignis, Bailey said, "Time and fate are complicated things. Is there just one future . . . or many possible futures?"

"This is all moot," Ignis said. His face had gone pale. Fine beads of sweat stippled his brow. "I will not let that future happen. It will never come to pass."

Bailey said, "Which came first—the work you did to ruin the future or your glimpse of that possible future where the One rules? Did you make that future before we saw it . . . or after seeing it, have you now been inspired to make a 'better' future?"

"What are you saying? Look, I'm in pain here. I'm not thinking clearly. I'm not following you."

"Time and fate," Bailey repeated, "are complicated things. Do you think each of us, every person in the world, is an instrument of destiny?"

Shaking his head, Ignis said, "I don't know what that means."

"I do," Padmini said. "I am an instrument of destiny, Mr. Hawks. We all are."

"What power employs you?" Bailey asked Ignis. "What dark destiny works through you to be born?"

"Don't be stupid, Bailey. I know you're not a stupid man. Don't talk to me about crap like destiny. I'm not doomed to that future we saw. I have the power to shape a better world, a freer world, a world as safe and clean as Eden, a world where the human impulse to corrupt and destroy is put back in the bottle forever."

Bailey shot him three times point-blank in the chest with Mickey Dime's pistol, perhaps saving the world as he had been unable to save his mother from a drunk and violent father.

Hugs had never felt so good to Sparkle Sykes. After a minute or so, Iris stiffened in her mother's embrace, but the girl continued to allow the affection. No less amazing, to the degree that she was able, she returned it.

Thereafter, the eight of them worked as one, not as a single mind, but as a community with a mutual purpose.

Tom erased the past twenty-four hours of recordings from the security-video archives.

With welding gear provided by Tom and with some assistance from Twyla, Bailey repaired the underset hinges of the iron manhole cover that had been blown off by the blue surge that rushed out of the lava pipe.

Because she was a novelist with a vivid imagination, Sparkle sat on the floor of the vault with Mickey Dime, explaining in what order and for what psychopathic reasons he murdered Senator Blandon, Logan Spangler, Sally Hollander, Julian Sanchez, and the Cupp sisters. For a cold-blooded professional killer, he was surprisingly sweet, almost like a child, and was fascinated to be reminded of how he had shot all those people and then dropped their wrapped bodies down the lava pipe. As sweet as he seemed, she nevertheless kept a gun on him the entire time. He had, of course, actually killed Jerry Dime and Vernon Klick, and she talked with him about them as well, and about how he had shot Dr. Kirby Ignis.

"My mother liked Dr. Ignis," Mickey Dime said.

"You mention her so often. You must have really loved her."

"I did. I do. I love her so much that I wanted to kill Ignis a long time ago."

"Is that so?"

"Because she liked him. I didn't like her liking other men."

"Yes, well, of course."

"She liked Senator Blandon, too."

"Did she really?"

"I wanted to kill him from the moment I caught them kissing."

"You might want to mention that to the police."

"I've always wanted to know who my father was."

"It's sad not to have a father," Sparkle said.

"He's my father, whoever he is, so he must have had sex with my mother at least once, and I'd love to kill him for that."

"Understandable," Sparkle said.

"Do you think they'll let me take her lingerie to the sanatorium with me?"

"They very well might. What could be the harm in it?"

There was nothing to be done with the ruined chesterfield in the Cupp apartment. Who could say what had happened to it? Perhaps Mickey Dime tore the upholstery apart in his murderous frenzy. Even in a homicidal fury, however, he wouldn't have had the strength to mangle their heavy ornamental fireplace screen; consequently, Silas and Padmini pried it out of the firebox and conveyed it to the storage room in the basement.

Through all of this, Winny kept silent company with Iris, who said no more to him for the rest of the evening.

The bodies of Jerry Dime and Vernon Klick were wrapped and waiting where Mickey had left them earlier, before the transition to the future. With them and the corpse of Kirby Ignis, with Dime's confession and plea of insanity, the authorities would have all they needed and would not be likely to mount an expensive and dangerous exploration of the perhaps bottomless lava pipe. And even if they did, they would find nothing.

After finishing dinner at Topper's, when Mac and Shelly Reeves walked back to the Pendleton through the chilly rain, police vehicles clogged the street in front of the building.

In the lobby, behind the reception counter, Padmini Bahrati greeted them with the terrible news of the murder spree. There was a moment of confusion when they thought Fielding Udell must have taken one last long step into paranoia, but they weren't surprised that it was Mickey Dime. Who would have been?

His mother always said he should not trust men in uniform. But they were very nice to him. Of course, the ones questioning him were plainclothes detectives. When his throat began to feel dry from so much talking, they got him some nice herbal tea with a lovely lemony fragrance. And when he complained that his hands felt dry, they were able to locate a bottle of hand cream, which he enjoyed very much. They insisted he had to have an attorney, too, but the man was such a buttinski that Mickey had to keep telling him to shut up. They were not just interested in the killings at the Pendleton but also wanted to know about the other murders Mickey had committed, and it was rather fun reliving his career. After all, though they were on the other side from him, and though they were sane while he was not, they had for a while been in the same business, the business of homicide. Everyone loves sharing war stories.

Having gotten by on too little sleep for too many days, Fielding Udell woke well after dawn, rested as he had not been in a long time. Curiously, he had fallen asleep on the floor in a corner of his office. He woke in the fetal position, drooling like a baby.

Either everything had been a dream or the Ruling Elite had been able to repair their Spin Machine. His apartment was as it ought to be, all his files in order, his computer ready for the workday.

At the window, he saw that the courtyard had been restored. The plants were not otherworldly anymore, and the fountains worked. Had it been a glimpse of the truth or a dream? Time would tell. Anything could happen at any time in this world of perpetual instability.

After a shower, he ordered his lunch and dinner delivered from two different restaurants. His lunch was moo goo gai pan, and when he ate it at his desk, he could neither see nor smell, nor taste, anything about it that suggested it was Soylent Green.

As the day progressed, his guilt grew. He had awakened with the conviction that he should donate 90 percent of his three-hundred-million-dollar inheritance to Dr. Kirby Ignis, for that good man's most important work. It was the One thing he could do to make amends for being born to wealth that he had not earned. It was the One possibility that he had for redemption, yet he procrastinated. By four o'clock in the afternoon, he was so tormented by this strange new bout of guilt that he left his apartment and reluctantly set out for Apartment 2-F. In the hallway, he encountered his neighbor, Shelly Reeves, and was greatly relieved to hear that Mickey Dime had killed Ignis during the night.

He returned to his apartment and poured a fresh glass of his homemade cola.

Oak View Sanatorium proved to be delightful.

The meals were tasty, and everything was pre-cut into bite-size pieces, which saved time at dinner. A spoon worked well in place of a fork because all the dishes had sides against which Mickey could scoop the food.

He could not have hoped for a more cozy room. His armchair was wonderfully comfortable, his bed a dream. They changed the linens every day, just like in a fine hotel.

His private bath featured a polished-steel panel instead of a mirror because mirrors could be broken, the pieces used as weapons. The door to the shower stall was safety glass, which if shattered would dissolve into a gummy mass of tiny fragments useless to either an amateur or a professional killer.

Care had been taken throughout his room and bath to be sure that all nails and screws in the walls, the floors, and the furniture had been countersunk and capped with glued-in plugs to make them inaccessible.

Anyway, Mickey had no intention of harming anyone. Even if he had not been on antipsychotic drugs, he would have behaved himself. He had been happy and content since he had acknowledged his insanity. All the tension had gone out of him, all the worry.

The court had barred him from using the money he earned as a hired killer. Likewise, he could not benefit from the portion of his mother's estate that had been left to dead Jerry, his brother. But Renata had left only 15 percent to Jerry, 85 percent to Mickey, and she had been richer than anyone imagined.

Charlie Criswell, Renata's attorney and Mickey's court-appointed conservator, visited once a month to make sure his ward was receiving good care. Mickey liked Charlie. Charlie was diligent and kind; he was also gay; he had never felt romantically attracted to Renata.

One warm day in the early spring, another man visited Mickey Dime while he was sitting on the veranda and watching squirrels caper across the lawn, in the shadows of the enormous oaks. At all times, Mickey wore a transponder on one ankle, so that he could be tracked by satellite if he escaped. When sitting on the porch, he also wore a vest of Kevlar straps securing him to the back of his wheelchair. The wheels of the chair were locked. Only staff members had keys to unlock them. All of these precautions made Mickey feel not like a prisoner but instead safe, safe from himself. The burly male nurse, supervising the veranda from a stool near the front steps, provided a chair for the visitor, placing it close to Mickey but out of arm's reach.

The visitor was tall, lanky, with sharply arched eyebrows as bushy as caterpillars predicting a bitter winter. His hands were pale, his fingers unnaturally long. He said he was Dr. Von Norquist, and Mickey had no reason to doubt him.

A month earlier, Mickey had sent a note to Norquist, by way of Charlie Criswell: *Your vision of a transhuman civilization with a greatly reduced and sustainable population will be realized beyond your wildest dreams. You will change the world more than any man in history. I have seen it, as did Kirby Ignis.*

Norquist said, "I don't know what I'm doing here."

"Yes, you do," Mickey said.

The scientist's eyes were the color of ripe plums, but there wasn't anything sweet about his intense stare. "You killed Kirby."

"Yes."

"Why?"

Mickey shrugged. "I'm insane."

"You killed those elderly sisters, a security guard, that helpless blind man. . . ."

"That's correct."

"And dropped their bodies down a lava pipe, for God's sake."

"I guess I did. I'm not as clear about that. It's what I intended to do, so I guess I did it."

"Why?"

"Insane," Mickey said, and smiled affably.

The scientist stared at him for a long time. Finally he said, "You don't seem insane to me."

"Well, I am. Totally. I'm okay with it."

After another silence, Norquist said, "How did you know I'm concerned about the need for 'a greatly reduced and sustainable population'? I've never shared those thoughts so explicitly with anyone, not even with Kirby."

In a low voice that sometimes sounded like that of Kirby Ignis and sometimes like that of Witness, at other times like other people he didn't know but that Norquist apparently did, Mickey began by recounting the waking dream that he'd experienced in Kirby Ignis's kitchen. The Pogrom. The destruction of the cities. The swift rise of the One. The resultant, profoundly simple ecology of that world of craggy black trees, luminous grass, and a single consciousness. His words were not his own. He repeated the more eloquent narrative of the One.

Riveted by these revelations, and reacting visibly to each new voice, Norquist leaned forward in his chair, seeming loath to miss a word. When Mickey paused, the scientist said, "How do you do that—such perfect mimicry?"

"The One contains the memories of billions of people and can speak as they spoke. I guess it conveyed that ability to me. Or I'm just insane. But for what it's worth, I have a further message for you."

"What message?"

It was a long one, but Mickey delivered it without

hesitation, without a mispronunciation, concluding with these words: "'I am plant, animal, machine. I am posthuman and the condition of humanity is not my condition. I am free.'"

Exhausted, Mickey slumped back in his wheelchair. Listening to himself, he had been amazed at just how insane he had become. It was kind of spooky.

For a while, he and Norquist watched the squirrels on the lawn.

Spangles of sunshine twinkled through the branches of the oaks.

From his distant station near the porch steps, the male nurse frowned at them, perhaps puzzled about what a reputable man like Dr. Norquist would have to discuss at such length with a crazy person.

Mickey wondered what was on the menu for dinner. He was hungry enough to need two spoons.

Then he remembered an additional message he needed to convey. "One more thing. There's a man named Fielding Udell who lives in the Pendleton. If you pay him a visit and ask him to help finance your research, he will be compelled to invest nearly three hundred million in the institute."

"How do you know this?"

Mickey's little smile was reproving.

"Right," said Norquist. "You're insane."

During the next silence, Mickey realized that Dr. Norquist was not watching the squirrels. He was staring at an SUV parked along the shoulder of the county road, far out at the entrance of the Oak View driveway.

"I parked on another road a mile west of here," Dr. Norquist said, "and walked overland, approached this place from the back."

That statement resonated with Mickey, reminding him of the days when he had carefully planned his murders.

Norquist said, "Lately I've had the feeling I'm being watched."

"Maybe you're paranoid. You should get diagnosed."

"Whoever it is, he's damn careful. I never get a glimpse . . . but I feel him out there."

"That SUV?" Mickey asked.

"Maybe. It's never the same vehicle."

"Who do you think he is?"

"I thought maybe you'd have an idea."

"Well, it's not my mother."

"I never imagined it was."

"She's dead," Mickey said. "But even after she died, I sometimes had the feeling she was watching me."

"From where?" Norquist asked scornfully. "From Heaven?"

"From somewhere," Mickey said.

Far out on the shoulder of the highway, a man got out of the SUV. He was hardly more than a shadow, too far away to be identified.

In the westering sun, something glimmered on the man's face. Mickey thought it might be the lenses of a pair of binoculars.

Winny continued reading too many books and avoiding manly musical instruments. He spent some time with Iris nearly every day. It wasn't a boy-girl thing and never could be. They were friends. They never talked about the world of the One, in part because she didn't talk much and because he didn't know what to say. Besides, if he did eventually know what to say about that experience, he couldn't tell anyone without ending up in a nuthouse like Mickey Dime. There was Mr. Hawks to think about, as well. He had killed Mr. Ignis, and if the true story were known, he might go to jail. Killing Mr. Ignis had been the hardest kind of right thing to do, and Mr. Hawks was the hero that Winny could never be. One night Winny dreamed of the Cupp sisters. His grandfather Winston, who died in the coal-cracker explosion when Winny was a toddler, was in the dream, too, and all he remembered of it was that it felt good, like it always felt when he visited his grandma Trahern on the farm that his mom had bought for her. But it was a strange dream, too, because a couple of times he woke from it, and the Cupp sisters were sitting on the edge of his bed, not any bed in a dream but his own real bed, sitting there smiling at him. He swore he could feel one of them smooth the hair back from his forehead the way his mother sometimes did, and he felt the other one kiss him on the cheek, not the way you feel things in dreams but as real as anything. One of them said, "Brave boy," and whether they were really there or only in a dream, Winny didn't know what to say to them. After that, however, he felt the sisters were all right. They weren't stuck in 2049 inside some tree or fungus or anything. They were somewhere better than either the present or the future. One day Iris got a socializing dog from an organization that provided assistance dogs to people with severe disabilities, and what a difference it made. If Iris had ever been happy before, you couldn't see that she was, but you could see how happy she was with that golden retriever. They said she could rename the dog if she wanted, and for a while Winny hoped that she would name it Winny, but of course that would have caused a lot of confusion. She named him Bambi, and Winny didn't have any hurt feelings. One day his mom showed him a newspaper story about this scientist who died when for some reason he drove his car over a cliff. His name was Norquist, and he'd worked with Dr. Ignis. Not long after that, his mom and Mr. Hawks were engaged to be married. Boy, the songs she started writing then were really something. She always wrote great stuff, but these were better than great. Old Farrel Barnett remarried, too, some girl named LuLu with big hair, and about four months later she hurried out two babies, twin boys. His mom had a subscription to *Variety*, and one day Winny saw an ad congratulating his dad on another hit, and it was a new publicity photo, though Winny never did get sent a signed copy. His new dad took Winny just about everywhere, to museums and amusement parks, to movies, you name it, the guy could wear you out taking you so many places. He called him Mr. Hawks at first, and then Bailey because they said that was all right. But one day he realized he was calling him Dad, that he'd been doing that for a while without thinking about it, and that was all right, too. He had two dads, and he loved them both—or wanted to—and that was neat in a way, having two, though old Farrel Barnett was dad with a small *d*, and Bailey Hawks was Dad with a capital. They got a dog of their own, a golden retriever he named Merle, after a dog in a book he read. And not long after that, there was talk of a baby sister. Life was just one thing after another. Sometimes there were baby sisters, and sometimes there were monsters, sleepovers with friends and stomach flu, student of the year at Mrs. Grace Lyman School and a bowling ball dropped on your foot. The way Winny saw it, the best thing and the worst thing were the same thing: nothing lasted forever, unless maybe he always would have skinny arms. So whatever came your way, you had to make the best of it, grin and bear it, smile through the storm. And the funny thing was, if you made the best of it, if you smiled through every storm, the bad things were never as terrible as you expected them to be, and the good things were better than anything you ever could have wished for yourself. He even began to think that the day would come when he would know what to say to anyone, any darn time, any place. Because what he came to see was that of the uncountable wonderful things in the world, the best of all were people, every one of them a new world and fascinating. That's why he had always read so many books: to meet new people in stories back in the day when he was not good at meeting real ones. He kept waiting for nightmares about what he had seen in 2049, but they never came. There were even good memories from that journey. The best were his mother standing there with the gun, looking tough and facing down the Pogromite, and Iris for the first time looking directly into his eyes, saying that she was scared, and then trusting him with her life. Really and truly, in 2049 or here in the present, it didn't get better than that.

ABOUT THE AUTHOR

DEAN KOONTZ, the author of many #1 *New York Times* bestsellers, lives in Southern California with his wife, Gerda, their golden retriever, Anna, and the enduring spirit of their golden, Trixie.

www.deankoontz.com

Correspondence for the author should be addressed to:

Dean Koontz
P.O. Box 9529
Newport Beach, California 92658

1

We are buried when we're born. The world is a place of graves occupied and graves potential. Life is what happens while we wait for our appointment with the mortician.

You are no more likely to see that sentiment on a Starbucks cup than you are the words COFFEE KILLS.

Sorry, but I have recently been in a *mood.* I'll cheer up soon. I always do. Regardless of what horror transpires, given a little time, I am as reliably buoyant as a helium balloon.

I don't know the reason for that buoyancy. Understanding it might be a key part of my life assignment. Perhaps when I realize why I can find humor in the darkest of darknesses, the mortician will call my number and the time will have come to choose my casket.

Actually, I don't expect to have a casket. The Celestial Office of Life Themes—or whatever it might be called—seems to have decided that my journey through this world will be especially complicated by absurdity and violence of the kind in which the human species takes such pride. Consequently, I'll probably be torn limb from limb by an angry mob of antiwar protesters and thrown on a bonfire. Or I'll be struck down by a Rolls-Royce driven by an advocate for the poor, knocked into an open storm drain, and washed out to sea, where my remains will be enthusiastically consumed by the teeming fish in a federally enforced no-fishing zone.

Anyway, at four o'clock that February morning, I was dreaming of Auschwitz.

My characteristic buoyancy will not occur just yet.

I woke to a familiar cry from beyond the half-open window of my suite in Roseland's guest house. As silvery as the pipes in a Celtic song, the wail sewed threads of sorrow and longing through the night and the woods. It came again, nearer, and then a third time from a distance.

These lamentations were always brief, but when they woke me too near dawn, I could not sleep anymore that night. The cry was like a wire in the blood, conducting a current through every artery and vein. I'd never heard a lonelier sound, and it electrified me with a dread that I could not explain.

In this instance, I awakened from the Nazi death camp. I am not a Jew, but in the nightmare I was Jewish and terrified of dying twice. Dying twice made perfect sense in sleep, but not in the waking world, and the eerie call in the night at once pricked the air out of the vivid dream, which shriveled away from me.

According to the current master of Roseland and everyone who worked for him, the source of the disturbing cry was a loon. They were either ignorant or lying.

I don't mean to insult my host and his staff. After all, I am ignorant of many things because I am required to maintain a narrow focus. An ever-increasing number of people seem determined to kill me, so that I need to concentrate on staying alive.

But even in the desert, where I was born and raised, there are ponds and lakes, man-made yet adequate for loons. Their cries were melancholy but never desolate like this, curiously hopeful whereas these were despairing.

Roseland, a private estate, was a mile from the California coast. But loons are loons wherever they nest; they don't alter their voices to conform to the landscape. They're birds, not politicians.

Besides, loons aren't roosters with a timely duty. Yet this wailing always came between midnight and dawn, never in the evening, never in sunlight. The earlier it came in the new day, the more often it was repeated during the remaining hours of darkness.

I threw back the covers, sat on the edge of the bed, and said, "Spare me that I may serve," which is a morning prayer that my Granny Sugars taught me to say when I was a little boy.

Pearl Sugars was a professional poker player who frequently sat in private games against card sharks twice her size, guys who didn't lose with a smile. They didn't even smile when they won. My grandma was a hard drinker. She ate a boatload of pork fat in various forms. Only when sober, Granny Sugars drove so fast that police in several Southwestern states knew her as Pedal-to-the-Metal Pearl. Yet she lived long and died in her sleep.

I hoped her prayer worked as well for me as it did for her; but recently I had taken to following that first request with another. This morning, it was: "Please don't let anyone kill me by shoving an angry lizard down my throat."

That might seem like a snarky request to make of God, but a psychotic and enormous man once threatened to force-feed me an exotic sharp-toothed lizard that was in a frenzy after being dosed with methamphetamine. He would have succeeded, too, if we hadn't been on a construction site and if I hadn't found a way to use an insulation-foam sprayer as a weapon. He promised to track me down when released from prison and finish the job with a different lizard.

On other days during the past week, I had asked God to spare me from death by a car-crushing machine in a salvage yard, from death by a nail gun, from death by being chained to dead men and dropped in a lake. . . . These were ordeals that I should not have survived in days past, and I figured that if I ever faced one of those threats again, I wouldn't be lucky enough to escape the same fate twice.

My name isn't Lucky Thomas. It's Odd Thomas.

It really is. Odd.

My beautiful but psychotic mother claims the birth certificate was supposed to read *Todd.* My father, who lusts after teenage girls and peddles property on the moon—though from a comfortable office here on Earth—sometimes says they *meant* to name me Odd.

I tend to believe my father in this matter. Although if he isn't lying, this might be the only entirely truthful thing he's ever said to me.

Having showered before retiring the previous evening, I now dressed without delay, to be ready for . . . whatever.

Day by day, Roseland felt more like a trap. I sensed hidden deadfalls that might be triggered with a misstep, bringing down a crushing weight upon me.

Although I wanted to leave, I had an obligation to remain, a duty to the Lady of the Bell. She had come with me from Magic Beach, which lay farther north along the coast, where I'd almost been killed in a variety of ways.

Duty doesn't need to call; it only needs to whisper. And if you heed the call, no matter what happens, you have no need for regret.

Stormy Llewellyn, whom I loved and lost, believed that this strife-torn world is boot camp, preparation for the great adventure that comes between our first life and our eternal life. She said that we go wrong only when we are deaf to duty.

We are all the walking wounded in a world that is a war zone. Everything we love will be taken from us, everything, last of all life itself.

Yet everywhere I look, I find great beauty in this battlefield, and grace and the promise of joy.

The stone tower in the eucalyptus grove, where I currently lived, was a thing of rough beauty, in part because of the contrast between its solemn mass and the delicacy of the silvery-green leaves that cascaded across the limbs of the surrounding trees.

Square rather than columnar, thirty feet on a side, the tower stood sixty feet high if you counted the bronze dome but not the unusual finial that looked like the much-enlarged stem, crown, and case bow of an old pocket watch.

They called the tower a guest house, but surely it had not always been used for that purpose. The narrow casement windows opened inward to admit fresh air, because vertical iron bars prevented them from opening outward.

Barred windows suggested a prison or a fortress. In either case, an enemy was implied.

The door was ironbound timber that looked as though it had been crafted to withstand a battering ram if not even cannonballs. Beyond lay a stone-walled vestibule.

In the vestibule, to the left, stairs led to a higher apartment. Annamaria, the Lady of the Bell, was staying there.

The inner vestibule door, directly opposite the outer, opened to the ground-floor unit, where the current owner of Roseland, Noah Wolflaw, had invited me to stay.

My quarters consisted of a comfortable sitting room, a smaller bedroom, both paneled in mahogany, and a richly tiled bathroom that dated to the 1920s. The style was craftsman: heavy wood-and-cushion armchairs, trestle tables with mortise joints and peg decoration.

I don't know if the stained-glass lamps were genuine Tiffany, but they might have been. Perhaps they were bought back in the day when they weren't yet museum pieces of fantastic value, and they remained here in this out-of-the-way tower simply because they had always been here. One quality of Roseland was a casual indifference to the wealth that it represented.

Each guest suite featured a kitchenette in which the pantry and the refrigerator had been stocked with the essentials. I could cook simple meals or have any reasonable request filled by the estate's chef, Mr. Shilshom, who would send over a tray from the main house.

Breakfast more than an hour before dawn didn't appeal to me. I would feel like a condemned man trying to squeeze in as many meals as possible on his last day, before submitting to a lethal injection.

Our host had warned me to remain indoors between midnight and dawn. One or more mountain lions had recently been marauding through other estates in the area, killing a couple of dogs, a horse, and peacocks kept as pets. The beast might be bold enough to chow down on a wandering guest of Roseland if given a chance.

I was sufficiently informed about mountain lions to know that they were as likely to hunt in the evening as after midnight, and in daylight, for that matter. I suspected that Noah Wolflaw's warning was intended to ensure that I would hesitate to investigate the so-called loon and other peculiarities of Roseland by night.

Before dawn on that Monday in February, I left the guest tower and locked the ironbound door behind me.

Both Annamaria and I had been given keys and had been sternly instructed to keep the tower locked at all times. When I noted that mountain lions could not turn a knob and open a door, whether it was locked or not, Mr. Wolflaw declared that we were living in the early days of a new dark age, that walled estates and the guarded redoubts of the wealthy were not secure anymore, that "bold thieves, rapists, journalists, murderous revolutionaries, and far worse" might turn up anywhere.

His eyes didn't spin like pinwheels, neither did smoke curl from his ears when he issued this warning, though his dour expression and ominous tone struck me as cartoonish. I still thought that he must be kidding, until I met his eyes long enough to discern that he was as paranoid as a three-legged cat encircled by wolves.

Whether his paranoia was justified or not, I suspected that neither thieves nor rapists, nor journalists, nor revolutionaries were what worried him. His terror was reserved for the undefined "far worse."

Leaving the guest tower, I followed a flagstone footpath through the fragrant eucalyptus grove to the brink of the gentle slope that led up to the main house. The vast manicured lawn before me was as smooth as carpet underfoot.

In the wild fields around the periphery of the estate, through which I had rambled on other days, snowy wood rush and ribbon grass and feathertop thrived among the majestic California live oaks that seemed to have been planted in cryptic but harmonious patterns.

No place of my experience had ever been more beautiful than Roseland, and no place had ever felt more evil.

Some people will say that a place is just a place, after all, that it cannot be good or evil. Others will say that evil as a real power or entity is a hopelessly old-fashioned idea, that the wicked acts of men and women can be explained by one psychological theory or another.

Those are people to whom I never listen. If I listened to them, I would already be dead.

Regardless of the weather, daylight in Roseland always seemed to be the product of a sun different from the one that brightened the rest of the world. Here, the familiar appeared strange, and even the most solid, brightly illuminated object had the quality of a mirage.

Afoot at night, as now, I had no sense of privacy. I felt that I was followed, watched.

On other occasions, I had heard a rustle that the still air could not explain, a muttered word or two not quite comprehensible, hurried footsteps. My stalker, if I had one, was always screened by shrubbery or by moonshadows, or he monitored me from around a corner.

And then there were the horse and rider that *only* I could see. I was alert for them, often looking behind me because the stallion's hooves made no sound, and the rider was as silent as any spirit.

I have certain talents. In addition to being a pretty good short-order cook, I have an occasional prophetic dream. And in the waking world, I sometimes see the spirits of the lingering dead who, for various reasons, are reluctant to move on to the Other Side.

Because my sixth sense complicates my existence, I try otherwise to keep my life simple. I have fewer possessions than a monk. I have no time or peace to build a career as a fry cook or as anything else. I never plan for the future, but wander into it with a smile on my face, hope in my heart, and the hair up on the nape of my neck.

If spurning a gift weren't ungrateful, I would at once return my supernatural sight. I would be content to spend my days whipping up omelets that make you groan with pleasure and pancakes so fluffy that the slightest breeze might float them off your plate.

Every talent is unearned, however, and with it comes a solemn obligation to use it as fully and wisely as possible. If I didn't believe in the miraculous nature of talent and in the sacred duty of the recipient, I would have gone mad by now.

Be assured that I am *not* insane, neither as a serial killer is insane nor in the sense that a man is insane who wears a colander as a hat to prevent the CIA from controlling his mind. I dislike hats of any kind, though I have nothing against colanders properly used.

I *have* killed more than once, but always in self-defense or to protect the innocent. Such killing cannot be called murder. If you think that it is murder, you've led a sheltered life, and I envy you.

A suspicion of homicide motivated me to prowl Roseland by night. The woman on the horse often manifested in a pristine white nightgown—but on other occasions the garment was mottled with blood. Surely she was a victim of someone, haunting Roseland in search of justice.

Far to the east of the house, out of sight beyond a hurst of live oaks, was a riding ring bristling with weeds. A half-collapsed ranch fence encircled it.

The stables, however, looked as if they had been built last week. Curiously, all the stalls were spotless; not one piece of straw or a single cobweb could be found, no dust, as though the place was thoroughly scrubbed on a regular basis. Judging by that tidiness, and by a smell as crisp and pure as that of a winter day after a snowfall, no horses had been kept there in decades; evidently, the woman in white had been dead a long time.

Roseland encompassed fifty-two acres in Montecito, a wealthy community adjacent to Santa Barbara, which itself was as far from being a shanty town as any Ritz-Carlton was far from being mistaken for the Bates Motel in *Psycho.*

The original house and other buildings were constructed in 1922 and '23 by a newspaper mogul, Constantine Cloyce, who was also the co-founder of one of the film industry's legendary studios. He had a mansion in Malibu, but Roseland was his special retreat, an elaborate man cave where he could engage in such masculine pursuits as horses, skeet shooting, small-game hunting, all-night poker sessions, and perhaps drunken head-butting contests.

Cloyce had also been an enthusiast of unusual—even bizarre—theories ranging from those of the famous medium and psychic Madame Helena Petrovna Blavatsky to those of the world-renowned physicist and inventor Nikola Tesla.

On an Internet search, I discovered that some believed Cloyce, here at Roseland, secretly financed research and development into such things as death rays and telephones that would allow you to talk to the dead. But then some people also believe that Social Security is solvent.

Being more familiar with the deceased than I might wish to be, I can tell you from personal experience that the spirits of the lingering dead don't talk. I don't know why.

Even when they have been brutally murdered and are desperate to see their assailants brought to justice, the dead are unable to convey essential information to me either by phone or face-to-face. Neither do they send text messages. Maybe that's because, given the opportunity, they would reveal something about death and the world beyond that we the living are not meant to know.

Anyway, the dead can be even more frustrating to deal with than are many of the living, which is astonishing when you consider that it's the living who run the Department of Motor Vehicles.

From the edge of the eucalyptus grove, I gazed up the long easy slope toward the main house, where Constantine Cloyce had died in his sleep in 1948, at the age of eighty. On the barrel-tile roof, patches of phosphorescent lichen glowed in the moonlight.

Also in 1948, the sole heir to an immense South American mining fortune bought Roseland completely furnished when he was just thirty and sold it, furnished, forty years later. He was reclusive, and no one seems to have known much about him.

At the moment, only a few second-floor windows were warmed by light. They marked the bedroom suite of Noah Wolflaw, who had made his considerable fortune as the founder and manager of a hedge fund, whatever that might be. I'm reasonably sure that it had something to do with Wall Street and nothing whatsoever to do with boxwood garden hedges.

Now retired at the age of fifty, Mr. Wolflaw claimed to have sustained an injury to the sleep center in his brain. He said that he hadn't slept a wink in the previous nine years.

I didn't know whether this extreme insomnia was the truth or a lie, or proof of some delusional condition.

He had bought the residence from the reclusive mining heir. He restored and expanded the house, which was of the Addison Mizner school of architecture, an eclectic mix of Spanish, Moorish, Gothic, Greek, Roman, and Renaissance influences. Broad, balustraded terraces of limestone stepped down to lawns and gardens.

In this hour before dawn, as I crossed the manicured grass toward the main house, the coyotes high in the hills no longer howled because they had gorged themselves on wild rabbits and slunk away to sleep. After hours of singing, the frogs had exhausted their voices, and the crickets had been devoured by the frogs. A peaceful though temporary hush shrouded this fallen world.

My intention was to relax on a lounge chair on the south terrace until lights appeared in the kitchen. The chef, Mr. Shilshom, always began his workday before dawn.

I started each morning with the chef not solely because he made fabulous breakfast pastries, but also because I suspected that he might let slip some clue to the hidden truth of Roseland. He fended off my curiosity by pretending to be the culinary world's equivalent of an absentminded professor, but the effort of maintaining that pretense seemed likely to trip him up sooner or later.

As a guest, I was welcome throughout the ground floor of the house: the kitchen, the day room, the library, the billiards room, and elsewhere. Mr. Wolflaw and his live-in staff were intent upon presenting themselves as ordinary people with nothing to hide and Roseland as a charming haven with no secrets.

I knew otherwise because of my special talent, my intuition, and my excellent crap detector.

When I say that Roseland was an evil place, that doesn't mean I assumed everyone there—or even just one of them—was also evil. They were an entertainingly eccentric crew; but eccentricity most often equates with virtue or at least with an absence of profoundly evil intention.

The devil and all his demons are dull and predictable because of their single-minded rebellion against truth. Crime itself—as opposed to the solving of it—is boring to the complex mind, though endlessly fascinating to the simple-minded. One film about Hannibal Lecter is riveting, but a second is inevitably stupefying. We love a series hero, but a series villain quickly becomes silly as he strives so obviously to shock us. Virtue is imaginative, evil repetitive.

They were keeping secrets at Roseland. The reasons for keeping secrets are many, however, and only a fraction are malevolent.

As I settled on the patio lounge chair to wait for Mr. Shilshom to switch on the kitchen lights, the night took an intriguing turn. I do not say an *unexpected* turn, because I've learned to expect just about anything.

South from this terrace, a wide arc of stairs rose to a circular fountain flanked by six-foot Italian Renaissance urns. Beyond the fountain, another arc of stairs led to a slope of grass bracketed by hedges that were flanked by gently stepped cascades of water, which were bordered by tall cypresses. Everything led up a hundred yards to another terrace at the top of the hill, on which stood a highly ornamented, windowless limestone mausoleum forty feet on a side.

The mausoleum dated to 1922, a time when the law did not yet forbid burial on residential property. No moldering corpses inhabited this grandiose tomb. Urns filled with ashes were kept in wall niches. Interred there were Constantine Cloyce, his wife, Madra, and their only child, Timothy, who died before his ninth birthday.

Suddenly the mausoleum began to glow, as if the structure

were entirely glass, an immense oil lamp throbbing with golden light. The phoenix palms backdropping the building reflected this radiance, their fronds pluming like the feathery tails of certain fireworks.

A volley of crows exploded out of the palm trees, too startled to shriek, the beaten air cracking off their wings. They burrowed into the dark sky.

Alarmed, I got to my feet, as I always do when a building begins to glow inexplicably.

I didn't recall ascending the first arc of stairs or circling the fountain, or climbing the second sweep of stairs. As if I'd been briefly spellbound, I found myself on the long slope of grass, halfway to the mausoleum.

I had previously visited that tomb. I knew it to be as solid as a munitions bunker.

Now it looked like a blown-glass aviary in which lived flocks of luminous fairies.

Although no noise accompanied that eerie light, what seemed to be pressure waves broke across me, through me, as if I were having an attack of synesthesia, *feeling* the sound of silence.

These concussions were the bewitching agent that had spelled me off the lounge chair, up the stairs, onto the grass. They seemed to swirl through me, a pulsing vortex pulling me into a kind of trance. As I discovered that I was on the move once more, walking uphill, I resisted the compulsion to approach the mausoleum—and was able to deny the power that drew me forward. I halted and held my ground.

Yet as the pressure waves washed through me, they flooded me with a yearning for something that I could not name, for some great prize that would be mine if only I went to the mausoleum while the strange light shone through its translucent walls. As I continued to resist, the attracting force diminished and the luminosity began gradually to fade.

Close at my back, a man spoke in a deep voice, with an accent that I could not identify: "I have seen you—"

Startled, I turned toward him—but no one stood on the grassy slope between me and the burbling fountain.

Behind me, somewhat softer than before, as intimate as if the mouth that formed the words were inches from my left ear, the man continued: "—where you have not yet been."

Turning again, I saw that I was still alone.

As the glow faded from the mausoleum at the crest of the hill, the voice subsided to a whisper: "I depend on you."

Each word was softer than the one before it. Silence returned when the golden light retreated into the limestone walls of the tomb.

I have seen you where you have not yet been. I depend on you.

Whoever had spoken was not a ghost. I see the lingering dead, but this man remained invisible. Besides, the dead don't talk.

Occasionally, the deceased try to communicate through the art of mime, which can be frustrating. Like any mentally healthy citizen, I am overcome by the urge to strangle a mime when I happen upon one in full performance, but a mime who's already dead is unmoved by that threat.

Turning in a full circle, in seeming solitude, I nevertheless said, "Hello?"

The lone voice that answered was a cricket that had escaped the predatory frogs.